CW01003199

'There But For The Grace ......'

'There But For The Grace ......'

JENNY ACKLAND

© Jenny Ackland, 2016

Published by Jenny Ackland

All rights reserved. No part of this book may be reproduced, adapted, stored in a retrieval system or transmitted by any means, electronic, mechanical, photocopying, or otherwise without the prior written permission of the author.

The rights of Jenny Ackland to be identified as the author of this work have been asserted in accordance with the Copyright, Designs and Patents Act 1988.

A CIP catalogue record for this book is available from the British Library.

ISBN 978-0-9955161-0-6

Book layout and design by Clare Brayshaw

Cover illustration by Stuart Trotter

Prepared and printed by:

York Publishing Services Ltd
64 Hallfield Road
Layerthorpe
York YO31 7ZQ

Tel: 01904 431213

Website: www.yps-publishing.co.uk

Chapter One

So, there it was, a tightly wrapped bundle being held towards me with thrusting hands. My own of course remained static, frozen and unable to respond. After so many hours of struggling to free myself from this awful load, any enthusiasm had been sucked out of me in company with the afterbirth. Why I hadn't elected to have a Caesarean escapes me. I thought it would be easy enough and anyway I was so busy at work that I really couldn't spare the time. What a joke that was. The midwife prattling on about all the choices I had, even giving birth in a bloody bath, became irritating. I lost half a day at the office because of her insistence in my making a choice. So I opted for the easiest, I thought. I noticed her eyes glazing over as she looked at me.

Now I know what she was thinking.

So, here I am, another nurse eyeing me, judgement unspoken.

To fill the emptiness I told her I wanted to sleep, in the firmest voice I could muster. She took it away, the bundle in white.

I could feel the thick pad between my legs becoming soft and squashy. There was nothing I could do as I'd dismissed the nurse and it appeared I had very little energy to move.

The nurse, who had obviously been assigned to me, returned minus the baby. She sat on the chair and, very presumptuously, I thought, took hold of my hand. That's what you get if you go privately, I suppose.

'I need a fresh pad,' I said. I didn't know what they were called but knew it was like having a large white loaf between my thighs.

Rather slowly she rose from the chair and rifled through my possessions. I have a vague memory of reading a list before I gave it to one of my staff to see to. She found what she was looking for and then cleaned me up with an expressionless face.

She didn't want to talk which pleased me. She had a brittleness about her. She'd probably done the same cleaning routine hundreds of times. Well paid too, I would imagine.

I could do with a jolly stiff drink. I hope Charles has the wits to bring something in with him. The nurse looks at me with a benign but blank glance. 'Your husband is coming in this afternoon.'

I say nothing.

'I'll bring your little girl in so you can give her a feed before he arrives. It is very important she has colostrum from you to protect her from diseases. It is the stuff you produce before your milk comes in.'

I didn't want to feed the baby. I didn't want my husband to see me like this, all fat and smelly, no hairdresser to see to my hair, makeup still in my handbag, wherever that was.

2

I just wanted to be left alone to sleep.

'I won't be feeding the baby,' I stated firmly. 'Can't you give it a bottle?' The nurse was very pinched as she repeated her education of me.

'No. It is essential that she receives the first feed from you. After that we can talk about what you would like to do.' Each word had ice ground through it.

My attention was drawn to a badge flapping above her chest.

Apparently she was called Charlie Smith. Well, that figures. With a name like that she stands little chance of making anything of herself. All the girls hanging about on the council estate, right at the other end of the City, have names like Britney, Chantelle, or even, God forbid, Chardonnay. One of my cleaners has children with the most awful names, mostly called after footballers or celebrities. As Charlie excused herself, I noticed the size of her bottom. That's another point against her. People like that shouldn't be allowed to have children. They are grossly obese, living on cheap fatty food.

I must remember to get Charles to book me an appointment at the clinic. My excess fat, caused by this pregnancy will disappear overnight. My nails need attention too. I must get out of here soon before I fall to pieces. Charles really must get things organised for me.

The nurse, Charlie, returned with the baby. 'Now,' the bossy cow said, 'we are going to have a go at breastfeeding. It's time you had a look at your beautiful little daughter.'

She unwrapped it and opened the front of my nightgown. That was a liberty, but I felt detached from it all. Firmly, she pushed the head against my breast. Something was happening but I averted my gaze. I found I was gritting my teeth. After a few minutes, Charlie removed the baby from me.

'Well,' she said, rather patronisingly, 'that was a good start.'

'I'm not actually feeding her myself. I thought I made that clear. She will be bottle fed so the Nanny can see to it. My husband is interviewing candidates today, so it will all be taken care of. Now, please go away, as I want to sleep.'

I noticed a wedding ring on Charlie's ring finger. Goodness! The man mountaineering over her hulk should get a medal.

My eyes seemed to close of their own volition and I sank into oblivion.

The husband Charles, at this precise time, was having extremely fast and not very comfortable sex with one of the applicants for the post of Nanny. She was conveniently offered the post, showing a willingness beyond expectations. His requirements were met.

'A good morning's work,' was the phrase that skimmed through his superficial mind. He showered, checked his 'phone as you never knew when the wife would be wanting something, and emailed the office to let them know he would be calling in to run over the figures. He felt obliged to call in, just to confirm in their minds that he had his finger on the button and their bonuses might be on the line if they became overconfident or self-satisfied in his brief absence. His system was managed in such a way that each individual was motivated to reach the maximum output. He smiled to himself, thinking that money was a most marvellous commodity. He found it amusing that there was nothing left for him to spend it on. He could let his wife have exactly what she wanted. She was happy, he was certain. It was just a pity that she got pregnant at a time when he needed to be in total control at work.

Oh well. It wouldn't lack for anything. A Nanny had been appointed and given a good seeing-to. She was gagging for it don't you know. He had done her a favour. She wouldn't cause any trouble. He hadn't heard many words of English coming from her. He intended to pay her over the odds anyway so she would be very grateful to him. Probably he might find a need for her in the future too; such a pretty filly.

A nursery with all the trimmings had been finished. There was absolutely nothing else he needed to bother his head about. His 'phone rang. Sod it. He thought he'd turned it off.

It was his mother. He knew it was his mother because he didn't have to say anything.

'Any news, darling? We didn't ring before as we know how busy you are.'

Charles pulled a face. Oh God! He should have rung her earlier just to stop her speaking like this. He didn't like his mother very much and his father even less, but couldn't bother to ask himself the reasons.

'You have a granddaughter.' Staccato. Information given and received.

'Well done Charles. A cousin for Zachary and Obediah. Have you checked my investments lately? I'm thinking of getting another property in Chelsea, so useful when I'm in town.'

'You spend most of the time abroad, Mother. I'll do it later today.'

'Must rush, love to' ……Charles could hear the pause, 'the new mother.'

The call, thus ended, Charles sat holding the 'phone, a bewildered expression on his face.

He felt suddenly empty, but hadn't the time to reason why.

Recently, a new emotion had appeared, which resulted in a tightening in his chest, always triggered by an unexpected call from his mother. How long was it since he had used his magnificent gym? After all, one doesn't have a fully equipped gymnasium just to look at. The same must apply to his pool. He had seen one of the staff cleaning it this morning, checking the chemical levels. He hadn't swum for ages and of course Cristabel, his wife, hated to get her hair wet.

A sudden thought attacked him. Perhaps his daughter would enjoy it. The phrase 'his daughter' seemed to ease away the pain in his chest. It hit him like a bolt. He was a father! Whatever it meant, he was in a state of ignorance.

They must have a celebration, a party. It must be very different from the last one, a few weeks ago. That had turned into a bit of a disaster really, when one thought about it. There had been far too much drug-taking and the guests got very silly. Charles couldn't remember much of the evening apart from looking at some of the faces and realising that he didn't know who they were; a fiasco really. He was now a father, so things might have to change.

Of late he had found himself becoming increasingly intolerant of some of the antics in which these supposedly sane adults were engaging. Of course Cristabel had cut down on some of her alcohol intake. One must accept that self- denial made her very grumpy and difficult to live with. Charles was certain that 'turning a blind eye' on his part was the most sensible. Cristabel, when riled, was not to be crossed. She was not the 'love of his life.'

She was, though, the mother of his daughter. He had a daughter!

Charles cast his mind back to the first 'love of is life.' He was still at school, aged fifteen. Cuddly, (actually Mrs. Cudmore), the matron, brought her daughter into school for Sports Day. Charles' parents were in the Bahamas, so obviously couldn't attend. Charles suppressed a laugh as he could feel Cuddly's daughter's lips on his. Ann she was called. She was simple, straightforward and totally wonderful to a sexually pumping adolescent. It was all so gentle. Ann was quiet and serious and very, very beautiful. She was studying at the local Comprehensive and intended pursuing a career as a doctor. This amazed

Charles. How could a girl from that sort of background achieve the grades necessary to become a doctor? Ann told him that her school was being renamed an 'Academy'. Charles hadn't a clue what she meant and wasn't interested, if the truth was known.

Cuddly never left them alone for more than a few minutes. How they filled those minutes! Charles remembered that there was no aggression with Ann. Everything was calm, accepting, quiet and kind. She was just there, accompanying him, listening, offering opinions, nodding her head in such a way that Charles didn't know if she was agreeing with him or dissenting.

Perhaps these thoughts unexpectedly filtering into his mind were a direct result of the baby being a girl, not a boy as he had expected. He hoped she would grow up like Ann. If it had been a boy he would go to boarding school. It was a relief that she wouldn't experience the bullying and homesickness that he had, though why he was homesick was anyone's guess, his parents not being the hands-on types. His Nanny was his guiding strength, strict but loving. He remembered his father telling him to 'Be a man,' in a very stern voice as, at age six, he was dispatched to a 'Good School.' Oh, and he was told to stop snivelling.

His daughter obviously would have to go to boarding school but not until later surely. She wouldn't be beaten nowadays. His hands started to sting as if the cane had just landed.

No. It was important he concentrated on his wife, Cristabel. The demands she would make were going to be difficult. He rinsed his face in cold water and decided on the most important priority.

An unwelcome thought slid into his head. Cristabel had been sent to boarding school, but at a later age, if he remembered correctly. She was tremendously assertive and successful in her profession. In fact it appeared at times as if this was the only important thing in her life. Charles wondered what the baby was named. Did one attach a name immediately, or wait, as he suspected he must do, until the family had been consulted? It would have to be a family name, his mother would guarantee it, but Cristabel would have an opinion, perhaps, although her interest in the pregnancy was superficial and more of a passing inconvenience than anything else.

Charles remembered asking what the sex of the unborn baby was when they met for dinner after some appointment or other that she'd had to attend. She didn't seem to want to talk about it and Charles knew better than to press her. He hadn't accompanied her on any appointments as she made it clear that it wasn't important. Cristabel had been told to make sure she didn't overindulge in the entertaining. There was a definite serious look in the consultant's eye. She didn't want Charles to hear as he could sometimes be incredibly boring about things like that.

Cristabel, trying not to remember anything, began to think Charles was deliberately keeping her waiting. How difficult can it be to pick up a packed bag and carry it to the hospital? Having done whatever it was that Charlie, or whatever the nurse's stupid name was, she was fully expecting to go home. Even the bloody office hadn't 'phoned or texted to see how she was. She was grindingly tired and uncomfortable and needed a drink to deaden all the thoroughly awfulness of everything.

She knew her parents wouldn't be calling. That's a joke. They weren't even in the country. They were hardly ever in the country. It was something to do with tax apparently.

Oh, for God's sake Charles. Where the hell are you?

Charles didn't come but a man in a very good quality suit arrived and planted himself by the bed. A bit close for comfort she thought. He was really quite attractive. Pity she wasn't able to give him the benefit of her charms. She vaguely recognised him.

'Er, Mrs. Courtney –Browne,' he stuttered, obviously nervous.

'Is it important? I'm waiting for my husband to come in and then I'll be going home.'

'There are a few things I need to discuss with you both. Will Mr. Courtney- Browne be in soon?'

'He's a very busy man, you know.'

'Mmm. Yes I know… but,' and he hesitated, 'it is important I talk to both of you.'

Cristabel sighed. It was really too bad. Her life was overflowing with irritating interruptions. She needed to get home and back to normal. She'd give her eye teeth for a decent drink. If Charles didn't bring some in, she would send him out to buy some.

' I'm Mr. McAlister, by the way, your consultant. We have met a few times.'

'Have we?' Cristabel thought she might have remembered as he was really quite personable.

'Yes, indeed. You remember we discussed pregnancy and alcohol?'

'Vaguely.' Cristabel knew she must seem disinterested, but she had just gone through the most awful experience of her life and wasn't up to trading platitudes. It was too tiring. Feeling as if her private parts had been on display for the whole world to see was enough to bear, apart from the still aching presence of the excruciating pain she'd endured. Was there no end to it?

'Yes... well...mmm.' Mr. McAlister ground to a halt.

Cristabel turned her head away.

'I'll come back later, after my next clinic.'

The door burst open and Charles, accompanied by Charlie, arrived rather breathless. Charles was carrying a large holdall.

'Charles!' Mr. McAlister held out a hand towards him. Charles, his face suddenly registering recognition, shook hands warmly.

'Not seen you for a bit, eh? How are things?'

'Not too bad.'

'I hear you're making quite a name for yourself in the city. Charles was taken aback that this old school friend was apparently looking after his wife.'

Charlie heard this interchange. So they went to the same school did they? She wasn't surprised as they seemed to speak in the same language.

'Well, how time passes. We'll try and have a chat later. Should trigger a few nasty memories, eh?'

Charles managed a small smile and left it at that.

Charlie felt she was waiting for her next orders. A silence followed full of different anticipations, each person in the room waiting for their own individual reasons. To the ordinary person it would have caused little discomfort. Charlie glanced at, and nodded to Mr.McAlister and left the room.

Mr.McAlister indicated a chair that he wanted Charles to sit on, extending his hand. 'You know, of course, I'm your wife's consultant paediatrician. I'm afraid you haven't seen me, as your wife wasn't the most enthusiastic about keeping appointments.

'Ahh. Jolly good,' Charles saw Mr McAlister place himself in the other chair, leaving Cristabel rather like a sandwich.

They both twisted their necks round so they could see her.

'What ?' she almost shouted.

Mr McAlister looked at Charles, which meant she would now be an interruption to the conversation.

'I need to discuss your daughter's condition with you both.' Mr.McAlister avoided looking at Cristabel, perhaps hoping that Charles would have a calming effect on his wife.

'Why?' Cristabel's face screwed up into a concentration of impatience.

'Well,' words were chosen with a practised skill, 'when Charlie was caring for your baby during the night, she noticed certain unusual reactions. She called me in and we are in the process of running some tests.'

'And......?' Cristabel snapped.

'Your little girl has been affected by your alcohol intake during the pregnancy.'

There it was, sounding cruel and cutting, just like the awful humiliating labour she'd gone through.

Charles and Cristabel's reactions were strangely muted. They appeared passive, as if someone was expected to enter the room and take over, making everything acceptable and perfect with nothing for them to do. They sank into partial attentiveness. The silence returned, this time it was solid.

'It is important that we make a more detailed assessment.'

'But I'm going home,' Cristabel whined.

'No. That won't be possible yet. We will do all we can to make you both comfortable in the assessment unit. I have arranged that Charlie can continue caring for the baby.

There is no finer nurse in the hospital.'

Charlie was standing by the door and had obviously heard this recommendation. A deep flush spread up her neck.

Cristabel found that she was almost relieved. At least somebody else was embarrassed by this ridiculous situation. She decided that they all needed to listen to her. After all, she was the one that had gone through the agony.

'I don't need to stay, do I? I have to get back to work.'

'It would not be sensible to return to work for several weeks. You have had a traumatic few days and need to recover your strength.'

'I know that!' Cristabel snapped.' I've been ripped apart and nobody listens to what I want. In any case, it's up to me if I have the occasional drink.'

She caught Charles expression of disbelief. So what? If he had been at home more in the evenings she might have not needed to soothe herself with a few glasses. In any case she made certain that the bottles were not in full view, empty or not, so how could he know?

'Well, that's the situation,' the paediatrician continued, 'I'll know more tomorrow.' Out he went, and in came the nurse, Charlie.

She quietly sat in the vacant chair. 'I'll organise the move in about an hour.' Charlie's voice was enclosed in calmness.

'I want you to go,' Cristabel shot Charles a glance that, at work, gained instant obedience.

'Leave the bag. It's got my clean clothes in.'

'Not you Charlie,' as Charlie was preparing to leave. Cristabel found it absurd to have to articulate this stupid boy/girl name.

'I'm going to take you to the unit shortly so you can get settled in with your baby. There will be other mothers there, so that will be less lonely for you and there will be someone to talk to, Charlie quietly told her.'

'I don't need to talk to anyone. I just need to get home and back to normal.'

'Well, let's get you rested then you'll feel more able to cope.'

Cristabel had always coped and to hear this nurse person imply that she wasn't in full control was very insulting.

'I'll leave you to sleep.' Charlie went out and closed the door quietly. It was as if she had taken all the calmness out with her but Cristabel closed her eyes and tried not to relive the nightmare of giving birth. Flashes of the intensity of the contractions kept attacking her and she rang the bell. She would get a sleeping pill.

Charlie was there in an instant. Could she have been waiting outside?

'I need a sleeping pill. I'm so tired that I can't sleep without going through all the pain of yesterday.'

15

'I'll get you one. Poor love, it has all been a bit much for you, hasn't it?' Cristabel was taken aback by the rush of emotion that sprung into her head making her eyes water. It was a bit disrespectful of the nurse to address her like that, wasn't it?

Later, after an enforced sleep, Charlie returned. So, there they were again, Cristabel and the nurse almost looking at each other. To be fair, Charlie was trying to avoid making the new mother feel under pressure. When she had finished washing her and finding a rather wonderful nightie in the bag, Charlie did look Cristabel in the eyes. Having just seen what accompanied the clothes, tucked away, but not secretly enough, she knew there were some awkward moments ahead.

Silence seemed to be occurring at regular intervals.

This was something that Charlie rarely met in her work. Ideally, she would have preferred N.H.S. work but she needed more flexible hours than were offered. Her husband had been made redundant the previous year and, what with the other problem, she thought they should spend as much time together as possible.

Like an arrow Cristabel asked, 'Are you married? I expect you are with loads of children.'

'Yes, I've been married for fifteen years. We can't have children.'

Charlie found herself speaking rather sharply.

There was another gap but of a different quality. It was full of unasked questions that even Cristabel refrained from risking.

'Oh, well I suppose you're one of the lucky ones. I was expected to have a child you know, family, and all that. I can tell you this will be the first and last.'

'Really?' Charlie had so many thoughts that should remain unspoken in her head that she moved to check the medical record on the end of the bed to avoid exploding.

The words forced themselves out. Looking directly at the girl in the bed Charlie said, speaking quietly, 'I would have loved to have children, so would my husband. We had even chosen names for them. We're not to be blessed with them though. We did think of adopting but with my husband being made redundant, the time isn't right.'

Why did she confess all that? Desperation, she supposed, to get this girl's thoughts away from the present. She knew she would have to tell Cristabel some unpleasant facts about her daughter's condition, but talking about her own life wasn't something of which she made a habit. It was even difficult to talk to her husband about the anguish and dragging sadness that attacked her at home. Before they were told that it was unlikely that they could conceive she had lost three stones in weight in preparation. Now, it didn't matter, did it?

Cristabel, for once, was silent. She thought to actually *want* children was, well, really rather strange. Charlie needed to remove herself from the room. She felt sweat dripping down her back.

Cristabel noticed the sweat. Well, fat people did perspire a lot, didn't they? All the cheap and rubbishy food they ate. She realised that she had forgotten to ask Charles to book a series of appointments at the clinic. Her mobile needed charging as well. Charlie can do that. She might as well make herself useful.

There were no circumstances under which she was going to stay in the unit. She would discharge herself. The baby was in good hands she was sure, and the nurse or Nanny or whatever Charles had appointed could take over when the baby was returned home. Such a bore, but Cristabel knew she'd had many stitches and her bottom was still extremely sore. She tried to get out of bed. If she practised, she would be able to walk out in a couple of days. Now, where was that drink ? If bloody Charles has forgotten it there will be hell to pay. Her body really hurt, all over, from head to toe. She must get some more painkillers. She knew Charlie had given her some pretty strong ones but the effect was wearing off. Drink first.

Cristabel looked around the room for the bag. Charlie must have put her clothes in the cupboard and left the bag somewhere. Damn it! She rang the bell. Nothing. She held her finger, that needed a decent manicure, down on the button. That should do it. It did.

Charlie came in, holding the baby. Oh. Cristabel had almost forgotten about that. Almost, but pain was a constant reminder.

'Your husband had a quick peep before rushing off.'

Charlie wondered if Cristabel would respond to the slight sarcasm.

Without asking permission, she placed the baby gently on Cristabel's chest, just above the static crossed arms.

It worked. The arms were instinctively uncrossed and there was the new mum, holding her little girl.

Cristabel looked stiff and uncomfortable. She looked down at her baby, which was a step forward, Charlie supposed.

'She looks fine to me. What is her problem? There seems to be a fuss about nothing. I need to get out of here and back to work. The baby will be looked after by the Nanny that my husband has employed as soon as I get there.'

'It's not as simple as that,' Charlie tried to make her voice calm. She chose her words with care and deliberation.

'She has a condition called Foetal Alcohol Syndrome and will need special care for some time. That was as far as she knew she should go but, silently, she thought the baby might have more long-term difficulties. Charlie had many years of experience and knew that the future was going to be uncertain.

To be as kind as possible, she said, 'Your little girl has been affected by your alcohol intake.'

'What? Just because I had a few bloody drinks?'

Charlie took the baby away from Cristabel. This was going to be a long haul.

'It's the same with any drug. The foetus can't develop along normal lines.'

'Well,' Cristabel said, pouting accusingly, 'they should have picked that up at my appointments.'

Charlie put the baby down in a little crib by the side of the bed and removed Cristabel's medical records from the folder.

'You only attended two appointments, so it was difficult to do all the essential checks.'

'Well the midwife kept wanting to come, but I was working, you know, and it was impossible to fit her in.'

'Yes, well, for the moment we'll keep an eye on both of you.'

'Where's my bag with all my stuff in?'

'It's been taken to the unit to be unpacked ready for you both. The alcohol, I'm afraid, was given to your husband to take home.'

Why was she apologising? They were not allowed alcohol in the unit and the vast majority of new parents couldn't give a toss about it. They were absorbed with the progress of their baby, leaving any need for alcohol on the side burner.

'Can you get out of bed if I help you?' Charlie was making an immense effort with this mum and hoped her real feelings were not visible.

'I'm in lots of pain you know. I'll only be staying a couple of days anyway. I need painkillers, strong ones, now.'

Charlie had the necessary medication with her and dispensed it with care and attention.

When she had told her husband she had a reluctant mother to deal with he didn't need to say anything. The expression on her face was enough without words.

She looked at Cristabel and tried to understand how she had somehow blocked out all her maternal feelings. Hormones were playing a part but the vast majority of new mothers, even after a traumatic birth, develop a modicum of affection for the baby. When she had worked in an Accident and Emergency Unit she had been impressed by the total dedication to the patient by the close relatives. If the patient happened to be a baby, it was heart rending to see the distress on the parents' faces.

She wracked her brains to try to find a way of getting this new mum actually to show an interest in the baby.

'I'm getting another nurse to help with the transfer to the Mother and Baby unit. We'll get the baby settled first and then collect you.'

No answer from Cristabel. Her breasts were uncomfortable and hot. She felt as though her vagina was full of white – hot needles.

She turned her face to the wall, closed her eyes and willed all the appalling insults to her body to vanish.

She was left in an almost empty room. There was no staff to see to her. There she was, marooned alone, in an uncomfortable bed. Quickly the nurses returned, just before she had managed to get herself out of bed. She was on the edge, balancing, toes reaching for the floor.

'Oh. Good,' Charlie entered the room with what Cristabel thought was a rather artificial smile, 'you've managed to get almost upright. Well done. Here let me hold you steady then you can walk a few steps.'

'Don't you understand the intense pain I'm in?'

'Yes, of course my dear, but it is important we get you moving.'

'My breasts are hot and very painful.'

'That's because your milk has come in.'

'I don't understand. I'm not feeding the baby. I've already told you that.'

'Yes I know, but your milk will dry up gradually. You will be a bit sore but it won't last long.' Cristabel, looking away, gritted her teeth. Here was a mother with abundant milk, who could probably feed the whole unit, showing no interest in doing anything for her baby. She wasn't the first and probably wouldn't be the last.

She held the mother gently and guided her round to the other side of the bed.

'Don't worry. We're not going to make you walk to the unit. We'll push you in this bed.'

'Really? But people will see me.'

'Yes, and they won't take any notice as they've seen it all before. It occurs quite regularly.'

Out the three of them went, sweeping deliberately gaily down the corridor, through countless doors, in the lift, more doors and corridors, until reaching double doors with security locks.

'Mother and Baby Unit' was prominently displayed on the doors. Charlie clicked in some numbers and both doors opened smoothly.

Nurse Winifred was waiting for them at the other side.

'You will have a lovely view from here,' she said. 'One of the best in the hospital.'

Another silence. Charlie decided not to try to fill it and instead bustled round putting various personal items away.

'I'm still in a lot of pain,' Cristabel's voice was high pitched.

'I'll get some medication for you lovey.' Oh.God! Did she really say that? Why not call her Mrs.Courtney-Browne? Charlie gave her a slightly apologetic look. She knew that Cristabel wasn't due for any stronger medication for another two hours at least. She needed to find some diversionary tactics.

'Your little girl has been very sleepy this afternoon. Perhaps you can give her a cuddle in a minute.'

No answer was forthcoming, so Charlie excused herself and hoped her absence was interpreted as collecting medication. The baby was asleep in the crib next to the bed. Perhaps some miracle would happen and Cristabel would look over at her.

Needing to have time to talk with Mr.McAlister about what the plan was for the next few days, Charlie searched through the duty list. Good. He was due in this afternoon and, hopefully, could offer some advice. She was feeling an antipathy growing towards this mother that she knew was unprofessional. The little, unnamed, baby was unnaturally quiet and Charlie was keen to understand the outcome of the tests.

She sat in the rest room, thinking how totally delighted she would have been if she had been able to give birth to the little girl in the crib. She knew that Cristabel had a serious problem with alcohol but knew that there was a reason behind it. Her husband was detached and anxious, but not particularly about his wife or baby.

She'd had enough experience in her nursing profession to know that bad parenting can be perpetuated. She was beginning to feel depressed by the frustration she felt and her own inadequacy.

She finished her cup of coffee, with four digestives. Well, why not?

Walking slowly back to the unit, she tried to fix a natural smile on her face. After all, this new mother was a victim herself, wasn't she?

In she went and was surprised to see Cristabel sitting in the chair.

'We've managed a few more steps,' Nurse Winifred said, looking surprisingly unfazed.

'That's good.' Charlie felt slightly easier. Perhaps this wasn't going to be quite as difficult as she had imagined.

Nurse Winifred had the wonderful cheery musical approach to her patients that all the black staff seemed to have without any effort. Charlie felt envious of her ability to persuade even the most contrary patient to co-operate.

'Well. I'll leave you to it, Charlie. Enjoy your day off.'

Cristabel's face looked perplexed.

'Don't worry, I'll be back tomorrow evening. You and the baby will be in expert hands. Have you thought of any names yet?'

'No, my husband's mother will probably see to that. I need my laptop. It has some important work on it that I have to organise.'

'Here's your mobile. I've recharged it, so you can contact your husband.'

Cristabel took it. No 'thanks' of course. Charlie handed her the day's menu, which Cristabel glanced at briefly. The girl must eat, thought Charlie and sat on the chair beside the bed. The baby was due to be taken out for feeding and more tests in an hour so she needed to make sure Cristabel ate something before then. There was no set time for meals. Patients could order anything they fancied, day or night. She read out certain sections of the menu to a blank face. When there was no response, she said she would order something tasty for her. After doing that she fussed around the baby a bit just to keep herself busy. There were no words to say to this mother.

The baby was still sleeping. Charlie was desperate to make some connection with the mother. Any sort of connection would do.

Post- natal depression entered her thoughts, being far more common that generally accepted. But her gut feeling was that this was a damaged young lady over whom she could have very little influence.

She realised that she was looking intently at the baby. Glancing at Cristabel she saw the girl fiddling with her hair, looking child-like herself.

'Your baby has a mass of black hair. Did you notice it? It really would be lovely to give her a name. Your mother-in law can give her opinion when she comes in.'

'Look at her tiny fingers,' Charlie persevered. Cristabel was obliged to look, a fixed emotionless expression on her face.

'I've got a book at home with all the boys and girls names in. I bought it when I thought I might be pregnant. I'll bring it in tomorrow night. Nurse Winifred will be here to look after you. I need to spend a few hours with my husband.'

The meal arrived and Charlie was surprised to see a rather submissive girl tucking in to it. She avoided watching, whilst waiting for some complaint or demand. Nothing was forthcoming and Charlie made herself busy with the baby. It was time for a feed and she really wanted this mother to give the bottle.

'I'll only be a minute,' she said and went to prepare the bottle.

A few minutes later she returned to find an empty plate and glass.

Probably the first time she's had a glass without any alcohol, she bitchily found herself thinking.

Removing the tray and getting the baby out of the crib, she sat in the chair nonchalantly and, unwrapping the little mite, started to tempt her with the tiny teat. Once the baby had latched on surprisingly easily, Charlie leant over and placed her in her mother's arms, hoping for the best. She was aware of the importance of 'bonding' and, if this mother didn't respond soon, there would be trouble ahead.

Cristabel, stiffly and with Charlie's help, held the bottle, looking down at the baby in a confused fashion. But Charlie wanted to shout 'hooray!' Of course she didn't.

The timing couldn't have been worse. Charles burst in. Why do men like him always have to make an entrance? He saw what was happening and looked embarrassed. Charlie put her fingers to her lips. This seemed to confuse Charles, so Charlie went, 'SHHHH', in the quietest but firmest way she knew. He rocked about a bit so Charlie indicated that he was to sit on the other chair.

He didn't know what to do, or where to look. Poor sod, thought Charlie. Here is a man, rich as hell, but totally deprived of any awareness of normal behaviour in a situation like this. He was carrying some flowers and, Charlie was pleased to note, no laptop.

Cristabel didn't even look up.

'Your wife is doing really well and we will be seeing Mr. McAlister later. He will be able to give you more information about your little baby.'

Charlie noticed that there was no eye contact between these new parents. Cristabel was looking at the baby sucking, rather lethargically now, at the milk. The hand holding the baby's head was moving very slightly. Without realising it, Cristabel was feeling the baby's downy hair. Charlie didn't comment but started to tell Mr. Courtney-Browne that the consultant would be coming to talk to them both later.

Charles had obviously been thinking, for once not about work. 'Oh, that's jolly good. We need to know what to do.' Charlie tried not to show how surprised she was at this almost normal comment.

Nurse Winifred breezed into the room and, for some reason, Charles blushed. Charlie wondered if it was because she was black and the only environment he was accustomed to seeing black people in his life had been as servants or cleaners.

Well, she thought, stuff it. It's about time these two entered the real world.

The baby was making hard work of the bottle. Charlie thought it would be a good idea to relieve Cristabel of her and give the parents time to talk in private. Nurse Winifred and Charlie both made a rapid exit, Charlie saying,' We'll leave you two in peace and take the baby to change her nappy. Perhaps you can think of a name.'

As she was changing the baby's nappy, Mr. McAlister popped his head round the door.

'Good, you're there. I wanted to discuss our approach to Mrs. Courtney- Browne and the needs of the baby. What have they called it by the way?'

'They haven't yet. Mr. Courtney- Browne is with his wife at the moment. I thought it better to let them have some time together. I really can't work them out. They seem almost disinterested in the fact that they are parents.'

'I had a word with him just now,' Mr.McAlister rubbed his hands together in a rather nervous fashion. 'He appeared to listen to me and nodded when I told him that I was concerned not only about the baby but his wife.'

'I'm at a loss to know what to do,' Charlie put the baby down on the changing mat. 'I worry that she won't get the attention she needs, certainly not from her parents.'

'Well, we might have to get the Social Services involved, or at least notify them that this baby might be at risk.'

'What from?' Charlie looked confused.

'Emotional neglect.'

' Even if they employ a really good nurse to care for her?'

'The nurse can't be there all the time.'

'But the Royal Family farm out their children from birth so what is the difference?'

'The difference is that this baby is going to have special needs, Charlie, so the sooner they realise that the better. I'm going to be very blunt with them.'

'Rather you than me. I'm off duty tomorrow so it will be interesting to see if there are any changes when I get back.'

'Don't expect miracles,' Mr.McAlister smiled at Charlie and off he went. Charlie was pleased he didn't expect her to follow him. Now he'd had time to think about the whole situation, he had adopted a confident attitude and wasn't going to beat about the bush. He was so sure of his ground that he didn't feel the least bit nervous at the thought of the possible confrontation ahead.

With a firm tread, Mr.Mc.Alister made his presence known. He had a distinct memory of being told at school the importance of a straight back and upright approach to problem solving. Ha!

He looked his old school friend in the eye. Eye contact was one of the other important facts that had been discussed during his training. Brief though this area was, it was, he thought one either had it or not, but it was important to be reminded.

So, it was handshakes again, spit in your eye attention, and assume the upper hand.

'Well, I'm pleased I've got you both together. Your baby is being looked after by Nurse Winifred, until Charlie gets back tomorrow evening. It is important you both spend time with your little girl so that you can bond with her.'

The consultant, even knowing he was speaking to an old school friend, couldn't manage anything but the formal approach in the circumstances.

'Jolly good, er... yes of course. The other nurse mentioned something about the baby needing some special care. That won't be a problem as I've appointed a Nanny and she can start immediately.'

' It's not quite as simple as that, Charles.' The consultant felt he was starting to waver. 'Your baby will need specialist care. A Nanny would have to be trained.' He thought he was asserting himself better now so quickly continued before he ran out of steam. 'You see she had certain weaknesses that will need constant surveillance to ensure she gets the best chance of making progress.' God! How ambiguous was that. He knew that if he was totally honest with this pair, they could just abandon the child at worst, or entrust it to the care of an untrained person.

The parents just stared at him, no comprehension being apparent.

He wished Charlie was still on duty. She was the best person to try to communicate with these parents. He'd leave it to her and, if they agreed on future treatment, a compromise could be achieved surely. Yes, that was the best plan.

Charlie and he could thrash it out between them and then he would feel confident in leaving it all to her. After all he had seriously ill children in his care and his time was limited.

'Have you thought of a name yet?' he asked as he was making an exit.

'Charlie is bringing me a book in tomorrow evening with all the girls' names in.'

'Oh good, then I'll leave it to her. I'll see you tomorrow,' and off he rushed, so relieved to be out of that particular situation. He'd noticed that the mother had been biting the old nail varnish off and there were shreds of it over the white counterpane. It looked like confetti, strangely inappropriate.

Nurse Winifred had been waiting outside and in she bustled. Even the noise of her oversized uniform was reassuring and Cristabel decided to give up fighting for the time being. When Charlie returned she would tell her about her plans.

Charles, meanwhile, had been doggedly silent. His mouth, at intervals moving as if to speak, was now almost pursed which could easily be confused with disinterest. What was he thinking, if at all?

Charles was in shock. The last three days had been a write –off There were numerous unanswered texts and emails queuing up for his urgent attention and he felt detached. It was not that he didn't care about the business, you know, but he wasn't able to concentrate his thoughts on any of it. He couldn't put his finger on it. The smell of the hospital and the sounds of babies crying, wheels on plastic, doors swinging; all these sounds were alien to him. He looked at Cristabel but there were no words. He cleared his throat, rubbed his hands together, and still the syllables were unformed. Nil, nothing, ziltch, came out from his mouth. He sighed and, with relief, noticed that Cristabel's eyes were closed. He glanced at Nurse Winifred. She was busy with the baby, doing something or other with a sponge. He coughed and the nurse turned to look at him enquiringly.

'Difficult for you, dear,' she said in a low relaxed voice.

'Mmmm. Yes... rather.'

'Well, you'll soon get the hang of it.' With that she wrapped the baby up in a blanket and placed her gently in his arms.

'Oh, I say, are you sure?' he mumbled.

Winifred thought she had never seen such an awkward and stiff body holding a baby.

'Don't worry, you won't drop her. Just rock her very gently and, if she looks at you, poke your tongue out.'

'Well I never. Why would I do that?'

'She will poke her tongue out at you too, if you're lucky.'

Charles felt the warmth of the baby through his jacket. He tried gently rocking but felt so self-conscious that he was forced to stop.

He glanced at the nurse. She was tidying up the washing equipment. He poked his tongue out at the baby. Nothing.

He started rocking her again and she opened her eyes. Winifred had gone out of the room. Charles put his

33

tongue out further. The baby returned the compliment. Charles was amazed and noticed her lovely blue eyes. He didn't know that all babies have blue eyes. They were staring directly at him in a disconcerting way. He started humming and realised it was a song that, at school, Ann had sung to him. 'Daisy, Daisy,' it was and he rocked the baby in time to his humming. Thank God the nurse wasn't watching. It would have been impossible to behave like this with an audience. It was really a very sweet little thing, this baby that he had helped, even if only by accident, to make.

Thank goodness Cristabel was in a deep sleep. He noticed the strips of red stuff on the bed; must be bits of her varnish stuff that she always had on her nails. He'd be in trouble if he didn't organise an appointment for her to rectify that particular problem. He looked at her more closely, the baby appearing to like it in his arms and sleeping peacefully. He knew he would have to get some people in to see to Cristabel's beauty requirements. She looked drab, more colourless than he could ever remember, with straggly hair, pale lips and what could only be described as a careworn expression on her face. He knew she had been through a tough time but, really, she should at least have tried not to bite her nails. He noticed that Winifred had returned and stopped all movement and noises.

'She did it you know,' he offered.

'What?'

'Put her tongue out.'

'That's wonderful.' Winifred offered up a secret prayer.

'My wife is still asleep. I need to get her some help with her hair and other things. I'll be in trouble otherwise.'

'I expect you will.' Nurse Winifred removed the baby from him.

He felt empty, the warmth still permeating his skin.

'Why don't you go and organise all the stuff you have to do and come back this evening?'

'Yes, jolly good. I'll do that...er... thanks.'

A quickly hidden old fashioned look flashed across Winifred's face and she smiled broadly at him.

'See you later, then. If you don't mind my suggesting it, why don't you bring one of your wife's friends in with you if possible?'

'Yes,..er.. I'll see what I can do.' His wife hadn't got any real friends; certainly not ones that would be there when you needed them.

Charles quickly gave Cristabel a peck on the cheek.

Winifred was holding the baby in her arms by the door. As Charles went out he involuntarily touched the baby's cheek.

The nurse's lips broke into a wide grin again, addressed to his back. 'There's hope there,' she thought, 'not a huge amount but a small flicker that could grow.'

She herself had never had any difficulty with recalcitrant mothers but, as she gazed at this new mother's dormant face, her natural optimism faltered. She would be glad when Charlie returned to duty the following evening.

Placing the baby in the cot she looked up to see Cristabel's eyelids fluttering. She noticed the downward thrust of her mouth and the overall expression of misery. As Cristabel gave a long sigh, Winifred knew she must be waking. Unexpectedly a low, rumbling groan came from her and spittle slid down her chin. Winifred was taken aback by her own response to this sign of humanity. She took one of the baby's wetwipes and gently smoothed away the offending moisture. Cristabel opened her eyes and shrank back into the pillows.

'It's o.k. honey, I'm just freshening you up.' Oh God. She knew it was unprofessional to address a patient in that manner. 'I'm sorry,' she babbled, 'I'll get you a cup of tea. Your baby has had a feed and a nap too. I think your husband enjoyed holding his daughter.' She couldn't resist that last bit.

A pot of tea, china tea cups, dainty biscuits, a slice of very delicious carrot cake were brought in on a proper tray.

Winifred frequently found herself questioning as to the morality of these apparently double standards. Half of her shifts were in the N.H.S. hospital over the road so she was constantly making comparisons.

Sick babies always got wonderful treatment in either environment. Winifred enjoyed the non-private mothers better though.

The tea and cake finished and obviously enjoyed, Winifred was surprised by a sudden outburst.

'I can't do this.' Cristabel had tears pouring down her face. It was about time for post birth blues anyway, but Winifred was disconcerted by the amount of water gushing from her eyes.

'Now, now, lovey.' Oh, there she goes again, whatever was she thinking? She must address the patient in a proper manner.

'Look,' she continued, 'we're here to support you. We won't abandon you yet,' she added trying to lighten the mood. 'We will help you to get into a routine so, when you go home, it will all come automatically.'

'But I can't do it on my own, she almost screamed, 'I will have a Nanny to do it all. My husband is not used to this. I have to entertain for him to win business.'

Charles was standing by the doorway. 'Shit', thought Winifred, 'now he'll take two steps backwards.'

But Charles came in, looked longingly at the teapot, sat down and took his wife's hands in his.

Winifred took the hint and removed the tray in order to replace it with a new set of tea and cakes. She returned briefly to take the baby out, explaining that she needed to take her for some monitoring, but would be back soon. She had decided to take the baby for the programmed tests then return with a tray of tea and cakes.

She fidgeted for about twenty minutes, hoping that there would be some signs of acceptance on her return. She called into the monitoring wing to see how the baby was progressing. There seemed to be no change in her functioning. She wasn't in any danger, but there were going to be concerns for some time. Waiting until the tests were finished, she collected some special milk and, with baby and warm bottle she returned to, as she saw it, 'the fray.'

Why she did what she did next she would never know, but walking purposefully across the room, she handed the baby plus bottle into Charles' arms. It was worth it just to see the expression of shock that crossed Cristabel's face, which, Winifred noticed, had been carefully made up. What a very beautiful woman she was with all the ' slap' on, she thought, then mentally rebuked herself. This was a disturbed young mother and it was her duty not to judge her.

'Chap in the office told me he was a "Hands on Dad", Charles whispered. 'Best thing he'd ever done apparently.'

Winifred leant over and helped tip the bottle up slightly. The baby was sucking weakly, but at least some nourishment was going in.

'I'm going to work late tonight so I can come in early tomorrow,' Charles rather apologetically muttered. He had a rather ridiculous expression on his face, but, as Winifred gently took the baby and bottle from him after a few minutes, she wanted to throw her arms around him and give him the biggest cuddle he'd ever had. It might kill him though. Charles, with a rather half-hearted wave of his hand, departed.

So there were just the three of them.

'Nothing venture, nothing gain,' Winifred thought as she lowered the baby into Cristabel's arms, hoping Charles' achievements would shame her into at least holding the baby.

The baby was in her mother's arms asleep. Winifred, ideally, would have liked to persevere with the bottle but knew any interruption would be counterproductive.

'Nurse, what's the matter with me?' Cristabel, very quietly, asked.

'We'll have a talk when I've got you ready for bed.' Winifred needed time to think and couldn't trust herself not to upset this mother.

So, the baby was put back in the little cot and Winifred bustled about getting everything she needed to make this mother comfortable. Cristabel lay passively as Winifred completed the intimate washing, creaming and gentle drying routine.

To ease any discomfort on Cristabel's part she said,' I've done this to thousands of new mothers.'

'Do you like it?'

'Believe it or not, I love every minute.'

'Really? I've never enjoyed anything very much.'

Winifred told herself to go slowly and thought carefully before saying, 'I've three sisters and we're all in nursing.'

'Really? How long have you been in this country? You haven't got an accent.'

Slowly, Winifred answered, 'Well, my grandfather came here in the fifties. He managed to support us as he was lucky and got a job as a bus driver. He always called Britain the "Mother Country." I didn't know what he meant, and he died before I was old enough to ask him.'

'Are you married?' Cristabel had a confused expression on her face.

'Never had the time.'

There was a long, long pause, one that Winifred didn't fill.

'They all think I'm a disaster, don't they?' Cristabel didn't look at Winifred as she asked this question.

'You are finding it all a bit of a challenge, but with your experience in business, I think it will get less irksome.' Oh. dear, there she goes again. She had never, in all her years of nursing, used the word 'irksome'. It wasn't a word that figured prominently in her vocabulary. 'You're having plenty of support and there will be frequent visits from the Health Visitor to make sure you are both happy.' 'Happy?' Again, Winifred was puzzled by the words she was using. What she really meant was the Health Visitor would visit to ensure the baby's needs were being met. That sounded a bit formal and it wouldn't take much to tip this mother over the edge.

'I don't want to be a mother. I don't know what to do. I'll be awful at it. My own mother hated bringing me up. That's why I was sent to boarding school.'

'Well, most new mothers wonder what on earth to do when they have a screaming baby to cope with in the middle of the night.'

'But you don't understand. I want everything to go back like it was.' Cristabel looked pleadingly at Winifred.

Winifred knew she must change the subject and talk to other professionals before unasked for words came out of her mouth. She handed Cristabel the menu and was relieved that there were no complaints about the meal she had already eaten. There shouldn't be any cause for complaints as the meals were perfectly prepared for these privileged new mothers.

Cristabel chose her meal and Winifred was happy to escape with the baby, which she knew was due for yet more tests. She went into the nurses' rest room after handing the baby plus records to the waiting registrar.

'Still no name, I see,' she said.

'No, but I think the Daddy might come up with something.'

'Good, it's a bit clinical to refer to her as Baby Courtney-Browne all the time. I expect you and Charlie will work your magic.'

'Not this time, I'm afraid. This is something different.'

'Yes. I got that impression.' The registrar grimaced and shook her head. We can only hope things improve. God knows what sort of life the poor thing will have if not.'

Winifred was silent, frustrated by the situation and feelings of impotence.

'You're really worried about this little one, aren't you? When Charlie gets back we'll have a heart to heart on the best way forward. Sorry Win, that is just more jargon.'

Winifred waited until the baby had finished with the various testing devices and took her, with the increasingly thick wad of hospital notes, back to the mother.

The meal had just arrived and Cristabel was tucking in with gusto. This fact annoyed Winifred. Did she really care so little for her baby that her own appetite was more important. She hardly looked up when Winifred and the baby entered.

The time until Charlie returned seemed endless. Cristabel had stopped threatening to leave which was a relief. Twelve hours passed more slowly than Winifred could ever remember. She knew she got personally involved with all her new mothers, a situation frowned on by the hierarchy, but she was unable to change herself into a more distant carer. It was impossible to pretend not to be upset when one of the babies died in the unit. Of course one kept in control and tried to be as practical as possible, but there were always tears bursting to escape. Winifred knew she could not be consoled if she had lost a child.

At last, with no real dramas unfolding, Charlie returned. She looked at Winifred's face and remarked,'Oh, so you're pleased to see me then?'

'You bet,' Winifred was gathering together all the latest test results, ready to discuss them with Charlie.

'Something radical needs to be implemented or I fear this mum will crack up altogether.'

'As bad as that, was it?" Charlie looked at the notes and screwed up her eyes, more in sadness than any other reaction.

'Not really, but I feel frustrated that I haven't managed to make a real connection. The father has surprised me though.'

'I've brought the book of baby names in with me. Come in with me and give me a bit of support. Please.'

'You know I'm a pushover. I'll not stay too long as there are loads of things I need to see to at home, much as I would love to watch you struggle.'

Charlie, refreshed from her short time off, grinned at her friend, knowing she could rely on her totally.

In they both went ready for a difficult time. Winifred was very quick to say, 'Look, Charlie's brought in the baby name book so we can go through it with you.'

'So she has. I think my mother-in law will over-rule any name I choose.'

'It is your decision, really, but you can always ask her opinion as well. You can always have her choice as a middle name.'

Cristabel gave them a look, no words needed. Charles' mother was used to having her own way obviously. Charlie was pleased that Cristabel showed an interest, however transitory.

Charles arrived. He had an assortment of packages with him and proceeded to hand them to his wife. She didn't bother unpacking anything but handed him the book of names.

'You choose. I'm too tired. '

'Mother will expect an input,' he offered.

'You choose and then she can stick her oar in for a middle name.'

Charles looked from Winifred to Charlie with an embarrassed expression on his face. He took the book and opened it on the first page.

In a very firm voice he stated, 'I'd like our little girl to be called Ann, no Annie, that's a bit softer.'

There was silence in the room apart from a quiet rustling sound from the crib.

'Well, she seems to approve, anyway,' Charlie laughed.

'When are we having the meeting with Mr. McAlister,' Charles asked.

'Probably tomorrow, when all the results are in,' Charlie said, knowing what the next sentence would be.

'I can go home then, can't I?' Cristabel had the closed expression on her face.

'We'll see what the consultant recommends. Hopefully it won't be too much longer until everything is in place to ensure you are both ready to manage. I know you will have extra help but it is important it is the appropriate type of support.' Charlie was sailing close to the wind and decided it was time for a distraction.

She lifted the baby, Annie, out of the crib and handed her to her father. He had actually stretched out his hands to receive the baby before Charlie assumed he would.

'Here you are, Daddy, your little Annie.'

She looked into Charles' face and was stunned to notice glistening in his eyes. Diverting her gaze to Cristabel there was no similar emotion waiting there. Of course not; there was no fragment of sentiment being allowed to show itself. Surely, soon, something resembling a human feeling would rise up, probably an accidental and unexpected reflex?

'I'll get Annie's next feed ready; won't be long.' Charlie left the three of them on their own, wondering what the conversation would be, if at all.

'You've organised the Nanny, haven't you?' Cristabel spoke in sharp bursts, as if these words had been imprisoned and they shot from her with desperation.

'Yes, I have, but we are going to need a qualified nurse as well so we'll discuss it with Mr. McAlister.' From what deep abyss had this courage appeared? Charles had never actually verbalised his thoughts to his wife a great deal as she always appeared totally in control and immune to any opinions he might have.

Even to himself his voice sounded different. It was firmer, resolute and he felt as if he were talking to his subordinates in the office.

Charlie returned with the bottle and gave it to Cristabel who wrinkled her nose up. Ignoring this, Annie was handed to her mother, as if it was her most natural thing in the world, and Charlie went out of the room. She noticed a slight flash of concern wash over Charles' face but it was fleeting. Out she went, knowing this must be the next step to helping the mother develop a connection with her baby.

'Back in a minute,' she called as she closed the door quietly. She almost felt like eavesdropping but forced herself to walk away.

She almost bumped into Mr.McAlister as he rounded the corner.

'Hello Charlie. I'm glad to see you're back. We must set up a meeting with the Courtney-Brownes as soon as possible. I've got several ideas, but will run them past you first.'

'Tomorrow evening would be good for me.'

Charlie knew this would give her time to collect all her thoughts together.

'Right, can you let them know? I'll get all the data together so we can be as explicit as possible. I have a feeling that it will be the father that will be he most approachable. Thanks Charlie, I'm keen to get this family out of here as soon as I'm happy that the home environment will be O.K.'

Charlie nodded her agreement and returned to the Courtney-Brownes. Cristabel was still holding Annie and looking marginally more relaxed. As soon as Charlie entered the room she held Annie up to be relieved of her. Charles jumped up and intervened with, 'Hey, let me. I can finish the bottle with her, or at least I can try.'

Cristabel gave him a black, sullen look.

Charlie quickly and softly said, 'It looks as if you've managed really well. The bottle is nearly empty. I'll show you how to wind her now.' She put Annie over Charles' shoulder and she obliged by throwing most of the milk out in a foetid shot. Charlie was speechless when Charles actually laughed, properly, naturally and spluttered, 'Ben, at work, said he thinks he stinks of milk most mornings. Funny thing, I've never really spoken to him before, but we had a long coffee break together today and he's such a decent chap.'

Charlie quickly wiped Charles' jacket and carefully made certain that she used the anti odour liquid, dabbing at the residue so as not to spoil the material. The strange thing was that Charles wasn't the slightest bit bothered by being vomited on. Cristabel was watching, frowning, but silent.

Charlie told them about the meeting programmed for the following evening.

'About time too; I can't think what is holding everything up,' Cristabel's face had a glassy sheen as she spoke in her clipped way. She was sitting in one of the easy chairs, fully made-up, with the highest heels on that Charlie had ever seen. As the nurse looked at them she wanted to say, 'What's the point, you stupid, selfish cow.' But, of course, professionalism won the battle and she just smiled sweetly, forcibly and totally insincerely. She knew these parents wouldn't notice much on this day. Tomorrow was to be a totally different scenario. Certain facts were going to be put on the table for discussion before the family could be discharged.

Chapter Two

The day passed so slowly and there was a growing tangible atmosphere in the room. It was as if the parents, at last, knew there were hurdles to overcome.

However, Charlie maintained her equanimity, was cheerful and confident in her handling of the mother. She was pleased, in a minor way, to see some very small points of contact between mother and child. Charlie assumed the mother would feed the baby now and just handed her over with bottle.

The next small step was to show how to prepare the milk formula. Cristabel was the clumsiest mother she had ever met. When Charles returned in the middle of one of these sessions he watched avidly and asked if he could try the next feed. Charlie was almost overcome but smiled at him, sincerely this time, saying, 'Of course, it is always a good idea for the dads to know how to prepare a bottle. I'll show you both how to sterilize all the equipment as well.'

So she did, Charles paying total attention, Cristabel tottering on her heels and shaking much of the powdered milk on the table. Charlie knew that she could take the easy way out and bring ready prepared feeds to them. However, she wanted to show them as much as possible of the sorts of routine they would need to know, regardless of whether a nurse or the whole of the medical profession was employed in their vast empire.

She did notice Cristabel, very secretly, sliding her heels off. A big step in the right direction she thought, amused, but a tiny one in the overall scheme of things.

The day passed, with Charles coming in and out at very frequent intervals. Charlie found herself warming to him. She wondered if he had been obliged, by family expectations, to marry this emotional cripple of a wife and then reminded herself that the poor girl was a victim of her own upbringing. She would make an even bigger effort to show her warmth and some sort of affection.

The evening came. Charlie noticed that Cristabel had replaced her shoes with a lovely pair of golden velvet slippers.

Her makeup was immaculate, hair sleek and shiny. How the hell she managed that Charlie couldn't be bothered to ask. She knew there had been several beauty consultants visiting and had taken Annie out of the room. Cristabel hadn't even noticed their absence.

Annie was, however, in the room as Mr. McAlister rustled in with all the medical records.

The next hour was full of facts and figures. The main consideration was to make certain that both parents understood that Annie had been in an environment during her development that had not been beneficial. He was as kind and as positive as he could be in the circumstances, especially when mentioning the little girl's future.

There followed a silence. Charles broke into it with, ' I'll make certain she has all the appropriate care she needs. If you let me know whom to contact, I'll do it immediately.'

Mr.McAlister indicated to Charlie that he wanted to see her in private. Out they went, leaving yet another silence behind them.

'I need to discuss an idea I have, Charlie.' Mr. McAlister was looking thoughtful. It was an expression Charlie had got used to over the years she had worked with him. He had obviously got some scheme of which Charlie was to be part.

The idea was that Charlie should go home with the Courtney –Brownes as a nurse and help the parents understand their baby's needs. She could also train another nurse to be on duty during the evenings and nights.

'The thing is,' she answered, 'these parents need to spend time with their baby or the bonding problems they have would just be passed on.'

'You're quite right as usual,' the consultant smiled at her, 'but I can't think of any other solution that would make me discharge them. Can you at least think about it and, if you agree, talk to them? '

'Yes, of course I will. I'll have to discuss it with my husband. It won't be an easy decision, as you know what their lifestyle is, and it is the opposite of mine.'

Mr.McAlister smiled. 'It's the opposite of most peoples' ways I think. At school Charles was a decent sort of chap, always trying to please. Parents hardly ever came to see him. Don't think much of his choice of wife.'

This was the not in the consultant's usual behaviour as he rarely offered any criticism of patients. He had a tendency towards being too clinical. This was a case where he felt it was necessary to become personally involved and Charlie respected him for it. She had known him for a long time but she still felt it was not in her capacity to call him by his Christian name, whatever it was. Henry had a familiar ring to it. She had heard other consultants call him by that name but she was unable to do it.

Going home, late that evening, she was relieved that her husband had gone to bed. She tossed and turned herself and woke him up with all her fidgeting. Luckily he was an understanding sort of man and turned on the light.

'Well, love, what's the problem?'

'Sorry, I think I might be going to work for the couple in the Mother and Baby Unit. I can't go into details but they will need some intensive support. They have plenty of money and Mr.McAlister thinks it would be a good idea if I worked with them until they get to grips with their baby's needs. There will be another nurse there that will do the nights. It hasn't even been suggested to them yet. I don't even like the mother but I can't bear the thought of that dear little baby not being looked after properly. I'm sorry to wake you up. What do you think I should do?'

'I think you know. Whatever you decide is fine with me. It's good to know Mr. McAlister appreciates you. Now go to sleep and start again in the morning.'

It was a relief to have talked with her husband, however briefly, and Charlie found she drifted off to sleep. In the morning her head was full of questions, suggestions, possibilities and anxieties. She got into work early and did the 'hand over' procedure quickly.

Going into the room, she was surprised to see Charles already there, Annie in his arms, smiling inanely.

'Well!' she said, 'you're an early riser.'

'I didn't go home.' Charles looked a bit sheepish. 'They made a bed for me here and I actually slept quite well. Oh, and I did the two o'clock feed.' He looked ridiculously proud of himself.

'Well done you.' Charlie saw that it would be a good time to make certain suggestions, but thought carefully before attempting any.

She sat down on the chair next to Cristabel. Charles was standing by the window swaying gently, Annie in his arms.

'I'd like to make a suggestion to you concerning Annie's future care. You don't have to say anything yet but think about it and then let me know. Well… what would you think if I came to help you for a little while just to get you through the first few months. Of course there would have to be a night nurse employed but I could train her. The arrangement would be that you would, between you, look after Annie for a portion of each day and evening, but I would be there to support you.'

Charlie paused, thinking she might have said too much. So what? It was out in the open now and they would probably huff and puff and think she wasn't out of the right drawer to be allowed house room.

The pause seemed to extend in front of her body and out of the window. Charles turned, looked at his wife and waited.

Cristabel had a smile on her face, an actual proper smile.

'That would be helpful,' she managed.

'Good. We'll talk about it later. You two have a think about what is involved and we can come to an arrangement as soon as possible as I'm sure you want to get home.'

Mission achieved. Charlie went out of the room, hoping some sort of agreement would be forthcoming when she returned. The more she thought about it the more her enthusiasm grew, for inexplicable reasons. She knew this was what she was intended to do with a bizarre certainty. She felt unreasonably happy and almost skipped along the corridor to see if Mr. McAlister was in his office.

He was and Charlie told him what she had suggested and that it would only be a temporary arrangement, so she would be back before too long. As she said this there was a calmness inside her and she knew the future was going to be unpredictable, but she was totally content.

So it all came to pass. Charlie went to work for the Courtney –Brownes, looking after Annie for part of each day, training another nurse in the needs of this little baby. She insisted that Cristabel was there for at least two hours in the daytime and every evening.

It was ridiculously easy. By being decisive, she obtained Cristabel's co-operation with no unpleasantness at all. It was all so unexpected. The reluctant mother, with help, gradually grew in confidence as she became accustomed to Annie's needs. To be honest she never relished being with her daughter but, as the little one grew and then learnt to sit up, at least she made an effort. The Nanny that Charles had employed and abused was kept on. Watching Charles, when the Nanny was close by, Charlie knew something untoward had happened.

This young Nanny was brilliant with Annie and Charlie felt confident that Charles wouldn't repeat the offence, even if it was by mutual consent. The girl was called Herta and her spoken English developed at a frightening rate. One day she told Charlie what had happened and that she felt ashamed of herself. She had needed the job so badly as money had to be sent back to her parents. She cried and begged Charlie not to sack her. Charlie told her that she had learnt a hard lesson and to tell her if Charles ever tried anything like that on again. Charlie knew that Charles wouldn't repeat the action as he sensed that she had been put in the picture.

One day, in a rare moment when all tasks had been finished, Charlie, very quickly, told Charles that she knew what he had got up to with the Herta and that it was now history, never to be repeated. He looked so abashed that she almost regretted saying anything. 'Message understood,' he said looking at the ground. Time passed, Annie's progress was slow but at least going in the right direction. The parents had few parties. The missing grandparents were almost invisible, thankfully in Charlie's opinion.

Things were almost too good. Herta and Charlie had formed a really affectionate relationship and worked perfectly together. The remuneration was incredible. Charlie, for the first time in years, could buy her husband a steak and they went out together for a meal on her birthday.

Even Cristabel was thawing slightly. Charlie recognised that this girl had never been in a naturally loving relationship, so she even started giving her a little cuddle when she came in from work. The response was truly amazing. After a few weeks, on coming home she came towards Charlie naturally waiting for her own welcome.

Then she started lifting Annie up and giving her a small swing up and down. It looked really awkward but Charlie was moved, and found tears pricking her eyelids.

Then something extraordinary happened, so extraordinary that Charlie was in denial for weeks until reality dawned on her.

She, Charlie, was pregnant. How it could happen to her after all this time and at her rather advanced age she didn't know. They had been told that they would never have children. At first she thought she had not been sensible with the food she had been eating. She had a queasy feeling in her stomach nearly all the time and felt more tired than usual. The food that Cristabel provided was of a very high quality and, strangely, Charlie had lost weight over the first few months in her new employment. Now she could get into her clothes of five years previously, being pregnant didn't come into her thoughts. She did think she could be pre- menopausal but was so happy in her work with the C.B's (as she had become used to calling them in private), that any other reason was not considered.

One morning she was just setting off for the C.B's when she had to rush for the bathroom, throwing up on the stairs on the way.

It was the most awful retching sort of sickness. Small rivers of vomit slid down the stairs, slowly sticking. Charlie watched, transfixed. She felt dreadful but knew she had to get to the C.B.'s establishment somehow. She called to her husband and, as usual, he immediately started to clean up, fetching a bowl and hot water and a flannel to get the worst off her. She looked at him and loved him, this man who had been nearly destroyed by redundancy, still able to jump up and give total commitment to his wife in the most disgusting state.

'I'll get you some clean clothes,' he said and brought her the practical garments she wore every day to work. She changed into them and looked at this man, this man who was so dear to her, knowing how lucky she was.

They went downstairs, Charlie becoming more and more thoughtful.

'A penny for them love,' he said.

'Nothing really. I feel much better now. I'll get to the C.B.'s and have something to eat there.' She gave him a long hug. As she went out of the front door she caught him looking at her with a very strange expression on his face.

Charlie made an appointment with the doctor and her hidden hopes were confirmed. She was so full of joy that evening that she had to force herself to walk, not rush madly, into the house.

She was overcome with a stupid embarrassment and called quietly for her husband, not wanting to worry him. She was rather late home, not having told him about her appointment with the doctor.

'I've some good news, or rather we have some good news.' Charlie heard herself speaking in a deliberately restrained voice, 'We're having a baby.'

There it was, words floating and spinning out in the air; words that were impossible to imagine ever being freed in that house.

'What?' Her husband stood, transfixed.

'It's true. That's what all the throwing up has been about.'

Her husband gathered her, literally, in his arms and held her there for so long that she had to ask him to let her sit down.

The next few hours were spent in mutual amazement, and the most rewarding sense of total happiness.

This couple, ordinary, honest and gentle people were being given the most welcome gift they had ever desired.

The Courtney –Brownes were told and, to their credit, reacted positively. Cristabel had a worried look on her face for a little while which disappeared when Charlie told her that she wasn't going to desert her. If the C.B.'s agreed she would stay on and, when the baby was born, return to them, plus baby of course.

'Gosh, we'll be growing into a proper family!' Cristabel said, her face taking on an almost enthusiastic expression.

'Don't worry,' Charlie said, aware how easily everything could go wrong. 'My husband intends to take over all the shopping, cleaning and cooking, so it will be easier to fit everything in.'

That was the theory, but Charlie was aware that sometimes events would mess up the intentions and she was determined not to get stressed by any of it. After all, there was nothing in life she could possibly want now.

The next event that Charlie had been invited to was Annie's Christening. Her husband, Bob, had been invited too which surprised her. The Courtney-Brownes had never met him and Charlie wondered what sort of initial judgements they would make of him. It no longer worried her and she knew that she was the only person that mattered to him and others' opinions of him were irrelevant.

Before that she knew that they had to tell both sets of parents about the pregnancy. Both were getting on a bit but would want to be fully involved. Charlie knew her own mother would worry herself silly about this unexpected and very late pregnancy. Charlie herself had seen many older mothers with problems but was determined not to be one of them. Her diet would be closely monitored and she would be sure to take the recommended vitamins and supplements. The rest was largely up to nature and luck.

When she telephoned her parents she phrased her words very carefully.

'Mum, I've got something to tell you. When you came for lunch at the weekend, I thought I had a stomach bug. You told me to go to the doctor. Well, I did, and guess what?'

Her mother calmly and quietly said, 'You're having a baby, my love. I've known for a bit, but didn't want to say anything just in case I was wrong.'

Charlie shrieked, 'Mum! How long have you guessed?'

'Well, you look different and I asked your Dad what he thought and he went all coy and wouldn't say. Have you told George and Mary? Bob better do that. They'll be so pleased. How many weeks are you? About fourteen, I'd guess. I'll help you clear the spare bedroom out and decorate it if you like. I'll pay for new stuff for you. Oh. I'm so happy. I'm going to be a Granny!'

'Mum. Mum. Slow down. We've only just heard ourselves. Bob will 'phone his Mum and Dad tonight.'

'Sorry, love, I am just so excited!'

The Christening day arrived. Annie's dress was exquisite and Cristabel had organised a magnificent cake to accompany all the other goodies. Herta had decorated the reception room with beautiful white roses and green and silver ribbons. The guests arrived and Charlie and Bob shrank against the wall.

Bob muttered,' If the bloody hats were any bigger, we'd be knocked down.'

Cristabel was holding Annie and she looked stunning in a very simple cream suit, no hat. She saw Charlie and Bob and immediately came towards them. She handed Annie to Charlie and held out her hand, 'Hello. You must be Bob. Your wife is my right hand. Actually she's both my hands. I don't know what I'd have done without her. Congratulations, by the way, I hear you are going to be a father.' This speech from Cristabel was the longest that Charlie had ever heard. She smiled at her. She knew it was difficult for her to talk to people, any people, not just those from a different background.

Charlie asked if there was anything she could do to help. ' No, you two are our guests. My husband wants to meet Bob. We had better rescue him from his parents.'

Charlie was overcome by this change. She had noticed subtle variations in her behaviour, but only today did she see a fundamental shift in her priorities.

So, Bob and Charlie, still carrying Annie, were pulled towards four very stiff looking adults swamped by hats and grandeur. Charles was standing, almost to attention, at his father's side.

'Mother, I want you to meet Charlie, the nurse that is helping us look after Annie. This is her husband, Bob.' Charlie held tightly on to Bob's arm as he was trying to slide behind everyone.

'How do you do? Nice to meet you', Bob managed.

Both sets of grandparents stared, intently with where their third eye would have been if they had had one.

Again, there was a silence broken by a shrill voice, 'Gosh, you two. What do you think of the awful name they have fixed on the baby?'

'I love it,' Charlie quickly intercepted any other opinion, 'it's simple and sweet and won't be shortened.'

Cristabel's parents were looking at her as if they were surprised she could string a sentence together.

Charles was hopping from foot to foot, obviously uneasy. 'Here,let me take my daughter,' he said and Charlie was only too pleased to give her up. She was getting heavy.

'Good God, man, she'll probably be sick over you. Give her to the Nanny.' Charles ignored this remark.

Cristabel said, very firmly,' We don't have a Nanny. We have two of the most wonderful nurses in the world. They are helping me to learn how to be a better mother.'

'Oh, Cristabel', thought Charlie,' be careful. These people are the result of centuries of neglect and cannot help being boorish and self- opinionated. It is how they have been brought up.'

How proud she was to hear Cristabel's words. She'd promoted Herta to a nurse, which of course, she was in many ways. With Charlie's teaching she had learnt as much as Charlie could teach and, if the truth were known, she probably had more potential. Charlie knew she wanted to study further and encouraged her to think about further qualifications when the time was right.

After the Church service and the poor child being named Annie Rosamund, Delilah, Courtney-Browne, the reception was a relief.

Gifts were laid on a white-clothed table with cards to indicate the donors. Charlie thought that was in pretty poor taste, but what did she know about tradition? Her gift, nearly invisible, was a photograph album. It stood out like a sore thumb in amongst the silver mugs and egg cups, Christening spoons, table napkin rings and shiny stuff of no use to a baby. Charlie had also bought a ball run, which stood there on the floor, inviting hostile comments. Charles had put Annie on the floor next to it and she had picked up one of the balls and tried to put it in the groove to run down to the bottom. Charles helped her by showing her how to do it. She smiled up at him and Charlie was constantly surprised at the effect this had on her father. He sat on the floor with her and said, 'That's it. Clever girl.'

Cristabel's father pulled a face and moved away. Charlie could have punched him.

Bob touched her arm and whispered, 'Can we go soon?'

'Yes, in a minute, I'm feeling tired and need to sit down.'

'Let's go then.'

So off they went, with parcels of baby clothes that Cristabel had packed up for them. Charlie was taken aback by the developing generosity and thoughtfulness of this mother. It was something she would have denied vehemently a few months previously. She had all the traits of a spoilt child herself, in Charlie's opinion, and this new slant to her behaviour was confusing.

The next day Charlie was on duty early as Cristabel had several important meetings. When she arrived the place was immaculate.

The pleasure of not having to clear up any mess was something Charlie could get used to, but still couldn't get rid of her feelings of guilt. Who had swept up all the crumbs, spilt drinks, dead flowers?

It was good to be back to normal and she had brought her swimming costume with her as she had decided to ask Cristabel if she could take Annie in the pool. The exercise would be very good for them both.

Cristabel looked surprised. 'Of course you can. I'll come in with you next time.'

Surprise after surprise. Now this spoilt brat is going to join them for a swim. Whatever next? Slowly, almost indiscernibly, Charlie was actually warming to this young mother.

It happened. The following week, there were the three of them in the pool. Annie loved it and laughed when the water was dripped over her head. Cristabel was an excellent swimmer, telling Charlie that they had their own pool at school. Of course they did! She was elegant and swift in the water and Charlie praised her abundantly. Cristabel's expression was very surprised as if normal people don't bother to flatter others very often.

'You're really good. I wish I could swim like you. My parents took me to the local pool but we always seemed to get there when the wave machine was on and I didn't like it. I taught myself when I started nurse training at the pool just near to the hospital.'

'I envy you, you know,' Cristabel spoke quietly, looking at Charlie holding Annie in the water.

'You mustn't say that. You have everything you could possibly want.' Cristabel swam away, speeding up the pool gracefully.

There was a quiet footstep and Charlie noticed Charles had been standing behind one of the pillars.

He came out and watched the scene. Annie started laughing again as Charlie showed Charles how she enjoyed water being dripped on her head. Cristabel returned, hair soaking and streaming out behind her. Annie saw her coming and laughed even more.

Charles was overcome. It was probably the first time he'd seen his wife enjoying her little girl. Herta was waiting at the poolside. She lifted Annie out and took her away to be dried and dressed.

'I'm so pleased you are enjoying the pool, darling,' Charles addressed his wife in the contrived affectionate manner in which he had been indoctrinated.

'Can you get a pot of tea organised, Charles? ..... Please.' The 'please' was an afterthought. Soon they were sitting in comfortable chairs, tea prepared in a proper china teapot and cups, as relaxed as they had ever been with each other.

'This is nice,' Cristabel offered. Then all three of them burst into laughter, none knowing the reason why.

Cristabel looked at Charlie. 'I know you don't think much of me, but I'm trying really hard.'

Charlie, softened by all the laughter answered, 'You are an amazing lady. You just need to have more faith in yourself as a mother. Don't you know how much you've changed?'

Charles interrupted by saying, 'I've noticed how much happier you are. Cutting down your hours at work has helped a bit, don't you think?' Charles knew he was skating on thin ice.

Cristabel looked closely at Charlie, hesitated and then said, 'Can I tell you something, Charlie? I worry that you won't want to come here after your baby is born. I know Charles feels the same.'

Charlie got up and hugged her. 'I love coming here. To be honest, I didn't think I would as our lives are so different. My cup of tea for example would be out of a mug! I was actually frightened of you. You seemed so detached somehow.' Charlie knew she had probably said too much but she gabbled on, 'However, I really love my job and I know Herta does too. She wants to go on to further education. We won't leave you. I feel Annie is part of my family somehow; that probably sounds a bit presumptuous but watching her make all her progress is so rewarding. It's as if she wants to please.' Charlie stopped talking suddenly as if she knew her words were running away with her.

'That's it!' Charles almost shouted, 'she makes me feel as if I'm important.'

Cristabel just looked thoughtful. Charlie knew she was thinking almost the same but was not quite as prepared as her husband to appear so vulnerable.

One of the cleaners knocked on the door and said there were two ladies outside wanting to speak with Cristabel. She was not really in the state of dress she would usually consider presentable, but she got up and went to the door to welcome whoever these people were into her home.

Surprisingly, they were two colleagues from Cristabel's work. Rather sheepishly they entered the house carrying parcels.

'Come and meet my husband and the nurse that helps me with Annie.' This was said naturally, without any concern that she must look totally bedraggled compared with the pristine state in which she went to work.

The two girls were rather overawed by the opulence of these surroundings.

'We've brought you a gift for your baby. We know it's a bit late but we didn't know what to get.'

Charles introduced himself and then left them to it. Although it was good to have a few minutes with the family, he knew he should get to work and make certain the wheels were being turned in the right direction.

The gift was perfect. The two girls were worried that their choice might not be quite right, but Cristabel had begun to learn not to be so impetuous with her comments and was very gracious with her thanks. The gift was a coloured ball that had bells inside it.

'Annie will love it and can take it into the pool.'

More tea was called for and a cake magically appeared. Charlie made herself scarce as there were certain duties that needed attention.

Some days later, after Cristabel had returned from work, and she had taken Annie up to spend some time with her mother, she saw her looking puzzled.

'It's the first time anyone from work has shown any interest in either Annie or I,' she quietly said, ' I didn't even know their names until recently. They were so nice. I really liked them and they genuinely seemed to like me for some reason.'

'Of course they did. You could see they were a bit scared of you at first but that didn't last for long.'

' Mmm, I wasn't interested in any of the others at work really. They all seemed rather, er… I don't know, distant I suppose. I didn't make any effort to make friends with anyone. I knew they thought I was a snooty cow.'

Charlie laughed, 'Well, I thought you were when I first met you.'

Enough said.

Chapter Three

The weeks went by. Annie made slow progress but at least it was in the right direction. Cristabel attended all the paediatric appointments and Charles managed to join them for several in the months ahead. They even went on their own on one occasion as the appointment clashed with Charlie's twenty week check.

She was constantly waiting for something to go amiss but nothing did and she knew she looked blooming. She tried not to put on too much weight but was incredibly hungry all the time. Being surrounded by all the gorgeous food at Cristabel's house made her will power shake many times but then she remembered that this was her one and only chance to produce a healthy baby and, at her 'advanced' age she mustn't put on too much weight.

One morning she was looking at her latest scan when Cristabel looked over her shoulder.

'What's that?' Cristabel peered at the printout.

'It's my latest scan. Here look, you can see all the limbs and head now. Amazing, isn't it?'

'I wish you had been around when I was pregnant with Annie. I might not have done so much damage to her then. You could have stopped me.'

'No, I don't think I could. You were in a different place then, probably worried and unhappy and feeling you didn't want to talk to anybody.'

'Yes, I was. My mother isn't the easiest person to talk to especially if she thought I wanted her help over anything.' Cristabel laughed a hollow laugh and Charlie realised how much this absent Grandmother lacked in normal human feelings. She was certain that she had probably had a pretty detached childhood herself; best not to enquire too much. It was enough that these new parents were showing promising signs.

'Why don't you come to my house one afternoon, when you're not working? Could you take a couple of hours off, just for a cup of tea and a chat. Herta could come as well. She hasn't seen where I live.'

'I'd like that. Will your husband.....er..... Bob, be there?'

'Yes, but he won't get in the way. He's busy decorating the baby's room at the moment so he won't feel he's overrun with women!'

The following Tuesday, a day to everyone's convenience, arrived. Bob had vacuumed the floors until the carpet must have been inches thinner. Charlie had made a cake, which had sunk in the middle. She sensed that this might be a good thing so that Cristabel knew that all people make mistakes and it didn't really matter. She mixed loads of chocolate icing and splodged a good lump of it in the crevasse, the rest smoothed roughly over the top. She was tempted to put something silly on it but decided that it was enough of a joke in itself.

She wondered what the neighbours would think of the latest BMW model outside.

Everything went to plan. The cake was laughed at but tasted surprisingly good. Cristabel was slightly uncomfortable initially, but Annie saved the day by trying to crawl. She also had a tiny piece of cake, no icing. She smeared it all over her face.

'I see she is going to have a sweet tooth,' Charlie smiled at her and Annie smiled back. 'She really is the sweetest little baby,' Charlie said as she went to get some baby wipes.

'I know,' Cristabel was staring at her daughter,' I can't remember what it was like before I had her. Strange isn't it? All I know is that we can't do without you and Herta. I'm really scared that everything might fall apart when you leave to have your baby and I might revert to my bad old ways.'

'I've told you before that Herta will be helping you and I'll return as soon as I feel able. You will manage, believe me, and Charles is besotted with his daughter anyway so between you you'll be fine. I bet Charles would take a couple of weeks off whilst I'm getting into some sort of routine and then perhaps you could take a few weeks off before I come back too.'

'But what if she's ill or there's something that I miss and Herta is on her day off?'

'Well, you telephone the Medical Centre's Help Line. You remember, I gave you the number in case you are ever worried and feel you need support? I'll always pop round if I can, but if I'm in the middle of labour, you will get a raspberry.' Cristabel laughed. 'I'll wait until it's over, shall I?' Charlie was so pleased to hear this lady make a pretty feeble joke. She had never heard her say anything even remotely funny, so laughed with her. They all became absorbed in watching Annie thump her legs behind her as if this would help her move.

'Why is she doing that?' Cristabel didn't understand the various stages in a baby's development and the thumping of the feet against the soft carpet seemed pointless to her.

'She's developing her leg muscles. It won't be long before she's crawling and then watch out!'

'Why, what will happen then?'

Charlie went out of the room and found one of her Mother and Baby books, which she gave Cristabel. 'It's a bit thumbed but you can borrow it for a bit. I've got several. ' Charlie knew she mustn't make Cristabel feel guilty, even if it was deserved. She was hoping that her developing attachment to Annie, possibly as a result of lessening feelings of failure, would be self motivating and destroy, even if at snail's pace, her reluctance to be a mother. The realisation that Cristabel didn't have any books on child rearing was a shock. Perhaps, when considering the contradicting advice being scattered around, it was a good thing.

Bob popped his head round the door. It was a weird experience to see Cristabel and Bob in the same room in their humble home but Charlie found herself at ease and, possibly because of her hormones, relaxed, took her shoes off and rested her feet on a chair.

'Hello there.' Bob, pleasant as always, greeted them. 'Nice for some people, I see.' He smiled the smile that had melted Charlie's heart so many years ago.

'Want a piece of cake, love? There's tea in the pot. I'll make another brew if it's gone a bit cold.'

'Did you tell them about the hole in the middle?' Bob grinned at his wife who was expecting some silly remark or other. He couldn't resist any opportunity to make people smile.

'Hello, Annie. My goodness, you're growing fast. It must be all the cake!' He'd noticed smears of cake on her dress and tights. He'd also noticed that Cristabel had smears of chocolate on the front of her blouse too, but was aware that keeping silent was the best option.

There seemed to be no hurry for Cristabel, Herta and Annie to depart. Charlie was getting tired but didn't want to do anything that would be interpreted as not wanting their company. Eventually, moves were made, stimulated by Annie who had started to grizzle.

'She's getting hungry,' Herta, said and started clearing up the tea things and packing Annie's bags ready to go. Cristabel, Charlie noticed, paid close attention to this. Soon they were in the car. Charlie and Bob went to the end of the path and waved them off.

'That went well,' Bob commented accurately, 'she's not so bad, is she?'

'No, but I still think there is quite a lot of stuff she has to accept and deal with.'

'Mmm. You go and have a rest. I'll get some tea on. I need the practise.'

The next two months seemed to fly by. Annie started to crawl. Some of her movements were rather stiff, but physiotherapy had been organised, without any reluctance from the parents. Herta was starting at evening classes and had brought a friend to see the Courtney- Brownes with the intention of getting them interested in employing her for Annie's swimming lessons. It was almost too easy.

Charlie knew the time was coming when she must give up working. She had been healthy throughout but was aware that it was not a good idea to carry on too long. She knew she would always have a job with the C.B.'s, but was not intending to go back to nursing at the hospitals as before. Not until her baby was at school perhaps.

The baby was very active, so much in fact that she was kept awake many nights. Nothing could go wrong. Her weight and blood pressure were fine. No, nothing could go wrong. So, why was she becoming increasingly anxious?

Another month passed. Charlie was getting breathless at simple exertions. She mentioned this to the paediatrician but he assured her that all the tests were perfect. She was quite old to be having a first baby, after all. She felt like saying, 'Oh, I should be on my sixth should I?'

So, she stopped working at the C.B.'s. When Cristabel knew she was leaving she was given an envelope and told she wasn't to open it until she got home.

When she eventually opened it a cheque fell out and Bob had to bend down to pick it up. There was also a letter. The cheque was for a ridiculous amount, but Charlie knew Cristabel would be deeply hurt if it was returned. The letter was mainly concerned with Charles wanting Bob to act as a maintenance man at the house, in charge of the buildings and pool staff. Charlie saw the expression on Bob's face and anticipated his reluctance.

'It's not that I can't do the job, and the money would be brilliant. It's that I want to be here with you and the baby for a couple of months. Will they let me do that?'

'Let you!' Charlie exploded. 'They'll be lucky to get you at any time.'

So they sat down, weary with thought. Nothing was said for some time. In truth, Charlie felt too exhausted to think about anything very much. She, in the last few days, had felt a detachment about most things. It was as if her body was telling her that she had overstretched it and it needed to close down for a bit. She was sure it was just being in the last stage of pregnancy. All the books said that you felt just like a blob of lard, or words to that effect.

She had even shouted at Bob. He had got into a mess with the wardrobe. It needed to be assembled but three of the integral parts were missing and Charlie heard him curse. This was so unusual that she started to cry. Hormones again, she supposed. She decided that she needed to be busy. She had rested for most of that day and was completely bored. All the baby books were all well and good but she needed a baby on which to practise.

A week later, as she was writing a letter to Cristabel, she found she was sitting in a pool of water. She had wanted to actually write a letter to Cristabel as it was essential was something more tangible than an email.

She quickly wrote, 'Waters broken, baby on the way,' and called Bob.

Panic ensued. They had been so incredibly well prepared for this, but for some reason, they just stared at each other.

'It'll be ages yet. First babies are always a long time. Have you got a stamp?'

Of course neither of them had a stamp, but Charlie knew it was imperative that she finished the letter and got it in the post. Bob had been primed as to what to do and he efficiently produced towels for Charlie. She wrapped herself up and told Bob to get the car packed up.

'I'll wait for a bit to see how long there is before the contractions start in earnest.'

'Don't you think we should get to the hospital anyway?' Bob was naturally anxious and had visions of him having to deliver the baby on the sitting room floor. No, they must get to the hospital sooner rather than later, despite what Charlie wanted.

Charlie looked at Bob's face and knew she must do as he wanted.

'I'll take the letter to finish with me. There's bound to be a postbox in the hospital.' Why had she never noticed one?

So, Charlie wrapped in an assortment of towels, the pair of them inelegantly shuffled to the car. Charlie knew that, when the waters broke, labour usually followed fairly quickly.

They reached the hospital with no problems. She was quickly settled into the ward and a midwife greeted her warmly.

'Well, we were expecting you a few days ago. Baby not wanting to come into the world? Have you had any contractions yet?'

'They're just starting; nothing much to fuss about.'

'I'll get an epidural organised for you and then you can relax. There is plenty of time, I assure you.'

Charlie asked Bob to unpack her nightie and washbag. 'I feel as though I need a good wash. I'll just go to the bathroom and clean myself up a bit. If anyone comes for me, tell them where I am.'

Charlie took her dressing gown and wrapped it around her. She felt like a ship in full sail and couldn't tie it round her middle. There were plenty of other women and girls in various stages of labour and she felt comfortable in the familiar surroundings of the hospital. She wondered if she would have time to finish her letter to Cristabel. Of course she would, this was a first baby and they were notoriously slow to arrive.

She felt much better after her wash and returned to the ward where Bob was chatting to one of the nurses that had worked with Charlie. Word soon got around and very soon she had seen a succession of visitors, all of whom she had, at one time or another, worked with.

Suddenly, there was Winifred. 'Oh, Win, how I've missed you. I'd hug you but can't really get near enough with this luggage.'

'I'd heard you were in and came straight over. Is everything going to plan?'

'I think so. I just want to get on with it. I'm having an epidural later.' She hesitated as a contraction hit her and surprised her with the intensity.

'Ouch. I must do the breathing. That was unexpected. I shall be much more sympathetic to other mothers in labour after this, if that was one of the initial ones.'

Another contraction came within three minutes and Win rang the bell for the midwife on duty, who looked at Charlie, told Bob to wait outside for a minute, examined her to see how far she was dilated, and said, 'Too late for an epidural. You baby is in a real hurry.'

Lots of bustling about, machines attached, blood pressure monitor at the ready and Charlie felt as if her body was being punched by heavy weights then squeezed by a grudge fuelled adjustable spanner. She had never imagined that there existed a pain so intense. Why anyone would go through this more than once was beyond her. But she breathed, thought of beautiful things, breathed again and wanted it to stop. She was given something to breathe in, but it stopped her feeling in control. Then she wasn't in control at all. Bob appeared as she was wheeled to the delivery unit, held her hand and tried to be helpful. She felt really angry with him but didn't know why. She thought she might have shouted at him, in fact she screamed at him, saw his stricken face and tried to restrain herself, but couldn't. He hadn't any idea of what she was going through. How could he? He was not helping at all and she told him to bugger off.

There was a strange lapse. Everything went quiet. Nothing seemed to happen until the most overwhelming tearing, pulling, wrenching cramps attacked her vagina.

'Don't push,' she was told.

'I can't help it.'

'Pant, that's it. In, out, in, out, that's brilliant. We'll have a baby very soon now.'

Bob was by the end where everything was happening. Charlie saw an ashen face. She knew she was groaning very loudly and could hear the midwife telling her what to do. It was stupid. She knew what to do. Hadn't she trained in all these techniques? She groaned even louder and thought her bottom end was going to split open and all her guts slide out over the floor, the baby hidden amongst them. It all seemed to go on forever. Then, after an eternity, when she thought she might actually die with the pain, a voice saying, 'One more push and we're there. That's it. Here's the head crowning, lovely. Rest for a moment and, when I tell you, give just one more push and your baby will be here.'

One more push, God, it hurts so much. Please come out and let me alone. I can't do this any longer.

Charlie knew she had let out the most horrendous scream as the need to push overcame her whole body.

So, a baby was born. Then the interval, waiting for the first cry and the signs that air was being taken in.

The cry, loud and strong, came from the red-faced bundle wrapped in a towel. Then she was removed for the various tests to be quickly completed before returning her to the drained mother. The afterbirth came away with no problems and Charlie looked at Bob. He was leaning against the wall, looking as if he would slide down it any minute. He came towards her, peeping at his new daughter. He gave them both a kiss and Charlie saw tears glistening on his cheeks. He was very, very quiet.

Charlie realised that she had had no idea of the intensity of the pain a mother in labour goes through. Obviously Bob had been traumatised by it all as well. She was so tired, indescribably so. She just wanted to sleep but knew both sets of parents must be told. They would be overjoyed. Bob went out of the room for a minute to 'phone people, hearing Charlie, rather weakly, call out, 'Don't forget Cristabel and Charles.'

Charlie, like most mothers, recovered well from her exertions and tried to reassure Bob that she was fine and had suffered no ill effects. He, however, was of the opinion that women must be mad to put themselves through it, even once.

The following day, Cristabel and Charles arrived, laden with gifts. Charlie was touched by Cristabel's concern at her obvious unkempt appearance. She had brought in just about everything she could possibly want and Charles was the first to look at the baby. There were six new mothers in the ward and a great deal of attention was attracted by Cristabel and Charles' entrance.

'I'm so pleased you've had a girl. It will be lovely for Annie to have a ready-made friend.' Cristabel knew she was the centre of attention and this made Charlie smile.

The new baby, named after Charlie's mum, was called Lily. She was a hungry baby and Charlie worried that she might not have enough milk for her, but she fed well and Charlie was surprised how easy it was. Perhaps she was just lucky, but she thought most mothers could feed their babies, they just didn't want to and the human race would be extinct if bottles hadn't been invented.

The C.B's didn't stay long and Bob was good at providing chairs for them. He didn't resent doing things for people. He was secure enough in his own skin not to mind in the slightest if it appeared subservient.

Cristabel would have liked to have a more private talk with Charlie.

'Ghastly, was it?' she asked.

'Not what I expected. I'll talk to you about it later.'

Cristabel gave her a secret smile, one that only women can appreciate.

Two days later it was time for the new mother to take her baby home. She still felt shell shocked, but was determined not to spoil Bob's obvious pride in his daughter. She was continuously doing silly things due to tiredness and it was a good job that Bob was coping on the domestic front. How the hell Victorian women coped with having a baby every year she couldn't imagine. Well a great many of them died in their forties or fifties didn't they?

Charlie loved little Lily almost to distraction. She could barely leave her out of her sight for a second, even to go to the toilet. Bob had a firm word with her and she managed a quick shower without imagining Lily was being stolen by some imaginary baby thief.

Gradually, she gained in confidence and stopped leaning over the crib every few minutes during the night to see if she was still breathing. The letter she had started writing to Cristabel was continued, Lily in the crib next to her. There were so many things she wanted to say, especially now she had experienced childbirth herself.

The words were almost impossible to find. She knew what she wanted to say but getting the appropriate words was harder than expected. Charlie was amused to see the first sentences were about her water breaking. She decided to leave them explaining that she had been writing just before going to hospital. It seemed years ago now and she knew she had changed in herself, perhaps gaining a little more understanding of the difficulties that new mothers face.

She wrote to Cristabel and Charles thanking them again for their generosity. She hesitated over the next words as she wasn't certain what it was she wanted to say. Eventually she found the words almost wrote themselves. She explained that she valued their friendship and hoped they would be able to continue a close contact for many years. It sounded a bit formal but Charlie knew they would understand, even if the notepaper was a bit cheap. It really didn't matter and Charlie knew that Cristabel had reached a stage in her life that was a watershed. She asked if she could return to work in about three of four weeks' time, when she had got herself and Lily into a routine. Bob was eager to start work and he knew Charlie was missing Annie. It was almost as if she felt responsible for the little girl. Bob posted the letter, catching the evening post.

Cristabel telephoned the following evening. Charlie was feeding Lily, but managed to have a reasonable conversation with her. Of course, said Cristabel, it would be wonderful if the three of them could come back when they could, the sooner the better. Charlie noted the phrase 'the three of you' with the greatest of pleasure.

Charles had been talking about their return that very morning. Herta had been wonderful and Annie was responding well to the physiotherapy. Cristabel actually sounded as if she really cared about her little girl. 'Well,' she said, 'there's surprise waiting for you. Not going to tell you. You'll be pleased. Oh, and my mother and father have actually taken an interest in Annie, as much as they're able. Charles' parents are in Bermuda so they haven't seen her much really. I don't want Annie to have the feelings of sadness that I can remember.' Cristabel stopped abruptly. Charlie knew she would talk more when they met in person and was reassured.

'Lily needs winding. I'll have to go or she'll throw up all over me. I seem to be covered with milk trails anyway. See you next month, all being well.'

The next month passed quickly and Charlie and Bob were welcomed as long lost friends. In fact, Cristabel rushed out of the front door, throwing her arms round Charlie, possibly the first time she had actually initiated a hug by herself.

Charlie was touched and squeezed her shoulders. 'I'll get Lily in and then you can show me the surprise. I bet it's to do with Annie.'

Charles had taken the morning off and he and Bob disappeared to talk about the responsibilities Bob was expected to take on.

Herta came in with Annie and Cristabel nodded to her, a signal that the surprise was imminent. She put Annie down on the floor and the little girl rolled over, tucked her knees up under her and started crawling over to where Lily was still in her car seat.

'Wow, that's wonderful!' Charlie was equally impressed by Cristabel's pleasure as by Annie's performance.

The weeks passed, again with little upset. Could life be too full of good things? Could perfection last?

Charlie found an uncanny atmosphere surrounding her in increasing bouts of anticipation. She couldn't put her finger on it, but it was taking on a more solid shape. She tried to forget it and enjoy the present but everything was too good. Once she tried to talk to Cristabel about how lucky she felt and that she thought life must have something in store for her that was not planned.

Cristabel tried hard to empathise with Charlie but Charlie could see it was outside her experience.

' I mean, you have been so good to us and Bob is so happy working here. My parents can come for a roast dinner at the weekends now as we can afford it. It is all up to you and Charles. I don't think you realise how we struggled financially before I met you.'

Cristabel, out of character said, 'Poo, I didn't feel as if I had anything in my life until you tried to sort me out.'

'It's like the comment that those poor kids make on game shows. You know, '"It's like a dream come true".' They both laughed.

Nothing else was said but Cristabel gave her a long look, too inexplicable to translate.

So many things seemed unimportant. It didn't matter one jot if the dirty dishes were left stagnating in the sink. Lily's equipment was the essential consideration. She was pleased she could breastfeed so easily. It got a bit sore and engorged but she knew that, by feeding Lily more frequently, the soreness would go. She was such a good baby, almost too good. Colic never occurred and Charlie looked at all the 'essentials' she had bought before the birth and knew she wouldn't need much of it. Bob was so helpful and, gradually, Charlie felt he was able to do some of the more physical tasks with his daughter. She even trusted him to take Lily for a walk in the very smart buggy that they had bought with the generous gift from the C.B.'s, although she was looking out of the window all the time until he came back.

Working at the C.B's was fitting in very well with the two sets of grandparents. Occasionally, one of them would have Lily for a morning and then Charlie felt she wasn't cutting them out of her life by the hours she was with Cristabel and Annie.

Chapter Four

The premonition, that Charlie had harboured almost secretly, came to fruition almost at the same time that she had managed to push it to the back of her mind. She was feeding Lily and noticed that she kept going limp and falling off the breast. Thinking it was nothing, she held her over her shoulder to wind her. Bringing her back down she noticed a patch of purplish rash at the back of her neck. Panicking, she pulled up her top and looked under her vest.

There it was; the rash that Charlie had seen on too many occasions. She got a glass and pushed it against the baby's skin. The rash didn't disappear. She called Bob and told him to get the car ready. There was no time for discussions. Bob knew by her face that something was seriously wrong.

At the hospital, which it took hours to get to or so it seemed, the A. and E. staff were put in the picture by Charlie. She tried so hard not to shout or panic. She screeched for a paediatrician to be called immediately because her baby had meningitis. 'Now!' she yelled at the top of her voice. She knew that every second was vital. She didn't care if she sounded rude or disrespectful.

Her darling baby died that night. There was nothing anyone could have done. It was certainly not her fault. She had moved very quickly and done all the right things.

The paediatrician took Bob to one side and explained the procedure. Lily would be prepared for both parents to hold her and say their 'goodbyes.' Charlie knew the procedure, but never expected that she would have to suffer it. She couldn't describe the black hole at the pit of her being. She would wake up in a minute, surely?

Bob had already told the parents and Charles and Cristabel. Their reactions made it all worse.

She was in a black abyss from which she never wanted to crawl out.

The funeral was organised in a clinical fashion. She wasn't aware of anyone that attended. Her days were automatically filled with nothing of any importance whatever. Bob, that was his name, wasn't it, got rid of all the baby stuff. Got rid of it; just like Lily was despatched.

The weeks and months passed as expected. Nobody spoke about what had happened apart from one person.

One morning, several months later, just before Bob went to work at the C.B.'s as he must keep things as normal as possible, mustn't he, the doorbell rang and there were Cristabel and Annie, right there, in her face.

Cristabel pushed past her, handing her Annie as she went into the sitting room. 'I've come to ask you to please come back as we all miss you so much and we know what you've been going through and I can't bear it.' All said in a rush, as though it had been practised.

Cristabel took Annie from her and told her to sit on the floor and play with the box of toys she'd got in her bag. It was such a risky move, but Charlie found she was diverted from her overriding grief for a brief second. Annie was looking at her and smiling, questioningly. Charlie went over to her and stroked her hair.

She was unable to speak but accepted that it must have been an extremely difficult thing for Cristabel to do.

Slowly, with some considerable effort involved, small sentences formed. They were both overcome with fear. Charlie sat down and looked at Cristabel.

'Why?' she asked. 'Why me?'

'I don't know. All I do know is that you were the person that saved me and my daughter and there is no explanation that I know of to make you feel any better.'

The silence that followed was filled by Annie, making a grunting noise and lifting her arms to be picked up. Automatically, Charlie picked her up. She could never explain how it felt to have a little body in her arms. Did Cristabel know? Did she actually feel the anguish, deep, deep down lodged in her soul?

It would never leave her, she knew that, but looking at Annie she felt a certain tiny ripple of warmth.

She went back to work with the C.B's. Herta gained her A. levels and started medical training.

Bob maintained his high level of commitment to everything and everybody. Distractions were many and welcome as they diluted the developing melancholy, which she knew must not be given in to. She managed to act out the part of happy child carer.

Sometimes, involuntarily, she was aware of how old Lily would have been on certain days. It must all be hidden. But, however successful she thought she had been, she knew that Cristabel was aware of her pain and how she needed all her strength not to be overcome by it. There was a part of her that always had Lily lodged in it. It was just behind her heart and would never go away.

What the future would hold no one person can predict. Charlie wondered if she would ever be able to think about Lily without weeping.

It is said, 'Life goes on,' but there is a certainty held by many that it is a second rate one after a child has been lost.

Chapter Five

Eight Years Have Passed

My nam is Annie I am 8 yrs old and i liv wiv my mum and Dab. We hav a dig hows and i hav a nurs how is cald charlee she is mi bets frend. I gow ridding on hoses. Charlee cums wiv me she hads a bady. He is sow sweet. I cawl him miy bady borther. Hes doptid. I cud play wiv him charlee sasy wen I get hom from scool and mummy givs me muy tee. I downt hav eny druthes to play wiv. Daddy is gud at gaymis. I wihs I cud rit myself.

Charlee is ritting this fro my as I tell her the wruds.

I am writing this diary as Annie dictates her thoughts. It's difficult to keep up as she is very enthusiastic to see her spoken words printed in front of her. We will try to do this every day and, for my part, my thoughts will be recorded at a different time. Perhaps it will help her to try using the computer herself. I know she finds it almost impossible as her thoughts streak ahead of any small ability she has to organise them on the screen. It was her own idea to tell people about her life but, as yet, she cannot write it down herself. She says making words doesn't make any sense to her.

So, here we go.

I was born eight years ago and my Mummy and Daddy called me lots of difficult names as well as the first one which is Annie. I have a nurse to look after me as I was ill when I was born. Mummy keeps telling me she will tell me all about it when I'm older. I think I'm older now.

My nurse is called Charlie and she comes to the house every day. Mummy and Daddy go to work. I think Daddy does money. I don't know what Mummy does but Daddy says it is very important. My Daddy has the same colour eyes as me. They are blue and he calls me 'blue-eyes' sometimes. He is very kind and Mummy says he spoils me but I don't know what that means. I thought it meant like when Herta spoilt the cake she was making because she left it in the oven too long. I wish she still worked here. She comes to see us lots. Herta is a doctor. She used to look after me with Charlie when I first came home from the hospital. She has a husband. He is called Mr.Crowlink but he lets me call him Crow which makes him laugh. They haven't got any babies but Herta says she might surprise me soon. Charlie has a little boy. His name is Robert. His Daddy is called Bob. Charlie says that is short for Robert. Charlie says she will tell me all about him when I'm older. There are lots of things that people say they will tell me when I'm older. I would like to know what adoption means.

I have to have my bath now as Mummy will be home in a minute. She arrives home just after I get home from school but today she has gone Christmas shopping so Charlie is writing this for me. Mummy and Daddy know nothing about it as it's going to be a surprise. Charlie says it will be a wake- up call but I think they are already awake so I expect that is another thing that I will be told about when I'm older. Charlie is laughing at me.

It is the next day. Charlie says it is Tuesday. We went to school this morning. Robert was in his buggy. I hold on to the side. I help Charlie to look both ways when we cross the road. Charlie says that Robert will come to my school when he's older. It is only fifteen minute's walk away from my house. We walk through the park to the other side of the town. Once Mummy took me to another school but I heard Charlie telling her that I would be happier at the local school. I have a nice lady that waits for me at the gates and then takes me into the classroom. I can't remember her name but Charlie says it doesn't matter as she has a difficult name to remember. She helps me get undressed if we are having P.E. I have to try and get my own shoes on and off. I can just manage it but it takes a long time and all the other children are in the hall before me.

Jasmine Ellis called me a snail. Charlie says I must ignore her and we won't invite her to my party after Christmas. I try very hard to be quick but my hands only work slowly. I get very tired.

Today is the next day. I'm not sure but Charlie says tomorrow never comes. I think that's a joke. She's looking at me and laughing. Robert is playing with my old ball run. I'm going to stop this and play with him. He is so sweet.

Today at school, Mummy and Daddy came. I was helped onto the stage and our class which is called Bluebirds sang to all the parents.

I can hear my voice and I think it sounds good. I saw Mummy with a tissue on her eyes. She must have a cold.

I have a Mummy *and* a Daddy which is lucky as most of the children in my class only have a Mummy. Ryan Smith has a Daddy but no Mummy. His Daddy brings him to school and sometimes Ryan plays with me at playtime. I shall ask him to my party. Sanjit Patel is one of my best friends too and he wants to marry me. I take packed lunch to school and my helper sits with me and helps me unpack my sandwiches. I must stop now.

Charlie (that's me) is writing the next bit.

Annie gets very tired when she has thought up a few lines for her diary. She wants to present it to her parents as a gift but it is going to take rather a long time. It is so important that we achieve this so that they can see what progress she has made. She has amazing determination and gets frustrated when she can't physically record her thoughts on paper. We have tried the computer but it is too difficult for Annie to separate her fingers quickly enough to use the keys. We are going to get a special machine which will enable her to touch type on the screen. She is adamant that she wants to learn to write normally, just like everyone else in her class but I am hoping to persuade her to use both methods. She is so lucky to have parents that have access to any piece of equipment she might need. Money is no object.

It is the next day. Charlie says it is the day we are going to start some special exercises in the pool with Robert. I can swim but he can't because he's only small. I can swim one long bit of the pool. My Mummy is a very good swimmer. She comes in the water with us sometimes. When I started to swim without my armbands Mummy laughed so much. I haven't seen her laugh very much before. Charlie said it was because she was so happy. Her eyes didn't look happy.

Today, Annie is showing signs of understanding when her mother is genuinely happy. Herta is brilliant at talking to Annie about the reasons she isn't quite the same as other children. She understands how Annie needs to feel accepted. We are going to see a professional counsellor at some point but I personally think it might do more harm than good if Annie's mother, Cristabel, is involved, as she has only made initial inroads into her feelings of loss and disappointment at her own failure, as she sees it, to produce a normal child. It doesn't matter how many times we tell her that Annie is normal and she just needs more time to complete tasks. We get a withering look.

None of my comments in this diary will be seen by anyone. They could be misinterpreted. I need to record my thoughts as much as Annie seems to. I am so closely bound up with this family now, as is my husband Bob, that I would never risk damaging the relationships we have built up between us. When I think of the day that Annie was born and the awful realisation by her mother that the excessive amount of alcohol she had been drinking during the pregnancy had damaged the baby I know I would never want the mother to relive it. She has been punished enough. The fact that I was the nurse that looked after the mother during labour made me even more aware that there are many factors working against a serene life in some families and apportioning blame is not the right way to proceed.

Charlie says that it is time for me to tell her what makes me happy. I told her that, at school, we had to write about the things that make us happy and the things that make us unhappy. I can think of lots of things that make me happy. When I sing it makes me feel as if I'm somebody else and important when they listen and stop talking. Charlie has helped me remember my helper's name. It is Mrs. Winter. Charlie says I must think of the seasons but I might call her Mrs. Summer by mistake. She is very kind and wouldn't mind. Now I have to think of more things that make me happy. Little Robert makes me happy when he giggles. Charlie makes me very happy when she lets me lick the spoon when she's made a chocolate cake.

My head starts to ache if I think too much. Charlie says just one thing will do that makes me unhappy but I can only think of one thing and I don't want to tell her. I might tell her tomorrow; that's the next day.

I'm reluctant to ask Annie today about her happy and unhappy thoughts. Lately she has started to have little quiet periods in the day; times when she becomes very thoughtful and introspective. I'll wait and see if she suggests it.

You must let me tell you, Charlie, all about the things in my head. Well, I heard Mummy saying something very strange and when I asked her what she meant she went all quiet. She was late home one day, I can't remember which day, but she came up to me and gave me a much longer cuddle than normal. Daddy came in and asked her how

A.A. had been and that was when she gave him a funny look. You asked me to tell you something unhappy and that is it. Mummy looked really unhappy when Daddy asked her about A.A. I asked Daddy what A.A. is and he said he would tell me when I'm older.

Well, how on earth do I answer that? Annie is definitely not ready for any grown up discussion about Alcoholics Anonymous. I must tell her a little lie. I will tell her about the breakdown company that her parents belong to that come and rescue a car if it has a breakdown.

That's a very good idea, Charlie. When I'm older I can drive a car when my legs get stronger. I will join the A.A. like mummy. My teacher asked me to sing to the class today. I sang the song that Daddy taught me; you know 'Daisy ,Daisy'. All the children clapped. I'm going to sing all by myself at the Christmas concert. When I'm singing Charlie, I'm really, really happy. Will you practice my Christmas song with me? We have to keep it a secret.

I said to Annie that I thought it was a good idea. It would be a lovely surprise for her Mummy and Daddy. I said I hoped I could come to the concert as well. She sings so beautifully and when I look at her I know she's in her own world, encompassed by the music. I'm going to suggest she has piano lessons soon as the movements will help her finger muscles. The teacher will have to be of a particularly sympathetic nature. I'll ask her class teacher if she knows anyone suitable. What a boon it is that Annie's parents have abundant money. What about the vast majority with developmental problems? If they could all have swimming and music lessons, what amazing progress they would make. I know my Robert is in a privileged position because of my job here with the Courtney-Brownes. He is such a dear little chap and we are so lucky to have him; especially after what happened to little Lily. There! I've actually written it down; Annie's diary idea must be helping me too. I haven't ever actually written Lily's name down before. My darling baby; she died so, so young. Meningitus.

Come on Charlie. I need to write my diary and then do some singing before Mummy gets home. Robert likes listening to me too. We can sit him in his chair and he can be my audience. My teacher told me that I'm going to sing, 'Away in a Manger'. What's a manger? It sounds strange. Can you ask Mummy to buy a piano? Then you can play the notes for me?

They would buy the all the instruments in the orchestra for you if you asked for them. They have amazed me; these two self- absorbed people that I met when you were being born. I disliked Cristabel because of the way she rejected you, even when she was aware of the problems you were going to experience as you grew older. Your daddy was a different kettle of fish, and it only took one look into your lovely new born blue eyes to transform him into a more sensitive human being. Cristabel, oh so gradually, worked her way into my heart. I learnt from her also; mainly that being denied a loving home can do irreparable damage. There are still times when I have to catch myself to stop correcting her when she makes an unnecessary caustic comment. Mainly though I have genuine feelings of concern for her and a desire to support her in her need to overcome her alcohol addiction. I must remember how wonderful she was when we lost Lily.

Charlie! Are we going to write my diary today? There is something I need you to write down for me. It's important because I need to ask Mummy if I can do it. Here it is then. I want to have all my class to my party after Christmas because I was ill last year and I couldn't have one. I don't want to leave anyone out and I want Herta and her husband to come as well. Why are you looking like that? Will thirty two children be too many? I know we can't go in the pool with such a lot, but I really want everyone to come. Can Bob come too? I know he is working here but I bet Daddy will let him off. Charlie is nodding so that means Mummy probably will say 'yes' too.

Annie is desperate to have all of her class to her ninth party. I expect it will be the first one that she will really remember as she has been ill for the last three and in hospital before that. After Christmas always seems to be a bad time for her health but she is getting more resistant to the infections that seemed to attack her then. I expect Mummy and Daddy will pull out all the stops but I will have to think of a way to prevent them from going over the top as there are children in Annie's class that could be totally overawed by her environment. Annie herself is unaware of the materialistic possessions surrounding her. She has the kindest nature, one I suspect inherited from her father which he would have developed even more if he had come from a caring background. He shows this gentleness more and more especially towards his daughter. I watch his development as much as Annie's and that of my son. There are times when he is with Robert that I know he is relating to him as if he was his own. I keep very quiet at these times as, on reflection, I know there is a well of envy underneath his calm exterior. However much I try, I find it difficult to cast aside my memories of Herta confessing how he had encouraged her to have sex with him when she was being interviewed for the post of Nanny after Annie was brought home from hospital. It all seems such a long time ago now and I know he regrets his overbearing attitude to her. It was not rape, Herta has told me; she thought it was inevitable so got it over with as quickly as possible. Her guilt was tangible as she tried to explain it to me after she started work here. She has 'moved on' as they say and maintains an extremely professional attitude towards him when they are in the same room. Charles treats her with almost overwhelming respect which is most amusing at times. It is almost ingratiating. I wonder if Annie notices. She is coming towards me holding Robert's hand as he has just started holding on to the furniture and trying to walk, so I'm hiding my part of the diary very rapidly.

It is Sunday today and Charlie, Daddy and me have been swimming. I think I'll ask Daddy first about my party as he always lets me have what I want. Charlie stops me sometimes as she says it's for my own good. I don't think that's true. What is my own good? I expect it is the next thing that I'll be told when I'm a hundred. Charlie is laughing at me again and has told me that it is not good for me to always have what I want. I understand that. I think I understand that it means I will be spoilt like the cake but not in the same way. Charlie says I'm growing up and can understand much more. This diary still makes me tired though.

Annie continually surprises me with her comments. She is developing her ability to comprehend much more abstract thoughts and emotions. I wonder if Cristabel has noticed. I will ask her later. She is spending much more of her time actually trying to have a conversation with her daughter. Perhaps she also has noticed that Annie is becoming much more receptive to complicated thoughts and expressions. I doubt it but I intend to discuss lots of things with her and that will be one of them. Cristabel is still enclosed by guilt which, I imagine, makes it more difficult for her to ease off the alcohol. There have been some evenings recently when I've heard her sobbing to Charles that he doesn't understand her. She could be right about that but he tries his best and has flowered into a wonderful father. I think this fact may contribute to Cristabel's feelings of inadequacy. Robert is looking up at me with an expectant face; it must either be teatime or snack time. He is constantly hungry but incredibly patient. I'll get him his snack and then he can watch Annie get on with her diary. She has almost become obsessed with it. My comments are only written when I am sure she has finished. Her pages are separate from mine. Mine are hidden. I suppose there might be a time when she would find them interesting. The C.B.'s (as I call Annie's mother and father) might not! I wonder how many in Annie's class have their own swimming pool, a team of cleaners, and a personal physiotherapist. I think there will be a time very soon when she will notice the luxury in which she lives.

My teacher gave me a special badge today. I am showing it to Robert and Charlie. I can't let Robert hold it because it has a sharp pin at the back. I have asked Charlie if she can put something else there. The special badge was for saying sorry to Leroy Carter as I kicked him as he went past me. I meant to do it but I said sorry straight away and Leroy said, 'That's O.K. I expect it was an accident.' I felt really silly then but our teacher said Leroy had been very kind as he didn't kick me back. My teacher gave Leroy the badge but he asked if he could give it to me to make me feel better. He handed it to my teacher and she handed it to me. She said that Leroy was a very understanding boy as he realised that I felt sad because I wasn't able to put my jersey back on after P.E. All the class were looking and I will never do that again as I felt so ashamed. My helper isn't with me in the afternoons so I have to do all the things the other children do. Sometimes I find it hard; especially the dressing and undressing. I hope the children will still want to come to my party after Christmas.

Dressing and undressing is one of Annie's most challenging activities. She tries really hard but I have seen her with tears on her cheeks, silently wrenching at her vest to get it to go down her back. I delay helping her as it is important she perseveres. I'm itching to give her a hand. If do interfere she bites her lips and scowls at me. I suppose it is all about getting the timing right. I must wait until she really cannot cope without help but not intervene until it is obvious that she can't manage without me. She will find it hard when Robert catches her up physically.

I have just come home from school and it is my favourite day. It is Friday and Bob, he belongs to Charlie, and Robert and me all have pizza. I'm only allowed it on Fridays and I have to eat some fruit afterwards, I don't know why but it is something to do with being healthy and 5-a-day. That's right, isn't it Charlie? Bob and me always have kiwi and banana. Robert has some smooth stuff; I think it is apricot. I don't like it and it looks like sick. Bob always makes me laugh. He looks at Charlie a lot as if he isn't sure she's all right. I hope she will always be here as I love her lots. She is giving me a hug but I don't know why. I expect she will tell me when I'm older again. I think I will be doing a lot of listening then.

Bob does look at me frequently; he is that sort of man, unusual in this day and age but I'm eternally grateful that he is there. His presence is total and enduring, even after what I put him through after Lily. Then, I stopped functioning completely for months until Cristabel arrived with Annie. There they were on my doorstep, waiting to come in. In they came and they will never know how instant the effect was on me. Perhaps, one day, I might again reiterate how she virtually saved my sanity. I have broached the subject more than once and thanked her but there was still the impenetrable barrier of our basic differences. It is true that we can actually touch without feeling awkward, but even though a quick cuddle is willingly given and received, the memory of our early meetings at Annie's birth still acts as a barrier to totally open communication. Bob and Charles however are like two old mates together. They seem to have a genuine respect and affection for each other. That is another unexpected outcome from the last eight years.

It is the day before the weekend. Christmas is getting nearer. I am practising my song with Charlie. We have to make certain that there is no one around as it is a complete secret. Robert is allowed to listen. He waves his arms around and makes me laugh. I have to look somewhere else or I can't sing. 'Away in a Manger' is the song I will be singing on the stage to the parents at Christmas. All the school will be on the stage. In the middle there is a crib with baby Jesus in it. It is a doll really and I said that Robert could be baby Jesus but Charlie said, didn't you Charlie, that he would climb out and then all the parents would have hysterics. What's hysterics? Is it people laughing? Well, that might spoil it and I really, really want it to be perfect for my Mummy and Daddy and you of course. I have to wear a special dress. It is long, right down to my feet and I mustn't trip over it. Herta made it for me. We have to keep it in a special cupboard so that Mummy won't find it. It's white and I'm supposed to be an angel. Charlie said that's a joke. Yes, you did Charlie. Can I stop now as I want to practise my song?

I'm crossing everything that Annie will be fit on the day of the School Nativity. Annie's school must be one of a minority that are performing the traditional story. I expect they will choose another religious festival next year so that all the children from the ethnic minorities feel they haven't been forgotten. At this time of year Annie sometimes gets a really nasty infection. She seems to be prone to bronchitis but I'm giving her extra fruit and vegetables whenever possible and Cristabel is giving her a vitamin supplement. It is lovely to see the enthusiasm that Annie is devoting to her singing. She is determined that her parents will not get any inkling of her starring part in the performance. Her parents will think she has been forgotten as she has told me that she doesn't sing her solo part until the end but she just stands in the background at various scenes. When the letter came home asking for a white dress to be made, if possible, I was so delighted to realise that Annie had hidden the letter from her parents. She had actually taken the initiative and stopped her parents from seeing it. I was so impressed by that action of hers; small that it could seem to others, but to me it showed that there is a forward looking anticipation of what is needed for a future event. It is a good omen.

I gave Mummy a note from school yesterday. It was about the tickets to the Christmas Nativity. She wants four tickets but I think each family are only allowed two. Charlie will sort it out, won't you? There was also a note about a school trip after Christmas. It asks for parents to come and help. I haven't said anything to Mummy or Daddy about it. I want Charlie to see if she can sort it out as I really, really want Daddy to come. I know Charlie would come and help but she has Robert to look after and it wouldn't be fair to drag him along as the trip is to a museum in Bristol. It is a 'Hands On' museum but I haven't asked Charlie what that means but I think I know. I hope Charlie can persuade Daddy to come. Tom Johnson's daddy is a scientist and I know he comes to all the trips. My Daddy can be friends with him and help with some of the naughty boys. Why is it nearly always boys that are silly Charlie?

Annie always asks me to act as her middleman when there is an issue about something she feels she is unable to articulate with her parents. She is approaching the stage when she will be able to reason with them herself. The progress, in this respect that she has made recently, has astounded me. I have been wondering if it is something to do with the music and her intensive singing practice. She has also recently started piano lessons. She must be very unusual as she has to be persuaded to stop practising. The piano teacher has a little Down's syndrome girl. She is wonderful with Annie, whose fingers can go into spasm and unclenching them is only recently showing signs of improving. Swimming is helping her and, along with everything else, I am continually amazed at how we manage to fit everything in to her days.

Charlie will get some more tickets for us. She is going in to school today when she meets me and will ask my teacher. Herta wants to come too, so with Mummy and Daddy and Charlie we will need four. Bob will look after Robert as he is much too young. Charlie has told me that Bob is good at putting Robert to bed, just like my Daddy when he is home in time. My Daddy is especially good at reading stories. He is nearly as good as Charlie. He says I have to teach him to read in a proper voice but I'm not certain what he means. I think it means he needs to use that word that I can't say but I know it means the story seems to come alive. Charlie says the word I need is 'expression'. My mouth goes all funny when I try and say it. I bet I could sing it though. My piano teacher has given me some more songs to sing. Her little girl loves music and we are going to do some singing after Christmas. I will help her. She is not my age. She is younger than me. I've told Mummy about the singing but only so she wouldn't really notice. Charlie says I'm getting to be a 'clever clogs'. It sounds good so that's all right.

Annie and her parents are seeing the paediatrician tomorrow. Annie hates going as she says it means she misses school. I've told her it is only for a morning so she won't be too grumpy. I'm going also as it gives me a chance to catch up with my old colleagues as well as be a part of the appointment. Bob is taking the day off; a rare occurrence. It is always a rather surreal atmosphere in the clinic, with long silences; everyone, including Annie, full of private thoughts. As it is with Mr. Mc.Alister it brings back dreadful memories for Cristabel. I try and have a private word with him before the appointment as I feel it is extremely important that he is positive with the three of them, particularly Cristabel. Last appointment I noticed her hands were shaking and she kept visiting the toilet. She will always have a problem with guilt but Mr. Mc.Alister could lessen it slightly by praising all the help the parents have obviously been able to arrange for their daughter. I have spoken to him several times before about his input. Whether he really understood what I was saying was debatable. He probably thought my amateur psychology ideas were ridiculous. I persevered though as I was the one person seeing the progress on a daily basis.

Today we had to go to the clinic to see the man who looks after me. He was there when I was born and Charlie was too. We had to wait and I tried very hard not to be grumpy. Charlie went to talk to Mr.Mac; I can't remember his whole name, and then she came in to the clinic room with us. I had to show how much more I can move my hands and I had to jump in the air and do lots of other things to show him how I could move. Then I had to walk along a line. He kept looking at my body and I had to take my jersey and trousers off. Charlie said it was so that he could see how much I had grown. He kept asking me questions but I didn't tell him anything about the Nativity that I'm singing in. Mummy told him about the music lessons I'm having. He asked me how far I could swim now and I told him. He kept looking in his folder and flicking the pages over. He spent a lot of time looking at his computer. I wanted him to look at me. Sometimes he didn't look at me when he was asking me questions at all and I know Charlie noticed because she winked at me. He asked my mother how she was but Charlie suddenly got up and said that she would take me to the cafe for a drink and biscuit. There was something happening that they didn't want me to hear. I will ask Charlie later. She helped me to get dressed. She seemed to be in a hurry.

Annie asked me about the clinic and why her mother was asked how she was but her father wasn't. I was very careful how I answered and deviated from her questions. I hope she didn't notice. I did receive a couple of strange looks from her though. I did tell her that Mr.McAlister was delighted with her progress and that he didn't need to see her again for another six months. Annie said she thought he was a bit rude when he kept looking at his computer screen when he was talking. I tell her always to look at the person when you're having a conversation with somebody. I was very pleased to note that she had remembered what I'd said. We have to go to another screening appointment; this time with an educational psychologist. It is an annual event but we play it down so Annie doesn't feel she is always being examined for one thing or another. She acts in a very subdued manner which is out of character. She had told me that she doesn't like the way this particular woman asks her silly questions. As I am in the room with her I try to appear as if it doesn't matter. Bob, my husband, thinks it is all a waste of time but I explained to him that her extra help at school will be taken away if it is thought she doesn't have special needs. More and more I feel it is her physical needs that benefit from the support. I have great faith in her ability to overcome her writing problems. Charles, Annie's father, came with us this time. I anticipate what the letter will say, when we eventually get it. I have been aware of Annie's 'problem' with organizing her letters and sequences in the correct order for a long time. I've spoken with Charles and Cristabel about it and tried to explain that, with support, Annie will overcome it. My father was diagnosed with Dyslexia when he was at school. I've kept some of his writing as I found it fascinating. There were times when he was small that he used to get extremely frustrated. My Mum told me how she had to help him write a letter or fill in a form when she first met him. It is strange as my Dad reads all the time. He just can't seem to retain an image of the 'right' order of the letters when he's writing. Mum told me that she thought I might inherit it as it is a genetic condition, but I didn't, although I was pretty rubbishy at spelling for a long time.

Charlie and Daddy are coming to the appointment today. It will be boring as the lady will keep asking me all sorts of questions and I don't know the answers. She gives me bricks and stuff to play with as though I'm a toddler. I hate the way she watches me. If she could play the piano, I could sing to her. She is kind though and Charlie and Daddy look at me as if I'm being tested for something. At least when I go up to see Mr.Mac he doesn't nag me. He doesn't look at my face very much either, so I should be pleased. The lady today had a computer too but hers was a laptop and she peeped at me over the top of it. She had a nice smile. I heard Charlie say that I could sing and I gave her a stare as I thought she might let Daddy know about the Christmas Nativity. The lady just said, 'That's nice,' and wrote on the screen. I was relieved when Charlie and I were allowed out of the room and I could hurry back to school to the Nativity practice. My Daddy looked pleased when he came out of the room a few minutes later. I know they were talking about me. Daddy said that he just wanted a few words on his own with the lady. He worries about me and I expect he wanted to know if I was doing all right. That's what he said anyway. Daddy drove me back to school and then took Charlie to pick up Robert. I notice that he always looks sad when he drops me off. There is no need as I know how to get in past the security system. I have to go to a special box on the gate and press a button to let them know I'm back; then in I go when the automatic gates open.

Annie is getting very observant as she matures. It is promising that her perception of different situations has developed so quickly over the last year. Her visual memory of words hasn't kept up though but I suppose things develop in different areas at differing rates. My main concern is that she keeps her sunny disposition most of the time. She is beginning to ask more searching questions and I know I must be as honest as possible with my answers. My little Lily would be seven now.

Charlie waved me goodbye with Daddy as I went to the office window. They both looked a bit sad. I will cheer them up when I sing in the Nativity. My legs ache a lot because I have to stand on the stage for ages. They asked me if I wanted a chair but that would be stupid as they didn't have chairs in those days. I know I can manage to stand up for all the time but I must keep smiling so nobody can guess my legs hurt. Charlie says that it wouldn't matter if I had a chair to sit on but I really want to be the same as the others. Tom's family have got a little Shetland pony and they are bringing it to school to be the donkey. I hope it doesn't poo on the stage; that would be so funny. It wouldn't matter really as it is what donkeys do in real life. What if my singing makes him bray; or is it whinny? Charlie says she's not sure but she says it will add to the atmosphere. I don't know what she means. I don't get quite so tired when Charlie and I do our diary. Charlie says it's because I'm getting fit. I know it won't be long before I'll be able to type on the computer as I'm getting one that I only have to touch the letter on the screen and it will do it for me. I'm not sure if I want to do it though as it makes me different. Charlie helps me aim for the letters W and E on the top line of her laptop and I can do it. I know it spells 'we'. Sometimes I hit the Q by mistake but Charlie says to look first; then aim. She says it's just like crossing a road; the more you practise the better you get. I watch her using spellcheck sometimes. When she uses it I can't see the difference from the word she thinks she has spelt wrong. We have written so much today and my head is tired.

Christmas is approaching fast and there always seems to be so much to do. The only thing on my mind is to ensure Charles and Cristabel are kept in the dark about Annie's part in the Nativity. It has assumed a ridiculous importance to me. It's as if everything in the future depends on keeping the secret. Annie's voice is truly that of an angel; I feel my eyes welling up with tears just remembering her last practice with me. She put on her angel costume, much to the amusement of Robert. He thought he could pull himself up from the hem as it nearly reaches the ground. He swung himself around and giggled. He is such a good natured little boy and I feel so lucky to have him. He feels like my own son, not adopted. Annie put her dress over his head so we couldn't see him and played 'Peek-a-Bo' with him. We thought we could hear Mummy coming so we had to move very fast indeed. We rushed into Annie's bedroom and I quickly put some other clothes on her. She didn't protest at all, knowing that it was all part of the game we were playing. Robert entered into the spirit of it and hid under the bed. It was so good to listen to spontaneous laughter from those two; it does my heart good.

Charlie says we won't have so much time today to do the diary. I really don't want to miss a day. It is very important to me that I tell Charlie all my thinking. Charlie says that we will 'find time'. That's another thing that I think I understand. We have found some time as Mummy is downstairs cooking a special dinner for Daddy as it is his birthday. I made him a very colourful card and bought him a bar of chocolate as he says he is not really allowed to eat it as it makes him fat, but I think he should be allowed it as it is his special day. I asked him how old he was and he wouldn't tell me. I can read much better now. At school today, I had to take turns reading to the class. I know lots of words now but I still can't remember the right order of the sounds to write them down. I don't know if the words are right or wrong. I look at them but they don't remind me if they look right.

That was such a good explanation of Annie's spelling problem. The best thing about it all is that she is reading much better and has a real love of books. I am hoping that, with repetition, her visual memory will catch up, eventually. That's what the educational psychologist reckons anyway and she should know. I'm not certain that is accurate as, if her visual memory was good, she would be able to recognise a word that she had spelt wrong. My father was in his twenties and engaged to my mother before he made real inroads into his spelling problem. He says it is all about repetition and avoiding letting Annie write anything incorrectly.

With this new computer that we are hoping to order, automatic spelling correction will happen. I don't understand if that will help her when she wants to write independently. I am asking Charles to get her a child's dictionary. He'll probably buy up the whole of Smiths stock. I've seen one online but I think it is a good idea for him to research it more thoroughly himself. It is a good exercise for him anyway. Cristabel is also looking into it and had asked her colleagues at work for help; that in itself is pretty remarkable. Annie will have shelves of dictionaries but it is the principle of the thing; I don't want to appear to be taking decisions like this on my own. Even if it does result in a shelf full of dictionaries it doesn't matter; Annie will love working her way through them. I often wonder why it is that Annie has never misspelt her name. It must be because of the frequency of her writing and seeing it. If this was undertaken for other words, in blocks, could that have the same outcome? I might try it with just one group of words, like 'would, could and should'. The more I look at English spelling patterns, the more I realise the total insanity of them. For example, look at these words- thought, through, rough, bough, and cough, to name just five. Having just written those down, I know that the task I'm eager to undertake might just be a bit too much. Perhaps I need to start with the more straightforward groups. Daunting, that's what it is.

My singing is coming along very well. We had a Dress Rehearsal today and I sang like a nightingale, so Mrs. Winter said. Charlie told me a nightingale is a beautiful songbird and we looked it up on the internet and it showed a picture of one. They are birds that are not seen very often as they are shy. They have a lovely song and if you ever hear one you are lucky. I felt so good and really peaceful after my singing. Charlie wants me to say more. Well, it feels as if my whole body is calm and happy. It's like I'm owned by the lovely musical notes. Charlie is smiling and had said that is a very good description. Robert has just woken up from his nap so we are going to play with him until tea-time.

It is getting near to the time when we can be certain that Annie isn't going to have one of her nasty infections. I am hoping with every breath of my body that this dear little girl can be granted her wish of performing in front of her parents. I have managed to get four tickets to the performance. I don't care if the other parents give us dirty looks! As the days pass, it appears that Annie's body is so geared up to this big event in her life that it will wait until she has achieved it before letting her down. If I sound pessimistic, it is because she has never been well before, during or after Christmas. There are only two days now until the most important day of Annie's life; at least it seems so to her. She is well; blossoming in fact. Everything is ready; her dress is on a hanger to take into school today. There are also some rather floppy wings that she doesn't like so we won't take them. She said that, if angels were real, they wouldn't be able to fly with them anyway. She is amazing me on an almost daily basis in respect of her single mindedness.

Charlie has got all the costume ready for me. We went out to get some little white shoes but I'm sure angels didn't have those in the olden days, whenever they were. Charlie says I can have bare feet if I want. She started laughing and said that I might change my mind if the donkey did a poo. Mrs. Winter is going to help me put on my white dress. I hope Mummy and Daddy and Herta get good seats. If they are late the best seats will all have gone. I want them to be proud of me, but most of all I want them to be surprised and happy. Mummy will be looking very smart. I hope she doesn't sit next to Liam's mummy because she doesn't get proper clothes for him and Mrs. Winter got him some from the box in the office. He doesn't seem to mind. If I have children, I will work very hard to earn money so they can have proper clothes. Liam told me that his mummy is at home all day as she can't get a job and she lies on the sofa. She forgets to pick him up from school sometimes. Charlie, Robert and me waited with him and Mrs. Winter once, until his mummy came. She had two other children with her and she did a lot of shouting. Charlie was very kind to Liam and gave him a biscuit. She always brings me a chocolate biscuit or a banana when she meets me. Robert likes Liam and Liam is very funny to him. He pulls silly faces and makes Robert laugh. I am sorry for Liam but Charlie says she thinks he is a survivor. I'm almost sure I know what that means. Sometimes Liam gets into trouble in the playground because he pushes other boys. He sometimes hits them and uses naughty words. I try to be kind to him because Charlie says that if I am kind to him it will make him feel better so he won't want to hurt other children. His mummy has a scary face. I know I mustn't say that to anyone. The two children that his mummy brings to meet him are boys and they are very dirty and

116

they push and shove a lot. Charlie gives them all biscuits but she asks his mummy first. Last week his mummy said, 'If you must,' and Charlie was very kind and gave Liam's mummy one as well. She smells. Charlie says I must not say that. She does though, Charlie and I don't know why. If they came to my house they could all have a wash. Why are you looking at me like that, Charlie? Charlie never gets cross. I think I understand why Liam's mummy gets cross. Liam doesn't have a kind daddy like I do. I asked him where his daddy was and he ran away from me.

Annie is such a sensitive little girl. Although she is emotionally immature, she has a wonderful outlook on life. Her world is inhabited by kind and generous people in an almost magical environment. I do hope the day when she finds disillusionment is as far away as possible. The family attached to her little friend Liam is one that represents many, I fear. I am pleased she is having the opportunity of experiencing the other end of the social spectrum. I wonder if she realises just how privileged she is in the material sense. Bob says I should stop worrying about her. I cannot do that as I was one of the first adults to see her at her birth. I still feel we are closely bound together. Her mummy, Cristabel, has made great progress in overcoming her alcohol problems but still has bad times. It is only a matter of time before Annie finds out more details about her problems or deduces it herself. Whatever will happen then? Looking at Annie and Liam's situations, they couldn't be more different, materially, but both mothers have a problem with alcohol. I know Liam's mother has a problem because she smells strongly of alcohol at the school gates, when she eventually gets there. We always wait now, at Annie's insistence. I wonder if Social Services are involved. I also wonder how I would cope if I found myself in the same situation. What if my parents hadn't encouraged me at school; even worse, what if I hadn't met Bob? I shall always be thankful of my life, apart from the one blackness that involved Lily. I try not to let Annie see me move away from Liam's mother if she is really stinking of smoke and alcohol. Her two other little boys are passive and just kick each other apathetically out of habit. They almost seem too tired and disinterested to bother about anything. I try to talk to the mummy but she is very wary of me. It is good that she can see Annie has problems. Liam is in the Nativity but his role seems to be a mystery. The whole school is taking part apparently. Annie has told me that there is more than one surprise. I can't see Liam's mummy coming to watch. What will she do with the other children? When I meet Annie this afternoon, I'll ask her. I have to write this very fast as I have to get organised for tonight.

Later

Liam's mummy is coming. Her sister is babysitting. I am amazed. All I said to her was that I was looking forward to seeing Liam and Annie on the stage. I tried to joke a bit and say I hope they would all remember to go to the toilet before. She gave me a strange look. I feel so sorry for her but mustn't be patronising. I find it difficult. I know I must look out for her tonight. Charles and Cristabel will think I've lost my sanity. So be it.

Tonight was the best night ever. We've just got home and Mummy says Charlie can talk to me a bit before she goes home so we can now do our secret diary. I love secrets. Mummy and Daddy were overcome by my singing. The parents all stood up at the end and clapped and clapped. I saw Mummy with lots of tissues. She told me that she was crying because she was so happy. She talked to Charlie a lot on the way home. I was so pleased because Liam's mummy saw him with me on the stage, having a very important part. Nobody knew that Liam was helping me with the singing. He had to come on with a big golden lantern and then hold out a hand to me to help me step up on to the golden stone that Mrs. Winter had made. He had to open the book of music and hold it towards me so I could see the words. I knew them all anyway, but I smiled at him and he had to nod to me. I don't know why. Then he had to put his hand up to the pianist so she knew it was time to start. I know I sang well. Charlie would say I sang my heart out. Charlie spoke to Liam's mummy afterwards and I saw Liam's mummy smile. I have never seen that before. Liam's next important part was that he had to help me down from the golden stone. I couldn't manage it on my own. Liam smiled all the time when he wasn't looking at the audience to see if his mum had really come. He told me that he bet she wouldn't. Mrs. Winter kept moaning about something called 'Health and Safety' but I think that is why she was behind the curtain at the back. The curtain was at the back of the golden stone and I could hear her breathing. I've got lots more to say but I'll save it for tomorrow as I'm so, so tired.

This has been the most surprising day for numerous reasons. There are so many emotions fighting each other to be recorded that I might just write about the most overpowering one. I never imagined, in any circumstances, that I would witness an atmosphere of complete enthrallment from an audience at a Junior School Nativity. Usually, and frequently in the past, there are rustles and fidgeting noises coming from the audience and the performers simultaneously. Towards the end, on this night, even a pin being dropped would have sliced through the enclosed expectancy. It was as if the audience knew something very special was about to happen. It was led by Liam's contained walk to the golden stone and his slow and perfect support that he gave to Annie, helping her to climb up to stand on the top. He was watching her all the time and only handed her the music when she smiled at him to let him know she was safely balanced. It was a tremendous achievement and he performed it perfectly. I think that was when I knew I was about to experience a unique event; one that would remain with me forever. When the music started, very slowly and deliberately setting the scene and engaging the audience's total attention, there was a stillness surrounding the whole hall. When Annie started to sing there was a respectful hush. Her voice soared above the audience and she looked possessed by the music. When she finished the second to last verse, she looked at Liam and he asked the audience to join in the last one. I know I couldn't have sung a note and I suspect there were many others similarly affected. The staff joined in with gusto which was just as well as there was a lot of sniffing going on. I sneaked a glance at Charles and he had his arm on the back of Cristabel's seat and was patting her lightly. His head was down and I suspect his emotional control was fragile. It was strange how nobody moved for at least a minute after Annie had finished. Even after Liam had helped her down there was little noise. Then, it was as if the lid had been taken off a head of steam and the applause ripped through the hall from front to back. It went on and on until the Headmistress came on to the stage and gave a speech of thanks to the children for working so hard. Then she turned and looked at Annie and Liam and thanked them for finishing the evening off so perfectly.

As we were leaving, Liam's mum came up to us, but then backed off when she saw what a formidable cluster we made. I quickly said to her, 'See you tomorrow, I expect. Liam did very well, didn't he?' She rushed off.

Chapter Six

When I got to school today I felt a bit sad but I didn't know why. Last night was so special and Mummy and Daddy were so pleased with me and my singing. I was proud that I had managed to keep it a secret from them. Liam did his part perfectly. I hope his mum is nice to him about it. Everyone is very quiet this morning in class. Mrs. Winter said that we were all perfect and that we would have a double playtime. I wanted to do something else but I didn't know what. I just felt that there was a hole that needed filling. I was going to ask Liam if he felt the same but he didn't come to school today. I was tired as well but Mummy said it was important to keep to my routine. She gave me the biggest hug I can ever remember last night and kept saying, 'Thank you'. I must ask Charlie why she looked so sad when she was saying it. Daddy looked very happy and he had such a wide grin on his face. He told me he felt like the Cheshire Cat. I think I have read that book but I can't remember what it's called.

Now I'm at the C.B.'s house with Robert, after taking Annie to school. It will perhaps be possible to organise my thoughts better. Last night I was almost overcome and my thoughts were knocking against each other. When we got back to the house, I helped Herta get Annie to bed. It was obvious s that no conversation was possible as I noticed Cristabel's red eyes when she had kissed her daughter goodnight. I expect Annie noticed too so I will be prepared for a question or two. This morning the parents have gone off to work and there were only few seconds to converse. I just said,' What a wonderful evening, wasn't it?' then left it at that. Last night Herta gave me a lift home. We hardly said a word on the way. She gave me a look which I know from experience means she doesn't particularly want to talk. I know there will be many opportunities for further discussion. I have so many things I want to talk with her and the C.B.'s about, mainly Annie's obvious singing ability. Not to push her in any way but just to ensure she knows we will help her in any way if she decides she wants to pursue it further. I think it will be some weeks before her parents recover from the experience of the Nativity. I'm taking Robert in for a swim in a minute. It helps to get my thoughts in some sort of order. It won't be long before he is swimming by himself at this rate. He watches Annie swimming and tries to copy her, flapping his arms and legs around and laughing. It took such a long time for us to be accepted by the Adoption Committee that we nearly despaired. I am eternally grateful that he was only two weeks old when we got him. His birth mother died in childbirth and, apparently, there are no known relatives. I was told the father was unknown which is such a shame, especially if we need to know any genetic details in the future. I must stop this train of thought. Bob is very good at diverting me. I think it is quite unusual to be given such a young baby but it was on a fostering basis for the first sixth months. It is only now that I am beginning to feel that he might actually belong to us properly. Apparently, the process can take more than a year, often up to two before potential adopting parents are fully investigated. Can that be fair on the child? I know potential parents have to be fully screened, but is it really not possible to achieve this in a shorter time? Bob and I actually felt as if we were criminals at certain points during the investigations. I think he was on the point of throwing in the towel; noticing the desperation I was showing made the situation very difficult for him. I tried so hard not to show my emotions to him but he knows me too well.

Today I was talking to Mummy and Daddy about my party after Christmas. I am waiting for Mummy to tell me that thirty children are too many. I know she is going to but Daddy gives her long looks and that seems to stop her. Charlie said to Mummy that she and Herta would help and we could hire a long table. I can't remember the name but it would let everybody fit round it. Charlie says I should wait until after Christmas is over before sending out the invitations. I know she thinks I'll be ill like I am every Winter. I have been well for the first time this year and I'm not going to miss another party. I won't mention it again until after Christmas. Mummy is taking two whole weeks off from work; the week before Christmas and the week after. It will be good and then she can talk to me more. I am making her a calendar at school but Charlie is taking me shopping to buy presents so I can choose something for everyone. I want to get Liam a present. Charlie says that I mustn't expect anything from him as they haven't any money.

After the Nativity, Cristabel was very quiet and I waited until she asked to talk to me. I knew she wanted to as she kept hovering around me but not saying anything. After what seemed like an age, she blurted out,' Who was that boy helping Annie?' I played for time and asked, 'When?' Cristabel, knowing exactly what I was doing, repeated the question. I tried to be as casual as possible, but failed. 'Oh, he's Annie's friend. His family are very poor and Annie is being very kind to him. He has two little brothers and Annie makes me wait after school to make certain the mother picks him up.'

'But, he is so dirty,' Cristabel said, wrinkling up her nose. I laughed and replied, 'Oh, the school had cleaned him up when you saw him at the Nativity. What's the problem Cristabel? Annie is his friend and he adores her so I can't see what you're worried about.' This was the bluntest I had ever been with Cristabel and I mentally crossed my fingers that it wouldn't upset her. After all she was Annie's mother and if she wanted to select the most appropriate, as she saw it, friends for her daughter it was her decision. The conversation was closed and Cristabel had the frown I had become used to recognising, appeared on her smooth forehead. I added, 'Don't worry; she's got loads of other friends as well.' Then I felt guilty. I knew I mustn't accept the parents' artificial standards on Annie's behalf. I was privately confident that Annie would make her way in the world if she was left to make important choices herself. Cristabel only wanted 'the best' for her daughter and it was totally understandable.

I have brought a letter home. It is about the school trip which is the week after my ninth birthday. Daddy doesn't know but I'm going to ask him to come as a parent helper. I know he likes Tom's Daddy as he sat next to him at the Nativity. They can chat about things I don't understand. Daddy has told me that Tom's father is a very clever scientist. Daddy was a tiny bit afraid of him, I think. My Daddy is clever too, but with money. He said to me the other day that it wasn't his own money he was clever with but that seems very peculiar. To take other peoples' money isn't clever, is it? I have just asked Charlie and she says Daddy makes it grow. Well, that seems even stranger. I am not interested really but I expect I'll ask Daddy again as I think I need to understand it. I won't ask him yet as he gets a funny look on his face and keeps talking and talking as if he hasn't got a stop button. Charlie is laughing at me again.

There was a letter from school that came home with Annie today. There is a school trip to the museum in Bristol in a couple of weeks. Annie has got it into her head that her beloved Daddy must be a parent helper. The unexpected reaction from Charles is one of complete enthusiasm. Apparently Tom's dad always helps as he runs his own business so can take a day off when he wants. Annie thinks this is an excellent idea and has indicated to her Daddy that it will give him a chance to talk to Tom's dad too. Annie has great perseverance and gives Charles strong eye contact when she is asking him to do something for her. He is a lost cause where she is concerned; putty in her hands. I, increasingly, do wonder about the future though. My concerns are not concentrated solely on Annie. I will help at the trip to Bristol. Bob will have little Robert to himself for the day. He is totally reliable with him and it will be lovely for them both. Whenever this happens it is always interesting to see how exhausted Bob is at the end of the day!

Daddy is coming on the trip with me to Bristol. Charlie always comes so I'm really lucky. Mummy can't come as she is needed at work. I hope she can come one day. Tom's Daddy is going to sit next to my Daddy and I am going to sit next to Liam. I know a secret about Liam but I can tell Charlie as she won't tell anyone else. Liam's Mummy didn't have any money for him to come on the trip so Mrs. Winter paid. I'm not supposed to know about it but I overheard her talking to my class teacher and she said she would pay, but not to say anything. Why are you looking at me like that, Charlie? Liam has to come or he will be the only one in the class that has to stay behind and that wouldn't be fair. It costs a lot of money to pay for the coach and we have to take a packed lunch. I am going to ask Charlie to pack extra so that I can give some to Liam as he has free school meals and I know his mummy has so many children that she won't have time to pack sandwiches for him. I hope he has a clean shirt on as he can smell a bit strange and some other children laugh at him and call him names but I look after him. Charlie has just given me a long cuddle. She is so nice and I love her lots and lots. Now she won't look at me but I think she is pleased.

The little rascal has made me want to cry, again. She has the most ridiculous sense of wanting to please. I cannot believe how I would manage without her in my life. She brings a glow of light and happiness that is, sometimes, frighteningly intense. She would laugh if I said anything to her though. When I watch her struggling with her clothes or shoes, knowing I mustn't intervene, I get an awful lump in my throat. She almost fights herself to prove that she can do it. On the occasions that she is forced to ask for help she rarely thanks me, just mutters under her breath. I usually compliment her and gloss over any grumpiness, but I suffer with her and I'm sure she is aware of it, because, within a few minutes she will come to me and give me a hug.

Charlie says she will make extra sandwiches. She might even make a special cake for everyone to share. That's good so I can scrape the bowl if Robert doesn't insist he has the first lick. Charlie usually leaves plenty of the mixture in the bowl. Once Daddy came in when Robert and I were licking the chocolate mixture off the spoons. Charlie gave him a spoon too and Daddy joined in. I was surprised. He had one of his silly looks on his face and I couldn't help laughing. Charlie started laughing too and Robert didn't know what we were all laughing about. I like it when we have a secret like that. Robert got in a disgusting mess. Herta came into the kitchen. It all went very quiet. She went out again and said she would wash the goo off Robert when he had finished. Charlie picked Robert up and took him out of the room to give him to Herta. Robert loves Herta as she knows lots of things to play with a baby. Daddy looked at me and asked me if I was looking forward to the trip. It is next week so Charlie will be baking another cake but it will have to be much bigger as there are thirty children in my class and the teachers and helpers will want a slice too. She says she will make two cakes. We might need four. If she uses the massive tin we've got, two might be enough. Charlie has just told me to leave the cooking to her and she will make sure there is one slice for everyone. I think she thinks I'm getting bossy. When I have my birthday party, it will mean lots and lots of food. My birthday is after the school outing though.

All the arrangements for the trip to Bristol are in place. I'm quite looking forward to it as, on my only school visit to a museum that I went on as a child, the place was musty and boring. We weren't allowed to touch anything and most of the things were dirty and had lots of very small notices on them. that I couldn't read. I have heard very good reports about this museum in Bristol and it appears the children are actually encouraged to touch everything. That's progress! When this trip is over, we have the enormous event of Annie's ninth party to arrange. I am crossing my fingers that Cristabel doesn't want to book a theme park or something like that. I know Annie wants the children to come to her home. It seems incredibly important to her. As she has missed so many of her birthdays due to her ill health, I suppose she just wants her friends, which seem to be all thirty of her class, to visit her in her own surroundings. I can understand that, and I hope her parents will also.

We have just come back from the school trip and I'm very tired. Callum was sick on the coach but I wasn't sitting next to him. Mrs. Winter cleared him up very quickly. Charlie's cakes were brilliant. She had iced numbers on each of them. One cake had from number one to twenty on and the other one had twenty one to forty on. She did it all in very bright colours. We were allowed to do all the things at the museum. There was so much to do that we really needed more time. I liked the colour mixing game best. Liam and my Daddy talked quite a lot. Daddy kept looking at me but I told him that I was fine and to keep an eye on Liam. Charlie was given five children to look after. My Daddy was given three. Tom's Daddy was given four but I expect that was because he has done it before. I have noticed that my Daddy gets a bit nervous sometimes. I can't really explain it properly but I know what it feels like. He keeps moving his hands and rubbing them together. It's as if he is in his own bubble and can't break the skin to get out. After a little while he settles down; I think Tom's daddy helps him as he is used to lots of noisy children. It was strange to see Daddy looking frightened. Charlie has said that I must understand that school trips like this one is a new experience for him and I must tell him that I was proud of him and that it is something called 'role reversal'. I really don't understand about that but Charlie says it is as if I am looking after Daddy rather than the other way round. I quite like that idea.

Annie was absolutely shattered after the school trip. She coped really well and only asked for help once. She found it difficult to balance on one of the weight experiments but was determined to have a turn. I noticed she checked on her daddy several times and I caught her watching him closely to see what he was doing. I found myself doing the same, in the intervals between organising my little group. I was pleased that I had a group of children that didn't include Annie. If she was honest I think she was relieved that there was distance between us too. We have plenty of contact at home and I'm sure the class teacher separated us deliberately. Annie had her helper with her anyway and if I was included in the group it would have been claustrophobic for her. Her daddy became more relaxed as the day wore on. It was a good thing that Tom's father was there as they seemed to gel in the coach on the journey up to Bristol. Luckily, their seats were adjacent. I wonder if some perceptive teacher managed to arrange it. I listened to some of their conversation and it was apparent that they had both had a 'privileged' education, whatever that means. I find myself stereotyping when I hear a certain accent. I know this is pretty horrible of me but I have, at times, had a bucketful of clipped accents. It's reassuring to hear, but perhaps somewhat inexplicable, Annie speaking with what I would call a normal accent. When she was learning to talk, most of the time there would have been Herta, me and a variety of therapists about. We all had relatively indeterminate accents so I guess that is the reason. She also speaks softly and the tone is calm and relaxed.

Robert was pleased to see me when I got back from the trip. Both my boys were tired out. I suspect Bob was more tired than Robert. I am continually grateful to Bob, for more things than I can relate. If I started listing the qualities that he has, which he uses effortlessly, it would use up all the paper in the world! My parents also think he is a wonderful human being. Thankfully, he can swear a bit and get irate about politicians but he always finds a healthy balance. I think his dyslexia has made him more sensitive. All this love surrounding me makes me feel guilty as I always seem too busy to give him the attention he merits.

Charlie says we are going to buy the party invitations at the weekend. Actually she has asked Mummy to buy them and give them to her so we can write the names in them and I can give them out at school. Mummy said it is better if Charlie does it as she has met more of my class and can help me fill the names in. I think Mummy is too busy. We must start getting the plans together or we won't have time to decide what to organise. Charlie says we can play some games that she used to play when she was little. Mummy says we can use our two large tables put together and that should seat at least thirty children. She is going to speak to Bob about it. Bob is Charlie's husband and he is like a second daddy to me. I am very lucky. I have thought of something that makes me sad. We had to talk about it at school again and I wasn't sure if I should say anything because I wasn't able to find the right words. Well, I said that my Mummy's eyes looked sad sometimes. All the class went quiet and I thought I'd said something bad. Mrs. Winter said she thought all the children saw sad eyes on peoples' faces sometimes and then Liam said that his Mummy always had sad eyes. Tom said his Grandma's eyes were sad but not very often. Then Ryan said he didn't have a mummy so he couldn't say anything but his Daddy's eyes sometimes looked as if they were hiding a secret. I liked his words because they tell you exactly how my Mummy's eyes look. They look as if they are talking but only about private things. She looks far away as if she is having a dream. Daddy never has sad eyes with me. He has crinkly eyes that look as if they have done a lot of laughing. I have never asked my daddy where he went to school. Mummy told me once that she wasn't happy at school and that was the reason she was letting Charlie change her mind about where I was going. I can't remember exactly but I think Daddy smiled a lot when Charlie said I was going to the school across the other side of the park. It takes quite a long time to get there but Charlie says the walk will do us all good. When it is raining really hard we go in Charlie's car. She has special chairs for us and she moans a lot as there are lots of belts to do up. Robert always starts fussing but I give him one of my school books to look at and then he is quiet for a little while. Robert nearly always has laughing eyes that seem to tell you lots of things. I like it when we walk to school because Charlie tells us stories. I want to try and write properly like the other children in my class. Mrs. Winter says that I have lots of ideas. I feel them jumbling about in my head but my hand doesn't want to write them down properly. It doesn't matter as I can get help but I think the other children might start laughing at me. It's a good job I can sing a bit. At least I am fairly good at something.

Annie is increasingly beginning to notice that she isn't able to record her thoughts on paper like the other children. She is getting to the age when this might upset her, but I will watch her closely and, if it seems she is becoming distressed by it, I'm sure the school will find some way round it. The problem, if it could be called one, is that Annie has a desperation to be like the others in the class. Some of the eight and nine year old girls in the class are more like going on fifteen. They seem much too aware of themselves as mini adults and watching them on the way to school their dress style looks totally inappropriate, to me anyway. Perhaps I am old fashioned but I like children to remain as children as long as possible. Underneath their veneer are little children and I'm delighted that school uniform is compulsory beneath their coats. There seems to be an abundance of flicking hair and fussing about bands, slides and an unhealthy preening. I wonder what trash they have been allowed to watch on the various screens surrounding them. Many also have dark shadows under their eyes. Annie hardly watches any television and I am aware that this is unusual. There are computers and tablets in the house but she is so busy with her music and swimming that there is precious little time left to spend in front of them. I am absolutely delighted that this is so, but we spend time on this diary project so I suppose she isn't missing out completely. I would like to ban all screens until the child is at least a teenager. What an old fashioned woman I must seem. We seem to have gone to an extreme in so many things and I am determined that Annie will gain from all the other things we do to reach the summit of her potential. Luckily, both parents are happy to leave any decisions concerning screen time to me. Annie, at some point, will ask for a mobile 'phone, i-pod, tablet etc. and whatever other gizmos come on the market. To me it appears there are new inventions almost daily.

Charlie is looking puzzled. I will ask her what she is thinking about. I need to ask her something as I have a little problem. Well it is only a little one but I really need to know what she thinks. It's this- Jessica, in my class, goes riding. She showed me a picture of a beautiful pony that she rides at the stables near her house. She asked me if I could go with her one Saturday. Well, I have never talked to Jessica before as she is very quiet and shy, but I dropped my P.E. kit and she picked it up for me. Then we started talking just a little bit. Are you listening, Charlie? I would love to go riding. Would Mummy let me? I would save up my pocket money and help to pay for it. We could go and have a look couldn't we? I know we will have to wait until after my party but please can you ask Mummy about it? Daddy will say 'yes' I'm sure, but Mummy might not like the idea. I don't think she likes animals. If you ask, Charlie, she might agree. We could take Robert couldn't we?

I was thinking confusing thoughts and Annie has possibly come up with a brilliant idea. It certainly distracted me from worrying about what the next step should be for this nearly nine year old. If the parents agree, it would be another positive activity for Annie. I know it would help her balance and possibly increase her confidence. It is something I've always wanted to try but, if I'm honest, I'm scared of horses. There are no logical reasons why this should be so. I suppose, not ever being in close contact with them when I was young, I haven't any horsy experiences on which to draw. There was one girl in my class that had her own horse and she used to go to cross- country events. All I really remember was that she looked a bit like a horse herself. She was very pretty but her teeth stuck out. I'm sorry now that I was such a wimp as the exercise would have been very good for me and I wouldn't have got so fat as a teenager. I wonder about the safety side of things where Annie is involved. There are stables on the outskirts of town where there is riding for the disabled. I wonder if Annie might feel insulted if I suggest that her parents may agree to her having lessons providing she starts off at this special centre. I really don't know what to do. I'll talk to Annie later and test the water.

Charlie has got her serious face on. I expect we are going to talk about something important. Is it about me going riding, Charlie? I want to do it very much and I think it will help me to get stronger. Jessica has her own pony and she says I can have a ride on her when I've had some lessons. She is really nice and I wish we had talked to each other before. She is the sort of girl that just stays calm and thinks a lot before she speaks. I think I might be the opposite as Mummy says my words fall over each other sometimes. I think I'll ask Jessica to tea one day after school. Can Jessica come to tea, Charlie? She could come home with us and then Mummy could drive her home to her house afterwards. Charlie is still looking serious. She is laughing now so I expect she will answer my questions.

Annie and I have just had a conversation about riding lessons after her party is over. She seems to have accepted my suggestion that some lessons at the Riding for the Disabled Centre would be a good idea. I have told her that she would probably get much stronger quite quickly and then she would be able to go to the stables where Jessica keeps her own horse.

Apparently it is a pony as it is under fourteen two hands. Whatever does that mean? I shall get a book out of the library and encourage Annie to find some information on the internet. We still have to approach the parents with this latest idea. I'm sure it won't stop Annie's singing; it's almost second nature with her. She hums all the time and bursts into song at every opportunity, especially if there's a tune she recognises on the radio or television. I shall think carefully about the best approach to her parents as, if they veto the riding, I think Annie will react very badly. She is a good natured child most of the time but, having set her heart on this latest idea, she might get really upset if it is not allowed. It would only be for safety reasons anyway. If I visit the Riding for the Disabled Centre this week sometime, I can get more details and reassure them that the safety of the children is paramount. The centre is almost within walking distance but I think I'll get Bob to have Robert for an hour then I can get there much quicker. All I want is the information about what courses they put on for a child of Annie's age and disabilities. I'll tell Annie what I intend doing tomorrow whilst she's at school.

Charlie's going to the special riding school tomorrow. We are not going to mention anything to Mummy and Daddy yet until Charlie had found out all the information. I can't wait until tomorrow when I get home from school. Charlie must promise me that she will help me talk to Mummy and Daddy. She is looking at me with her funny expression. I can't explain it but she looks as if she would like to say lots of things but she's keeping the words hidden. I will tell Jessica what Charlie is going to do. She asked me last week who Charlie was and I told her that she was a nurse that looked after me when I was sick in hospital after I was born. She asked me what the matter was but I said I didn't know. Charlie knows because she was there all the time. She had said that she will tell me when I'm older and Mummy can help to explain it. Charlie said that it was something that was too difficult to describe at the moment. All I know is that my muscles and movements are stiff and that it is hard for me to move quickly. My hands are very ugly but I am helping them by swimming and doing piano exercises. Charlie was cross with me when I said that my hands were ugly. She said that everyone is different and that I mustn't judge myself by my appearance. She said my eyes were the most beautiful colour that she had ever seen. She said that a beautiful person was on the inside of everyone and then she made me laugh as she told me to remember the DVD we got called 'Shrek' and how the beautiful princess met him when he was really ugly and fell in love with his kindness.

What an experience that was! I really wasn't expecting to see so many heart-warming things in such a short time. When I arrived at the appointed time, there was the proprietor waiting at the gate for me. He was so kind and considerate that I immediately warmed to him. We went to his office and he, in a straightforward way, asked me about Annie. I obviously didn't mention the cause of her difficulties but filled him in about her present condition and how she was desperate to have riding lessons. He, without any prompting, mentioned that there were special rates for children if the parents couldn't afford to pay. Riding for the Disabled is a charity apparently, something of which I should probably have been aware. I explained that the parents would have no difficulty in paying the cost of the lessons but I still needed to discuss it with them. The owner of the riding stables was called Mr. Straw. He laughed and said, 'Well, that is appropriate really. My wife says that we spend so much on hay and straw that she's surprised there is any money left to feed our own children.' He let out a great guffaw of laughter which I found myself matching in enthusiasm. He was such a pleasant sort of man; open and honest with no contrived mannerisms. I found myself comparing him with the C.B.'s and would have liked to ask him about his own childhood. However, I refrained as it could have been interpreted as impertinent. My questions were silently answered when he led me to look round the 'yard'.

'Oh, good,' he said, ' Daisy's back. Daisy is my daughter. She's been off school with a cold.' Coming round the corner into the stable was a small white pony with a little girl on top. There was an adult with her, leading the pony. The little girl was wobbling about a bit but the adult had one hand on her back.

'Hello Daddy, can I go round the field again. I feel much better now?' Her father told her it was time to get off and go inside for a wash. He would come in to help her in a minute. As soon as Daisy dismounted, I saw what the problem was; her legs were very wobbly and bent and her feet pointed inwards. She hung on to the sides of the stable door as she made her way back to the house. Her father didn't help her and, on catching my look of surprise, said,' She can manage it you know. If she falls she will remember to hold on to something next time.' I thought that was very hard-hearted and Mr.Straw noticed my expression. He laughed and said,' Come with me and watch her.' We followed Daisy quietly and saw her slowly drag one foot after the other. She didn't fall but I was on edge the whole time. Her balance was much worse than Annie's. We went towards the house which I assumed belonged to the Straws. There was her mother waiting for her, holding out her hands towards her. Daisy grabbed at them as soon as she was near enough and her mother took her inside. I think I saw a young baby crawling on the floor.

'Daisy had difficulties during her birth and we thought we had lost her. She was born at twenty four weeks. She's great though, isn't she?'

Yes, indeed she was, and I had so much to think about. I knew I had to get Annie riding lessons. I saw how much it was helping Daisy. I would get Charles and Cristabel to visit the stables and meet Daisy's parents. I told Mr.Straw that I would contact him very soon to arrange a meeting between them, if he could arrange a time that was convenient. I was suddenly aware that, since spending so much time at the C.B.'s house and in their company, I had adopted their more formal tone of speaking. It was only on this day that I noticed myself using almost the same rather artificial way of speaking and how it affected the way the very nice Mr.Straw responded to me. I immediately decided to watch my language and tone. I had always felt natural, for most of the time, when speaking with people. Actually, the realisation that I was speaking slightly artificially, made me ashamed of myself and I vowed to return to my more relaxed methods of communication. When he replied to me about making an appointment I noticed a slight detachment in his glance and knew it was my fault. I decided to show him that I was an ordinary person and said, 'Your little girl is about the same age as Annie, the child I look after for some of the time. I know what you are doing with Daisy would be wonderful for Annie. I have to persuade her parents, Mr.Straw, but I know how beneficial it would be for her. Apart from that, I will be on the receiving end of non-stop nagging if we can't get something arranged. I expect you've a long waiting list, haven't you?' I felt I had returned to myself as I was speaking and Mr.Straw smiled and answered, 'We'll see what we can do.' I thanked him and he said he would telephone the C.B's the next day. He told me his wife used to do all the lesson times but, since having the baby, she was otherwise tied up. I told him that my baby was with my husband. How peculiar it is that a simple statement about something personal transforms another's reactions to a level of calm and sincere interest. The change can be quite dramatic as it was on this day and I made a resolution to be on my guard not to ape anyone else. I remember Bob quoting something to me. It was " Unto thyself be true". I'm not sure if that is accurate but it's near enough. It is only today that I feel I know what it means.

On the way home I felt hopeful that Annie would get her wish. There was another, stronger feeling, one of humility and a residue of shame. Here was I acquiring another skilled service for Annie with absolutely no thoughts about the thousands of other children in much worse situations. I could justify it very easily by saying that Annie's parents could afford it. If truth were known they could have bought the whole bloody stables, horses and all. It was then, in that absolute second, that my hidden agenda started squirming into life. If I could get the C.B.'s interested in Annie's riding, providing they agreed in the first place, perhaps there might be a way for them to finance other children. Going home I felt ridiculously cheerful and momentarily Lily was pushed to the back of my mind.

Charlie says we can talk to Mummy and Daddy tonight. Daddy had a special meeting so he might not be back until later but we can see what Mummy thinks. Charlie is staying on later than normal and Bob will be there. I think he's taking Robert swimming. I could go too but I really, really want to hear what everyone says. Charlie says I mustn't interrupt. She has taught me to write some words on the computer. My fingers keep touching two of the key things, but I'm getting better. It's the same when I play the piano. My teacher says she is putting me in for Grade One soon. Charlie says I don't need to do it if I don't want to, but I think I might want to. The words I can spell on the computer are- wet, was, and pot. I will like it better when my touchscreen arrives. Yes, I know it should have been here by now, Charlie. I really want to write with a pencil or pen like the others in my class. You should see

Jessica's writing. Miss says it is amazing. It is so neat and it looks really beautiful as if a butterfly has fluttered across the paper. Why are you looking at me like that, Charlie? Jessica says I can go to her house and see her pony at the weekend. Will Mummy let me?

Annie is in fast forward at the moment. She seems so motivated by all that is happening in her life. She has no idea of just how privileged she is, although I think she is beginning to have a deeper awareness of the fuller situations of others. Her friendship with Liam was a bit of an eye-opener for her. She definitely noticed his worn clothing. I think she was on the point, several times of asking me about it, but something else always interrupted her thoughts. I love this little girl so very much and every day I can see progress in some way, even if it is only her being able to walk along the balancing board, without falling off, that the physiotherapist brings. I have wondered, many times in private thoughts, what she would have been like if she hadn't been damaged in utero. I think she would have been a very able child but then my thoughts involuntarily meander. I know she wouldn't have had so much sensitivity and her friendship with Liam wouldn't have happened. She would have been like many others in her class; too busy with their own environment to show much concern about others.

Annie expects me to write her thoughts down almost as she thinks them. I am beginning to anticipate them and am increasingly impressed by her self-awareness. Her parents are so proud of her too but I know there are still immense problems with Cristabel and alcohol. How I wish I could wave a magic wand and make her happier. I'm afraid it is not to be though.

Chapter Seven

I am so, so happy. Mummy says I can definitely go to the riding school and have lessons. She said that when she was very small she had some lessons but then she was sent to boarding school and the lessons stopped. I didn't know Mummy was sent away to school. I hope they won't send me away. Poor Mummy; I gave her a cuddle and her eyes looked all wet. Charlie says that Mummy will never send me away. I heard her mutter, 'Over my dead body', or something like that but I don't know what that means. Charlie has said that I wasn't supposed to hear her say that but she only meant that it was never going to happen. Mummy says she will arrange a time so that Daddy can come as well. Charlie, I want you to come. Mummy and Daddy might not know what to say.

Well, that's a turn up for the books! Annie has noticed that her parents aren't the most adept, in certain circumstances, at communication. I would definitely like to go to the stables with them. I think it would be an excellent outing if I took Robert too. I'm not pussyfooting around anymore. I know Cristabel would possibly prefer it if she had centre stage but the more of us that can dilute any atmospheric stress the better. I shall have to take Robert with me anyway as Bob has had him once this week and there are jobs he needs to catch up on at the C.B.'s.

I'm really looking forward to the trip to the stables. Just the smell makes me contented. Many people will find that ridiculous but the simplicity of the smell of horse dung and the total lack of sophistication or falseness of the ethos of horses is a mystery to me; one which I would love to investigate further. There will be precious little time for anything like that in our full to bursting daily timetable. I'm just grateful that Robert is such an even tempered little chap. His speech is developing very well and he is starting to try to put words together. He absolutely adores Annie. She is the perfect older sister for him. I know the time will come when he will notice that he can do certain physical things that Annie will never be able to achieve. I'm hoping that he won't say anything that might upset Annie. I'll deal with that when and if it happens. For the moment, all the anticipation levels are set to high until we get the confirmation about the visit to the stables.

There's such good news. We are all going to the stables on Saturday. Jessica says that she will ask her mummy if I can go to her house in the afternoon. Robert is coming to the stables too. Charlie says there is another baby there. There is a man called Mr.Straw and Charlie thinks it is a good name for him as he has lots of ponies and horses and ponies and horses sleep on straw in the stables. Charlie says the smell of the stables is one of her favourites. I don't know if the baby is a boy or girl but Charlie doesn't know its name. I have to buy new wellies as the yard is very muddy and my wellies are too small. Charlie told me that there is a big concrete yard where the stables are. I really can't wait but I know I have to. I think the

146

next few days will go really slowly. I am going swimming now and then I have some homework to do. Robert has a cold so Charlie wants to take him home to bed as soon as Mummy comes in. I have been told to keep away from Robert as I must not catch it before Saturday. He likes to be near me though and doesn't understand about germs. I don't either but I think they are tiny little things that we can't see that can make you ill if you breathe them in. You can catch them from other people that are ill but Charlie says she will explain it to me later. She said the germs are microscopic, that's right isn't it Charlie? She will bring me the microscope that is in their sitting room that Bob uses to look at the night sky. I think Bob is very clever and he knows lots of things. He probably knows more than my Daddy but I would never tell him that, would I Charlie? I'm trying to be patient and wait for Saturday without nagging everyone. I will do some more piano practice. I have a new chair that has a special back. It sort of props me up so I don't sag. My back aches as my muscles aren't very strong. Charlie says they are getting stronger all the time.

Annie is getting over excited about Saturday and she will not be able to control herself soon. She knows she must be quiet infront of her mother and she senses the times when she must be extra quiet. I watch her looking at her mother's face sometimes and trying to read the expression on it. I don't make any comments to her at this time as it is important that she alters her own behaviour to accommodate her mother's varying moods. Cristabel tries so hard not to let Annie see when she is having a bad day. I think she has made friends at work now as she has mentioned that she had lunch with a couple of them. It is so hard for her to maintain her feelings of being in charge when she sometimes, I know, is on the brink of losing it. I wish I could find some way of helping her.

It is Saturday at last. We are all ready. Mummy has got on her very best clothes. She has a smart jacket and some very high heeled boots that I haven't seen before. Mummy has a wall with things. What are they called Charlie? Oh, it's 'compartments'. It's got about three hundred pairs of shoes. I heard Daddy say to her that she could only wear one pair at a time so what did she need so many for. Mummy didn't say anything that I could hear but, when I was in bed, I heard her crying.

We are all going to the stables in a minute and Robert's cold is better. My wellies are getting too small for. I really would like some proper riding boots. Mummy says that I probably won't have a lesson today as we are only going to have a look. I am definitely taking my wellies just in case. Charlie says you never know and it is better to be prepared. Daddy had a worried look on his face but he seems quite happy. He has got some very large boots in a very large bag. He has told me that he has never been on a horse and all that he knows about them is that they have a leg in each corner. He told Mummy to put some wellies in but I don't think she's got any. Yards are always muddy, even in the Summer, Jessica told me. It's because the yard has to be washed down every single day to get all the poo and muck out of the way and into wheelbarrows to take to the big pile. Jessica says her daddy buys some bags of it and puts it on his potatoes. I have been waiting here for ages and ages.

I have such a strange detached feeling about this trip to the stables. It's almost as if I have had control removed from me. We all fit into Cristabel's other car which is a massive off-roader. I feel very high up and almost important. My feet are firmly on the ground though. Robert senses something is happening. He has a closed expression on his face and it is rare that he keeps silent for so long. Annie played with him all the way, but he just looked distant and appeared to be fascinated by all the things that we could see. It is difficult to explain the following two hours. A dreamlike atmosphere seemed to enclose us.

On arriving The Straw family were there waiting for us. I noticed Mrs.Straw looking at Cristabel's boots. After saying hello in a very friendly way, she disappeared and came out with a pair of wellies for Cristabel. I watched with some trepidation as she handed them to Cristabel, saying, 'You'd better put these on. Your feet look the same size as mine. Well, about anyway.' Then she roared with laughter and said, 'Come on then, we'll have a nice cup of tea afterwards and then the babies can get to know each other.' The wind was completely taken out of Crisabel's sails and she passively allowed Mrs. Straw to help her off with the stilettos and on with the boots. I noticed Annie looking a bit worried, but after her daddy had got his own boots on and deposited his others in the Landrover, we all made our way to the stable where the pony that was reserved for Annie was waiting.

I noticed that Mr.Straw was watching Annie as she walked towards the stable. Mrs. Straw was talking easily to Cristabel and everyone's faces were full of expectation. I was the only person that was nervous, I think. That was unusual but I had such premonitions about this trip and no evidence on which to base them. There was a teenage girl in the stable, getting the pony ready. I noticed that she had a very awkward way of moving. It was as if her legs weren't quite sure about what they were doing. She had the most wonderful smile though and welcomed Annie like a long lost friend with, 'I'm so glad you're here; Poppy has been looking forward to meeting you.' Watching Annie's face, full to the brim with happiness, I moved away with Robert. The outcome of this was not in my power to alter. I hoped there was somebody, somewhere looking after this precious little girl.

The next two hours were spent with Annie being taught how to respond to the pony. When Annie was helped up on the pony's back I was amazed how she managed to balance. Poppy was so incredibly gentle with her. She must have sensed that the little girl on her back was vulnerable. I overheard Mrs. Straw saying to Cristabel that the ponies were all chosen and especially trained to react to vulnerable humans. I noticed, inexplicably, that she didn't say,' children'. I heard the words, 'At liberty', but didn't know what it meant. I noticed that Cristabel had walked to another stable door where there was a large horse. She just looked at the horse, nothing else. She just very calmly looked into the horse's eyes, then quickly came back to where we were all watching. It was a frozen moment. I noticed that Mr.Straw was watching Cristabel. I wondered why. I know she is exceptionally beautiful but there was something else in his gaze. The morning ended with Mr.Straw writing something down. He did a lot of smiling. I noticed the ponies that were in the stables, all watched him. Mrs. Straw said, 'Let's go inside and I'll put the kettle on.' So, after Annie was shown how to get off the pony, we all congregated in the kitchen. A cup of tea was almost magically prepared and a massive chocolate cake appeared on the long farmhouse table. Two high chairs appeared and Robert was put in one next to the Straw's baby. We all sat down, higgledy piggledy, around the table, comfortable because of the relaxed and easy manner of the owners. 'Well,' Mr.Straw said, ' that was very good, young lady. Do you think you'll want to come again?' Annie's response was a squeal with an,' Oh, yes please.'

I noticed that Charles had been very quiet, but, after a cup of tea he seemed to perk up. In fact he started a conversation with Mr.Straw about how he had started the riding school. He asked in a genuinely interested way as well which, I noticed, made him feel better in himself and Mr.Straw reacted in a warm and friendly way. After all, he knew nothing about this family apart from their obvious affluence. So, there we all were, being warm and friendly, perhaps each one of us knowing this was going to be the start of something mysterious, especially to the C.B.'s.

I am so happy. Mummy says I can go to Jessica's house to tell her about my morning. I have tried to tell Charlie about my riding on Poppy but it is difficult to remember all the stuff. I do remember that when I get off it is called 'dismount.' Charlie didn't know that, did you Charlie? On the way home, Mummy said she was going to buy some proper boots. I saw Daddy smile. Mummy was very quiet but I expect that was because she was doing the driving. We are going to have some lunch and then Charlie is going to drop me off at Jessica's house. Daddy is going to pick me up later. Robert fell asleep on the way home and Charlie said that all the excitement had made him tired. This day was one of my very best days.

We have to start on the preparations for Annie's Ninth birthday party. Goodness knows how we would cope if there were any more children in the house. Catching myself thinking that, I immediately thought of Lily. There was an instant drowning of all the preceding happiness. It was all washed away, destroyed. I managed to grasp a little control and fixed a smile on my face. Nobody would ever know the extent of my sorrow, hidden softly away. I really must keep myself busy, even more than before as the sudden slicing into my memory of little Lily, in my arms as I whispered goodbye to her, was more poignant than I can remember. Surely the memory should become less painful, rather than so suddenly arriving with a silent smashing into my mind? I had to think of Annie and direct my energy into her life as well as Robert's. Was I being self indulgent by allowing myself to concentrate on the past? It would not happen again; at least I was able to anticipate it and therefore control it. There were invitations to write and distribute. As the whole of the class were being invited, this task will take some time. It is important that Annie contributes to the task to a meaningful extent, although it will make her very fatigued. I will, with her help, design an invitation so all she had to do is sign her name. To do that thirty times will test her patience but I think it is essential for her to do it. It will help her realise the effort needed to accomplish it. She will probably surprise me though. Often, the outcomes I expect are the opposite of what I think is inevitable.

We have to write thirty invitations to my party. We have made some pretty ones on the computer. I tried to help but my fingers got in the way. I did choose the, what's it called, Charlie? Oh, yes, the layout. I chose all the different colours. Computers are able to do lots of things. Charlie said that if we had time we were going to draw one card and then she would photocopy it thirty times. No, twenty nine times. We didn't really have enough time to do that so we just printed off the one that we like, after adding my address and the time of the party and our telephone number. Now I have to put my name on the bottom of each. I really don't want to do that; it will be so boring, but Charlie has a very serious face on and I know I must do it. Next year I might only ask three friends, but I have loads of friends so I really want the whole class to come. Charley has just said that the sooner we start the sooner we finish and then we can have tea. Robert is grizzling so Charlie is going to give him his tea whilst I get on with this job. I expect I will starve to death before I finish. Charlie has just brought me a drink and a biscuit as she says it will help keep my energy up. My energy is always up but not for this sort of thing. It makes my hand ache and then I feel all sort of muzzy as if I need to lie down. If I write my name ten times before tea and then ten times after tea, there will only be another nine to do. I think that's right. Charlie has said to get on with it.

If it appears that I'm being a bit hard on Annie, there are good reasons. It is important she doesn't expect everything to fall into her lap. She has not noticed the extent that her privilege exceeds that of all the other children in her class. She knows that she has all sorts of extras but hasn't quite realised how many of the other children only have a fraction of what is provided for her, discounting her special needs. She does know Liam's background but is somewhat detached about it. It is as if his situation is only temporary and somebody will come along and wave a magic wand. If I took her to the area in which he lives, I think she would be speechless. If he comes to her party, and I'm not convinced he will, I must make sure he takes home some party bags for his two siblings. Who am I kidding? Throwing a few crumbs at the family won't solve their problems.

I left Annie for half an hour and, bless her, she'd signed her name ten times. She looked totally exhausted. The touch screen computer came today but I'm hiding it until all the excitement of her party is over. Cristabel agrees with me that there is enough going on at the moment without adding to it. I shall need time to read the instruction book myself as my skill with technology is pretty basic. Bob laughs at me but understands how I almost feel as if my personality is being eaten alive with all the gadgets around. It seems as if there is less and less time to actually talk to each other. I'm not a lazy person but the extent to which people rely on computers for simple communication messages worries me. The voice must be the most genuine vehicle to make a connection with another person, surely? Using a computer seems such a cold method, if one wants to get a proper response. Using Skype becomes obsessive; I know this from watching Cristabel when she is working from home. The extent to which she will prepare herself seems ridiculous to me, especially as some of the girls at work have seen her totally dishevelled. I think any privacy or personal space is destroyed. I really don't want Annie to grow up without developing sensitive listening and speaking skills. It is difficult enough for her at the best of times so making her totally dependent on screens seems like taking the easy way out. What about Robert? Will he become immersed within the screen culture? I'm not sure if Bob will understand how strongly I feel about it. Annie will have to rely on her new computer to a great extent but I would love her to actually want to commit pen to paper, even if it is in small bursts, as it is at present.

When I get home from school tomorrow, Charlie says I can finish off the invitations. I want to ask Mrs. Winter to my party but I don't expect she will be able to come. I've just had my tea and Mummy has just come home. She is very quiet at the moment. Perhaps she is thinking about all the food she will have to order for the party. It doesn't matter because Charlie will do it all anyway. I heard her ask if the parents will stay and if she should order drinks and nibbles for them. What's nibbles Charlie? The parents won't be staying as we are all old enough to be left on our own, aren't we Charlie? Mummy looks very worried but I know everything will be fine. Daddy will help and Bob is going to stay on late. Herta and her husband are coming too so there will be plenty of people to get everything organised. We are putting two long tables together and carrying all the chairs from the other rooms to put round them so there will be enough for everyone to sit on. Mummy has asked me what cake I would like. She looked very strange when she said it and I don't know why. Her eyes were sort of stretched open.

Annie will be very surprised as her Mummy is going to help make the cake herself. That will be an interesting exercise in itself as I can't remember ever seeing her in the kitchen actually following a recipe. I heard her on the telephone asking Herta if she would come over to give her a hand. She has absolutely no experience of decorating and actually spending time on a creation that is edible. Apparently the cake is to be a fairy castle. Oh, dear, I hope Herta knows what she is taking on. I heard Annie telling her mother that all the girls' mothers make the cakes for birthdays. I wonder how accurate that is or if the little girl is putting her mother through a test. I have a vague suspicion that Annie thinks it would be a 'good thing' for her mother to do. Let's hope it doesn't backfire. When Annie is at school tomorrow Cristabel and I are ordering the party food off the internet. What an admission after all my opinions about that! My main worry is the entertainment. If all the children turn up, however are we going to occupy them all? I know we could hire a party entertainer but it seems like cheating as this is Annie's first proper party. Are the children too old for 'Pass the

Parcel' and 'Musical Chairs'? What about 'Hide and Seek'? That would be too dangerous with the pool so near. Do we need to make party bags? Oh, my God!

This is stupid. It's not rocket science, but it feels extra important that everything is successful. I'll talk to Herta tonight. It seems awful that I can't talk to the mother of this child. Poor Cristabel's face would be overcome with confusion and anxiety. She has absolutely no experience of what is involved. Well, this party is throwing her into the deep end, and she will be involved whether she likes it or not. That applies to Daddy as well. Herta and I will probably be on the 'phone for a couple of hours tonight. Why am I so determined that this party has to be such a success? There are all sorts of reasons that I'm not sure I feel comfortable with but I know that, if Lily had lived, this would be my way of ensuring she had a party to remember. She would have been of an age that would have made it possible for her and Annie to be really good friends. I am certain that this would have been so. I still feel her little dead body in my arms before they took her away. Now I must stop this train of thought. I have been more able to blank the more morose thoughts away recently. They serve no purpose whatever and Bob especially, mustn't see that I am still affected by them. No, I shall keep very busy and involved in this extended family of mine, knowing all the time that I'm so lucky when thinking about how many other families are on the edge of existence.

My birthday is getting nearer. I have finished writing the invitations. Well, I mean I've written my name hundreds of times as neatly as I can. I hate it because it takes so long. Mummy says I can have my new touchscreen computer after my party. I can't wait but I think it might be disappointing as I really just want to be able to write like the other girls in my class, not like some of the boys as their writing looks as if a spider has walked across the page. I know how I want my writing to look; just like Jessica's does but I know that is probably impossible as my hand wobbles and the letters look like scribbles. Charlie has just said that I mustn't think about it as the most important thing is what is in my head. I think she means what I'm thinking. I like what we are doing now as it means I can see my words going down on the screen almost at the same time as I'm thinking them. I think Charlie must be very clever. She has just pretended to push me off the chair. She is just like a second mummy to me. Yes, you are Charlie; you're always there when I need you.

I nearly said that she was like a daughter to me but it is not appropriate, especially with the difficulty Cristabel has had in forming a natural bond with her. Annie is, in spite of everything we have all gone through in the last nine years, truly special and I would be devastated if anything happened to prevent her being in my life. I know Bob feels the same but he is more able to keep his emotions under control. I think that is probably why he jokes a lot. It acts as a barrier and stops him showing what he feels. I know him well and I recognise the times in which he feels uncomfortable. Having been on the receiving end of teasing at school, he is especially sensitive if a child's feelings are involved. He always looks at the ground, not trusting himself to stay dry-eyed. I constantly thank fate for putting him in my life. I cannot imagine any other man understanding how important little Annie is to me. I know he loves her dearly, but it's not the same; I cannot think why, but perhaps it's a woman's maternal instinct.

Cristabel's maternal instinct has developed slowly and reluctantly. She still has the alcohol problem to overcome. I'm not sure she knows that I am fully aware of it. It is not my place to talk to her about it. She goes to A.A. meetings regularly. I've also found out, through Herta, that she also has counselling. She has never broached the subject with me and I feel she has a need to keep it private for the present. I wouldn't know what to say to her anyway. Telling her she was being a selfish cow ran through my mind but, of course, that would only make it all worse. So, I try to boost her confidence and be at her side when she asks. Charles is hopelessly impotent in this respect. He does try his best and has improved in his ability to show affection to his daughter; not his wife though, infront of anyone. I often wonder if they have any sex life. This is absolutely none of my business and I cannot think of any circumstances in which I would creep into a discussion about it with her. Annie is accurate about her mother's eyes looking sad. That's another thing I can't talk about in this house. Bob says that time will have its own plans and that my worrying over any of it is unnecessary and could be the unwanted rustling in the wind, upsetting but unheard by those unwilling to listen. There are a multitude of thoughts in my head that I would like to discuss with him. The more

I concentrate on them, the more they fragment into lateral shafts of disconnected and flimsy parts of sentences. No sense can be gleaned from the jumble. Only if I deliberately ignore these words, swooping and swilling, like flocks of roosting, murderous starlings, will they settle eventually, alertly, waiting for me to achieve some sort of order.

It's really funny, Charlie. Mummy says I have to keep out of the kitchen. I really want to watch her make my cake. She says she will need to concentrate and I might put her off. Anyway, she says that I'm not supposed to see it. Herta has arrived. She gave me such a big hug and then disappeared into the kitchen. Everyone seems to have such silly looks on their faces. I know exactly what they're doing but I'm not allowed to look. Charlie says I had better do my piano practice. She's going home in a minute. When I get to school tomorrow I expect there will be lots of answers to my party invitations. Charlie has to get Bob's tea and bath Robert, so this will be the last bit she'll write for me. After my party I'm going to try and practise spelling words on my special computer. I still don't know if I really want it as I can feel some power coming into my hands more and more every day. That is when they don't seem to take over and do lines that I don't want. Charlie has shown me some cards that some grownups made. They were painted with the brush held in their mouths. They couldn't use their hands at all. Yes, Charlie, I'm going to play the piano now. See you tomorrow.

At last we've managed to get away and come home to do all the things that are piling up in this house. Bob is giving Robert his bath and I'm trying to make a pasta dish quickly as it is something we can all eat. I'll cook a few carrots and peas too. I need to get Annie's present wrapped up tonight. I suspect there will be a million things waiting at the C.B.'s house tomorrow. I hope the damn cake is a success. It is obscenely important that Cristabel has a triumph on her hands. If she manages to keep off the alcohol it will help when the trickier bits are being designed. Herta is fantastic in this department and could rustle up a birthday cake fit for a queen. Unfortunately, she has an inept mother to teach the art of decorating. It has always amazes me that a mother exists who has never made a cake. Cristabel has a vacuum of confidence in the kitchen, even though Herta and I have both tried to show her some simple ideas for a quick meal. I reckon Marks and Spencer think this family have a major shareholding in the company. The amount that is paid to it every month would keep Bob and I in good food for a year. That's an exaggeration, I know, but it frustrates me when I can see the wastage in the bins at the end of a week.

There is a cook starting shortly, at my suggestion, as I think it's time that this family sampled freshly prepared meals, especially vegetables. Opening wine bottles is Cristabel's speciality. A case is delivered every week at least. After the party I'm going to talk to Bob to see if he can come up with any new ideas about how we can stop the drinking routine. I see clearly that is what it is. Cristabel comes home, goes into the kitchen and immediately opens a bottle of wine. That is even before she acknowledges her daughter's presence. I wonder if Annie notices the drinking. Perhaps she has got so accustomed to it that it is accepted as normal. I know, at secondary, school there is a programme of drug and alcohol abuse. I'm jumping the gun a bit but Annie is nearly nine and within three years she will be going to secondary school. A friend of mine has a son at the school and she has told me about the lessons in health care which include the dangers of excess drinking. I was surprised how young the students were that were exposed to all manner of topics that certainly weren't in my school curriculum. 'Times move on', I'm told, with an increasingly frequency, but I think we might be taking away childhoods.

Bob goes very quiet when I tell him about the topics addressed at the secondary school. He won't offer an opinion and I can't work out the reason. He must have an opinion. I'm actually too tired to bother any more. I think the thought that Annie might inherit her mother's alcohol problem fills me with horror, and that is probably at the bottom of my concerns. However, we are going to be really busy for the next few days so there will probably be a great deal for Annie to write when she next sits here next to me.

My cake was the most magical thing you ever saw. Herta and Mummy decided that it was going to be very pink. I mean very pink. Mummy said that she didn't realise that such a small amount of colouring made so much pink. There were fairies and monsters all around the side and there were three cakes all balancing on top of each other. Mummy said that she liked cutting out the scary monsters. Herta did all the fairies and butterflies and then Mummy cut out some scary spiders and insects. We took some photos of it to show Daddy. He looked very surprised and then pretended to be frightened of it. It made Mummy laugh. It is the first time I have heard her laugh for ages and ages.

We played lots of games and I won 'Pass the Parcel'. We actually played that three times as everyone wanted to keep doing it. Charlie looked surprised. The best game was 'Musical Chairs'. Daddy helped me but I really couldn't manage it. Liam won that game. He didn't turn up until much later than everyone else. Daddy went to get him from his house. He didn't tell me until later, but he had to ask Mrs. Winter where he lived and then he went to get him. When he came back he took Charlie in the kitchen for a couple of minutes. They didn't think I noticed but, after the party had finished and everyone had got their party bags, I went with my Daddy to take Liam home afterwards. I know now why he wanted a talk with Charlie. I hope he has a talk with Mummy as well. Well, Liam lives in a very dirty house. Charlie has told me to be careful what I say for her to write and I will but it was so dark and dismal in his road. There were lots of bins and old cars lying about. Lots of the houses didn't have gardens but just a little strip of rough grass at the front. There were children crying and Daddy said that it was probably their bedtime and they were tired but he had a very worried look on his face, just like Mummy has for a lot of the time. When he came to my party and Daddy came in through the front door with him, he was holding his hand. Liam didn't seem to mind. Daddy took him into the downstairs bathroom and I think he gave him a wash which was very kind of him because he really smells some of the time and the other children might tease him. They wouldn't do it infront of Mrs. Winter though. I made a special welcome of Liam and sat next to him at the party table. I'm going to use the new computer tomorrow so Charlie won't have to help me so much. My party was another of my very best days. Charlie told me not to forget to thank Mummy and Daddy for making it such a special day. Oh, yes I must just tell you about the candles. They were the sort that you blow out and then they light up again. You don't have to use a match. Mummy said that Herta bought them. I had so many presents and Charlie made a list of the childrens' names and the gifts. She says I can do a 'Thankyou' card on my new computer. I have lots more to say but am going to do it tomorrow.

Well! Everyone is thoroughly washed out from the last couple of days. What a success it all was and surprisingly enjoyable, even though the mess to clear up was knee deep in some places. That didn't matter as the army of cleaners came early in the morning to fulfil their magic. When I arrived this morning everything was sparkling again. As it was only eight o'clock when I got here, the cleaners must have had a very early start. Cristabel hurried off to work with something that almost resembled a tiny smile on her face. Annie was in overdrive and the computer in all its glory was placed on a special table, waiting for us to set it all up. That duty will fall to Bob as I'm useless at technology, mainly because it bores me. I have a secret thought that Annie might feel disappointed in her latest gizmo; she expects some immediate result in her ability to form words quickly. Her problem is recognising the order of the letters, just like Bob had when he was her age.

That is possibly a good thing as he can sympathise with her and, if he can manage the time, help her. Goodness knows how; it always stuns me how a person can learn to read eventually, but the ability to record words never seems to improve. Bob carries a dictionary round with him and uses wordcheck on our computer all the time. I used to think that was not helping him but now I have accepted that his memory of what a word looks like, when correctly spelt, is almost negligible. I am not looking forward to our session on the new machine tonight. No-one will notice as I'm expert at hiding my feelings. Ever since Lily's death, I find it easier to shut my darkest thoughts away. I expect Annie will find some way of coping with this new technology. The fact that she only has to touch the right sequence of letters on the screen to 'write' doesn't actually confront her basic problem. I know it is only a problem if we make it one but I think disappointment may be the result. Her memory of letter sequences is virtually non-existent. Using the predictive program will only confuse her more and shouldn't she, with her great tenacity, be persevering in the conventional route.

I cannot think about this any more as there are things to do and we'll be late getting to school if I get distracted. I want to get Robert's name down on the pre-school nursery register this morning as I know there is a waiting list. It will feel strange when he goes to nursery. There is more than another year before he will start and it will only be for two mornings a week to start with. Why am I worrying about this now?

When Charlie met me from school, she told me that I could have a turn on my new computer after I'd had my swimming lesson and done my piano practice. She has a serious face on so I know she has other things to tell me. Daddy is coming home early tonight as he wants to see me swim all the way from one end of the pool to the other. I expect Robert will come in the water as well. He only has two blue floats on his back now and he doesn't mind when I splash water on his face. My swimming teacher is very kind and we always have fun. I love the feeling of the water holding me up and my body does what I ask it. I don't have to force it like I do out of the water. I want to go on doing my diary like this as it means Charlie and I sort of talk together as she writes things down for me. It will be much quicker too. I know Charlie is worried about the new machine as she keeps looking at it and frowning. Bob has set it all up and it's 'ready to go'. I feel quite sad that this computer won't be needed so much. Daddy came to watch me swimming and he had one of his silly grins on his face. He helped to get the tea for Robert and me whilst I was doing my piano practice. I heard Charlie and Daddy talking about the new computer. I am getting scared of trying it. It is very new and shiny and looks as if it is waiting for something.

Charles made the fish fingers for tea. It took quite a long time but I didn't interfere. I discreetly prepared the sweet potato and peas and we actually had a good chat at the table. Charles asked Annie about Liam. He was surprisingly careful when choosing his words. Taking the boy home after Annie's party had obviously caused him to think. Annie knew her Daddy was trying to find out more about this boy and she told him virtually nothing. I respected her loyalty. In a perverse way I was pleased that this father had, probably for the first time, come into contact with a needy family. He dropped the subject and then we all went very quiet. We all knew it was time to introduce ourselves to the new computer.

There was a ring at the front door which I think we all welcomed. It was the new cook who was starting work the following evening. She was a jolly, smiling lady and I knew that we were all going to get on together. It didn't matter about Cristabel as she was completely detached from that side of the running of the house. The birthday cake was her summit of achievement and, although she showed a sliver of pleasure at the result of their labours, it was obviously going to be a 'one off'. Annie thought the new cook was going to be good fun particularly as she asked her what her favourite foods were. The name Mrs.Cook was perfect and Annie said, 'Is that really your name?' Mrs. Cook said it was indeed her name and people laughed when they found out what her job was. Annie said that she thought a good name for her would be Mrs. Jolly as she had such a jolly face. Mrs.Cook laughed a great big guffaw and we all found ourselves joining in. It is an immediate, warming reaction to people like her. You know instantly that she is a lovely person, totally trustworthy and honest. Her beam lit up the whole room. At that moment Cristabel came home from work and, the second she entered the room, the atmosphere changed into one of a cool tense watchfulness. Annie rushed to her mother and shrieked, 'Come and meet our new cook.

She's called Mrs.Cook but I'm going to call her Mrs. Jolly because she is so happy.' Cristabel was forced to laugh. She put out her hand to shake Mrs. Cook's and smiled, 'Welcome, I hope you'll enjoy working here. We are a very busy house so I'll leave you to manage on your own most of the time.' I wanted Cristabel to shut up. Without realising it, she was immediately forming a barrier between them. She didn't even know what she was doing. It was just another example of the damage her parents had inflicted on her. Luckily, Annie remembered the promise of the introduction to her new computer and dragged her father out of the room. Cristabel then asked me to show Mrs.Cook the various areas and tools that the kitchen possessed. The room looked as if it was an advertisement for 'Homes and Gardens'. Every possible piece of equipment was in place, most of it unused. I noticed that Mrs. Cook gave a little grunt of barely suppressed surprise at all the gleaming tools, pots, pans and shiny surfaces. I did notice a rapid glance at the rack of wine bottles and had a thought that might have meant Cristabel didn't feel the need to hide them away any more and perhaps she wasn't drinking in secret as in the past. I knew that wasn't true though as her furtiveness was always there as a cloak. The day she had a spontaneous and natural reaction to anything was still in the wings. I had a permanent wish that somehow, something could be done to help her feel genuinely content and confront her guilt about Annie, once and for all. It was quite dreadful to watch as she held her emotions under control. I tried to remember the girl, nine years ago that had given birth to Annie, and I knew that this new mother had made enormous strides in her ability to form a loving relationship with her daughter; the daughter that had been nameless for days; the daughter that had suffered dreadful damage because of Cristabel's alcoholism. Her guilt would never disappear but, surely, she could continue to come to terms with it. Charles had, seemingly, accepted the situation and I had never heard him blame his wife. I was not there all the time though. What about at night time? He must have an opinion about the selfishness of his wife, surely? Perhaps he didn't know just how serious her drinking was during the pregnancy. Could he be as much to blame? He had developed a wonderful relationship with his daughter and it was a joy to behold, especially as they seemed to have the same sense of silly humour, a characteristic missing totally from Cristabel's makeup.

I've just come home from school and Charlie says that we will have a shot at the new computer again when we've done a bit on this one. She says we will choose two words every day and practise touching the screen in the right order. I don't know if they are spelled right or not. Bob says, 'Practise makes perfect'. He says that he had to write a word lots and lots of times before his brain remembered it and even then he still got it wrong, but it is not important really as it is the words in your head that are vital. I like the sound of that. Bob says that I can always spell my name right so that means if I write another word lots and lots of times I will start to remember that too. We are going to have some tea now as Robert is getting hungry, isn't he, Charlie? Then we are going to have a go at shooting the new computer. You did say that Charlie; you said have a shot or something. Why are you laughing?

this is the frist tim I hav ysd this. Bod ses Im dowing wel.

Well! That was short and sweet. I stopped Annie after this first attempt as I have this idea of establishing two words a day and then writing sentences. I don't know if it is a good plan or not but I'm going to give it a go, or a shot as Annie would prefer! I thought I'd choose words that she uses a lot and build up a list of them that are firmly rooted in her memory. I know that lots of things seem to fly in and out of her brain but I am determined to at least try my idea. The first words will be very simple and she can access them easily as this new computer comes with special supports for her arms. Her hands are very near the screen and all she has to do is touch with her fingers to find the right letter.

I am annie I am 9 I am a gril

That was brilliant for a first proper turn. I must think of more common words for her. I wonder if I can make up a silly poem for her so she can say the words as she types them?

Here goes....

My name is Annie

I can spell it now

Annie, Annie, Annie

WOW!

I expect we will leave out the punctuation marks for the moment. I'm not sure about the capital letters as it means she has to think of getting both her hands touching the screen simultaneously. I know she finds playing the piano difficult for this reason and often one hand is out of timing with the other. I'll play it by ear and change things as we go along.

Mrs Cook, or, as I suspect Mrs. Jolly will be her name, is going to be a great help. Her two boys go to the same school as Annie but are two years above. She was such a lucky find as we will be able to work together during term time and make sure all the expected tasks are completed. This house occasionally feels as if it is a business, being run in a strictly programmed routine. As the C.B's have radically altered their own routines to fit in with Annie and my own demands, time needs to be carefully organised. I am reluctantly impressed by the growing emotional attachment I catch sight of, almost as if by accident. Last week I saw Cristabel looking at one of Annie's horse storybooks. She wasn't aware of me and seemed absorbed in what she was doing. Later on that day I saw her looking at the same book but with Annie next to her. She had her arm round the back of her daughter, which is the first time I have seen such a natural pose. When she saw me she immediately removed her arm; a pity I thought. It was as if she felt guilty about touching her. Cristabel asked me when it would be convenient to go to the stables again on a regular basis. I told her that I would organise it for a Saturday afternoon as this was the best time for everyone. Bob could look after Robert and I could then accompany the others.

As I heard myself saying these very normal words, a wave of something indefinable washed over me and I thought I was going to faint. I took some deep breaths and focused on the wall for a moment. The weird feeling passed but a residue of my head and body not being connected still remained. Thinking that keeping busy was the answer, I telephoned Mr.Straw to find out if he could fit us in on a regular basis. He is such a kind man that I knew he would move heaven and earth to accommodate us. Then I felt guilty. Was I using the influence of money and the C.B.'s obvious power over events? Of course, if they could change their situation with their daughter they would, so really they could be considered at a disadvantage in the overall scheme of things. I felt confused at my mixed emotions. However, after having the most relaxed and normal conversation with Mr.Straw, I felt better and convinced myself that we were doing what was best for Annie and she was the most important consideration. I still had the feeling as if I were floating above a situation over which no-one, especially me, had any control. I knew I wasn't dreaming, but I felt as if things were being passed across my face, out of control and of no relevance to me. I remember, as a child, trying to catch bubbles in the garden that my Dad had blown for me. I never caught one, not a single one. My Dad used to laugh as I sprung in the air, twisting and flapping my arms about, getting more and more frustrated. It was exactly how I felt at this moment. I had absolutely no skill at catching and taming whatever was going to happen. All I knew, with certainty, was that the future was tied up with our visits to the stables and Annie's riding lessons.

Today, Charlie told me that I am going to have riding lessons every Saturday. I have made Mummy promise to come with me. I didn't know it before but she really loves horses. We read a book together yesterday and she had a proper smile on her face and then she gave me a cuddle. I can't remember her doing that before. No, I can't Charlie, and it was so lovely. Why are you looking at me like that Charlie? Mummy and me are going to the special shop that sells jodhpurs and riding boots and hats, so if I fall off I won't hurt myself.

Now we are going on the other computer and Charlie is going to give me some special words to spell on the screen. She says I have to practise them a lot and then I'll be able to write about my riding. We are going to do the same for my swimming. These are the words...

Jodhpurs, riding, horse. Now I have to do it myself and then Charlie is going to delete them and I have to try to remember the order myself. Here I go.

| Joderps | ridding | hoses |
| Jodphs | riding | horses |

We are back on the other computer now as I want to talk to Charlie. Charlie has helped me out a bit but she gave me the really difficult one deliberately to test my concentration. I got two right but I probably won't remember them tomorrow. I don't know why riding trousers are spelt so funny. Charlie says we are doing the same three words tomorrow with one more added. I am looking forward to Saturday and I would like my Daddy to come as well but I think he has a conference in

Birmingham but I don't know where that is. He is going to come the next time we go. He has promised. Charlie says that I can remember how to spell jodhpurs by doing 'jod' then thinking ha.. ha.. for the next letter and putting the stupid 'h' in. Then I am half way through the word and just have to add 'purs'. It is that bit that is difficult. Charlie sounds it out for me but it looks the same whatever order I write it in. She has started singing the spelling out for me which I think is funny as her voice sounds scratchy. I'm not being rude Charlie but you need to open your mouth and breathe out as you sing. My teacher says that you have to sing from the heart and the music will float out on its own. Sing jodhpurs again please.

Annie is taking the role of teacher this morning and I appear to be having a singing lesson. I will sing the word jodhpurs but wish to hell I hadn't chosen it! I'm using the tune of 'Jingle Bells' as most of it seems to be on the same note. Annie is joining in with gusto and my voice fades into the background with gratitude. It doesn't really fit but it is our first attempt after all. Now I must find a tune for 'horses'. Annie reckons 'Three Blind Mice' will do. There's only 'riding' and we are done. This is exhausting!

I think Charlie doesn't know that I'm practising writing the words in my book as well. I still make mistakes all the time but it helps if I sing the order of the letters. When I try to write with my special pencil that is shaped like a sort of triangle, my hand goes into a spasm. Now I've told you, haven't I Charlie? Don't worry about it. I am getting better at it. I'll let you look at my book one day soon. I didn't mean to tell you. Mummy and me are going to the shop that sells jodhpurs tomorrow and she is meeting me from school. She has never met me from school before. Will you come as well Charlie as she won't know where to park the car? It will feel very strange to see Mummy waiting outside the gates with all the other parents. I'm worried that they won't talk to her. I'll tell the girls in my class to speak to her.

Poor little girl; worrying about her mummy feeling left out. I'll make sure Cristabel knows where to park and to get there early. I don't think it is a good idea to accompany her. It will seem as if she needs me to look after her, although I instinctively act out the part of her carer as well as Annie's. I haven't really thought about it much until now. Being there, at the sharp end, at Annie's birth was such a deeply traumatising experience, even for me with all my years of working in the profession. I never thought my little family would become so closely tied up with the C.B.'s. We seem to have become mutually interrelated. I know Charles adores Robert and I have become genuinely fond of Charles, even though we had a sticky start. There is a small part of me that knows he is still vulnerable in the presence of an attractive woman that is not Cristabel. It can't be much fun at times, knowing of her alcoholism and being completely unable to give the sort of support she needs. Poor Charles is also a victim. The difference is that he has mellowed into a lovely Daddy, probably in spite of his own rotten experiences as a child. A doubt of the authenticity of the Birmingham conference activities flashed through my mind but I shunted it to oblivion. He is basically a kind and thoughtful man, his deficiencies caused by parental neglect. The little snippets that I've picked up in general conversation tell me that family life was pretty low on the agenda. So, all in all, he's made exceptionally good progress and if he strays during these absences, I can understand the reasons. I will cross everything that is possible that nothing is ever suspected, especially by Cristabel.

Well, Mummy came to meet me from school and some of the other mothers came over and spoke to her as well as the girls in my class. She looked very smart. Perhaps she looked a bit too smart but it didn't matter. I noticed that Liam's mummy was late. I wanted my mummy to talk to her as well but I didn't think that would happen. I noticed Liam's mummy running and wobbling as Mummy and me were going towards our car. Jessica's mummy asked my mummy if I could go for tea after riding on Saturday. I felt all warm and glowy when my mummy said 'Yes and thankyou very much'. When I looked out of the back window of our car, I saw Liam's family all looking at us. He was smelling funny today at school. It was a bit like chips. His shirt cuffs were nearly black and they were all torn round the edges. His shoes always have holes in them.

There was a lady on Monday that came into the classroom and she sat at the back. After a little while she went to talk to Liam and he showed her his book. I have had people come in to see me but they are different from the lady that came in to see Liam. I don't know how to describe it Charlie. It's just that my lady seemed more friendly. A man came in about a month ago, and he was whispering to our teacher at the front of the class. He kept getting in the way of the white board that Miss was printing our group work on. He had a very big beard and if it had been white he could have been Father Christmas. He never smiled, not once. Miss told me to stop staring and to get on with my work. Is Liam in trouble, Charlie?

Oh! Annie is far too observant at times. I expect Social Services have been called in as well as the Educational Psychology Department. Liam could have been such a 'normal' little chap if he had had some proper care. It is difficult to say anything to Annie without appearing to condemn the situation. As the boy must be nine or nearly so, I wonder why it has taken so long to get help for him and, of course, the family if the children are really at risk. Just because they are dirty and Liam is often absent or late, doesn't necessarily mean that something awful is happening at home. Or, does it? The mother shouts and smells of alcohol but she doesn't actually fall over. I know the area in which they live is dirty and run down but perhaps she copes as well as she can in the circumstances, whatever they are. There is no husband but there may be someone in this mum's life that keeps her from going totally overboard. The problem is that nobody knows. With three little boys it must be hell if she is on her own. Do I know that there isn't a husband? No, I am making assumptions. I will try to find out from Annie in a subtle way, but how without arousing her suspicions and appearing to be pushing my nose into something where it is not wanted? At the Christmas show, the little boy's face was a joy to watch. He was completely absorbed in his role and proud as Punch to have the responsibility of looking after Annie at certain times. I'll never forget his face.

It seemed unusually confusing that the two ends of the privilege spectrum were closely relating to each other, the richest one depending on the poorest. The richest had a debilitating poverty of movement whilst the poorest had total fluency. What a strange diversity of interdependency. Who would dare to judge which one of them was the more fortunate? I am uneasy about Liam. I know Charles was speechless when he saw where Liam lived and the conditions surrounding his house. I mustn't interfere, but it is another thing that I know is interconnected with our lives over which I have no influence.

Mummy and me have just come back from the riding shop. Mummy must have spent thousands of pounds. She was smiling a lot and looked very happy when I tried on my jodhpurs. They felt a bit tight but the lady said they have to be tight so that your legs can feel the horse without flapping clothes. My riding hat is brilliant. I am going to practise writing 'riding hat' on my new computer and then in my writing book that is secret but now it's not because I've told you haven't I Charlie? There is another thin cover that can go on top of my riding hat and it is called a silk. Isn't that funny, Charlie? Does that mean it is made of silk? I chose a stripy one with a toggle on the top. Mummy laughed and put the riding hat on her head. I was surprised as it nearly fitted her. It stuck on the top a bit, so the lady in the shop asked Mummy if she was going to ride. Mummy went very peculiar and said, 'We'll see'. I don't know what she meant but it would be nice if she could manage to ride with me. It would be something we could do together a bit like the swimming we do together sometimes. Mummy is very, very good at swimming. I can't keep up with her at all. If Daddy is watching, he shouts at me to beat Mummy. We don't do it very often though. Mummy tried on some very special boots. I know they were very special because they were over one hundred and fifty pounds. I saw the price on the label. Mummy bought them but told me not to tell Daddy. I expect she wants to surprise him when she is walking about in the mud at the stables. She will walk better in the boots. My boots are black and are quite difficult to get on and off. We decided to get ones that only come up to my ankles as the lady said they would be perfect for me. We also bought socks and some really soft gloves that were specially for riding so you can grip the reins properly. That's what the lady in the shop said. I'm really aching now so I have to stop.

Annie looked really tired when they came home. She rushed her tea that Mrs.Jolly had prepared and spent longer than usual wanting me to write her thoughts down. She enjoyed the trip to the shops with her mother; a rare occurrence but one that was very important to the little girl. She spent a long time telling us all about the purchases and then I had to record it for her so it has been a long day. Robert wanted to see all the riding stuff and he was very interested in the boots and gloves. I hope it's a fine day on Saturday as it will be Annie's first proper lesson and if it is pouring with rain it will take the edge off it. Cristabel can wear her lovely new boots regardless. We have lots of other things to fit in before that though. Robert needs some new clothes and I really must have a few hours to kit him up before he looks like an urchin. He seems to have been on a growth spurt recently and is starting to look like a little boy rather than a baby. That makes me sad, as I'll never be able to retrieve the innocence that he had as a totally dependent little soul. I should be pleased that he's growing up into a strong child with lovely blond curls that I never want to cut. He is lucky to have Annie as a big pretend sister as she is always chatting to him and his speech is coming along very well. I know I'm expected to accompany Cristabel and Annie to the stables on Saturday so I must find time to buy myself some wellies. The days are never long enough to fit everything in.

I'm not complaining as I love my life completely and am aware of how lucky Bob and I are to be able to afford things that were impossible before we came to work with the C.B.'S. I just wish I could get through one day when I don't dwell on my little Lily's death. I know there was nothing I could have done any quicker as, with my nursing knowledge, I got her to the hospital immediately. Meningitis is a killer and there is very little that can be done even if treatment is rapid. I still feel hurt by the way fate took our little angel from us, especially as we had waited so long for her. I tell myself that we wouldn't have Robert if Lily had lived and that gives me a shred of comfort. I often reflect on the day that the paediatrician suggested that I went home with the C.B's. and supported them through the first few months with their little baby. Dear little Annie, damaged permanently by her mother's alcohol intake. Little did I know then how things would develop and that my husband and I would both become closely involved with this family and all the additional therapists that Annie's condition would need. I know she has made and indeed is still making remarkable progress. The fact that the parents have abundant finances make it easy for them to employ all the staff needed. They had both been affected by their own cold upbringing and the more I found out about their childhoods the more I knew how seriously the absence of warm and close parenting had damaged them. Cristabel still had severe problems with alcohol but the relationship I never thought would happen had, so slowly, gathered impetus, especially since the Christmas concert. Perhaps the riding lessons would be the next catalyst. I laughed silently to myself, assuming that was wishful thinking. If Annie learnt to ride independently, surely her mother would get some satisfaction from that, especially as she was going with her daughter every Saturday.

Saturday never seems to get any nearer. Charlie says, 'A watched kettle never boils,' and I think I know what she means. So, I'm keeping very busy and swimming, playing the piano and doing my homework. Daddy helps me sometimes if he's home. He is very clever and can do my number work in his head. He is not so good at actually writing as it is very untidy which makes me feel better. He told me that he was very bad at spelling at school and that he uses 'spellcheck' on his computer all the time. Charlie says that is very interesting. I don't know why she said that. Now she says that I'm like my daddy and that, if he can learn to spell, then so can I. Bob is rotten at spelling too so I think I'm not so rubbish at it after all and I will get better soon. Well, not straight away, but when I'm grown up. I can look at spellcheck and find out the right way to spell a word but the problem is that it still doesn't look any different to me. Charlie spelled my name wrong yesterday and asked me to look at it. Then she spelled it the right way and put the two words close together. Then she asked me which one was my name and I told her straight away. Then she wrote 'went' and 'wnet' and asked me which one looked right. I told her. She said that it is when a word is on its own that makes me get in a muddle sometimes. I know that when I read I often guess a word. Charlie is looking puzzled so I'll tell her. Well, if the sentence goes like, 'I am very tired so I'm going to.......' then I can guess the word 'bed'. Another one could be, 'My puppy loves me to.........him'. I could guess that one wrong but I normally get it right and nobody knows. I look at the first letter and think of a word that starts with that sound. Do you get it Charlie? My teacher says that my reading is really good now. I hope she doesn't find out how much guessing I'm doing.

Annie has this appealing ability to tell me things that I would never think of asking her for fear of trampling on her fragile privacy. Her reading is indeed progressing very well and, like my husband Bob, won't be the main obstacle to her communicating digitally in the future. She has such a feisty personality that she may well get impatient with the monotonous effort she has to make just to get the right letter on the screen. I know technology is moving at a frightening pace and her thoughts will be interpreted and recorded without her having to move any part of her body.

The point is that she is able to move her hands and arms so she must be encouraged to do so. It is the finer motor control over her fingers that causes the most impatience. The fact that she keeps repeating that she wants to write with a pen like the others in her class is what will cause the greatest frustration. There have been so many positive signs that her body is finding different ways of succeeding that I'm hopeful that she will reach her target of writing with a 'proper' pen. There must be others in her class that have difficulties with writing. She probably will only judge herself by the best in the class. This will be, needless to say, Jessica. This is the girl who is, inevitably, going to be the best rider in the world also. There is virtually nothing I can do about any of it so I shall just continue encouraging her and let nature take its course. Thankfully, Jessica is a kind little soul. She appears to like Annie so I should mind my own business.

I have been ready for my riding lesson for an hour. I don't know why Mummy is taking so long to get ready. She always looks very beautiful so she needn't worry about looking her best. We are going to be trampling around in mud anyway so it really doesn't matter. Charlie is going to see what the holdup is. I am going to wait here and read what I've written.

Yes, we eventually were ready to go. What a performance it was. Cristabel seemed very nervous for some reason. I can't for the life of me think why as everything has been done for her to ensure we can get off smoothly. Mrs. Jolly even prepared a thermos flask of coffee for us. So, off we, eventually, went. It had been raining in the night and I had remembered to pack a change of clothes for Robert as I knew Bob would be finding the muddiest place possible to take him. With the nappies, wetwipes, towels, plasters, drinks and other necessities, it looked as if the poor child was being sent away for a month. The riding lesson lasts for an hour. This meant that Cristabel and I were alone in each other's company. Usually there is at least one other child around to act as a barrier to us speaking about anything too personal.

I still can't forget the ghastly first few days when I met Cristabel. I have to mentally kick myself to bring the progress she has made to the forefront. The residual problem of the alcohol is always there, the reminders entering my thoughts unbidden. Bob tells me to take each day at a time and not to be too judgemental. He wasn't there at the birth and afterwards when Cristabel was only interested in herself and when she was going to get her multitude of beauty appointments organised. I couldn't put the memories out of my mind completely but I knew Bob was right and that it served no purpose whatever to wallow in them now. I tried to think about the time, shortly after I had lost my little Lily, when Cristabel arrived at my house unannounced, and made me think about something else. It was as simple as that. What Cristabel did was of even more value as there isn't a person in the world that would have found it more of a challenge than her.

The riding lesson was full of surprises. Initially, Cristabel and I stood watching as Annie was helped to understand the various bits of equipment that a pony needs. The pony that Annie was going to learn on was called Poppy. She was a pretty little animal and exceptionally quiet. Mr.Straw came over to us and told us that Poppy immediately knew that Annie needed looking after. Cristabel and I both stayed quiet. We didn't know what to say. I felt rather foolish as I found tears welling up in my eyes when he said that. He was looking directly at Cristabel, thank goodness, so he wouldn't have noticed. At least I hope he wouldn't but there is something very 'knowing' about Mr.Straw and I don't think he misses much. We were invited into the kitchen as it was important that Annie formed a good relationship with Poppy without distractions. Mrs. Straw was a gentle, kind lady and I noticed a cake had just been taken out of the oven. Cristabel also noticed and her gaze seemed fixated by it. It could have been that she didn't know where else to look. I wish I could explain her reactions to what most people would consider normal experiences. It is as if she is hiding a secret terror and by appearing detached she hides it. I know her well enough and have seen her with her parents to know her basic instinct is to cover her real thoughts behind a screen of platitudes. Only once or twice have I seen her let down her guard and show immediate natural reactions to things. Once was when she was swimming with Annie. I watched, as did Charles, as they giggled together because Cristabel's goggles got in a muddle and she had them on all twisted. Annie was trying to help her and Cristabel let her. It was a magical but rare moment when all defences were down. As soon as we were seen, it was as if a sheet of glass came down between us. I tried to act naturally but the atmosphere was thick with anxiety.

Mrs. Straw's kitchen was warm and welcoming. We were told to sit down on the squashy sofa and not worry about taking our boots off. The floor was tiled and I noticed a mop and brush in the corner. Life must be easier with that casual attitude. Cristabel had a bevy of cleaners so she wouldn't be aware of the more mundane chores of keeping a floor reasonable clean. We had tea and cake and the little baby crawled around our legs playing with an assortment of toys. He was a happy little soul and reminded me of Robert's easy going nature. His mother picked him up and gave him lots of cuddles and he struggled to be put down. She laughed and said, 'Typical boy; only wants to be cuddled when it suits him.' It was time for his morning nap and, whilst she put him in his cot, I tidied up the tea things. Cristabel watched me. When Mrs. Straw returned she asked if we had known each other a long time. I decided to make Cristabel answer that one and left a space which, luckily, she filled by saying, 'Oh, Charlie has been my life-saver. She has helped me since Annie was born.' This obviously exhausted her and she looked at her boots. Mrs. Straw then told us that her name was Nancy and that was what everyone called her. So, we introduced ourselves and from then on were obviously going to be on more familiar terms. Cristabel kept looking out of the window and Nancy told her that we would be going out to the stables very shortly as the hour was nearly up. We thanked her for the tea and cake and, looking out of the window, saw Annie on Poppy looking through the window at us. We all laughed, even Cristabel managed an almost natural snigger. Annie's face was covered in an enormous smile. I don't think I have ever seen her smile so broadly. She was sitting very confidently and holding the reins in what looked like a natural grip, but I know nothing about riding so it was just an overall impression. We kept very still for some reason as if the moment had to be captured in time. Another pony arrived with Daisy on top. I'd forgotten all about the Straw's little girl. We waved and Nancy went outside to ask her what she'd done with her pony. Daisy was not as articulate as Annie and had difficulty in getting the words out. She persevered though and managed to tell her mother that she had trotted on her own. Then Mr.Straw led both ponies away and we said our goodbyes to Nancy and followed them back to the stables. He showed Cristabel how to use her hands to support Annie back. She obeyed the instruction to the letter and didn't take her eyes off Annie for a second. We watched as Annie was helped to dismount which I thought she managed very well. She was very stiff as she almost staggered over to us. Cristabel went towards her. I stood still. I knew that if I interfered now it would ruin everything. They hugged each other, really hugged properly and tears cascaded down my cheeks. I quickly blew my nose and turned away as it was not the right time to be seen to be losing control. This was a private time between mother and daughter, perhaps one of the first to follow. Oh, I did so hope it was! We looked at all the horses and ponies before we went, at Annie's insistence. She knew nearly all their names and obviously would have moved in with them, given half a chance. This was a day that needed to be bottled.

Today was one of the best days ever, wasn't it Charlie? I loved riding Poppy. She was so gentle. Her mouth looks as if it is smiling all the time. She was very smooth to ride and I only bumped about a little bit. Mr.Straw says that I'm a 'natural'. What does that mean? I think it means that I find it easy as I'm not nervous. I'm really not nervous at all. Can I practise some riding words now please? I know I have to go on the other computer but that's fine. I feel as if I can do anything.

riding hat   riding hat   riding hat

boots   boots   boots   riding boost

That stuff on the other computer took me half an hour. But I did it! I know I will have to practise on Poppy for a long time before Jessica can see what I can do. She is coming to tea on Friday and Mummy says that I can ask her mummy if she can bring her swimming things. Charlie and Robert will come in the pool with us and my swimming teacher will be there too so it will be good fun. Mummy says that I can ask Mrs. Jolly to make anything we want for tea. Mummy smiled a lot after we got back on Saturday. When Daddy comes home from Birmingham we will have lots and lots to tell him. I think he will smile too. I hope he can take me to the stables as well as Mummy. I want him to see what I can do. I think he will be surprised. I have a new friend. Her name is Daisy and she can't talk very well. She is a much better rider than me though because Mr.Straw is her Daddy and she has been learning for much longer than I have. She is a bit wobbly on her pony. Mr.Straw says that we might go out on a ride together in a few weeks. I have to learn how to muck out the stables and put new straw down. It will take me quite a long time because my legs get very tired.

What a day we have had. There seems to be so much to think about. It was nothing short of amazing to see the expression on Annie's face. I am reluctant to say the same for Cristabel as it might all backfire, but there was a difference about her when we got home. There is no other way to describe it. We have all been very thoughtful and quiet. I have Sunday off tomorrow so we are going, just our little family, to see my mother and father for the day. It has been three weeks since we last managed a visit and I know Robert misses them, as I do. We will probably go to the park which is fairly near and then have a lovely roast that my Mum is so brilliant at making. It is good that Bob gets on so well with them; but he gets on well with everyone so that's no surprise.

I have been told that there is going to be a visit from Charles' parents very soon. The preparations will be ridiculous. There will be nothing like 'take us as you find us' about it. Everything will have to be organised down to the last table napkin. We will all hide within our respective glass bubbles waiting for the next comment and thinking about the most appropriate response. It is almost annoying that Bob just chatters away to the children seeming to be oblivious of the adults. It is we adults that seem to do a lot of staring into space. Bob has told me to relax and be myself. That is impossible. I know too much about this fragmented family. The visit isn't going to happen for a couple of weeks, so I will have time to think about something to say. In reality I have absolutely nothing to say. We have nothing in common, a fact that I am very pleased about. I can talk at length about Annie and how wonderful she is but their faces assume a blankness and I know they are neither interested nor involved in anything concerning their granddaughter. It is their loss and I would dearly love to tell them that. Poor Charles does try. His ability is weak at best, but at least he makes an effort. The problem is that the more effort he makes the more forced it becomes. I do have some sympathy for him though. He married a girl from the right social class, with an accent that could cut glass. He did what was expected, knowing no better and having no experience of anything else. Cristabel came along at the appropriate time, looking stunning. He was obliged to ask her to marry him. Did either of them know what real love was?

I can't wait until next Saturday. I know I've got to wait patiently and do all the other things that are on the calendar. Mummy says that Daddy is coming next Saturday. I like that because I don't often see them at the same time. I want Charlie to come as well. I can't tell you why Charlie. I might tell you later. I want to see Daisy again. She is really nice and I think we are going to be good friends. I like the way she speaks. She takes lots of time to say anything but it doesn't matter. I take a lot of time to get from one place to another so we are nearly the same. I saw Mummy looking at one of the big horses. She went right up to it and then quickly came back to us. It was just before we got back in the car to go home. She put out her hand to touch the horse's face but then she took her hand away and turned back to us. I don't know why she did that. I know she's not frightened of horses. I think perhaps she really likes them. That would be good because then she might come with me every Saturday. I'll tell you why I need you with me, Charlie. I feel funny telling you but I must. I know that something special is going to happen, just like when I sang in the school concert. I feel as if I could do anything and I need you there just in case I disappoint everyone. I can feel a warmth coming up through my body from Poppy. Mr. Straw laughed when I told him but he said horses were good at keeping warm and knew how the rider was feeling, especially a new one that wasn't used to sitting on a horse. He asked me if Mummy has ever ridden and I told him about when she was younger. He didn't say anything else but just looked like you do when you're thinking important things.

We had a lovely time with my parents on Sunday. They adore Robert and he chuckles at them which is lovely to hear. The weather was mild and sunny which always helps. Robert ended up in some muddy area, as he always does, but my Dad just laughed and helped change his trousers when it was certain he wasn't going to repeat the adventure. My Mum is very good at talking to Robert and pointing things out to him. They have made a common bond over anything that resembles water. They found a stream and spent ages throwing little stones into it. Bob smiled a lot as he watched them, and I thought my heart might burst with the sudden thrust of love I felt. It is exactly that experience which the C.B. adults have had denied to them. That is why I must be there, in that palace of a business- like house and try to bring some warmth to it. Will that be possible?

I am determined that Annie will have a better chance as she grows up of understanding and relating to others in all sorts of environments. She already has an ability to perceive situations that might need sensitive handling. But, it is not up to me. What will I do if it is decided that Annie's best interests will be served by her going to boarding school? I can't even think about it. I am hopeful that Cristabel respects my opinions enough to take my well meant advice if she asks for it. I am certain that Charles won't want his daughter going to boarding school. He knows the help she receives now is part of her established routine and must know that she is making progress, especially in her communication skills. In fact I have heard her contradicting her father over some minor event and he seemed pleased that she had got her own opinion. He absolutely adores this child and I cannot envisage a time when he would want to cause a separation. I fear, if it did happen, his relationship with Cristabel would be even more barren. He tries so hard to make a connection with his wife but the barrier is mountainous. The unexpected glimpses of contact between them, when they both appear to be appreciating the same thing, are too few and far between. Perhaps there is a miniscule drip of hope. After all, I did see them laughing together recently. It still saddens me when I see the over-reaction from Annie; her response is extreme as she is not used to her parents showing happy spontaneous behaviour.

Mummy says I can have Jessica back to tea after school on Monday. She is coming home early from work. Mrs. Jolly is going to make a special chocolate cake. Her two boys are coming as well. I heard Mummy saying that it would be fun as everyone could go swimming.

Mrs. Jolly says both her boys are good swimmers and that she will watch as well. She said something about 'Health and Safety' but I don't know what that means. Charlie has told me that there are special rules for swimming pools and children have to be watched, even if they are strong swimmers. Daddy says that our pool is a private pool so it doesn't matter but Charlie told him it is better to be safe than sorry. Mrs. Jolly says her boys eat anything that isn't nailed to the ground and we couldn't stop laughing. She says we can have our tea after the swim and she will lay it in the kitchen. I wonder if there is a Mr. Jolly?

I loved that little tale that Annie told. Her face was alive and animated. I expect the other children will be surprised when they see Annie in the water. I suppose being weightless helps her to move more freely. I am pleased that Cristabel is making the effort to be home early. I will take Robert in the water with them as it will be good for him to watch what they all get up to. The deep end is over three metres so I'll need eyes in the back of my head. I'm not sure Cristabel will pay enough attention to what is happening. Perhaps I'll ask Bob to go in the water with Robert and I'll act as lifeguard. I remember watching them on their high chairs at the pool where I learnt to swim. They were very free with the use of their whistles and stood no nonsense from anyone, especially children jumping in too near others. Perhaps I should get a whistle or, better still, get the C.B's to employ a lifeguard. What a joke! They could employ the whole staff from the local swimming pool. No, this is going to be a proper family affair and it will all work out perfectly as long as I stop worrying. I will never forget the expression on Cristabel's face when we were at the stables. She almost, but not quite, succeeded at feigning disinterest. I shall watch her reactions when the children come for a swim. She will be almost forced to become involved. Perhaps that is the answer; don't give her a chance to become detached.

The day for my friends coming to tea has arrived. I have two days, one next to the other that good things are happening. Next week I have lots of doctors' appointments again so I will enjoy these two days as the appointments are boring. Now Charlie says we can finish this tonight when my friends have gone home.

This is becoming a habit. Recording Annie's happiness is a joy to me but I mainly want to see her mother get emotionally involved and it so nearly happened today in the pool. Cristabel was persuaded by Annie that she really, really must go in the water as she wanted her friends to see what a brilliant swimmer her mummy was. Amazingly, she obeyed her daughter's instruction. All the children were very well behaved and watched as Cristabel swooped from one end of the pool to the other. She did a tumble turn at the end too. It was all so fluent and graceful. The children all clapped as she finished at the shallow end. She looks slightly embarrassed and told them all to get in and enjoy themselves. Then she wrapped herself in a large towel and watched them, actually concentrated on it. Even this mother was aware of the dangers that water and unsupervised children can cause. I told her that Mrs. Jolly and I would watch as I'd notice her shivering and she needed a hot shower. So, off she went. Annie's swimming teacher turned up and proceeded to entertain the children by giving them various fun activities. I felt much better then, especially as she taught them the first stages of diving. They were all impeccably behaved and I sense this might become another regular date on the calendar. Charles had been sitting on one of the lounger type chairs but his body was upright. He watched his wife and I noticed that he touched her gently as she disappeared to have a shower. That was a first. There was no reaction from his wife but no flinching either. Charles then got changed and had a swim. He was rather flabby and in obvious need of exercise. He swam the lengths relentlessly, perhaps because of his wife's behaviour. When he'd completed goodness knows how many, he got out and disappeared into the shower room.

Cristabel and Charles were a long time in the shower room. It crossed my mind that, perhaps, they were having unexpected sex, and I couldn't stop a smile spreading across my face. That could be a perfect end for them both on this day. It was probably wishful thinking on my part. I'd never had sex in our shower and I can't think why I should be hoping the C.B.'s were having unbridled passionate sex at that precise moment, in their luxurious shower suite. Well, I did, and both their faces had slightly secretive expressions on them when they returned, fully dressed, to the pool. I tried not to stare at them but their body language was interesting. Charles put the most comfortable cushion on the lounger next to where he had been sitting and they both sat down, silently peaceful. It was definitely food for thought, but strangely worrying.

Chapter Eight

I haven't had time to do this diary for a few days. I have practised on the other one but I still find it awkward. My fingers are definitely getting looser, but I'm still very slow at remembering the order of the letters. Charlie says it doesn't matter a fig. She doesn't know what that means either. I have ten more words that I can write on the new computer. They are-going, mud, straw, reins, Daisy, mount, get on, bridle, and bit. I can't remember reins as I get muddled as it sounds the same as when water is coming down from the sky. Rein sounds the same as rain. Charlie says there are hundreds of words that sound the same but are spelt differently. I know one and that is a very difficult one. It is through and threw. I will never learn to spell those. I have so many other things to think about and going to tea at Jessica's house is the best one apart from riding on Saturday. I know that Grandmother and Grandfather are coming to see us soon and I'm not looking forward to that. He doesn't like me and he stares at me all the time. I know that I must be very polite and quiet but they do too much frowning. Charlie says that I must be on my best behaviour as we don't see them very often. I'm pleased that we don't see them very often. Poor Mummy. They don't even give her a kiss or a cuddle when they haven't seen her for ages. I don't think Daddy likes them either. The best person is Bob. He keeps very quiet, just like a well-behaved cat. He stands in a corner and answers any questions with a 'sir' at the end. Why does he do that? Grownups are very peculiar sometimes and when I'm grown up, I'm going to do lots of talking. Daddy says I could talk for England. I think he was being funny, but I'm not sure. I will tell you all about going to Jessica's house next time. I have to do some singing now.

Annie comes out with such funny things sometimes. She is still so innocent in many areas and I hope she stays like that for as long as possible. Her Mummy has bought her a tablet but she has hardly looked at it. In one way I'm pleased because there are so many other things for her to do and becoming immersed in yet another screen will only distract her. She can hardly fit in all her additional activities now, so another distraction might not be helpful. I sound really miserable and I think it is because Annie's language development is so good that any further piece of equipment might be counter-productive. I often wonder if all the fast moving colours, figures, sounds and images have a detrimental effect on a brain. Not just Annie's vulnerable brain but all young impressionable people. Perhaps the fashionable ADHD syndrome is caused by the young immature brain becoming over stimulated and going into free-fall. I noticed that there was a lot of fidgeting at the table during Annie's birthday party and I'm sure it wasn't caused by the excitement. It was continuous twitching of fingers, feet, eyes and bodies. It seemed impossible for a child to keep still even for a second. There was one child with an eye tic. A blink every couple of seconds. He also drummed his fingers on the table, very quietly, but insistently, and then, after stopping that, tapped the sides of his head rhythmically. I watched to see what the next movement would be but the cake arrived and he was distracted for a little while. It disturbed me that nearly all the children were what I would call 'wired'. Was it really because of the rather, to them, unusual surroundings? I don't think it was. Annie was the calmest in the room and appeared to be the most at ease. I will make a point of watching other children when the opportunity arises as I have a growing fear of these electronic gadgets and the damage they might be doing without us realising it. Of course Annie must have her instrument to help her record her thoughts. A mobile phone is the next possession which, at secondary school, will be considered vital if she is not to feel excluded from her peers. I'm please to read that many schools don't allow them in the classroom. Where on earth do they keep them securely? Whatever is going to happen to eye-contact? I've noticed that the checkout person rarely looks at me when I'm doing the weekly shop. I must look ridiculous as I make a point of staring her in the face and throwing in a few pleasantries. She probably thinks I'm a mad old bat. They all look about ten anyway. Unexpectedly, the boys are better at eye-contact than the girls.

I had a brilliant time at Jessica's house. Her bedroom is all pink and frilly. She's got loads of pictures of horses and ponies on the walls and some of herself riding at the stables she goes to once a week. Her mother was very kind when we went upstairs and helped me. I was quite fast and I think it surprised her. She told me to call down if I needed anything. We had a lovely tea and her Daddy cooked it. He laughed all the time and had a very jolly face like Bob. Jessica is an only child and a bit spoilt her Daddy said, but he was laughing when he said it. I'm still not absolutely sure what being spoilt means but it isn't anything too bad or he wouldn't have smiled when he said it. When we were in Jessica's bedroom she told me a secret and that I was never to tell anyone. She had a baby brother but he died. Jessica couldn't remember him but she said that her mummy sometimes got sad because she missed him. Why are you looking so sad Charlie? Oh. I've just remembered. You lost a little baby didn't you? Mummy was talking to Daddy about it the other day. I won't say it again if it upsets you. We had better stop now.

Yes, it was hard to hear that little bit from Annie. She won't have any recollection of Lily at all. She was only a baby herself when Lily died. One day I will tell her that her mummy helped me so much during that awful time. It is not the right time though. She will ask me too many questions and I still feel raw. Indirectly it was partly her presence that got me clawing myself out of the black pit I had been curled up in. I wonder if I will ever need to tell her about the reason for her disability. Will she ever get to the age when she notices or realises that her mummy has a problem with drink and then put two and two together? I suspect that time will come eventually as she, in the rapidly approaching future, will be part of whatever 'Sex and Relationship' classes are called nowadays. I imagine cucumbers and condoms play a prominent role. I'm starting to get depressed by the thought that, inevitably, this little girl will lose her innocence, however much we try to protect her. If she goes to the community college it is certain that her education will be broadened rapidly in respect of sexual awareness. Is that a bad thing?

Chantelle, in my class, wears a bra. I heard her friend saying that she has nothing to put in it. She is only nine. You don't mind me telling you this, do you, Charlie? You said I can say anything I want and you will try not to interrupt me. She showed it to Jessica in the toilets and it made Jessica laugh. Chantelle said that Jessica was jealous but that made her laugh even more, so Miss heard them and told them to go back to the classroom at once. Miss is going to speak to them both after school. I wonder what she is going to say? Will I have to wear a bra? It looked very uncomfortable. I think Chantelle must have a mummy that wants her to be grown up. Chantelle is not very well behaved in class. You haven't met her Charlie as she had gone on holiday when it was my party and she didn't answer the invitation. Saturday is getting nearer and my favourite day of the week is nearly here.

I suspect that Saturdays are going to be the highlight of Annie's week. I expect there will be lots of news for Annie to tell me on Monday mornings as I won't go to the stables every Saturday. I think it is important that Robert and I spend as bit of time together although he seems to prefer to be where the action is. It's being a boy I suppose. Cristabel will be with Charles on Saturdays and three adults are more than enough for one little girl to have hovering around. I will try to go with them this Saturday as it's a very enjoyable couple of hours. There is a wonderful atmosphere about the place, difficult to quantify or describe. There is a definite tranquillity between Mr. And Mrs. Straw that they seem to take with them wherever they go. There's a calmness, even in the way they walk. Certainly they both speak quietly and kindly, especially to the animals so it's as if the whole environment is contained in a protective sheath. I'm looking forward to my next visit. I know with absolute certainty that Saturdays represent something in this family's life that is, as yet, inexplicable.

It was brilliant on Saturday, Charlie. Mummy led me on Poppy. Mr.Straw, his name is Tommy by the way, asked her to help me as he had to get a splinter out of Daisy's hand. Mummy was so good and she didn't say anything at all. She just walked very slowly with me on Poppy. I wish I could have seen Mummy's face. Did you see her, Charlie? She did keep looking back but all I could see was a smile. Tommy, he told me to call him that, came back very quickly and took over from Mummy. He thanked her and then told Mummy and Daddy to go into the farmhouse with you for a cup of tea. I wonder how Tommy knew that my Mummy could manage to lead me. Why didn't he ask Daddy? Next week you will be able to see what I can do now. I have been taught how to muck out. It is lovely and smelly and Mummy came into the stable at the end and just stood and looked. She still had a smile on her face. She gave Poppy a carrot that she had brought in her pocket. Her hands got all wet and slimy but she didn't seem to mind. Are you surprised, Charlie? Mummy said that you all had a lovely cup of tea with Mrs. Straw in her kitchen with the baby. I don't know what Mrs. Straw's name is yet. Daisy played in the stables with me whilst we were waiting for you all to finish your tea. She was very shy when Mummy came in but I don't know why. Daisy showed me how to hang up the tack. Did you know that all the stuff that the horse needs is called tack, Charlie? I helped Daisy because she was a bit wobbly. We managed to hang it up together. Daisy told me that none of the horses or ponies in the stables has any shoes on. Most horses have metal shoes. She told me to ask her Dad the reason. I think she was getting tired from trying so hard to talk to me. She opens her mouth but nothing comes out. Sometimes some of the words sound as if she has food or something in her mouth but I can understand her if I'm patient. I try and smile at her so she knows that I don't think she's silly. Her mouth does look a strange shape though if she's trying really hard to tell me something. I saw Mummy watching her. I was pleased she didn't say anything. Mummy smiled and asked me later if I wanted to have Daisy home for tea next Saturday. I think that might be all right. Will you be there Charlie? Daisy's mother might have to come the first time because I think she might worry about it.

Annie is showing real concern about her new little friend. I think she realises that Daisy has some serious challenges in her life. I wonder where she goes to school. I would really like to know as it is obviously not the one that Annie attends. Perhaps she goes to a school that offers her more specialist help. I'll get Annie to ask her. I must also make sure that I'm around if the little girl comes back after riding next week. It would be good if the whole Straw family could come. Is that taking on too much for Cristabel? We could ask Mrs. Jolly to come and get the tea. Her husband would have to look after their boys as I think there would be too many children for little Daisy to cope with on her first visit. There I go again, worrying, probably unnecessarily, about things that might not cause a problem. I'll suggest to Cristabel that we ask Mrs.Jolly in for the Saturday anyway. I hope she can manage it as she is such a brilliant and efficient cook, instinctively knowing what children like to eat and making it look so attractive. I know Bob is going to tell me off for trying to organise everyone. He says I was born being bossy. I know my Mum was run ragged when I was very little. It seems I was 'into everything'. I would have thought that was a good thing. I must ask her exactly what I got up to. Bob says we will manage perfectly next Saturday and that life is full of surprises. I don't know what he means but I have complete confidence in his judgement. Annie is managing to fit in all her extra-curricula activities. She still doesn't like her new computer and I have a certain amount of sympathy for her. I wonder if she realises that there are computers that recognise the voice and that she wouldn't have to do anything but speak to it. I know, without asking her that she would refuse one. She has an indestructible need to be like other children. I do fear for her within the next four or five years though. I was overjoyed by her progress with spelling. I know she is years behind her peers but the determination she has shown to spell the twenty or so words that she now can manage is nothing short of miraculous. She can sequence the letters in the right order most of the time. We practised five more tonight. She chose them herself and they are all what I call 'horsey' words. We try to add all the others that she has learnt and she is getting quicker and quicker. Her latest words are…. shoes, hooves, trot, lead, brush, carrot. I think most of her written work will have to include horses. It doesn't matter of course as the most important fact is that she is beginning to be able to spell even in a rather restricted way. Bob says that writing about horses is more interesting than writing about people. Annie's teacher called me in to have a quick word last week and said how she had noticed the improvement in her spelling. I didn't ask how the writing was produced as I would imagine it was on their special computer.

I must spend some time with Robert this week as he is getting very mobile and is starting to explore. When the weather improves a bit we can go outside into the lovely play area that the C.B.'s had built especially for Annie.

My teacher told me that my spelling is getting much, much better. She doesn't know that I have been practising using a pen at home and I will soon be able to surprise them all. I know it won't be as good as Jessica's but it would be funny to see their faces. I'm looking forward to Daisy's family coming to tea on Saturday. They are not coming until later in the afternoon as Tommy has to give more lessons and the baby has to have a sleep. Mrs. Jolly is making everyone tea and she has promised to make one of her special cakes. They are all bringing their swimming things. We are going to be a very large party. I love it and I want everyone to be happy and laughing, especially Mummy. My swimming teacher is coming as well so that makes a lot of us. Mrs. Jolly's boys are going to a football match with their Dad, so I won't see them. When I see them at school they always says hello to me and are very polite.

I like boys like that and I will marry one that is like Mrs. Jolly's when I'm much older. How old were you, Charlie, when you married Bob? Have you been married a long time? I love Bob and, if I didn't have my Daddy, I would like Bob to be my Dad. Mrs. Jolly's boys call their daddy Dad. I call mine 'Daddy'. I expect I'll call him 'Dad' when I'm older. Do you think Mrs. Straw will be a good swimmer like my mummy? I wonder if the baby will go in the water. I know Charlie, we'll wait and see.

Annie is getting very persistent in her demands. She is so charming when making a request that it is very difficult to deny her anything. I am dreading the next few years and the disappointments that life might throw at her. I hope she is aware of how privileged she is in the material area. It's lovely how she enjoys sharing her home with others and doesn't appear to show any selfishness. I know her one worry is that her mother isn't happy. I, more and more frequently, catch her looking at her mother behind her hands, knowing that if her mother noticed it would cause anxiety. Cristabel has an almost permanent expression of an imminent threat, watchful and bordering on guilt. This is her problem, of course, and I would do anything in my power to alleviate it if it were possible. We certainly are going to be a large party on Saturday afternoon but, considering the rejecting attitude that Cristabel had until recently, all the lucky stars in the firmament must be thanked that she has willingly agreed to the arrangement. I can't be the only person that has noticed a subtle change in her, surely? When I mentioned it to Bob he just said it was wishful thinking and I obviously hadn't seen the number of wine bottles stacked by the recycling bin. Unfortunately, Cristabel is the sort of woman for whom Bob will never have any respect, or even forced fondness. He does like Charles, increasingly as the months and years have passed. Cristabel however is a type of person that Bob had never met in his life and, as he had said to me, hasn't missed. He is always polite and shows a sympathetic level of concern and politeness when in her company but he is never at ease. I know she respects him and is grateful for all the work he undertakes but it is an attitude of employer towards an employee. She would be surprised if she knew what he thought. Poor Cristabel, she is such a victim. I wonder what she would have turned out like if she had been removed at birth and thrown into a large happy family with a mother that actually wanted to stay at home and nurture her brood. I am convinced she, at least, would have managed to avoid morphing into an alcoholic. She might also have been able to develop some of her senses, which will always be stunted. I sound very hard-hearted, but I get frustrated to see this mother's inability to behave naturally, even towards her own daughter; especially her own daughter. I suppose every time she looks at Annie the guilt reminds her of the damage she did during pregnancy. I must keep reminding myself just how much she has improved from when we first met, during the extended labour and subsequent difficulty with bonding with her baby. I had never had such an awful experience with a new mother and was lucky to have the support of a wonderful paediatric team.

I wonder if Cristabel's paediatrician ever questions his suggestion that I went home with Cristabel and Annie. I am willing to bet he didn't imagine I would still be working with the family after nine years. Now they are all part of my life and I admit to having developed a fondness for every one of them. After the weekend we all have to get ready for the visit of Charles' parents. I am determined that I shall be sweetness and light at all times and not let them irritate me. I must look on them as a couple of very emotionally disadvantaged adults. This will help me to stay polite. I hope they are kind to Annie. That is the one area in which I will not be able to keep quiet if they say anything stupid or inconsiderate to her. I think Charles will act as protection for her. His awareness in this respect is flowering rapidly. It is almost as if Annie is demanding it without either of them being aware of it.

It is nearly time for us to go to the stables. Everything is ready for my friend to come here afterwards. Daisy's parents and her little brother are coming later in the afternoon. Charlie has spoken to Daisy's Mummy and she said it would be alright for Daisy to come back with us after the riding lesson. I'm going to have lots to write about next time. Mummy has cleaned her special boots. Daddy is going to bring his old ones. He says that there is nothing wrong with them that a good scrub won't cure. Mummy is smiling again this morning. I hope I remember all the things that Tommy taught me. I want to do really well at my riding and I want Poppy to like me on her back. I will write about it all later.

I have to write this down now, while it is fresh in my mind. We had a really lovely time all day. Everything went like clockwork. Robert had a ride on a little Shetland pony. That was a surprise as he hadn't got anything with him. Tommy had a hat that was just the right size and Robert was very keen to do what his big 'sister' was doing. They both walked round the ring, Tommy leading and helping Annie and I led Robert. When we had finished I lifted Robert down. As I did so, my glace was taken by Cristabel. She was outside one of the stables that housed a rather large horse and was just standing isolated, almost as if made from stone. As soon as she saw that I was looking at her, she quickly moved away. I only write this down now as it was such a strange thing to see. Afterwards we all waited until Annie and Daisy had done the chores. Daisy had been out in the ring with one of the other trainers, doing some trotting. I heard her tell Annie that she would soon be able to do it too. It took her a long time to actually get the words out and I was proud of Annie when she didn't interrupt. Annie told Daisy that she should go and get her swimming things and she would help her. There was a massive lump in my throat as I watched them, side by side, working their way towards the farmhouse. They had to avoid a gang of clucking chickens on the path and I was impressed at the way they both waited until the path was clear. I suppose they both instinctively knew there was no point in hurrying.

Oh! What a lovely time we all had in the afternoon. The Straws are such a refreshing family. They just relaxed and joined in everything. It even made Charles get his trunks on and go in the water. One of the best things was the nonchalance that the Straws treated the opulence of the house they were visiting. It was as if the occupants were the most important thing and the surroundings immaterial, which of course they were. It was lovely to see how little Daisy's body relaxed in the water. She had a permanent smile on her face. Annie's swimming teacher showed her how to relax on her back holding something apparently called a noodle. Annie stayed by her side most of the time and only swam a couple of rapid lengths when Daisy was involved with the teacher. It was a peculiar situation in many ways as no-one seemed to question the reason for the presence of Amanda, the swimming teacher, and who, in fact, asked her to be there. I suspect it might have been Cristabel. All I know for certain is that it wasn't me.

This was another brilliant day, wasn't it Charlie? Did you see Mummy smiling? I saw her watching Daisy and me all the time. I think she was pleased to see what Daisy could do in the water. She hasn't had many lessons but I know she would like to have some. Perhaps Daddy can arrange for her to share my lessons after school on Wednesdays. I know she goes to a school at the other side of town but she told me she goes in a minibus and that it could drop her off here. You could drop her home afterwards, on your way home with Robert, Charlie. Why are you looking at me like that again? I'm glad you're laughing. Is it because I'm being bossy? Oh, it is. I really like Daisy and she tells me all sorts of things that she can't tell anyone else. Please try and ask

Daddy if he can arrange it. Next Saturday I'm going to have a try at trotting. Mummy is going to make sure I have my gloves with me. She says it is important as I must hold on gently but firmly. How does she know that? I remember now. She had lessons when she was my age. When I look at her face when Mummy is talking about riding, it goes all soft. I don't know how else to describe it. When I saw her giving the carrot to Pablo, that's the name of the huge horse that is in the last stable in the corner of the yard, she had the same look on her face. I wish she could always have that look.

Well! Here we go again. I will, of course, try to arrange to take Daisy back on Saturdays but I'm planning on spending some quality time with my own family on that particular day. I think it should be up to Charles or Cristabel to do the taking home and I intend to make sure this happens. Everything can't be arranged around Annie's wishes. Now I feel as if I'm being mean. I've spoken to Charles and he agrees that it will be easy for one of them to return Daisy home. I suspect the Saturdays will develop into a 'sleepover' if Annie has her way. It will be interesting to see if my prediction is accurate. I'm definitely not going to the stables next Saturday as Bob's parents are coming for the day and we are going out to the countryside park. The C.B.'s have seen it written on the large calendar in the kitchen, so know of my plans. I need to take a step back as I have an instinct that now is the right time to let others in this very complicated family. There always seem to be approaching events that are almost dreaded because of the things that could go wrong. Bob says my cup has got to start being half full instead of half empty. I know he's right and I honestly do feel more joy in my life as the years pass. There are so many things that make me happy. I'm insulated from so much that other families have to endure. Bob and I have no money worries now. The C.B.'s pay us a ridiculous amount as salary. Bob says it must be considered as 'salary' rather than 'wage' as the amount surpasses anything that could be only considered a 'wage'. He always roars with laughter when he says that for some reason as he seems to think it a great joke. I don't actually 'get it'. I'm really pleased that he has formed such an unlikely bond with Charles. Then again, I wouldn't be surprised at any unlikely bond that my dear, kind husband could form. The next hurdle to jump will be the rapidly approaching visit of Charles' parents. I'm not exactly sure of the date as nothing is on the calendar. That in itself is strange as events months ahead are written in. It depends on when they are in the country, I suppose. I wonder if they realise what they are missing. They haven't heard any of Annie's singing or piano playing. It is probably a good thing as they wouldn't recognise effort if it smacked them in the face. There I go again; my cup slopping about half empty. It is such a relief that nobody can read this, but such a comfort that I can write it. Apparently, the grandparents are visiting in three week's time. That's good; at least we will have got into some sort of routine by then. With all the additional activities recently I hardly know what day it is. I am relieved that I seem to be relatively healthy and don't suffer from aches and pains very often. I'm sure if I entered into the riding craze, my body would protest fiercely. I'm more than happy to watch occasionally. Bob thinks it as all very slanted towards girls until the highest level. When I asked him what he meant, he said that he'd noticed the vast majority of the top show jumpers were men. It is irrelevant to all of us anyway. I have managed to get another pair of wellies so at least I'll be waterproof next time I go up to the stables. My main concern at the moment is to have a meeting with Mrs.Jolly to put her in the picture about the ghastly visitors descending in a short while. I will have to watch my language as there are no redeeming features about them and all I can think of is the damage they have caused to their son. They stand, instant judgement on their faces, arrogance pouring out. I think, by writing this down it might act as a waterfall of dislike and then it can be stemmed. Unfortunately, the instant they open their mouths my dislike gushes up and overflows into my facial expression. I can feel my mouth turning downwards and my eyes screwing into slits, however hard I try to control myself. I will warn Bob to act as a buffer. He is sublime in that sort of situation and seems able, without any effort, to slide away. I simmer, waiting to boil over, anticipating a crass comment from one of them. Of course I can control myself, being a reasonably intelligent adult, and here comes the 'but'. If they make any damaging remark relating to Annie and her difficulties I will not be answerable for my actions, Bob or no Bob. I'm looking forward to having a little talk with Mrs. Jolly. She will understand straight away the type of person that is about to invade our peace. I have an empathy with her and she will instinctively know what I'm anticipating. Perhaps she will help dilute the immediate antipathy I feel towards these people. I do hope so. Nothing must upset the progress that has been made. Even Cristabel is smiling more. I feel better already. My self-absorption must stop this instant.

Grandmother and Grandfather are coming to stay. Daddy says we will still go to the stables and do all the things we normally do. I can remember them a little bit. Grandfather is Daddy's father and he talks in a very loud voice. It booms and is quite frightening. I haven't seen them for ages and ages. I think Grandmother is a long way away. I had to look up to see her. I have never sat on her lap. I think she must have one. I wonder if Daddy ever sat on her lap. I hope they like my piano playing because my teacher has been helping me practise a special piece. I can play it all the way through without making too many mistakes. Daddy says it doesn't matter if I make mistakes as he thinks I play it beautifully. We are still going to the stables during their visit. I hope Daisy can still come home with us afterwards. When I asked Mummy, she went very quiet and looked worried. It won't matter if Daisy misses one Saturday afternoon but I know she enjoys the swimming and she is already nearly swimming on her own after just one lesson. My swimming teacher says it is fine if we share the lesson. What do you think Charlie? Daddy can take Grandmother and Grandfather out for lunch can't he? Oh. That's fine then. I'll ask Daddy tonight. Daisy will be so disappointed if she can't come back with us. It will be strange to meet my grandparents. Will Daddy find it awkward too? I'm a bit frightened of them really but if I play the piano nicely to them perhaps they will want to see more of me. Isn't it sad that Daddy never sees them? He told me that he was sent away to a boarding school when he was only six. I shall never send my children away. Daddy says he will never send me away as he wants me to be near to him all the time and not miss any of my growing up. I wonder what Mummy thinks. I won't ask her at the moment.

Annie instinctively knows that her mother would find the question confusing. She also is constantly aware of her mother's frailty. I've decided not to worry about the black cloud of the grandparents' visit until the day before they arrive. There is always a small hope that they will find something more amusing to do. I know I will immediately be judged, for my clothes, accent and general inability to know my place. Unlike Bob I'm much too sensitive when summing up others' opinions of me. As he says, my cup is half empty. My one worry is that Annie will feel rejected. It is inevitable as, if my memory serves me right, they are incapable of showing genuine affection. Charles' father is afflicted by an assortment of deficiencies in my opinion, which nothing in the world will be able to penetrate. It would be like trying to smash a glass against a moss bank. I wonder if Charles' mother ever has the smallest inkling of his impediments. As she is of a similar disposition it is unlikely. I don't even know how long they will be staying and if Charles and Cristabel are intending to take time off work to entertain them, for entertained they will need to be, I'm sure of that.

Now it is time to take Robert to the park before collecting Annie from school. It's a lovely sunny day and he has just woken up from his nap. This is the time when I enjoy my own space, along with Robert of course. Mrs. Jolly will have prepared the tea when we get back and she will then leave to feed her own boys. It seems a strange way to live; feeding another mother's child before your own. I read a book recently that reflected a time, in South Africa, when black mothers looked after white children whilst their own were looked after by someone else, possibly grandparents. It is a vile situation that still continues in many parts of the world. Until we respect motherhood and give children a nurturing childhood, there will be these awful inequalities in the world that lead to violence and a disdain for others. The book was so upsetting that Bob told me to stop reading it as there was nothing I could do about it anyway. I am pleased to have finished the book and will, at the next chance I get, read more.

I would have been a controversial politician if I had followed one of my early ambitions. There is no equality. A person is dealt a variety of situations over which he has very little control. Forcing the mothers out to work, in order that they can help to support their children, is already showing signs of being counter-productive. Children show anxiety, become alienated from education, have an experience of film and video content that is unsuitable, and are generally unhappy. We wonder why. These are the reasons that I will be with this family for as long as possible. When I met an old colleague of mine from my midwife days, she told me about some of the young girls coming into hospital to have their babies. It was very sad as she said that most of them were far too young to have children anyway and that the vast majority had left school at the first possible opportunity. That must be an indictment of our education system. They probably had mothers that farmed them out to a nursery at a few weeks old, to be watched over by a rapid turnover of staff. All the supposed training in the world is no substitute for the first few years with the mother and perhaps, father. In the long term, to pay mothers to stay at home would save money, possibly vast amounts in childcare costs, later truancy, obesity, antisocial behaviour, alcoholism, and suicide. That about covers it! I'm sure Cristabel's problems were exacerbated by her being looked after by a selection of adults that weren't her parents, although any other adult would have made a better job of it, I suppose. There is no obligation to have children and there are plenty of preventive methods on the market. I wonder exactly how much irreparable damage Cristabel's childhood had on her. I can hear Robert singing, so will get lunch and then go to the park.

We had a good day at school. Liam has been absent for a week and there was a bit of a fuss when he came back today. He had very red cheeks and his nose was very snotty. He smelt awful and even the classroom assistant moved away from him. I didn't know what to do as he is my friend, so I went and sat next to him and asked him if he was better. I noticed that he had a green bruise on his cheek. He said he had fallen down the stairs. The head teacher came in and asked him to go with her. I felt so sorry for him as he looked frightened. He came back and he was wearing a different school jersey and I think he had had a wash as he didn't smell. He was smiling and Miss was very nice to him and said we had missed him and it was good to see him back. Her voice was weird though and I saw her giving the head teacher a long look, but I don't know what it meant. I stayed with him all day as I know there is something the matter and you have told me, haven't you Charlie, that I must always be kind to people. We saw his mother after school and she looked raggedy. The two boys in the buggy were screaming but, when you went up to them Charlie, they stopped and ate the biscuits you gave them very quickly. Liam's mother didn't want to talk and shouted at Liam to hurry up. I think I will look after Liam tomorrow as well. I know that I have to have a helper to help me but I think he needs help too. In the playground he always stays close to me and my helper. I think he expects the bigger boys to bully him. So, that is why it was a good day at school. Do you think I did the right thing, Charlie?

I had to look away or she would see my wet admiration on my cheeks. This little girl is developing a maturity beyond her age and I am so proud of her. We have done most of the essential things today and I have noticed that Annie has something on her mind as she keeps looking at me and smiling. When I asked her what she was thinking, she quickly looked away but then said that she supposed she had better tell me. Then she disappeared and came back with a piece of paper. On it were about twenty lines of words that she has learnt to spell, sometimes not with total accuracy but it was the physical writing that impressed me so much. It must have taken her hours and when I asked her how she had found the time, she looked a bit guilty and said she had a torch in her bedroom and had been practising every night for a month. I told her that it was a wonderful page and to keep it a secret from her parents for a bit longer as perhaps we could write an actual story for them or even a diary about all the things she is doing. I've told her that I will help her but only for a few minutes every evening before her mummy and daddy come home. Robert likes to try to scribble with some of Annie's big crayons so he won't feel left out.

I showed Charlie my writing today and she said it was very good. We are going to do a bit after school on some evenings when I get home. It will only be a little bit because there will be new words that I will need help with. I think I'm going to write about the stables. There is so much to say and I can spell quite a few of the words that I'll need. Mummy and Daddy will be surprised. They don't know that I'm learning to write like the other children in my class. Jessica is doing joined up writing which is very pretty. I won't be able to do that but she says that it doesn't matter and she will still be my friend. I really like doing my diary like this with Charlie writing it on the computer. She writes it at the same time as I say it, or nearly. I never seem to run out of words, do I Charlie? When Grandmother and Grandfather come to stay, will I be able to tell them things about what I do? I do so many things that it would be good to talk to them about it. I know I'm going to feel very shy with them but I'll try not to irritate them. Why are you laughing Charlie?

I've just told Annie that her Grandparents aren't used to children so she mustn't be upset if they don't take much notice of her. I think it is important that she is prepared to be ignored, or worse, belittled. Having seen their reactions to her when she was a few weeks old, I have no illusions about their inability to relate to her. How wonderful it would be if they had both magically had a personality transplant. Perhaps they will have mellowed in recent years, or at least absorbed some sensitivity from somewhere. I suspect that the people with whom they mix are of the same calibre. Stiff upper lips, backbones and anything else that can be paralyzed from showing warmth, will be on prominent display, I suspect. Having got that out of my system I will not prejudge any further. I do hope I won't be looking for the worst in them but, as Bob would encourage, react to the best. I was awake last night for at least three hours worrying that I wouldn't be able to stay in the same room as them. Then I dozed off and dreamt that the visit was cancelled because their plane had crashed.

We are off to the stables in a minute. Now the nights are getting lighter, Daisy and I can play outside after swimming. We have a really busy day on a Saturday and we both get tired early. Mummy says that Daisy can stay the night after my grandparents have gone. I love it when we are doing lots of things. Mummy is ready to go and Charlie is coming this week, aren't you? I like it when you're with us as Robert looks so sweet on the little pony. Daddy isn't coming as he has to go to a meeting, I can't remember the word. It's 'conference', thank you Charlie. I will never be able to remember how to spell a word like that. I will write more when today is over. We can do it on Monday, after school, can't we? I will try to do some more spellings with Daisy, but they have to be horse spellings as we're going to write a story about a lost horse. I'll tell you the ones I want.

I've written some words for Annie on a piece of paper as I will be going home straight after going to the stables. It's Bob's birthday and we are going out for lunch with both sets of parents. I noticed that Cristabel seemed very withdrawn this morning, happy enough, but detached. I hope there will be an abundance of positive things to write about on Monday. I am determined to follow Bob's advice and only notice the good stuff. As it was such a lovely sunny day we all stayed outside for most of the riding session. When Mrs. Straw suggested we had a cup of coffee, Cristabel said she would stay outside, which was a surprise. I don't know why she wanted to do that but didn't question her. Mrs Straw didn't seem surprised at all and told her to wander wherever she wanted. Annie was overjoyed when she came in with Daisy as she had managed to walk with Poppy without anyone holding on to her. She was holding Daisy's hand as they came into the kitchen. They looked an unusual pair, in their jodhpurs, boots and riding hats, tottering a bit but with beaming smiles on both of their faces. I think that was the most noticeable thing; their smiles filling up their faces. Cristabel was ages coming back into the kitchen. I didn't question her as where she had wandered off to as it was none of my business. She looked detached but managed to join in the general atmosphere in the kitchen.

Annie burst out with all that she had been doing and asked if Daisy could come home with us again. Cristabel said, 'Of course, if her mummy says she can,' with such a placid expression on her face that I immediately, and probably unfairly, thought she had been at the gin in one of the stables. After all, she had been 'missing' for a long time. Then it was time to pack everything up and go home. Daisy got her swimming things and was eager to get in the water again. Cristabel actually said to Mrs. Straw that she would be going in the water as well and, as the swimming teacher was going to be there, all would be safe. I could barely conceal my amazement at the length of Cristabel's verbal engagement with Mrs Straw. She would also make certain that Daisy was returned home safely after tea. I kept quiet, any words being chased from my brain by my feeling stunned at the unexpected communication between the two mothers. Tommy came over to the car as we packed everything in and had a quiet word with Cristabel. I couldn't hear what he said, which was infuriating. I did notice that she looked down at the ground though as if she had been found out doing something she shouldn't. I forgot all about it then. It did seem a bit strange not to be involved with them all in the afternoon but I felt reassured that Amanda, the swimming teacher, would be there with them. Mrs. Jolly would have prepared a nice lunch for them before going back to her own family. I remember her saying that they played football every Saturday so she was happy to be preparing another family's lunch. I knew I would be taking over in the Easter holidays and knew my cooking didn't meet up with the standard of Mrs. Jolly. I had watched her and tried to learn about being more adventurous and experimenting with new recipes. She never seemed to waste anything and Robert attacked the food she prepared much faster than when I'd rustled up something that I thought he'd enjoy. I know he watched the other children when they were eating and copied them.

It was another brilliant day on Saturday. Mummy didn't see me ride by myself. I expect she was having a cup of coffee. I will surprise her next Saturday. Daisy and I are going to be best friends. She has learnt to float on her back all by herself and her legs are much straighter in the water. She doesn't talk at all when she is in the water. I expect she is concentrating. I am going to learn words that are to do with swimming. Charlie will give me some. I will be able to write a good story then all about riding and swimming. I could write a diary. The words I want are not the ones that I always get wrong because they all look the same. Charlie knows what they are. She calls them my enemies. I have asked her to write them here for me. They are:- her, here, she, this, me, my, was, saw, then, there, and some others but this list is enough. I type them ten times each and sometimes I remember what they look like. I really want to do it myself without having to look again and again but I know I won't be able to for some more months. I keep thinking that I never spell my name wrong so I must be able to get the other words right, even if it takes me a long time. I saw Mummy was speaking to Tommy on Saturday. I expect he was telling her how I'm getting on. I love Poppy so much. She is always gentle with me and very still when I wobble. We had a good time on

Saturday, in the pool. Amanda brought some things for us to play with. There was a massive ball that we had to push along the water. It had little coloured balls inside it and we had to make them roll around. We laughed so much that we swallowed lots of water. Mrs Jolly had left us a special home-made pizza. It tasted much better than any I have ever tasted before. She is going to teach you how to make them, Charlie, so that will be good.

We also had a lovely time on Saturday. In the afternoon we went to the countryside park and I had remembered to take a load of extra clothes for Robert to change into. He kept saying Annie's name. I expect it is because he is so used to her being around and she is just like a big sister to him. I think 'Annie' is an easy name for a baby to say. He just opens his mouth and says 'Ahh' with a 'm' at the end. This makes it 'Ammy' but I love it anyway. He has quite a few words now and it won't be long before he'll be stringing words together. The parents all adore him and he is the centre of attraction. He is very affectionate towards them and I'm so pleased that he is a cuddly little boy. Both grandfathers are affectionate towards him; an essential part of his experience, in my opinion.

Annie noticed that Tommy was talking to her mother at the stables. She, like me, is slightly confused as to the reason. It will all be revealed in good time, I expect, but I can't work out why I feel slightly apprehensive. I think it was because of the expression on Cristabel's face and the fact that it was obvious that it was a very private conversation. I can hear Annie practising her piano piece that she is preparing for her grandparents. I have Robert next to me with some Duplo bricks. He, like most boys I suspect, likes to build things to knock down. They have just been scattered all over the floor which is a sign for me to stop doing this for the moment.

Chapter Nine

Mummy says that my grandparents are coming in two weeks time. I can't make my brain have a picture of them but I know they bought me a silver egg cup on my christening day. We don't use it but it is in the cabinet that had all sorts of shiny things in it. Mrs. Jolly says it makes more work for the cleaners. I don't see the cleaners very often as they come in to the house very early, even before I get up. They have to see to the chemicals in the pool. Daddy says that the water has to be looked after. Bob helps to see that everything is something called 'shipshape' but I don't know what that means and I keep forgetting to ask him. Amanda came in the water with us on Saturday afternoon. She showed us that she could swim on the bottom of the pool. Her goggles are a pretty pink colour. Mine let the water in a bit but Mummy says Amanda will get me some better ones. Liam hasn't been at school today. The headteacher came into the classroom and was whispering to Miss. I know it was about Liam because they looked in his drawer that has all his work in it. I hope he is not in any trouble because I like him. He is the only boy in our class that spends time with me. Charlie says she will try to find out about why Liam wasn't at school today. His mummy must be very busy with the two other little boys that are always crying and shouting. I am very lucky to have a Robert as a little brother. He hardly ever cries. Now Charlie says I have to go to my other computer and do my spellings. She wants talk to Bob about something.

Mrs. Jolly is going to prepare some meals and freeze them ready for the grandparents. I suspect she has worked out the likely scenario. When the Easter holiday arrives we will miss her but she says she will be able to help out a bit as her husband has flexible shifts. She has asked if, occasionally, she can bring her boys here for a swim. I think that would be a brilliant idea as they are very well behaved most of the time and I'm sure Charles would like the pool to be used more. He has started having a swim early in the morning. I only know that because I've seen his trunks hanging in the changing room. It makes me feel so much better about working for this ultra-privileged family, in the material sense. I wonder if they would give it all up to have a little girl that was physically normal. I'll never know and certainly will never ask. Although Cristabel and I have an ever improving relationship there will always be the barrier between us because of her awareness that I knew in detail the depths of her ignorance and selfishness, brought about by her refusal to attend adequate obstetric or midwife appointments. The fact that I saw, hidden away in her case, a bottle of vodka and that her baby was seriously affected by her alcohol intake during pregnancy, will always be a wall between us. As time goes on, I will work on knocking down some of the bricks, but I don't think I'll ever get to a stage that I'll feel able to scrape out the residue of the hatred I felt for her at the time. The obstetrician had told her about cutting down on the alcohol as her file has a record of it. It appears to be the one and only appointment she condescended to keep. Of course I know she had and has deep psychological issues caused by her own lack of parenting and I must understand. My vigilance over Annie is ever present as I will never trust Cristabel completely. I watch her before we go to the stables in case she has had a drink. However, I think we have at least achieved a few hours of sobriety as her driving was careful and considerate. I do wonder if the fact that I'm like a judge sitting in the back of the Landrover could seem as if she is under surveillance, and she keeps off the bottle until the afternoon or evening.

Daisy and me are going to start on an exciting story. It is about a pony that gets lost. Charlie says it has to have a happy ending, but Daisy says that we have to get all the words that we need before we start, so we are going to talk about it lots of times before we write it down on my new computer. I am getting better at using it but I still like to tell Charlie what I want to say because she can write it on the new computer much quicker than I can. Daisy had a turn on it and is much better than I am, but her spelling is rubbish, just like mine. I'm quite pleased about that as it makes me feel I don't need to say sorry to her. Her fingers work better than mine, but they jerk about a bit. We started to laugh on Saturday as we both tried to write something and it looked as if the words had been shaken up. I let her use my special pad that I rest my arms on and she is going to ask her daddy to buy her one. I don't know what shop you have to go to though. Can you tell her parents, Charlie? We are keeping our story a secret from everyone but you, Charlie. We are going to try to write most of it ourselves on the new computer but we will need your help.

This is very good news about the two girls using their imagination to write a story together. I'm not sure how long it will last before boredom sets in as they haven't yet realised how tiring it will be. It takes ten times more energy than a normal nine year old, of the physical and mental kind, for them to achieve anything very much. I hope to be proved wrong. I think I'll be in the close vicinity when they are attempting it so that I can divert them if it all gets too much. I do love their ambition though and will do all in my power to distract them if I sense they are getting discouraged.

The nearer the grandparents visit looms, the more anxious I feel myself becoming. I wish I could switch off and let things follow whatever course is planned. I know the bedrooms and the dressing room have been redecorated and there is a disgusting smell of brush cleaner throughout the house. All sorts of people have been rushing round hanging new curtains, putting expensive toiletries in the two bathrooms and generally making me feel irritable. These are Charles' parents and should be accepted without this ridiculous need to present a perfect antiseptic environment for them. I do wonder if Charles and Cristabel know that whatever they do, fault will be found, or at least silent criticism which is the worst kind. I would love to be able to talk to Charles about this but I can't find the right words. I imagine saying to him that his parents will love to see him whatever condition the house is in and it is him and

229

Cristabel they are coming to see, not a redecorated house, but these words are not the right ones. I want to find sentences that explain parental affection, but not in a lecturing sort of way. Well, I'll do what Bob recommends and relax, keep in the background and know my place, whatever that is. I keep repeating it silently but the more it is embedded in my mind, the greater the worry it causes me, stupid though it is. I even went shopping to buy a new dress for the visit. It is as if we are being invaded by royalty. The dress is definitely not a success and I'll have to find time to return it. Why don't I just wear a T-shirt and jeans as usual? I can't seem to answer that question. It is as if I'm absorbing Charles and Cristabel's stress level, accidentally. At least I've now decided to take the damn dress back and buy a new top instead. There! I feel better already.

Today at school I felt sad because Liam wasn't there again and the headteacher came in to have a whisper again with Miss. They had very serious faces and I knew they were talking about him. I wish I could hear what they were saying. I did hear his name mentioned so I knew they were saying stuff about Liam. I wanted to go up to them and ask them to tell me if he was in trouble but I didn't dare as we were doing some special test paper for 'SATS' and we weren't allowed to talk. I have help with my test. One day I might be able to put the answers down myself. I know I'm different but I think I can make my muscles work really hard and then they will let me write properly, like the other children. Amanda says that my muscles have got much stronger in the last year. I feel my leg muscles aching when I get off Poppy but Tommy says that shows that they are getting stronger. I am worried about Liam. Do you think that we could go round to his house, Charlie, just to see if he is ill or something? Your face tells me that your answer is 'No'.

I will go into the classroom and ask about Liam. I'm sure I can justify it as I'll say that Annie is really worried. I can't think of any other way to find out. Nothing would surprise me as I'm convinced that he is at risk, as are his little brothers. When is it right to interfere in another family? If something awful happens will I be partially to blame? Will the school and the Social Worker also be at fault? There are families at the other end of the social scale suffering from abuse, probably of a different type, but abuse all the same. Who is the judge? Well, tomorrow I'll pop into the classroom and ask a few simple questions. I'll have to tell Annie to wait outside but Robert can stay in the buggy. It won't take long and then we can reassure Annie. Her class teacher is very approachable and I'm sure she won't be breaching any code of conduct. All we want to know is that he's not ill. I hope there are not any other parents wanting to speak to the teacher. It will not be possible to say what I want to if anyone else is in the room.

We are finding out if Liam is ill after school. I have to wait outside the library. I'm not sure why I have to do that but Charlie says that Miss won't tell her anything unless it is in private. I don't see why I can't be there. He is my friend. I'll do what Charlie says but I hope she will tell me why later. Sometimes grownups have funny rules. I hope it's not because she thinks there might be something nasty happening to him. We are going to tidy my bedroom in a minute and we are finding some of my old toys for Robert. I have grown out of lots of toys and they are all in a jumble in my cupboard. We have a big bag to put them in and then I'll have lots more space in my room. I would like to give some of my toys to Liam and his little brothers too but Charlie says we have to be careful not to hurt their feelings. That is another thing I really don't understand, but I know Charlie is good at working out what is best for people and she will explain it to me when I'm about a hundred and fifty. You are laughing again, Charlie. When we go riding on Saturday, I really want you to see me trot. I can almost do it on my own. Will you come soon, so I can show you? Guess what, Charlie. You never will, so I'll tell you. Mummy brought a big bag home with her on Tuesday. I pretended I didn't notice as I saw her hide it under the hall stairs. When she was in the kitchen getting a drink because she always gets very thirsty, I took a peep and there were some jodhpurs in there. Who do you think they are for? They were big ones so they aren't for me. Perhaps she has bought some for Daddy as a surprise. What do you think?

I think that Cristabel is hatching something, goodness knows what, but Annie has noticed that there is a change in her mother, very subtle but noticeable if you are on the lookout for it. There isn't time to worry about it at the moment. The house has to look even more like an advertisement from 'Homes and Gardens', before the grandparents arrival. They will not be in a particularly good frame of mind and Bob has been asked to collect them from the airport suffering from jet-lag no doubt. There I go again; expecting the worst. Well, the next two weeks will be spent enjoying ourselves before their arrival. Then, they can do their worst. We will be immune. I am going into see the class teacher after school tonight. At the back of my mind is the certainty that the news about Liam is not going to be what I would like to hear. I don't think I am allowed to be told anything of a sensitive nature anyway so I'm probably wasting my time. However, Annie won't leave me in peace until I have at least tried to find out the reason for his absences Robert is smearing paint over his feet. It is entirely my fault for thinking it would be fun to print his footsteps on paper and hang it in his bedroom. Floor tiles are a wonderful invention and won't take long to wipe clean. Now I need to concentrate on my son.

Charlie went into my teacher's office after school and I had to stay outside. I tried to hear what they were saying but they were talking very quietly. I went into the library as I love it in there. There are hundreds of books all quietly waiting for someone to take one off the shelves and open it. I am a bit clumsy and I have to choose books that are light or I might drop them. There are lots of really fat heavy books looking at me and wanting me to take them down to read. There are some huge books. I wonder who writes them. They must take a very long time. Perhaps I can ask someone to take one down for me. When Charlie came out of the office, she looked sad. Yes, you did, Charlie. I can't think of another word to tell you how you looked. Was it because Liam isn't coming back to school? Our teacher told us this morning that Liam is going to start at another school. I am really sad about it and I will miss him. It wasn't his fault that he was smelly and dirty. What about his mummy? Won't she feel sorry that he has to start again somewhere else? Is it because she can't look after him properly and he was often late?

Yes, that's about the top and bottom of it. All three boys have been taken into care. They were on the 'At Risk' register apparently. I was surprised that I was allowed to be told this bit of information. Liam is already with another family but not in this area. I am so disappointed that he has been forced to leave the school as it was one of the places that he appeared to be happy in. He certainly enjoyed the music and Annie's company. I don't know whether this arrangement is permanent but I suspect it is. At least he will have his physical needs met. I wonder if the other two boys will be kept together. It has put a real sadness in this atmosphere. I'm afraid that Annie's knowledge of the cruelty in the world is only just beginning. She knows as much as I do now as I told her about Liam's new family. She looked very confused and it will be better if we don't dwell on it. She came to sit on my lap just before tea and was desperate for reassurance. I suspect her imagination was at full throttle as she thought of her own situation. She is fully aware that her own mother has problems, but is not mature enough to comprehend the exact nature of them. I shall do my best to prevent her from ever getting any suspicion of her mother's alcoholism until it is absolutely necessary. Even then, it will have to be handled exceptionally carefully. Oh. Today has not been one of the best for us. At least Robert doesn't seem to have picked up on our rather depressed expressions. I have told Annie that we will go for a swim and then have one of Mrs. Jolly's pizzas, to cheer us up. She gave me an old fashioned look as if to say she knew exactly what I was up to. We had a good swim and Robert laughed so much as Annie splashed him that the sad news about Liam was forgotten temporarily. When Cristabel came home Annie rushed at her and threw her arms around her neck. Her mother, thankfully, responded after an almost unnoticeable pause. She looked at me enquiringly but I decided that to smile enigmatically was the best policy. Annie, of course, burst out with all the news about Liam. Cristabel looked genuinely shocked and said how sorry she was. She kept looking at me, expecting me to fill her in with the gory details but I had already decided that we had grieved enough for one day. Annie held her mother's hand and dragged her into the kitchen to show her that a pizza was waiting for her and that she wanted her mother to sit down next to her to eat it. As it was time for Robert and me to go home, we made an unusually rapid exit. Bob came into the kitchen to take Robert to the car so it probably seemed like a mass exodus to Annie. I gave her a quick hug and told her to tell her mummy about the lovely swim we had.

Charlie was very sad when she came out of the school office. Robert was in his buggy so he didn't notice her face. I knew that the news about Liam was going to be sad but I'm glad I know. I wonder where he lives now. His little brothers will be very sad if they have been taken away from their mummy. It is not their fault. Do you think we will ever see any of them again, Charlie? I wish I could understand why things like this happen. We had a good swim to take our minds off feeling sad. Robert was really funny in the water and tried to make me laugh. I think he noticed that I was sad. Mummy and me had a lovely pizza. Mummy put it in the oven herself. We sat together in the kitchen. It was the first time we have ever done that.

I told Mummy about Liam. She went very quiet and didn't say anything for ages. Then she just said that lots of adults have problems and when I was older she would have a chat with me about it. I didn't like her saying things like that. Then she told me to go and do my music practice. I don't think she wanted to talk to me at all. I made lots of mistakes with my music. If I don't get better I won't play for my grandparents. I don't suppose they would mind at all. I tried to sing one of my favourite songs but my voice sounded miserable. I practised my spellings instead and felt even more grumpy. After I've written this down with you Charlie, I'll feel better won't I? I know it is because I'm not old enough to understand about Liam and that he had done nothing wrong. I asked him about the bruise on his face Charlie but he wouldn't tell me anything. His Mummy wouldn't hit him, would she? I am going to be a very kind adult when I grow up and I'll try not to shout. Mummy and Daddy have never shouted at me. Bob never shouts at anyone. You never shout, Charlie unless we have to get out of the pool and we aren't listening. I think I'll go and practise my song again.

Poor little girl. She has been more affected than I thought. I think it is the abandonment she feels as Liam was a special person in her life, even though she has made more friends recently. I doubt if we will ever see him again, but one positive aspect of it all is that he will be safe and clean. It is no compensation for being separated from his mother and siblings, even though I suspect there were unacceptable levels of aggression in the house. I am relieved that the intervention came when it did after the recent tragedies of little children being killed by their parents. It is inconceivable to most people and too horrible to spend time imagining the hell that the little children must go through, but I know from my years at the Accident and Emergency Department at the hospital that worrying injuries were investigated and children removed to a place of safety. There was one occasion when the baby was actually dead on arrival, obviously having been assaulted. All the staff members on duty were emotionally distraught following any episode of that nature and we never got hardened to it. Being encouraged to be emotionally detached was impossible. I know I met some complicated family situations that were inevitably going to break down but aware that I was impotent at that time to intervene. It seems ironic that it is only when a tragedy happens that the professionals pull out all the stops, too late. I think it will be some days at least before Annie will recover her joie de vivre. I wouldn't be surprised if she broods about it all for a long time.

Charlie says I'm broody. I thought only chickens got like that. I have an idea about Liam but I'm not going to tell anyone about it until I'm sure I know what to do. Charlie is giving me funny looks. I'm going to tell Mummy about Liam later as I think it is important that she knows I am upset about it. She never asks me if anything is bothering me. I wonder why. I know something bothers her and she will never talk about it. I see Daddy looking at her in a funny sort of way and I wish I was older then they might tell me and then I won't feel as if I'm being kept in the dark. Charlie has just said that it is nothing for me to worry about. She always tells the truth so I will stop worrying about it all. Last month when Daddy went to get Liam for my party he was very quiet when he came back but he didn't say anything. I wish he had spoken to me and he could have stopped Liam being sent away. No, I know Charlie, I have to stop thinking about it. You wouldn't like it if Robert was sent away, would you. Why is it different? Now your face is looking cross so I really will stop.

Goodness me! This child is getting far too inquisitive. I need to protect her from the possible awfulness of Liam's family breakdown. I wonder what is happening to Liam's mother. Will she be left at home all on her own probably to get into another abusive relationship or will there be a team of supportive therapists alongside to give her the help she obviously needs? I know the answer to that with only a rapidly passing thought. The chances are that she will be left to fend for herself, knowing she is totally inadequate. She will inevitably find some inappropriate 'friend' that will be as unable to cope as she is and, together they will pretend to be a couple until she gets bashed up again. It's the inevitability of it that is so bloody depressing. There will be a strong chance that a court appearance is programmed. I will be looking in the local newspapers to confirm it. I must make certain that Annie doesn't see any reports of the hearing, if there is one, as I confidently suspect. What is so predictable is any likelihood of Liam's mother having a decent childhood herself. It is impossible to conceive that her experiences were anything but abusive and lacking in real affection. It seems especially ghastly to me because of losing my baby. Mothers have babies with, sometimes, little knowledge of what motherhood entails. I suppose, being so long in the midwifery profession I have seen, and listened to, so many differing combinations of attitude and backgrounds that my opinions are indelibly imprinted on my brain. That life isn't a level playing field is becoming increasingly obvious. With all the political side-swiping that goes on, I sense that the politicians have lost sight of what is important. That is, if they have any awareness of how the average family lives. They are forced to go to work when their children are far too immature. I think mothers should be paid to stay at home for three years until the child is emotionally ready to go to nursery. No choice is given because of financial necessity. Is the world producing adults who will produce unfeeling offspring because of being surrounded by unidentifiable adults themselves? Forming close emotional relationships is the cornerstone of a happy fulfilled adulthood. I get frustrated and depressed every time I read about the number of youngsters on drugs, using alcohol to do something called 'binge drinking' and unable to communicate with anyone apart from their peer group. We, the generation ahead of them, are responsible for this crisis; for that is what it will turn into. These youngsters won't be able to form any sort of meaningful relationship with their children because they have never experienced it themselves. There is such an easy solution. If, as a woman, you want to pursue a career and forge ahead in the achievement stakes, then wait until you are absolutely sure you can devote three years to being a mother. If you find this horrifying, then don't have children. No-one is forcing you to procreate. The government will pay you a fair wage for nurturing your children. Your employer will be obliged to employ you at the level at which you left, and of course, at a significant increase in salary or wages, as is more likely. Now, what would be the longer term outcomes of this approach? A huge saving in mental health costs to the country, fewer families needing intervention, happier children who will be in a better state to benefit from the learning experiences at school and possibly fewer couples fighting because of stress. Utopia? Well, why not try to improve the conditions under which so many of our young children suffer. At present everything is done in a hurry, parents have to get to work, children have to get to the nursery, shopping and cleaning must be done, washing cooking and perhaps ironing are all waiting in a queue. When is there any time left to spend quality time with these deprived children? Parenting by appointment is the only option or, more likely, no parenting time at all. Inevitably there must be a build up of resentment, tiredness, anxiety and guilt. Buying expensive and ill-affordable presents is no compensation.

I must see if Robert has woken up from his nap. I seem to have had longer today to get this off my chest. The C.B.'s are fully aware of their responsibilities and when Annie was brought home from hospital, each took time off to bond with her. One of the conditions I insisted upon when I came to work for them after Annie's birth was that they both had to spend time with her. The situation was so fraught that I think they would have agreed to any conditions. I can hear Robert babbling to himself. I think we will go to the park again after lunch. He has just learnt how to climb up the ladder steps of the slide. I am impressed at how brave he is as he had only been walking for a little while.

Charlie and Robert had red cheeks when they met me from school. Charlie had a biscuit for me and a new sort of juice. She said it was made from carrots but it was orange and tasted really nice. I expected it to taste like carrots but it didn't. Robert was kicking his legs as he wanted to get out of the buggy. We walked home through the park so that he could practise his walking. He tried to run which was funny as he fell over every few metres. I didn't mind as it meant that I could keep up. Charlie was looking at me a lot and I think she expected me to talk about Liam. I didn't because it made me feel like crying. I asked Miss where he had gone to school and she said she wasn't sure but I think she just didn't want to tell me. She didn't look at me when she was saying it. I am going to ask again until she gets fed up with me asking and tells me in desperation. Why are you laughing, Charlie? I am definitely going to find out what had happened to him. Can we do our spellings now, Charlie? I have some new ones to add to the list. The list is getting very long. Can we stop doing some of them because I think I can remember the riding ones now? I want to add Liam's name. I want to be able to spell it without trying, like I can write my name. Can you write some other words for me please? I need- left, school, bruise, cheek. Just those four will be enough as they are horrible words to spell. It really helps me when you write on the computer for me, Charlie. It is like I'm talking to you but you don't really know what I'm saying but you still understand. When words are written down it makes a space between them and the person you are with. When we talk it is much more difficult. It is like double strength orange squash not being mixed with water. Can we go on the other computer now please?

I know exactly what Annie means. A face to face conversation can be too intense. She is developing an ability to reason and explain her feelings very nicely. She will need all these skills in the future, I anticipate. The weekend is approaching and Annie has already got all her kit waiting for her to put on. I think Robert will enjoy another outing on the Shetland pony. Tommy has said it is 'fair exchange' for the swimming that Daisy has on Saturday afternoons. I also noticed that there was a bag of neatly folded stuff in the utility room that my fingers itched to open. I asked Annie as she was in there getting her boots ready and she, very casually, in a throw-away line said, 'Oh. That's Mummy's stuff for riding.' I nearly shrieked, but managed to control myself. It seems that Cristabel is going to be having a riding lesson as well as her daughter. I am more than amazed. At least she will have to keep off the pop when on top of a horse. The weird anticipation I had about Tommy and the stables is coming to fruition.

Cristabel is still attending A.A. meetings. I always know when she has been by her distant expression on her face afterwards. She never says a word to me about it but she must know that I am fully aware of it. She affects a rather childlike stance, upright and defensive when she comes home afterwards and we both keep our distance, extra politely. She builds a barrier between us and the fleeting cuddles on greeting that we have had in the past are never achieved after an A.A. session. Her misery is shining from her immaculately made-up face. I would like to throw my arms around her but know she is not ready. I wonder what will happen at the stables?

Chapter Ten

It was amazing on Saturday. I learnt to trot with one of the helpers. Tommy said that I was ready and he wanted to get Robert sorted out on the Shetland. I didn't see Mummy ride at all. I wonder if she has got scared? Daisy and I went into her house afterwards and played in her bedroom and got her swimming things ready. Her baby brother is quite sweet but not as sweet as Robert. Daisy's mummy gave us a hot drink and some biscuits that she had made herself. They tasted of ginger and were shaped like little men. Her baby brother made a mess on the floor but his Mummy didn't even notice. I like her Mummy as she is always the same. Her face never changes very much. I wonder why Mummy didn't ride? Charlie didn't see me do my trotting either, so next week they will both be surprised.

I watched Robert on the Shetland pony and saw, in the corner of my eye, a very smartly turned out Cristabel. She was standing by the stable in the corner, nearly out of sight, giving the massive horse Pablo, some carrots. She didn't see me watching her. After a few moments Tommy came up to her with the Shetland pony with Robert perched on top and said something to her and opened the stable door for her to go in with the horse. He was saying lots of things to her and looked down, shaking his head. He came back to me and asked me to take Robert round the yard. The little Shetland was so well behaved and I loved being in charge of my son. It was lucky that it wasn't a bigger pony or I might not have felt so confident. All the time I was wondering what on earth Cristabel was up to in the stable with the monstrous beast, a gentle giant of course. He must be for Tommy to risk encouraging Cristabel to go in with him. I wouldn't find out on this Saturday and I wondered if Cristabel would say anything to me. On the way home, Annie asked her mother why she didn't watch her trotting and Cristabel, thankfully, answered kindly that she would definitely watch her the following Saturday, but she had got involved with one of the other horses and forgot the time. Annie seemed satisfied at this and we arrived home in good spirits, starving hungry and ready to wolf down the pizzas left by Mrs. Jolly.

Saturday was another fantastic day. Next week Tommy says that I can trot in the field with Daisy. We will have one helper each as we both are a bit wobbly. I am so happy that I can do it and can't wait to show Mummy and Daddy. We had a good swim in the afternoon and then Daisy and me wrote some more of our story. It is so slow and it doesn't look very neat but I'm going to ask Charlie to write it on the computer. Daisy and me are going to practise writing it with a pencil until we get it looking a bit better, then we will surprise our parents.

We might keep it until Easter and then give it to them for a present. Daisy is very good at thinking up words but then we both start laughing because neither of us can spell them. If we look them up on spellcheck it takes ages and we still forget how to spell the word the next time we need it. I know I can have a really clever machine that can recognise what I'm saying but I want to learn to spell and write like Jessica in my class. Daisy says that they have machines like that in her school but she wants to learn to spell like me. If we work together we might surprise people. Mummy is getting ready for Daddy's parents. It seems strange that I hardly ever see them but I will try to be polite and quiet just like Mummy says.

The visit is approaching with horrible speed. Bob suggested that I might curtsey when introduced to them. He is only trying to get me to put everything in perspective. I don't expect they will remember me from when Annie was a baby. I know they have been back in this country several times as I overheard Cristabel talking to Charles about the fact that they couldn't even be bothered to come and see their granddaughter, let alone their son. Cristabel's parents aren't much better. They have literally popped in a couple of times during a weekend but again only staying an hour or so, as if visiting a hospital patient. I have never coincided with them luckily and Annie has never referred to them. It's as if they don't really exist. It is such a shame that she has missed out on having a relationship with them. Robert loves spending time with his grandparents and they are looking forward to him having a sleepover when he is a bit older. I'm willing to bet that the two sets of absent grandparents had virtually no contact with their own grandparents.

We have just one more riding lesson for Annie before the visitors descend upon us and probably disrupt everything. Bob says I'm behaving as if I'm jealous of any time they take away from that which I spend with Annie. He's right of course and I am instilling into my mind certain behaviour patterns so that I keep up a wonderful appearance of calmness and relaxed acceptance. I am going to the stables again on Saturday as Robert keeps getting his wellies out of the cupboard and trying to put them on. When I asked him if he wanted to go on the horse again he shouted, 'yeth'. I explained that it was on Saturday and that it was two more days to wait. He started galloping up the hall and fell over the rug. So, that was the end of that, apart from a nasty bump on the head. I have been surprised at how enthusiastic he is about riding. It is probably because of Annie's almost obsessive attitude. She is obsessive about most things, I've discovered. She has a tremendous energy, driving her to aim for almost impossible targets. I don't want her to suffer disappointment, but know it is normal for everyone and almost inevitable for her.

We haven't managed to write our diary for two days because I have been practising my special piece on the piano. I don't know how long my grandparents are staying. I will still go riding because Mummy says it is all booked up. Daddy is coming this Saturday morning but Daisy can't come back with me for her swim. Mummy explained to Tommy that it would all be back to normal the following Saturday. I don't see why Daisy can't come back with me, but Charlie says that it is important that my grandparents see me by myself. I don't see why, Charlie, but I think you know more than I do. At least I don't have to miss my riding. I expect they will come and watch.

It is the morning of the 'Arrival of the Grandparents'. It feels just like that! Luckily it is a school day so the meeting between them and Annie is delayed for a little while. I will meet her from school as usual and walk home through the park as usual; delaying the evil moment for a little bit longer and giving me time to prepare myself. Well, as we go into the house there they are, sitting in their majesty, sipping tea. I notice that Mrs. Jolly had been coerced into being a bloody waitress. As we go into the sitting room, Annie freezes and stands motionless in the doorway. I hold her hand and we go towards these two elderly people. Then Annie sees her father is home and runs to him, throwing herself on his lap and giving him a big hug. He responds wonderfully by saying, 'Oh, my little cherub, you missed me did you?' I could have kissed him. The two visitors watched impassively. Then Annie, as she had been practising, approached her grandmother and held out her hand. Charles' mother didn't know what to do. Cristabel reacted well and told Annie to go and change out of her school uniform and then come down for a drink and a biscuit with us. I saw both grandparents watching, as if mesmerised, Annie wobbling her way through the door. She had made such amazing progress with her balance but, by the expressions on the grandparents' faces, they were less than impressed. When Annie came back, she was neat and tidy and clothed in her best dress. I had accompanied her up to her bedroom to brush her hair, thinking all the time of how unimportant all this stupid presentation was. Annie was a very pretty child, with her father's lovely blue eyes and dark, curly hair. When we returned to the sitting room all eyes were on her and she was aware of being the centre of attraction. She worked her way over to her grandmother and reached up to her face and aimed a kiss on the aged cheek. 'There,' she said, 'I managed it.' Her grandmother looked confused as if she had never experienced anything like it before as was probably accurate. Then Annie walked over to the table where her juice was waiting and casually started to drink it. There was silence in the room which I decided to cut through, saying, 'I hope your journey wasn't too tiring.' This was received by a couple of grunts which I thought meant I could interpret any way I chose. My determination to retain my composure made me enter a conversation with Cristabel and Charles about the homework that Annie had brought home. Meanwhile, Robert, bless his little natural heart, had staggered over to the grandfather, assuming I suppose that he was of a jolly nature like my father, and leant against his knees. I held my breath anticipating rejection, but was overwhelmed by gratitude when this elderly man ruffled Robert's hair and said, 'Well, young man, and what is your name?' I was even more affected when Robert, looking him straight in the eyes, said, 'Wobert'. I quickly picked him up and said it was time for us to go home and I hoped that they would enjoy their visit. The truth was that I couldn't wait to get home to tell Bob what had happened. Luckily, I knew he would already be getting the tea ready as he wasn't needed at the C.B.'s until the following morning. As soon as he saw my face he knew something good or unexpected had occurred.

Well, my grandparents have arrived and I met them after school. They are very stiff but Charlie said that they aren't used to little children and so I acted as a grownup and just watched like they seem to do. I don't understand why they find children difficult because they had Daddy and he must have been a very little child before he grew up. My grandfather has a voice that booms, but he seems quite kind. My grandmother looks bored all the time and I don't know why. When I get home from school tomorrow I'm playing the piano after a special dinner we're going to have to welcome them to our house. It feels so strange to do things like that when they are our family. It is like me having to do a performance for them like when I sang at school but it is different because all the children were in it I didn't feel nervous at all. I think Charlie will be watching me too so that will make it feel better. I'm pleased I am at school all day as I don't think I could be so quiet and polite all the time. Charlie says that now I am nine I will find it easier to pretend things if it is really important. I don't have to pretend with you Charlie or Bob, or my Daddy. Sometimes I have to pretend with Mummy.

Annie will find the pretence increasingly wearing. She is right about it being good timing that she is at school all day. I hope she doesn't feel under too much pressure to perform to these elderly relatives. I suspect they wouldn't be able to discriminate between a piano and a drum anyway. I shall make a point of having fun with her before her piano playing ordeal. The problem is that I know when she is hurting and it tears at my heart strings also. Her finger must be warm and I will make a point of massaging them as her physiotherapist has taught me. I shall also

250

be very positive if she makes many mistakes and quickly find something else to do with her. There is such a big fuss about the meal tomorrow night. These elderly people seem to need exceptionally intensive attention, to which Cristabel seems obliged to pander.

The long table in the dining room has already had the ridiculous silver candle sticks placed on top of the mirror like polished wood surface. It is the worst way to make people relax in my humble opinion but I am going to fulfil my promise to myself that I'll keep my distance. Eating in the kitchen with Bob and Robert will be a treat. I was dreading Cristabel asking me to join them at the massive, silent table. Even worse she might have asked me to be a waitress. No, even Cristabel wouldn't risk that. She has employed a team of waitresses. I saw them with Mrs. Jolly; being instructed I suppose. The flowers look beautiful on the table and cancel out a small amount of the sparseness. I will be listening in the kitchen for any normal family sounds but will drink all the water in the swimming pool if I manage to catch one small sound of laughter.

When I got home from school, Charlie helped me change into my best dress again. Then we played Snakes and Ladders with Robert. He was very good at watching and learning the rules. Actually he didn't play but Charlie moved the counter for him. He really seemed to understand that his counter had to go up ladders but down snakes. The problem was that he didn't understand that he couldn't choose when to do it and had to land on one of the squares first. It was very funny and we laughed a lot. It ended up with lots of counters all over the place and the dice under my bed. We are going to teach him to play animal dominos where you have to match the animals and put them next to each other. I expect we'll stand them all up in a line and then push the first one so that all the others topple down. I remember Charlie teaching me that. Robert is still too young to play games with rules but I like him to try as he is so funny. Mummy came into the bedroom and told me it was time to come downstairs for my dinner. I was sitting next to Daddy so I was really happy about that. There were some girls dressed in black and white that served us. Mrs. Jolly has made some food that I didn't know what it was but I tried most of it. She had made a lovely fish pie which is my favourite. Daddy kept looking at his mother in a worried sort of way but my grandfather said, in an enormous voice, 'What a wonderful pie. I can't remember having such a treat for years and years.' The problem was that my grandmother just stared and stared at him but said nothing. Daddy told them about Mrs. Jolly and what a wonderful cook she was. Grandmother said a strange thing. She asked if they no longer had chefs? I don't know what the difference is anyway but Mummy said that we don't need a chef as Mrs. Jolly is the best cook in the world. I saw Daddy smile at her and it made me very happy. We had two special puddings with fancy names. I tried both of them but the one that was covered in lots of chocolate made me feel sick. I'm not allowed lots of sweet things so I suppose my tummy was telling me not to do it again. My Grandfather seemed to enjoy himself as he spoke to my Daddy a lot. He didn't seem to notice my Mummy. All the adults were very thirsty and drank a lot of wine but I had my normal juice. They all started laughing a lot but it was strange laughter; it sounded as if they were trying extra hard. When we had finished our meal we went into the drawing room for me to play the piano. I wasn't nervous any more as the grownups seemed so happy. I played my piece as well as I could and there was a silence at the end. Then my Grandfather started clapping and my Daddy and everyone else joined in. I felt like crying but I didn't know why.

Then I saw Charlie in the doorway beckoning me and I went over to her as I knew it was past my bedtime. As we went out of the door, I heard my Grandmother say, 'Aren't there places you can send children like that?' but Charlie closed the door very quickly so I don't know what else was said. I think they must have meant me because I was the only child in the room. Robert had gone home with Bob. He is still a baby anyway. I don't know why she thought I should be sent to some other 'place'. Charlie read to me and told me that I played the piano very well indeed. Then she said she thought my grandmother couldn't understand music but my grandfather smiled all the way through. I felt much better then but I still noticed a nasty expression on my grandmother's face. She doesn't talk to my Mummy much and hardly ever speaks to anyone else. Charlie says that she possibly thinks a lot and will talk more when she is used to us. I have told Charlie that I think my grandmother is like a witch and I got told off but only a little bit and you were smiling, weren't you Charlie, just like you are now? I need to see Poppy again as she understands everything.

I could swing for that bloody woman. Has she no compassion at all? Didn't she realise the effort that Annie had put into her piano playing? The overall impression she gave was one of total boredom. She must have been topped up with alcohol to the limit as her eyes kept half closing. I notice some of the amber liquid sliding down the cracks that were etched on each side of her pouting mouth. I was pleased about that as it made her look pathetic, which, in my opinion, she was. I eventually managed to escape and told Bob about the ordeal Annie and I had endured. He asked me how the adults actually spoke to each other and it was interesting to me to relive the plastic conversation that stuttered between them.

The grandfather, apart from the booming voice, made a reasonable effort at communicating with his son. The content of their discourse was, inevitably, within the mutual comfort zone of business, the city, share prices and weather. It wasn't so much the content of their conversation but rather the stilted and jagged deliverance. There was hardly any eye contact as far as I could see, but I wasn't a witness for very much of it. What I was aware of was my immediate prejudice, on listening to the practised suffocated vowels, the ignorance of these people. Bob told me not to get personally involved with them but, as the effect on Annie was my main concern, I was inevitably drawn in, silently screaming and shouting. Bob, bless him told me to sense when there was an unhealthy atmosphere and remove myself. It's easy for him to say as he is not as emotionally involved as I am.

I've just had a thought; I've not had time to think about Lily. It must be the first day since we lost her that my grief hasn't gushed up and challenged me. I'm not sure if that is good or bad. Her memory is always just beneath the surface of my consciousness. Perhaps it is a good thing that all the frenetic activity of the last few weeks has submerged it further back in my mind. I know Bob would be relieved if I told him, but I can't as it will make me feel guilty. I am fully aware that my attentions to my husband have been neglected at times. I am constantly full of wonder at his ability to understand, without saying a word. Perhaps that is the secret of a good relationship. The ability to know when to be silent, but allowing the other person an awareness of the presence of understanding. I have explained it very badly but I know that Bob doesn't judge me when he picks up on my inner grief. He doesn't resent the exclusion he must feel. I try so hard to show him how much he means to me but there are times when things in my head take over and I have no control. I have been reassured recently though and think, after all these years, the sadness I've tried to hide from him is lessening. I used to think that people telling you to 'keep busy' after a tragedy was insulting but there is some truth in it. Grieving can become absorbing to an unhealthy degree and I know from experience that I am coping much better. I need Annie and Robert to keep me truthful to myself. Bob is at the top of that list of course but for different reasons.

When I got home from school, the grandparents were out somewhere. Daddy had taken them out for lunch and they hadn't got back. I was pleased and it meant that Charlie and I could get on with our writing. She gave me one of her special cuddles. Robert wanted one too so we sat in the big armchair and had an enormous cuddle. We didn't talk at all. Then we did this writing and I have to tell her something about Liam. Well, I went to the office at play time and asked if I could have Liam's address. The secretary said she would have to ask the headteacher. Then the headteacher came in and I asked her. She looked surprised and didn't say anything. Then she said she would try and see if it would be allowed and I was to come back to the office next week. I don't see why I can't have Liam's address because he was my friend. All I want to do is write to him and see how he is. I'll ask my Daddy to find out for me if the school don't allow it. My Daddy is very powerful and can get anything he wants. Charlie has said that it is the sort of thing that even my Daddy might not be able to arrange because Liam's new family might not want any contact with his old life as it might upset him. I don't think Liam would be upset if I just wrote to him but I'll wait and see what the school say. Sometimes I think that adults are very unkind.

We are going riding on Saturday and my grandparents are coming to watch. I don't think they will say anything nice about my riding as I still wobble a lot. Charlie says it doesn't matter what they say and that I am doing brilliantly. I have managed to learn nearly one hundred words. I forget some of the first ones but the important ones to do with my riding seem easier. I don't know why. I wonder when my grandmother will speak to me? Charlie says it doesn't matter if she only says a few words because she finds talking difficult. I really don't understand that, Charlie, because she is an adult. Is it because she doesn't like us? She never says anything to Grandfather and she never even looks at him. She hasn't said one word to Mummy, even after the lovely meal we had. She just sat and sat, a bit like Toad in 'The Wind in The Willows'. You are looking cross, Charlie, but I know you think I'm right. Let's take Robert swimming and then we'll feel happy again.

Well! Annie is noticing more and more about adults and their irrational behaviour. I'll have to watch her carefully to ensure she doesn't say anything rude to her grandparents, although I can almost feel myself wanting her to insult them. I secretly suspect that her mother might get a little buzz of satisfaction from it. Robert and I are going home when we've done all the routine activities. The repetition of all the physical tasks isn't onerous at all. I suppose it must be something to do with having established such a familiar programme that we just get on with it. It has occurred to me how much Robert would miss the variety in his life if, for any reason, it had to be curtailed. Of course this will eventually happen as Annie grows up. I know it is something that I dread. Annie will develop into an adolescent with all the attendant emotional turmoil. With her physical difficulties I do wonder how she will survive. Now I must stop this train of thought as it manifests itself as a bleakness of mind from of which there seems to be little relief. If I could wave a magic wand to ensure Annie's happiness I think I would be prepared to sacrifice just about anything, apart from Bob and Robert, of course. I am pleased not to be in this house during this evening's meal. Mrs. Jolly gave me an old fashioned look when she knew I was absconding. She is also leaving as soon as she has instructed the team of helpers as to their duties. She muttered, 'What a performance it all is', but I don't think I was supposed to hear. She, like me, has a very supportive husband. I wonder if she has to start preparing yet another meal for her husband and two boys when she gets home. I will be interested in Annie's news tomorrow.

I wish you could have stayed longer yesterday, Charlie. Mummy was in one of her very quiet moods and I didn't have anyone to talk to. Actually, Grandfather told me to get Snakes and Ladders after dinner and we had a good game, so it wasn't too bad after all. I don't want you to think I moan all the time. Daddy said that my Grandfather thought I was very good at the game and that he was going to teach me to play Draughts, but then Grandmother spoiled it by telling him he had to play a funny sounding game with her. It sounded like 'bread'. Mummy and Daddy played too but I heard Mummy say that she wanted to read me a story as it was my bedtime so she didn't play for long. It was a card game and they were very quiet. I tried to watch but it looked so boring that I told Mummy that I was going upstairs to get ready for bed. That was when Mummy said she was coming up to read to me. It was so horrible because my grandmother turned to my Mummy and said 'SHHH', in a very loud voice. I don't think I'll ever play cards. It makes grownups grumpy. When we were eating, Grandfather asked me about my riding. I think Daddy must have told him about it. I told him that I could trot a bit and that Mummy liked coming with me but she hadn't seen me trot and I was going to surprise her next Saturday. Grandfather asked if he could come and watch, which was a big surprise. Daddy said that we were all going in a very strong voice and Grandmother looked at him and I noticed that she frowned. I really don't think that I will ever like her, Charlie. Is that very bad of me?

I know she doesn't like me, but I think that Grandfather is a bit like a squashy teddy bear, that can look grumpy but when you get to know him he is really a softy. I am going to think of a name for him. I think I'm going to call him 'Grampy'. I know that sounds a bit like 'grumpy' but I'll tell him it's a nice nickname. He looks like my Daddy a bit and they have been doing a lot of talking. When we were eating our dinner last night they were having a secret together. I know it was a secret because their heads were close together and they didn't want anyone to listen to them. Grandmother didn't seem interested in anything. She put her food in her mouth and chewed and showed her teeth. I don't think the teeth are her own as they were moving up and down. I stopped looking at her. Mummy was very thirsty and kept drinking from the beautiful glasses that I haven't seen before. The glasses have long red stalks as if they have a flower at the top. I am definitely not allowed to have my juice in one. I was so pleased when Mummy said she wanted to read to me. I think she wanted to escape from something as well. We left Daddy to entertain his parents and we didn't feel guilty at all. At least that's what Mummy said. Mummy was so soft with me when I was in bed. She had her arm around my shoulders. I cannot remember that ever happening before. I can tell you this, Charlie, because I know you will understand what I'm trying to say. I can't wait for Daddy to see me trotting. He will be so amazed. I'm hoping that I can keep my balance. Poppy is so good. She never throws me about on her back, even when we're trotting. Daisy has told me that the next thing we will be doing is called cantering. I think it sounds too scary for me but I expect Tommy will help us. He is a very quiet person and I think Mummy likes him as she seems to watch him, especially when he is with the horses. Charlie has promised to come to the stables on Saturday, with Robert. I looked in the big parcel under the stairs again and the jodhpurs were still there. I am afraid to tell anyone but you Charlie, because I think they are supposed to be a secret and I don't know why. They are Mummy's but she hasn't worn them. Why did she buy them? Can we go swimming now please? I need to get my arms as strong as possible so that Poppy will trust me not to wobble too much.

We've been swimming and Robert and Annie are in the kitchen with Mrs. Jolly having their tea. I felt totally redundant as Robert wanted to sit next to Annie and wanted me to go away. I should have felt pleased but there was a pang of hurt, totally silly, I know. I should be delighted that he wants some independence. We are going home in a minute anyway so I'll just rush a few thoughts down. I wonder about the hidden jodhpurs and why they haven't seen the light of day yet. I know that things are going to happen over which I will have no control. The one thing I'd like to happen is that the emotionless grandmother could manage to dredge up a modicum of warmth towards her granddaughter. I think that is a losing battle, but at least 'Gramps' is showing positive signs of accepting his granddaughter. I wonder what their reactions will be on Saturday. Impressing her grandparents is so important to Annie, unreasonably so, but with all the adults watching, I'm sure we can give her some positive feedback between us. Tommy will be silently observing the situation anyway. I'm convinced he knows all the dynamics of this family so far and adding the grandparents will only be a small extra challenge.

On Saturday morning I sat in the hall with all my riding gear for ages and ages. We waited and waited for the grandparents. Mummy said that we would go on ahead with Charlie or I'd be late for my lesson. Daddy would follow on later with his parents. I was pleased about that especially after last night. Grandmother fell asleep in her soup. I very nearly laughed but I saw Mummy's face and so I looked out of the window instead. I think Daddy was cross as he gave a big, long sigh. Gramps just ignored her. I told him that I had a special name for him and he asked what it was. When I told him he said that he was honoured but I don't know what that means. He was smiling a big smile so I think it was a good thing. He patted me on my head, just as if I was a dog. I wonder what he would have done if I had pretended to bark. Daddy was smiling too and he held out his arms for me to give him a cuddle. Charlie, you'll never know how safe I feel in my Daddy's arms. I feel safe in your arms as well but my Daddy has a special smell. I don't mean he smells dirty. I mean he smells comfortable. The grandparents were quite late but they did manage to see me trot. Gramps clapped and I felt all warm inside and very proud. Mummy smiled a lot too. Afterwards we sat at a picnic table and Mrs. Straw brought out a large jug of coffee and a delicious cake. Gramps said, 'I could make a habit of this. What a lovely place you have here.' Then I was proud of him. After a little while Mummy got up and walked over to where the very big horses are in their stables. Tommy followed her, saying, 'Excuse me a moment. I think your Mummy wants to give one of the horses a carrot.' I thought that was a bit strange, Charlie, don't you? When she came back she was smiling a very big smile indeed. I don't know why. She asked Tommy about why none of the horses or ponies had shoes on and he said all the animals were kept 'At Liberty'. I'm not certain what that means but I know all the animals seem very happy and gentle. I did hear Tommy say to my mummy something about one evening next week but I couldn't hear properly. I wonder if she is going to have lessons. I am a bit scared of asking her in case I'm wrong and it might make her cross. Grandmother was silent. I don't know why she never wants to talk. Is she unhappy, Charlie?

Yes. It was an unusual morning. Everything went very well after the grandparents eventually arrived. It was probably a good thing that we travelled in separate cars as it seemed as if we were doing the normal Saturday routine. Luckily it was a beautiful morning, warm and sunny. Annie rode very well indeed, hardly wobbling at all. We explained to Daisy about missing the swim that morning but it would be back to normal the following Saturday. Annie and Daisy went to clean out a stable and I noticed that Cristabel went to where the larger horses are kept. When I saw Tommy follow, I wasn't sure what to think but nothing was amiss as when they returned they were chatting amicably about the excellent progress that Annie has made. I caught a few words, as Annie had, about Cristabel and one evening but that was all. When we were driving home

I noticed that she was looking at me more frequently than normal and I guessed that there would be something said when we were in private. I was right. She seemed a little shamefaced as she said, very quietly, 'Charlie, could you spare an evening a week to come to the stables with me? Just you and I. It will be an evening to suit you, of course.' When I didn't reply she continued.' Tommy thinks it would be a good idea if I worked with some of the horses. He realises that I have problems with Annie and he thinks that he can shed some light on them. Please say you can, Charlie. I have never wanted anything so much in my life. I know that must sound selfish but it's only since Annie started riding that I can feel something happening but I don't know what it is. I know you are the one person that has all my gory details lodged in your mind and you probably think there is no help for me, but I feel as if this might be my last chance at just about everything. Cristabel slammed her mouth shut, knowing she hadn't said as many words to me in months. She had a pleading, childlike expression on her face to which I instinctively responded, knowing this was all part of some plan or other. 'Of course I will. What about Charles and Annie? What will you tell them?' It was all going to be a massive secret apparently. I knew that this young mother had severe problems and that she knew I was fully aware of them. What choice did I have? Part of me was inquisitively desperate to watch the ensuing events, knowing that there were situations of which I had no experience at all. It was quite exciting at that moment in time but a wave of apprehension crept into my thoughts as I didn't want my time with Robert eaten away. There was no point in suggesting Robert came with us as I knew this whole arrangement had to be totally secret. Cristabel was going to tell Annie that she wanted to surprise her Daddy by showing him that she had learnt to ride, so Annie must be sworn to secrecy too. I thought Annie would relish the fact that she was party to adults' secrets. I know this is predestined and I will just 'go with the flow'. Part of me is trying to hide a growing anticipation but I can't think of anything specific that is causing it. There is a general atmosphere surrounding this family and I know it is more positive than I can ever remember.

Chapter Eleven

Charlie says that we have to keep a secret and it will be fun to show Daddy what Mummy can do. She is going to the stables with you, Charlie, once a week in the evening. We are going to choose an evening when Daddy is late so that he won't suspect anything. It is the evening when I have my physio and Mummy is going straight to the stables from work and meeting you there, Charlie, isn't she? It will be exciting to have a secret, just my Mummy and me and you. Mummy says she will be back before Daddy gets home. I'm going to check when the new jodhpurs disappear from the cupboard, so I'll know Mummy is really getting on a horse. It is starting next week after my grandparents have gone. I will miss Gramps. He is talking to me lots of times now, but Grandmother never even looks at me.

When we got home from school today, Cristabel looked very pale and asked to have a word with me in her office. Apparently, Charles' mother has terminal cancer and has refused all treatment. Charles has never been close to her and is very uneasy about what to do. Cristabel asked my opinion and, after much thought, I told her that there was a very good Nursing Home about two miles away. It had a lovely name which is why it came to mind so easily. I, ironically, thought it would be lovely for my own parents when and if the time came that they needed intensive care. Chance would be a fine thing, I thought, knowing the weekly cost was ten times even my present inflated salary. Cost was not an issue in this case though and I told Cristabel that we should discuss it with Charles. I mentally noted that I said 'we', knowing that I would be bound up with all the discussions. The fact that I didn't like the woman made me feel guilty, although I doubted, had she been fully fit, her behaviour would have been any different. So, it was decided that a visit to 'Hummingbird House' would be undertaken by Charles as soon as possible. I privately wondered what opinion his mother would have about decisions possibly being made without consulting her. I really didn't care that much, which is something not to feel proud about. From today, I shall try very hard to make some pleasant comments to this woman and try to remember that she is a victim of her own parents' lack of warmth. Whatever happens, Cristabel's attendance at the stables must not be compromised. It is all a question of time management; a subject I have heard Cristabel discussing over the telephone on several occasions. Her contact with her work colleagues is much more casual than before Annie was born and I know she has lunch with a couple of them occasionally. I would like to be a fly on the wall to see exactly how she relates to them. I am convinced the conversation would sound like cocktail party talk, although the C.B.'s experience in that domain is now non- existent, I'm please to say. I wonder if they miss all the meaningless chatter. From what she has inadvertently and briefly let drop, her life before Annie was one round after another of drug-fuelled parties. All she said was, 'We were drunk most of the time and I'm so sorry about it now, especially because of Annie.' Then she clammed up and quickly went into another room, away from my accidentally accusing glance. Charles will be discussing the possible move into 'Hummingbird House' this evening apparently, after the evening meal and Annie being safely in bed away from any possible unpleasantness. I have my parents coming for a roast at the weekend so I need to do some serious shopping. They are so good with Robert and he loves having them around. We are going to a model train centre in which my Dad and Robert are becoming mutually interested. Obsessed might be a better word but Thomas the Tank Engine is becoming an increasingly popular toy along with the numerous bits of track, tunnels, stations, signals and personnel, including one called 'Controller'. I remember he was called 'Fat Controller' when I was a child. I suppose it is politically correctness. I will take extra care of my parents, and Bob's of course, having suddenly become aware that, at their age, they are not invincible.

I had to do my homework straight after tea tonight and I'm not having the evening meal with the adults. I prefer it like that although it means Gramps won't be able to talk to me. Mummy says I need an early night as I look tired. I'm not the least tired but I can get on with my part of the story that Daisy and me are doing. We will do some more on Saturday after riding. I think the grandparents will have gone by then. I know there is something going on that they are all keeping from me. I think it might be to do with Grandmother as they only talk to each other in whispers when she is not in the room. It's as if they are expecting her to burst in at any time, but I don't think she could burst in anywhere as she always walks in a shuffly way with her head down as if she thinks she might fall over. I know all about that as I used to look down all the time when I was smaller. I can remember looking at the pattern on the dining room carpet when I was trying not to lose my balance. Now I don't have to worry about it any longer; only if I hurry too much. If I'm carrying anything, especially my stuff at school, I feel as if I might lose my balance. It is not a good feeling. I feel quite frightened because, if I fall, everyone makes a stupid fuss and it starts my eyes watering. Charlie says that it isn't important and that I must walk more slowly if I'm carrying heavy stuff. I hate it when I'm always last to get in line. Yes, Charlie, I know all about the hare and the tortoise, I just would like the chance to be the hare for once.

There seems to be a great deal to think about at the moment. Last night I was asked to join Cristabel and Charles in the sitting room. Bob took Robert swimming and Annie had a piano lesson, so I didn't have them to worry about. Charles' father was looking very grim and sat next to his mother. She looked grey and distant. Charles then told his mother about the Nursing Home that I had told them about and that they had visited to see if it would be the right place for her. She looked totally impassive and showed no flickering interest whatever. I thought it would be helpful if I told her a little bit about it. I told her the name of it hoping that would melt the atmosphere a little. An extremely small blink was the result and she actually looked up at me, but with no apparent recognition. She asked me who I was so I told her about my involvement with Annie. She then asked who Annie was which told us all that the situation was one that needed urgent attention. Charles then took over and told her that he was taking her to see Hummingbird house in the morning. 'That's nice dear,' she said. 'How are my shares doing?' It would have been funny if it hadn't been so unexpected and sad. She spoke gently and smiled at her son, a rarity at the best of times. Her eyes were vacant though and I wondered if the impending plan would be the right one. There was no time for further discussion with her and Gramps took her up to her room. Whilst he was out of the room, Cristabel said, ' She seems very confused. I think we must get all her stuff packed up ready as I don't think she will be coming back here.' I saw Charles give her a worried glance. He opened his mouth to say something and then snapped it shut again. Then he asked me what I thought and it was an easy reply for me as I knew that there would only be a short time before more intensive care would be needed. Charles accepted my comments and actually thanked me which made me hope I'd been right in my estimation of his mother's condition. Then Bob knocked and came in carrying Robert who was in a very relaxed and sleepy state, so off we went.

We talked all the way home about the situation with Charles' mother and Bob thought my advice was as good as anyone else's, which was not the exact response I would have liked. However, after Robert had polished off his supper and asleep in his bed, we managed a further chat about what, if anything, we would say to Charles and Cristabel if asked. Bob said that we must be a united front which sounded bit like a war zone but I knew exactly what he meant. We decided that to encourage Charles' mother to accept the move to Hummingbird House was the only option. I suggested that Gramps might like to live there with her as, in our opinion, it came across as more like a five star hotel anyway. Bob told me to keep quiet about that as it might not be what he wanted. I thought about what he meant and was too tired to question him.

Mummy has told me that my Grandmother is very ill and that she will probably be living in a Nursing Home near to us. It explains why she is so quiet and really rather grumpy. I will try very hard to be nice to her but I don't think she will notice. Everyone seems to be very busy with cases and fussing about what she might need. What will happen to Gramps? I like him a lot and he could live here with us, couldn't he Charlie? I know you said it's too early to make a decision but he is looking so worried all the time. Why don't my Daddy's brothers come and help? I know they are in other countries far away but they could get on a plane couldn't they? I have never met my uncles or my cousins. I don't even know how many I've got. I must have aunties as well, mustn't I? I'll ask Gramps when all this fuss is over. At the weekend, Daisy and me are going to start to learn how to go quicker than trot. I think it's called canter. Tommy says we have to learn how to send messages to the ponies with our legs even more carefully.

My poor legs will ache afterwards, I know, but I don't mind one bit. I'm writing a letter to Liam tonight to tell him all the things that I've been doing. I really miss him. I wonder if he's happy. I hope we can get his address soon then I can post my letter to him. It will be nice to write things down in my best writing even if it will take me a long time. If I get really tired, Charlie, will you help me?

I went into school with Robert in his buggy this morning. He seems to like going in with Annie but doesn't like it when she has to disappear into her own classroom. I had made an appointment to see the headmistress and had planned on what I was going to say. It turned out to be really difficult as she explained to me that she wasn't allowed to give me any information about Liam's whereabouts at all. All she would tell me was the name of his Social Worker and that she worked at the Town Hall and I could make an appointment with her. I had a definite feeling that my queries had overstepped the mark and she wasn't totally happy about giving me even that modicum of information. I convinced her, I hope, that I was a responsible member of society and wasn't in the business of abduction or any other illegal activity. I left feeling a criminal. I was, however, determined to follow up the contact with the Social Worker. We hurried back to the C.B.'s knowing that the visit to Hummingbird House was happening at that moment. Robert had suddenly become more vocal and said, 'Wimming, Mummy,' meaning a swim was the one thing he would like to do. It was such a luxury; stepping into warm water, with no-one else in there. Also a waste,

I thought, but thrust it from my mind as there were other important things to think about. Robert was enjoying the water so much and I removed one of the three little floats from his back. It made no difference and he merrily splashed away from me. I think he must have very good buoyancy. We swam alongside each other, right up to the deep end. He kept looking at me and laughing. My heart was so full of gladness that I knew my smile stretched from ear to ear. I kept telling him what a good swimmer he was and to keep kicking his legs. He laughed so much that he swallowed a gulp of water. I tried not to overreact as I had heard the swimming teacher say that if you fuss, it will make the child fuss and be frightened of the water. I just told him not to drink all the water as Annie would want to swim later. It seemed to do the trick and he spluttered a bit more then went on swimming. What a dear little chap he is. I must make some plans for his birthday. It seems like yesterday that he came to us, wrapped in a blue blanket and, even at that young age, looking around to see where he was. He smiled after two days with us. I'll never forget that magic moment. It was quite difficult to contend with all the checking that the Social Workers were obliged to do but, after one year, things became stable and we knew he would never be taken away. It would be a ridiculous coincidence if Liam had the same Social Worker we had with the adoption. I expect it's a different department.

Grandmother isn't at my house any more. She has gone to a home that sounds like a bird. Gramps looks better. He doesn't look so worried all the time. Mummy says I can visit Grandmother when she is settled. I don't want to. I expect I'll have to though because Gramps will be upset if I'm grumpy about it. I really don't like her and I know she hates me. I will go and see her but I hope she takes ages and ages to settle. Now I'm going to do my homework with you Charlie and then I have my swimming lesson. Robert said, 'Annie go wimming', to me on the way home from school. He is so sweet and I want to get him something really good for his birthday. When are you going to go to see Liam's Social Worker, Charlie? I promise I won't talk about it to anyone at all, even my teacher. I have started the letter to him telling him all the news. I hope it won't make him miss me too much. I'll tell him lots of silly things too. He can read you know Charlie. I used to practise in the same group with him and he was much quicker than me. His writing was better than mine too. My writing is getting better. I'll surprise you soon.

The visit to the nursing home and Charles' mother being deposited there was accomplished without any bother at all apparently. Charles filled me in briefly before rushing off to work. He's coming home early tonight but he has to sort out some financial matter. It always amazes me how he tells me things that I would consider confidential in most circumstances. Well perhaps these circumstances aren't considered to be needing secrecy. I'm honoured in a way that he speaks so freely to me. He obviously trusts my discretion.

I am looking forward to going to the stables tomorrow evening with Cristabel. It will be unique; just the two of us. I hope Bob has remembered that he is in charge of Robert. Mrs. Jolly will have left tea for Annie and the physio has agreed to stay until we return. I hope all this complicated set of arrangements is going to be worth it. There is no point in trying to get out of it now. In any case, I know something is going to happen and I'm intrigued to find out. All I know with complete conviction is that Tommy is going to play a massive part in the future and I intend to stick around to watch events unfolding.

I have had a very good day at school. We are doing another show for Easter. It is called 'Joseph and the Technicolour Dreamcoat'. I am going to be doing lots of singing. All the children from the top class are taking the main parts. Our music teacher has to write to all the parents to ask them if their children can stay after school on two nights a week because there is no time during the day to have rehearsals. All our music lessons have been cancelled as there is no time any more. I don't think it's fair as we all love singing and our music teacher is really brilliant at teaching us all the songs. She has helped me sing better as well. I have to learn all the words as I'm the leader of the chorus. It is so good to be chosen and I just wish Liam was still at my school so that we can do it together. I'll tell him about it in my letter or perhaps I'd better not or it might upset him as he can't be in it. Mummy and Charlie are going to the stables tonight. It is a special secret that I'm not allowed to tell Daddy about. The jodhpurs have gone from the cupboard. Daddy will be looking after Gramps anyway so they won't notice Mummy isn't home and I have my physio. It's very exciting. I can't wait until Mummy wants to talk about her riding. Charlie has told me not to ask and that Mummy will tell me when she's ready, haven't you Charlie?

Tommy was waiting for us this evening. He suggested that I watched from a short distance away. I didn't understand that but did as I was told. I expect he didn't want me distracting Cristabel, but don't really know the reason. As I listened to Tommy, his voice almost sounded musical and Cristabel didn't take her eyes off him. He asked her to go into the stable at the end of the yard and collect a grooming kit. This she did and when she returned he told her to go in Pablo's stable and groom him. Pablo. I know, is the largest horse at the stables. I crept to the corner of the doorway, out of sight, to listen to what was being said. I don't know why, but I knew it was important that I listened to everything.

'Brush him gently and talk to him if you like,' was all that Tommy said. Cristabel, after a minute, said, 'I know horses love being groomed. I remember when I was a little girl.....' she ground to a halt. Tommy said nothing and Cristabel continued grooming, staring at the horse's coat very closely and taking a huge amount of care as she rhythmically swept the brush downwards. I noticed that the horse, 'Pablo' was standing absolutely still, with not a muscle moving. I don't think Cristabel noticed me at all. It seemed as if she and Pablo were in a bubble together. I almost felt like an interloper. Tommy said, 'Why don't you put his headcollar on and take him into the top field?' Cristabel jumped at the sound of his voice and said, 'Oh, I was in a world of my own then, sorry.' She expertly put on Pablo's headcollar and off they went together to the top field. Tommy stayed behind. He saw me lurking, almost hidden by the stable door. He said it would be fine for me to watch but advised me to keep very still and quiet. I followed them up to the field, feeling rather self-conscious. After all I know nothing about horses and felt as if I had been put in the wrong place. I knew deep down that I was in the right place but I didn't know why. When I got to the corner of the field I saw Tommy putting poles on the ground. I didn't understand why as he made a row of poles about two metres apart, parallel to each other. I counted five poles. He went over to Cristabel and told her to step over the poles imagining they were all the things in her life that upset her. She looked up at him in surprise but did as she was told. She walked very slowly indeed. In fact I thought she was going to stop altogether but, without any warning, Pablo started following her, stepping carefully over the poles behind her. When she reached the last pole Pablo stood, absolutely still, next to her. They both seemed to be frozen in time. Neither moved for at least a minute. Then Cristabel put her arm slowly up to Pablo's neck. He lowered his massive neck towards her and gently rested it on her shoulder. There they stayed motionless. Tommy approached them slowly and murmured something to Pablo. I didn't hear what he said, but Pablo moved away back to the gate as if he had been asked to do a job and he had made a good start. Cristabel followed and I noticed that she, for the first time I could remember, had an almost serene expression on her face. I didn't comment at all as I felt I resembled a gooseberry. We stayed for another half hour, during which time Tommy and Cristabel were in close conversation. I thought it wise to keep my distance so I went to see some of the other ponies in one of the other fields. It was lovely to see them all, their coats gleaming in the sunshine, munching at the new spring grass. There was an atmosphere surrounding them that exuded peace and I felt totally relaxed for the first time in weeks.

All the built up anxieties about the grandparents' visit, locating Liam on Annie's behalf, thinking about Robert's birthday and trying not to count the number of wine bottles ready for recycling, dissolved into the far distance. I couldn't dredge up any enthusiasm to go home, but saw Cristabel walking away from Tommy and nodding, so I knew it was time to tear ourselves away. We didn't speak at all on the way home. In fact, if Cristbel had spoken I would have been extremely surprised. There was no need for any words between us. When we arrived back at the house, Cristabel turned to me and smiled. That was all; a smile, which I returned, and in we went. Annie rushed out and demanded to know how her mother got on. She was shushed and told to remember it was a secret. They went into the house arm in arm, which was a first. Whatever was happening I was totally and completely persuaded of its magnitude. Charles came in shortly afterwards. Cristabel had changed from her jodhpurs luckily.

Charles asked if he could speak with me and my heart dropped. What if he didn't approve of what we were doing? How could he have found out? I needn't have worried because he was only concerned to put me in the picture concerning the details of his mother's removal to Hummingbird House. He wanted to know

277

if I thought his mother had long to live as there were numerous financial matters that needed attention and he didn't want to appear to be hurrying her off. 'You know, of course, that I'm not very close to my mother, or my father for that matter, but I'm the only person they've got that is willing to spend time with them.' I wanted to say that if they had shown an interest in their children as they were growing up perhaps they might feel able to show more of an interest now it was desperately needed. Of course I didn't, there being not much point, although I must say that Charles has been a loving father to Annie.

I just spewed out a few platitudes and asked him if his mother had been seen by a doctor since moving to Hummingbird House. Apparently her consultant had been summoned, and attended very briefly and rapidly. He offered very little of a tangible nature. I told Charles that it was always difficult to put a time scale on these things but her overall appearance indicated, in my opinion, that she had a matter of months, if not less, to live. Charles said that he felt distant from her and was embarrassed that he felt unable to show her any affection at what was her most needy time of life. I didn't answer that as it was pointless. His father, I thought, had potential. I said,' 'Your father is a pleasant chap, isn't he? Annie thinks the world of him. Does your mother have anything that she shares with your father?' I didn't know how else to phrase it. What I wanted to ask was did Charles' mother have an atom of affection or interest in anyone apart from herself? Even though she was terminally ill, I knew instinctively that this woman had no ability to make connections with others. I wondered if she had ever been able to touch anyone physically and spontaneously but couldn't find the right words to ask her son. There was never a mention of Charles' brother and sister, or was it two brothers and no sister? It was a ridiculous situation considering the length of time I had known this family. I just found it impossible to ask him. What about his daughter? She had relatives that never made contact and probably cousins shut away in some boarding school somewhere that we could arrange to have for holiday visits. That's what normal families do, surely. It is none of my business, I am fully aware of that but will never accept that Annie should be kept away from her extended family. I am also fully aware that her uncles and aunties would probably not want to be seen with her. It is their loss.

Mummy and me are going to buy a new riding hat for her. She has told me all about her lesson. I have never heard Mummy talk so much to me and I can't wait to go shopping with her. It is so brilliant to have a secret with her too. Mummy says that I must ask Tommy what 'At Liberty' means. I think it is something to do with the horses not having metal shoes fitted on their hooves but I'm not sure. Daisy says it is a much kinder way to keep horses but she hasn't told me anything else apart from horses can help people to feel better. I don't understand what she means. I always feel better after I've been riding but I think she means a bit more than that. I know I have to be patient and everything will be explained to me, just like you keep telling me, Charlie, but sometimes I think it would be easier if everyone told me everything straight away and then I could work things out for myself. I know you will give me one of your funny looks Charlie, but it is very hard for me sometimes when I feel everyone is keeping things from me. Can we do some more of my letter to Liam now, please?

It's a sod of a situation with Liam. I went to the Town Hall this morning to get a brief appointment with Liam's social worker. She was in a hurry as she had ten families to fit in that day. What a system! When I went into her office which she obviously shared with the rest of the staff, she ushered me into a corner, trying to get a bit of privacy. That was after we recognised each other. She was indeed Miss Crouch, my Social Worker with whom I was involved during all the interminable investigations during our adoption of Robert. She smiled at me and I showed her a couple of photos that I kept in my purse. After making all the comments she asked me what she could do. I briefly told her about the situation with Annie and her friendship with Liam that had been severed. She was sympathetic, but said it was a very difficult case. I explained that all Annie wanted was to write to him but Miss Crouch said that it might open up all sorts of memories for the little boy that could be damaging. She told me that he was doing really well with his new family and that all three boys were hopefully going to be adopted together. This was a most unusual event, understandably, and my admiration for these new parents was immeasurable. Everything was working out very well and the new parents were one in a million. They didn't have any children of their own and when I remarked, 'In for a penny, in for a pound, eh?' she laughed and agreed. She then told me that they were living on a farm and that the natural mother had another partner and had shown no interest in keeping in contact with the three boys. She had also been sectioned just before the boys had been taken into care but was now managing to keep out of trouble with her new partner. When I looked dubious, she said that regular visits were made and the medication was having a calming effect. 'Of course, I haven't told you any of this,' she said. When I asked if there were any circumstances that the mother could get them back, if she ever wanted them, Miss Crouch said that she had learnt from experience never to say never, but in her opinion, there were very few circumstances that would allow them to be returned to their birth mother considering the history. 'She'll probably have more with this latest man.' she said. 'Who am I to forbid it? It might mean that any future child is taken away at birth. Unfortunately, her type only attracts similar dysfunctional characters as her history shows. We tried to encourage her to use contraception but she seems detached from any routine in that respect and we can't insist on her having the three year insertion in her arm. I sound bitter and twisted and apologise. There are an increasing number of families that just can't cope. Usually their food intake consists of takeaway rubbish, the children sleep deprived, nobody works, alcohol is an essential ingredient to their daily life and the kids grow up to perpetuate the problem.'

When I looked shocked, she stopped abruptly and said, 'Look, I'm talking to you as another professional and I know it won't go any further, but I get so frustrated when I know the inevitable outcome of bad parenting.'

I replied that I understood completely and that poor parenting wasn't limited to the more deprived end of the spectrum. I was pleased that she looked surprised, then thoughtful. This has been a trying morning, the result being the opposite of what Annie wanted. Although I didn't tell her that I was going to the Town Hall this morning, I know I will have to tell her that she won't be able to contact Liam. I might suggest she continues to write to him from time to time as we might bump into him in the future, accidentally and then she can talk about the letters she has written. That sounds pretty feeble but it's the best I can manage. It will seem very unfair to her, I know.

We had to go to see Grandmother after tea tonight and I missed all the things that I like doing. Mummy said we can make up for it tomorrow as we are going shopping after school. Grandmother stared at me and it made me wobble even more. She didn't say anything and just looked out of her window all the time. Gramps was so nice to her and asked her if there was anything she needed. All she said was, 'A gin and tonic, no ice and be quick about it.' I remember that because Gramps smiled at her and said he would see what he could do. I don't remember him smiling at her before. She has a lovely room that looks over the gardens. There are loads of tall trees and flowerbeds full of flowers. There are three bird feeders and I saw some birds that I didn't recognise, just like Grandmother didn't recognise me. There are lots of nurses that keep coming in and asking us if there is anything that we want. Gramps stopped Grandmother from speaking as he thought she might be rude. At least I think that is why he seemed to speak straight after the nurse stopped. Everything smells of disinfectant in Hummingbird House. I really love the name. I had a drink of orange squash and two chocolate biscuits. Mummy kept looking at me and winking and I think I know why she did that. It was because she knew I was cross at missing all my stuff that I usually do. Grandmother suddenly sat up very straight and shouted, 'Who the hell are these people? Get them out of here.' Gramps took my hand and quietly said that we were going to look around the garden. I was frightened of my Grandmother and liked her even less than before.

Gramps and me went all round the garden. It was good because as soon as I was out of that room my wobbling nearly stopped. The gardens are massive and there is a path with a rail that goes all around it. Gramps told me to hold on with just one hand and see if I could march, like he showed me. It was brilliant and I did it easily. Then he showed me how to do a 'silly walk' with his legs straight out in front of him. I laughed so much that I nearly fell over. He told me that Grandmother didn't know she was being unkind as she was ill and she had forgotten how to behave politely, so that made me feel much better. When I asked him if she was going to die he said, 'Yes, probably quite soon so we all have to be very understanding.' I am so pleased that Gramps isn't keeping secrets from me and is treating me as if I can understand. I don't think I do understand completely but it is much better than when people whisper and I know they are keeping things from me, like Mummy does sometimes. Mummy and Daddy came out into the garden to meet us and then we all went home. I didn't have to go back into Grandmother's room to say goodbye. I heard Daddy say that she wouldn't remember who I was anyway.

I feel sorry that Annie had to endure that particular experience but it doesn't seem to have done any harm. It wouldn't surprise me if the Grandmother passed away sooner rather than later. I noticed that her medication was one of the strongest ones and usually indicates that death isn't too far in the distance. What a pity that all Annie's memories of her will be of the unpleasant kind. At least that visit is over and hopefully she won't be expected to repeat it too soon. Perhaps Grandmother's death will release everyone, herself included. What a waste it all is. At least Annie seems to have formed a bond with her grandfather; a surprise to me but a pleasant one. He seems to have a hidden sense of humour and it may come to the fore in the future. I wonder if he will come and live with the C.B.'s. I can think of worse things. Every day I watch him and Charles making more relaxed conversation. It would be rather unusual if the death of one parent made the relationship with the other flower. It is something that I will be watching closely as Annie would benefit, I'm sure. The Grandmother is still here though, so I must not anticipate anything. So much seems to be happening at the moment that it is almost impossible to find time to think about it.

Hurray! Saturday is getting nearer and Daisy can come home with me for a swim and then we can get on with our book. We do a lot of laughing when we are planning what to put because we keep thinking of all the funny things that happen at the stables. We both have fallen over in the horse poo. We helped each other up though. When we were mucking out, we had to push a special wheelbarrow full of poo to the manure heap and tip it up. The first time we did it we tipped the wheelbarrow over and the poo went all over our boots. Tommy saw and said it was a good job we had our boots on. He didn't help us though and we managed to get all the poo on to the heap. Daisy said that he never helps when she does things like that as it is good for her to sort it out herself. I know exactly what she means. I will always trust Tommy to do the right thing. Charlie has told me about Liam and that I won't be allowed to see him or even write to him. She explained it to me but I don't really understand how it might upset him if I just write a short letter to him. When you said, Charlie, that we might bump into him when we were out shopping it didn't sound like you meant it. I will have to speak to him then, won't I, so what happens if that upsets him? You are giving me one of your looks, Charlie, so I'll shut up. Mummy and I are going shopping tomorrow after school to get me a back protector. If I fall off Poppy, but I won't, it will stop me getting hurt. Mummy said that it will feel a bit stiff to start with. I'll be able to wear it on Saturday, won't I? Daisy has one and she takes ages to get it on. I expect we'll get in a muddle with them at the same time, but at least we can help each other.

I felt really dishonest when telling Annie about not being allowed to contact Liam. There is no way around it, unfortunately and I can understand completely that the Social Worker has to keep his whereabouts confidential. Life must seem very unfair to a young girl in Annie's position. There are enough distractions in her life to avoid it becoming a serious problem, thank goodness.

Cristabel and I are due for another couple of hours at the stables shortly. I can't understand why I'm looking forward to it so much. All I do is eavesdrop. I find it incredibly fascinating for reasons I cannot put my finger on. Secretly, I would love to be in Cristabel's shoes. I know Tommy wouldn't mind if I gave the horses some carrots and even helped muck out sometimes, but I'd better ask him. We have an enormous calendar in the kitchen at home with all the various engagements we have. We run out of space sometimes and I have to write in red with arrows pointing to the appropriate date. However do parents with two or three children cope? I remember seeing on the white board, in Annie's classroom, a list of children's names. When I asked Annie why they were there she told me that they were the children that were being picked up after school by minibus and taken to after school care. This was a revelation to me and I found myself feeling angry. This list of children would only see their parents for a short time in the evenings. Were they the same children that attended the breakfast club? Soon the poor youngsters would be able to take their beds to school as well, so with a bit of luck, the parents would be able to earn lots of money and see their children as infrequently as possible. Society has got it wrong. I must stop thinking about it as there is nothing that can be rescued now. Seeing disaffected youngsters mooching round the precinct makes me sad. They are the binge drinkers of the future and we will all throw up our hands in horror at their bad behaviour when it is our neglect that has caused it. Although Annie had a rough start to her life, I'm hoping that she will have enough affection from all of us combined to help her develop into a happy, well adjusted adult. Why do I not have total confidence?

I'm getting my new back protector tomorrow night. Mummy is picking me up from school and we are going to the sports equipment shop together. Just Mummy and me are going, nobody else. It is the first time she has picked me up since I have been in the Juniors. When we have got the back protector we are going to go and have something to eat in a little restaurant that Mummy knows. She said that she knows the owner. It's the first time that Mummy and me, no-one else, has been out to eat together. I will be very polite and eat slowly and try not to spill anything or she might not take me ever again. I feel a bit nervous, but Charlie has just said that I must enjoy myself and remember to say 'please' and 'thankyou'. I am quite good at that now because I'm older. Mrs. Jolly tells me how to sit nicely at the table. But she giggles a lot and says I should see her boys. They eat as if they have never seen food and she tries very hard to teach them good manners. She thinks they will only learn good manners when they get a girlfriend who happens to have good manners and holds her knife and fork properly and not as if she's trying to kill her food. She makes me laugh but she has taught me how to hold my knife and fork so that I don't keep dropping them. I really need all my fingers and thumbs. If I'm nervous, my food tends to get thrown all over the place, but Mrs. Jolly has shown me how to rest my arms on the table, a bit like when I'm on the computer, and relax. It's easy for her to say. Her hands will do as she wants them to. Mine sometimes behave as if they don't belong to me. I will try to be relaxed and enjoy myself because I really want Mummy to be proud of me.

Charles asked if he could have a word with me tonight, just as I was going out of the door with Robert. He mumbled with his words a bit but eventually he asked how Robert got on with his grandparents. I thought it a bit of an unexpected question so I asked him why he wanted to know. He said that he had no recollection at all of his own grandparents and wondered if it was a bit unusual. I told him that, in the age we live in, grandparents are extremely important to act as surrogate parents especially for the picking up from school duties. The floodgates then opened and he said that he would have loved to have had grandparents but had never thought of asking his mother about them. He laughed when he said that he assumed she had a mother herself, but didn't I think it strange that he had no memories, pleasant or otherwise, of any grandparents. When I reminded him that he was at boarding school from the age of six, he went very thoughtful and quiet and slid away into the study. I don't think we've heard the end of it. As long as the end result is that Annie benefits from extra attention from her father, any further discussion will be worth it. Charles looks so sad sometimes; an infallible expression which I fear hides numerous hurtful images. I will prepare myself for further interrogation. Poor man; he has hidden secrets relating to his upbringing, I'm certain of that. The positive state he has arrived at is to be treasured. He seems able to address the unknown facts about his childhood with only minimal uneasiness. At least that is the superficial impression he gives. I'm sure he will continue to build on his relationship with Annie and I have noticed, of late, that there have been some flimsy pleasantries between him and Cristabel. I gave Robert an extra long cuddle tonight, for some reason, and read three stories instead of the usual two.

Mummy met me from school. All the other children were looking at her because she is so smart and elegant. I know that word because we had to find language to describe a swan in our Literacy group today. I felt so proud that she was my mother. I wished she could have held my hand though and then all the children would have known she belonged to me. We went to the shop called Saddles and Riding Gear. It was like a big warehouse and had a lovely warm smell just like in the stables. Mummy said that it was because they sold bags of horse feed and special stuff to clean the leather of the saddles. She knows so much about horses. Tommy must have told her. Mummy kept wandering off and I nearly lost her a couple of times. It didn't matter though because she called out, 'Annie, come and look at this,' and I went towards her voice. She wanted to show me some bridles and lead ropes. They were all in beautiful colours. I told Mummy that we hadn't got a horse to buy anything for and Mummy laughed. There was a very unusual expression on her face. I feel so good when she is smiling. We went to look for back protectors and I thought it was very boring after all the masses of interesting things we had seen. There are very colourful blankets, but they are called rugs if they are for horses. Daisy told me that. In the cold weather some horses and ponies have to have rugs on to keep them warm. I would like to buy Poppy a new rug for Christmas, or her birthday. I wonder if ponies have birthdays. We eventually got a back protector that fitted me. A man had to put it on me and fasten all the Velcro bits up. He pulled it very tight. He asked me where I went riding and I told him about Tommy. He said that everyone knew Tommy and I was a very lucky girl to have lessons with him. He showed Mummy some covers for my riding hat. They were all bright and silky and Mummy said that was why they were called silks and we could buy one for me and also for Daisy. I bought two exactly the same. They were pink and purple stripes and Mummy asked if I thought they were bright enough. I think she might have been joking. Then we looked around the warehouse for a bit longer and my legs began to ache. I asked Mummy if I could find somewhere to sit down and she looked surprised and said it was all right because we were going to have something to eat at the place she had told me about. Charlie, I had such a brilliant time with Mummy. I remembered what Mrs. Jolly had told me about good manners and how to hold my knife and fork so my hands didn't wobble too much and I did it. I had something called Lasagne which was delicious. Mummy had a salmon salad. For pudding I had three sorts of ice-cream covered in chocolate and marshmallows and Mummy had strong coffee. I know it was strong because I could smell it and it was what she had asked for in a very firm voice. I think everyone does what she says because she has a very straight way of speaking. It's as if she is giving orders. I don't think it sounds very soft though. Nobody seemed to mind. I was pleased to be able to sit down for a bit as my legs were not behaving very well. Mummy said we had better get home as Daddy would like to see my back protector and the silks I had got for myself and Daisy. She seemed to be in a great hurry now we were out of the big warehouse. I managed to keep up with her but it was quite difficult and I rocked a bit from side to side. Mummy didn't notice though and we were soon back at home. Mummy almost ran into the house and I was left in the car. I managed to get myself out without any help so that was good, but I don't know why Mummy was in such a hurry. Perhaps she needed the toilet. It was such a lovely trip with Mummy, Charlie. I wonder if we will do it again.

Annie was glowing when she came in. Her mother had rushed in before her and, just for a moment, I thought she had forgotten her daughter. Annie was so proud when she showed me the coverings for the riding hats and her back protector. I noted that she had chosen a cover for Daisy's hat that was exactly the same as her own. I expect it is all about little girls bonding and I'm so pleased that she thought of her friend. I'm looking forward to Cristabel and my trip to the riding stables this week. Now the evenings are so much lighter it seems as if the atmosphere is also of a more relaxed quality. Certainly, Cristabel and my trip out passes much too quickly and I find I'm getting almost obsessed by everything that surrounds the stables. There seems to be so much happening but nothing is measurable in the accepted form. There are no sudden achievements, no shouts of targets that have been met, or unrealistic stages to be mastered and very little conversation. It's all very strange and magical. There! I've admitted it. There is something almost surreal in the environment at the stables and I'm only just beginning to get adjusted to it with an increasing willingness. Watching Cristabel and the transformation of her facial expression as we approach the stables warms my heart. I hope I will be able to watch closely again this week.

Mummy and Charlie are so lucky. They are going to the stables this evening again. I wish I could go too but Mummy says that it is going to be a surprise for Daddy as he doesn't know that she loves horses. I think he might have noticed when he came with us the first time and Mummy disappeared to feed one of the big horses in the stables. I don't think my daddy misses much but he won't say anything as it might spoil the surprise. I wonder what Mummy will do. Perhaps she'll come galloping round a corner and jump a massive jump in the top field. She will look very smart in her riding gear. I wish I could watch her with Charlie. It was good in the pool tonight and my teacher says that it is nearly time for me to try and get another certificate. It was a really busy day at school as well as I had to stay later to practise the songs for 'Joseph'. I saw Charlie and Robert peeping through the windows of the hall. I love singing so much as it makes me feel loose. I mean all my body goes soft and it stops wobbling. Do you know what I mean, Charlie? Will you tell me how you and Mummy get on tomorrow night when you get back from the stables? I promise I won't say anything in front of Daddy.

Cristabel and I were very quiet again on the way to the stables. I decided not to initiate any conversation as it was obvious that Cristabel was in a world of her own. It was a comfortable silence, but one that was overflowing with our own individual thoughts. As soon as we arrived Cristabel turned and thanked me for accompanying her and said it helped a great deal to know that I was there with her. I didn't really understand why she said that but there was no time to probe further. I followed her to the stables and tried to keep in the background. She walked purposefully towards the stable where I know the massive horse, Pablo, she had been working with was waiting. Tommy was outside with the grooming kit in his hands. Nothing was said that I could hear but Cristabel immediately entered the stable and I could hear a low murmuring. In a few minutes out she came leading Pablo. Tommy walked towards the top field and I waited a few moments before following them. I tried to appear invisible as I stood hovering almost behind a bush. I must have looked pretty ridiculous. I certainly felt superfluous and awkward and, if I hadn't had my capacious handbag to fiddle with, even more gauche. In the field there were squares of poles. The poles were placed so that they formed squares of about four metres along each side, making a large and empty area of grass in the middle of each. It looked very confusing as it was totally different from last week. Tommy led Pablo into the middle of one of the squares and I just managed to hear him tell Cristabel to stand in the middle of the square next to him and think about the birth of Annie. I was horrified and thought Cristabel would run away but she didn't. She just stood, frozen to the spot with her head down, just like before. It seemed that many minutes passed before there was a slow movement from Pablo. He, so, so slowly lifted his hooves out of his square and joined Cristabel in hers. It was an amazing moment and my eyes were full of tears, for reasons that I couldn't immediately understand. Tommy was watching and immovable like me. Pablo lowered his head onto Cristabel's arm and she stroked him very slowly and gently. It appeared as if she was supporting Pablo's head with her other arm. They stayed like that for what seemed ages, until Tommy quietly approached them and whispered something to Cristabel. I noticed that she nodded and Tommy pointed to the stables. As Cristabel passed me I noticed her wet cheeks so I knew something important had happened to her as well. When she returned she had her riding gear on. Pablo was waiting for her, standing still as Tommy gave her a leg up. I never would have imagined this event happening until recently. Up she went, sitting upright as if she had spent her life on a huge horse, with a rather ridiculous grin now on her face. She walked around the field perfectly balanced, confident and secure. If this wasn't life-changing for her I would eat all the hay on the stables and her very smart boots as well. I noticed Tommy watching her closely. After a while he helped her down and I was too far away to hear what was being said. They seemed to be speaking about something very important as they were both so engrossed that they didn't notice me waiting and passed by me without any comment. I gave Pablo some carrots after I was sure the conversation was over between Tommy and Cristabel. The horse was so beautiful that I could understand how little girls especially loved to be in their company. I was jealous of Cristabel and felt very slightly ashamed. Tommy came over to me and asked if I would like to have a turn the following week. Then I knew that Cristabel had said something to him perhaps about the sadness in my life. When I answered that I would love to actually learn to ride he laughed and said that was what he meant. Cristabel told me in the car that she had mentioned to him that it wasn't fair that she was the one having all the fun and that she thought I'd get a lot from working with one of the horses. She obviously hadn't mentioned my sadness over losing Lily but I had a feeling that Tommy had noticed something about me that gave him a reason to suggest I could benefit from some sort of connection with a horse. It all seemed very confusing, but I felt as if there was a definite reason behind everything that was happening.

On the way home Cristabel suddenly cancelled the silence between us as if an immovable barrier had magically dissolved. She said that Pablo was going to help her overcome her alcoholism. Of course, she explained, that once an alcoholic, always an alcoholic. I kept quiet. She filled the expectant air between us by telling me that there are ways in which horses can sympathise with the troubled emotions of people and actually give some positive support. I still said nothing but, by her rare expressions of enthusiasm, was convinced. Anyway, I had so much respect for Tommy that I instantly believed every word. I wanted to know more of the actual evidence on which it was based, but having seen the effect Pablo was having on her, thought intense questioning was pointless. She asked if I would go to buy some riding gear with her as she wanted to repay me for all I had done. Now, it was impossible for me to answer as my throat had closed up with amazement. This lady, of incredible privilege, was asking if *she* could do something for *me*. Me, as an individual and seemingly a friend as well as an employee; it had never happened before, at least not in such a direct and unusual way. It was totally detached from anything in the home environment; something just involving the two of us. I smiled my acquiescence but was still unable to say any words. Just before we arrived home, I managed a quiet couple of words of thanks. She asked me if I would go to buy some riding gear on the Monday morning. She was going to take the morning off.

When I had got back from taking Annie to school, we could disappear for a couple of hours then. She was like a child as she spoke; looking pleased and shifty, as if planning something secret, which of course it was. So it came to pass and we contrived to buy me all the clothing I would need for this illegal escapade, for that it what it felt like, and I was more than the willing accomplice. As we started out on our mission, it was the first time that I can remember feeling on the same wavelength as my employer. We chatted amicably, like two old friends. It was

296

bizarre in the extreme. We were both relaxed; perhaps partially acting at this point, as it felt so unusual for me to be in such close proximity with Cristabel. The riding kit was purchased, paid for by Cristabel, even though I protested vigorously. I didn't continue protesting as there wasn't much point. Having an abundance of money meant the buying of a few items of obviously expensive clothing didn't mean anything to her. It was the fact that it was all on her direction that made it so incredibly touching to me. I knew her difficulties. I had watched them from the time of Annie's birth. I knew about the bottle of vodka hidden in her bag in the maternity wing. I had seen and dealt with the problems during and after Annie's birth. For the last nine years I was the one person that knew about the depths to which she descended. Now she was trying to help me. It was a situation that was almost too complicated to accept. But, accept it I would.

Charlie was very quiet when she collected me from school tonight. Yes, you were Charlie. It was unusual as you normally ask me all sorts of questions about my day. Well, I know you and Mummy are up to something. Last night there was something else that happened but I didn't mean to listen. I heard Daddy asking Mummy if she could remember her Grandparents. Then there was a long, long silence. I knew I shouldn't have gone on listening but I did. Don't tell me off, Charlie. Well, Mummy said something very strange. She said that she had never met them. Do you think it was because they were dead or something? Then Daddy said that he only remembered meeting his Grandparents once and he had to be very quiet and good and not say anything because they didn't really like children. I don't think *my* grandmother likes children and I know she is ill but I don't think she would like children even if she was well because she has never bothered to meet me and I know my cousins never see her either. I think Gramps is different and if he had married somebody else perhaps our family would be more friendly to each other. Daddy said to Mummy that it was important that we make sure that I keep up a good relat... relation... with Gramps. What's the word I'm looking for Charlie? Thank you. Relationship. Yes, that was it. I think it means that you look after people that are in your family especially carefully and see them often. It's like Liam and me. We can't have a relationship now because we never see each other and I miss him. I keep hoping I'll bump into him one day when I'm out shopping but I hardly ever go, so that's not going to happen. In a few years I'll be almost a grown up and perhaps I'll meet him then but he won't recognise me will he but he might notice my funny walk if it hasn't got better by then.

There are so many things to think about at the moment that I could do without Annie getting all philosophical on me! We heard tonight that Grandmother has taken a turn for the worse suddenly and now we have to make her top priority which I feel somewhat resentful over. I know that appears uncaring but I find it almost impossible to drag up any feelings for her at all, pleasant or otherwise. I feel a certain amount of pity for her but it ends there. Bob wonders what I would have turned out like if I had been so emotionally neglected. He has a point.

I heard Mummy and Daddy talking about their grandparents. I was standing by my bedroom door and they didn't see me. I kept very still because I don't often hear them talking to each other. It's called overdropping or something like that isn't it Charlie? It was very interesting because mummy said that she had only met her grandparents once and then Daddy said that he didn't do much better. Then, Charlie they started to talk about you and your mother and father and how Robert sees them often and has fun with them. Then, something very unusual happened. Daddy went over to Mummy and gave her a cuddle. I came out of my room then because they could have seen me. Mummy was smiling and Daddy opened his arms for me to get into the cuddle as well. I felt so happy. There we were, just the three of us all huddled together. It seemed to last forever until Mummy said it was time for my swimming lesson. I saw Daddy giving her a very kind look. Then I went for my swimming lesson that I have by myself during the week. On Saturday I think I might tell Daisy about what happened, but I might not. I might keep it a very special secret. Grandmother is very ill. We have to go and see her tonight and I have to go as well. I really don't want to but Daddy says that she might die soon so I must say goodbye to her. I asked Daddy that if I say goodbye to her tonight do I have to go and see her again. I think that might have been unkind of me as Daddy gave me one of his serious looks that I don't see very often. Then he gave me a cuddle and told me I was being very sensible and honest but sometimes we have to do things that we don't want. I understood that and felt very pleased that he talked to me as if I was nearly a grownup. I hope she doesn't die before my riding lesson on Saturday.

I nearly laughed out loud at that last remark but managed to control it. I am desperate to go to the stables with Cristabel tomorrow night and am wishing the grandmother's imminent death could be postponed until after that too so I'm just as guilty of unacceptable behaviour. I have a feeling that she will hang on a bit longer but, when she does die, it will be at the most inconvenient time for everyone. There! That's off my chest. Tomorrow night is the next riding lesson for Cristabel and I have to take my riding stuff as well. I have mentioned it all to Bob and he has seemed fairly detached with the comment that he is sure I know what I'm doing. That's a joke; all I know is that it is something that I am meant to do. I will be interested to see what the next stage of Tommy's 'treatment' for Cristabel will be. Can it be called that? It is more like a therapy. When I watch Cristabel's reactions I know something life-changing is occurring. All my riding gear is on the spare room bed waiting. There is an immense air of expectancy surrounding it.

Chapter Twelve

I can only write a little bit tonight because we had a long rehearsal at school for 'Joseph'. It is such beautiful music that I'm carried along by it. The words are difficult though, especially the long list of the names of Joseph's brothers and the colours of Joseph's coat. If I keep singing it, it helps to get it in the right order. Mummy is buying me the D.V.D.

Annie was very tired indeed last night and I hope the show isn't going to be too much for her. I'm off to the stables with Cristabel in a minute and we are both in a bit of a tizzy. I will continue this when I get home. Bob will have put Robert to bed and he is going to see his Mum and Dad so I'll have a couple of hours to put down what we got up to with Tommy.

Tommy was waiting for us and I felt extremely self-conscious in the riding gear. However, Cristabel was the first to gather her wits and collect two grooming kits, passing one to me. Tommy walked with us to the stables where Pablo and another horse, that looked too big for me, were standing still and watching us approach. It was as if they were waiting for us. Tommy told Cristabel that she could manage it on her own and he showed me what to do in the adjacent stable. It felt so comfortable, with the smell of the straw and even the poo. I took to it as a duck to water and he disappeared to see what Cristabel was doing. There were open windows between the stables so I could hear what was being said. Voices were very low and relaxed, Pablo puffing out of his nostrils every so often; I expect this was with pleasure at the expert grooming that he was being given. My horse was also very still and patient. I talked to her all the time and she bent her head round to look at me when I was brushing her sides. She was called Alana and some other names but I couldn't pronounce them. Tommy said that she knew her first name and that it was what she responded to. He told me he would take Cristabel and Pablo out into the field to do some work and he put a leading rope on my horse and told me to walk gently by her head and follow us to the field. I was quite proud of myself that I remembered the rope was called a leading rope and, after a few minutes, I followed them up to the field. Tommy came over and tied Alana up to a bar of the fence so she could eat some grass. He didn't say anything else to me. Then I saw what he had done in the field. There were the poles again but this time they were right up at the end of the field in the distance. They were parallel to each other, very closely positioned. I couldn't see how a horse could walk between them, let alone a person, if that was what was intended. At first, Cristabel didn't do anything and Pablo walked away from her up to the top of the field. Tommy said something to Cristabel and she followed Pablo up to the poles. Then Pablo, very slowly and carefully, walked between them and stopped at the end. He seemed to be waiting. Slowly and very, very carefully Cristabel walked between the poles and reached Pablo. He, again, lowered his head onto her arm and she stood immobile gently stroking the side of his face. I noticed that she was talking to him but couldn't hear what was said. It was a very private time so I looked at Tommy to see his reaction and he had the familiar beam on his face. He told me to wait where I was for a minute and he went into the field and up to where Cristabel and Pablo were. After a moment she got on Pablo and came trotting down to where Alana and I were waiting. There was the smile again.

Why is it that horses and some people have such a connection? Cristabel was told to take Pablo out of the field and off for a short ride around the farm. Tommy said,' His saddle is ready in the stable. I'm sure you can manage it. Don't worry, he knows where to take you,' and I was left with him on my own. Tommy told me that all his horses and ponies were looked after in a scheme called 'At Liberty'. This means that none of the animals are shod and some of them don't even have a bit in their mouths when they are ridden. Saddles are sometimes dispensed with as well. When he saw my look of amazement he laughed and started to talk to me about Lily. I had forgotten that I had mentioned it to him when he met Robert and I had told him that Robert was adopted. It had seemed easy to tell him about Lily then and now was no different. He walked away from me and put some poles into the square that I remembered him doing for Cristabel. It looked so straightforward. Then he told me to stand in the middle of the square and imagine that the poles represented a bad memory surrounding me. It became clear then when he let Alana into the field and let her free to go where she wanted. At first she ignored me and started to eat the grass, so I stood there thinking about my dear little baby and the intense pain her death had caused. I couldn't look up at all as the poles seemed to imprison me with my thoughts, but then something breathed out right next to me and there was Alana, totally immobile, waiting. I, without realising, leant towards her slightly and she stepped closer, one small step. Again she stood absolutely still. If I couldn't have heard her breathing, I wouldn't have known she was there. Hours seemed to pass, but it was probably only seconds. I felt my spirits lift as if a huge burden of guilt was being carried from me. I lifted my head and slowly put my hand on Alana's neck, then stroked it and, very quietly, murmured to her what I think was a 'thank you'. I felt no embarrassment at all. In fact I felt rather lightheaded and was pleased to see Tommy approaching. He patted Alana and gave me an apple to give her. It is so touching to see how the horses respond to this man. Alana walked as close to him as possible as we approached the gate. Tommy suggested that it would be a good idea if I sat on Alana. He didn't bother getting a saddle but took me to some wooden steps that I went up to be almost level with Alana's back. To just get the feeling of being on a horse's back is important, he told me. I felt extremely high up but absolutely safe. Tommy walked a little way ahead of Alana and she followed, very slowly as if she was aware that a total novice was aboard. Tommy told me how to hold with my legs and he gave me a great clump of Alana's mane to hang on to. I felt as if this horse and I were one. She was walking very calmly and smoothly as if she needed to look after me, which was definitely the case. I wasn't the slightest bit alarmed or anxious and couldn't fathom the reason why. At that moment however, I was completely detached from everything and questioning my innermost feelings was bottom of the list. I was, for the first time for ages, genuinely happy in an uncomplicated way that I had never experienced before. Perhaps I had never given myself time to just be, without questioning. Tommy was watching me, grinning. I caught his look and returned the grin.

He helped me get off, or dismount, I think is the correct term, and told me to lead Alana back to her stable. The whole session took just an hour but it was one that will stay with me forever. When Cristabhel and I met up in the stables, she called over to me to ask me how I'd enjoyed it and I replied that she didn't need to ask. We both laughed and no words were needed. I don't suppose much was said on the way home but, as she dropped me off at my house, we exchanged a look that needed no explanation. We had both experienced something very special and, for the first time, a sincere bond had developed between us as equals. From now on she would never be my employer first. Now we were confidants, our mutual secrets forming a strong connection between us. I couldn't wait for our next lesson. My wish that the grandmother's health didn't deteriorate for some time was impossible to chase away. I found myself thinking that if she could cling on to life for a few more weeks it would be very convenient. I told myself that these unkind thoughts were out of character but I couldn't dredge up any feelings of guilt. I wondered what Cristabel's honest thoughts were about her cold mother-in-law. As she had never experienced any warm, loving adult relationships when she was growing up she would probably think it was to be expected and her thoughts would be unaffected, unlike the malice that was under the surface of my own. My own opinions of Cristabel were mellowing rapidly, and the enthusiasm she showed in getting me to accompany her to Tommy's sessions, made me realise the hidden potential for affection there was hiding under the surface. I felt quite humble and almost ashamed that I hadn't made more attempts to understand just how much she had been damaged during her childhood.

I had judged her, almost against my normal nature, but I think it was caused by her attitude to Annie when she was born. Her desperate need for alcohol in the special care maternity unit made me intolerant. I should have shown more understanding and given her support. Looking back, I remember the desperate expression on her face. She had been through a very difficult birth and didn't know what was happening to her. The fact that she hardly attended any pre-natal appointments and was almost in denial that she was pregnant at all should have rung all the warning bells. The one appointment she did keep was with the obstetrician and by that time it was too late to stop her alcohol intake. We should have intervened earlier, but the whole midwife setup was so understaffed that I'm not exactly sure how we could have managed it adequately. I don't understand why I'm writing all this down now but I think, somehow, it is connected with our sessions at the stables. I feel so free and unfettered, possibly identifying with the horses that are also free. I'm hoping to understand it all more as the sessions continue. I actually hope they never end and I'm grateful that the C.B.'s are loaded with money to avoid my having to feel grateful, which of course I am, but it's not my overwhelming feeling. My main emotion is total pleasure, multiplied by the knowledge that Cristabel is also experiencing something similar and unique.

When Charlie met me from school tonight, she looked different. She laughed a lot and told me that Mummy and her had a very special time with Tommy. I could have told them that. Daisy and me always have a special time with the horses. I think that is what horses are for. They know what people are thinking. Tommy told me that horses are always in the moment but I didn't understand what he meant then, but now I think I do as it means they react to what is happening that very second. By the way, Charlie, can you hear me sing the order of all the colours of Joseph's coat? I don't know why he had to have such a fancy coat. We were told in assembly that Jesus thought that poor people were better than rich people so I don't see why Joseph had to have such a fancy coat. One of our Teaching Assistants is making the coat and we have to bring in any odd bits of material that we can get our Mums to find. It can just be bits of old clothes as long as they are made out of very bright colours. I've got an old blouse that is very bright pink and purple and it is made from a shiny material. I don't like it so I've put it in my school bag ready to take it to school tomorrow. It will be good to see it all cut up into squares. I wonder if Mummy will recognise it as part of Joseph's coat. Joseph's brothers are very jealous of him and try to kill him because he is his father's favourite. He has loads of brothers but no sisters. At the end of the story Joseph tricks them and they are sorry that they were nasty to him. I don't know the whole story yet but my friend Jessica is singing with me in a duet. I love the music so much. My music teacher is getting me some of the songs to play on the piano. At least she can play them to me and I can sing. She says that I can play the right hand and she will play the left hand. I think that's a good idea as I can't do it all together, even if it looks easy. I'm pleased that I can sing as I know I will never be any good at the piano. I can't do any other instrument either because I can't hold on to it. The guitar has a lovely sound but I know I won't be able to do that either. I won't moan about it because there are lots of other things I can do. Daisy and me are writing a story about horses and it is getting very exciting. I'll let you read it before we show it to Mummy and Daddy.

Today is the first time that I've heard Annie sound negative. I knew it was inevitable one day. Hopefully it is a passing phase and she will concentrate on the aspects of her life which are so satisfying and happy. I'm still in a peculiar state of semi-euphoria after the hour at the stables. I keep remembering something that Tommy said. It was almost a throw-away remark but I definitely heard him say, 'Horses are always in the present moment, always forgiving,' before walking away. The air around this man was still and quiet and had an emptiness that was tangible. It was a difficult sensation to explain. It was as if he had some special power over the animals in his care. It was much more than that though. He was father to a child that needed much attention but he didn't seem the slightest bit bothered or worried about her. For her part Daisy was well adjusted and happy, sociable and relaxed when failing to organise herself as she wished. This must be the result of Tommy's attitude and care. Of course her mother must have been of the same outlook. I marvelled at their ability to keep so under control and not appear to worry about anything. The truth of it was that they didn't seem to make any effort at all. Everything came naturally. Did it all have something to do with their contact with horses? Perhaps we have all missed some secret ingredient about special sympathies with animals but, for some reason that I don't understand, horses play a particularly powerful part. I must ask Tommy if his wife has always been involved with horses. I assumed she was but I need to ask him as she has never been out to the stables when we have been there for our lessons. There are several nagging questions pecking at my brain. The more I think about what is evolving, the more eager I am to learn more. I mentioned it all to Bob and he said that in World War 1 there were many special relationships formed between horse and rider. He went to see the film 'War Horse' with his parents. I remember that he was very quiet when he got back home. I think Cristabel and I should go to see it. It is all a wonderful learning experience for me but I fear the learning curve is vertical. I wish we could go to the stables every night and I suspect Cristabel feels the same.

I can sing all the right sequences of the colours of Joseph's coat and also all the names of his brothers. I expect he would have liked a sister. Charlie and Mummy are having a lovely time at the stables. I'm very jealous but I know that I have to keep the secret. When Mummy comes home afterwards she always comes up to my bedroom and kisses me goodnight. This is a new thing and I like it very much because she doesn't seem to be in a hurry to get downstairs like before. She even sat on the side of the bed, next to me and looked very hard at me. I felt a bit worried because she didn't look very happy but then she suddenly smiled and gave me a great big kiss and told me she loved me. I said it back to her and it felt very unusual as we have never, ever, said it to each other before. I have heard Charlie say it to Robert, haven't I Charlie, but Mummy has never said it to me. I haven't really thought about it a lot until now. I hope Mummy says it again as it made me feel all warm. I don't expect Liam's mummy ever told him she loved him. That's why he had to be taken away isn't it? Are you listening, Charlie? You seem very far away. Mummy has gone to see Grandmother. I don't have to go and I'm pleased because I think she is a cruel person. She never says anything nice to Mummy and she sent Daddy away to school when he was only six. Don't you think that's cruel, Charlie? You are writing this down for me but you are looking as if you are miles away. Can you hear me sing tomorrow, on the way to school? Robert is getting very clever because I noticed that he is trying to say the colour words with me. He even manages to say some in the right order.

Yes. I have been miles away. Coming down to earth after the last riding session was almost impossible. I understand a little now why some people need a God. It creates a support system that is unquestioning. I prefer to use something more tangible and preferably on four legs. I noticed that there was one of Annie's pretty blouses in her school bag. I didn't say anything as it is none of my business but I bet I'll see bits of it in the impending multi coloured coat of Josephs. I'm really looking forward to the show and we have already bought five tickets as Bob wants to come and Herta has offered to babysit Robert. I know Charles and Cristabel are anticipating something special as well. I'm amazed that they haven't started to make comments about Annie's future education. It is a constant worry to me that they might transfer her to a private school where she would not have the support she has now. I think they know my opinion about private education and how divisive it is, but mainly that Annie's needs wouldn't be met and she might be made to feel inadequate in that environment, surrounded by equally prosperous family offspring. All children can be cruel but I think being surrounded by a cross section of children is less of a challenge to her. She is certainly very happy at the present school, so why change. A change would be for all the wrong reasons, I think. It is a good job that these are my private thoughts. The best thing about this time is the, almost accidental, smiles that I catch on Cristabel's face.

It was good fun at school today. I helped to hold the material that I had brought in and Miss said that it was absolutely perfect as it was the brightest colour she had ever seen. That is the reason that I will never wear it. Miss cut it up into lots of squares and Jessica was very good at cutting too. I can't cut things. The scissors seem to be alive and dance around just to tease me. Miss told me to put all the squares into piles. Tom had brought in one of his Daddy's shirts which he said reminded him of sick. He made me laugh but Miss showed him what size squares to cut out and he was very good at it too. I think I'm the only person in the class that can't cut out. Miss saw me looking sad, I think, and said that I was one of the best singers in the school and that nobody was good at absolutely everything so I was to smile and be happy.

There is a boy in Mrs. Smith's class, in Year Three and he is in a wheelchair all the time. He can't feed himself at lunchtime and he has a special helper. He has one of the new computers and his stories are brilliant. Mrs. Smith read one out to the whole school at assembly. It was all about the solar system and all the planets and how many moons they each have. He'd made up a story about strange little men that lived on Jupiter that had three heads. One head was for seeing, one for hearing and one for speaking. Apparently none of the heads had mouths so I don't expect they could eat. They spoke out of some thin wires that grew out of the sides of the heads. There were no ears, but bright red flaps that waved about picking up any sounds. I could imagine exactly what they looked like and Mrs. Smith said he had a brilliant store of ideas and that he must write all of them down and the school would make them into a book.

Tomorrow, after school, there is a rehearsal for 'Joseph'. Miss says that she will be sewing the coat tonight on her machine and so he can try it on. She must be very clever to be able to sew all the squares together. I will see where my blouse bits will end up. I expect she will have to stay up all night to finish it. The boy playing the part of Joseph is called Christopher and he is in the top class. He is going to the Community College in September. He sings very beautifully and doesn't seem to get nervous at all. His Dad is a music teacher so I expect they do lots of practising together. There is one scene that Jessica and me sing a duet and we are the only two on the stage, apart from Joseph and he is in prison. We have to sing to him and he sings all by himself afterwards as Jessica and me go off. We sing sitting down on a golden board and we are slid off at the end with us sitting on it, because I might not be able to get up in time. The board has thick golden ropes tied to the ends and Tom's Dad has put wheels underneath so it is easy to pull us off the stage. It was very funny the first time we used it because Jessica and me nearly fell off. Now we hold on to each other and try not to laugh. Miss says if we fall off it will turn the show into a comedy. I think there are some very funny bits in it anyway. There are some camels in it that Mrs. Smith made and they are so fluffy that it makes the boys that are inside them sneeze. Some of the camels have boys in them that are so funny as Miss has taught them how to do silly walks. They have to prance about to the song we are singing. I'm not going to tell you any more about it. Tom's Dad is making a DVD of it so we can watch it at home but I'm not sure I want to see myself.

Early this morning we had a 'phone call to tell us that Grandmother had passed away in the night. I'm not sure if it's good timing or not but, when I heard Cristabel's voice on the other end of the line, I hardly recognised it. It sounded crumbly and distant as if she was holding the 'phone a long way from her. Perhaps she has never had to deal with this sort of thing before. I asked her how Charles was and she replied,' Well, you know Charles. He copes in most situations.' I couldn't work out if she was being sarcastic or whether she was genuinely replying automatically, and perhaps kindly. Her voice sounded so unusually constrained. Then she appeared to collect herself and asked if I could come in to work a bit earlier as she wanted to talk to me about arrangements. She really hadn't a clue as to what was expected and this knowledge came to me like a bolt. This lady had no experience of dealing with death, unlike me. The difference being that my loss was of a depth unimaginably painful. That of Cristabel and Charles' was a reaction to the death of almost a stranger. Wanting me to get to her house earlier than usual was difficult but, with Bob's help, we managed it, albeit with rather a great deal of huffing and puffing. As Annie and Robert had their breakfast together, Cristabel, unusually pale and disorientated, asked me to go into the study with her. As she closed the door she shredded into a mass of sobbing. I put my arms around her and tried to reassure her as to what was expected. She gulped, 'It's not that. We had to go to the Nursing Home and she was already dead and I have never seen a dead person and it was awful. She looked like she was asleep but when Charles lifted her thin, withered arm up he dropped it and it twisted out of his hand and fell back onto the bed with a horrible clicking noise.

It landed facing upwards like a frozen claw. The nails were bright red like pools of blood coming out of her stiff fingers. It freaked me out but I couldn't do or say anything. I seemed to be rooted to the spot. When we got home I drank a whole bottle of wine, straight off, infront of Charles. He just stared at me for ages, then came over to me and carried me up to bed. Now, I feel so ashamed. I know I should be strong for him but I can't, not yet. Do you think we can go to see Tommy for an extra session?'

After that lengthy speech, I had no choice and, as soon as I got back from taking Annie to school, I telephoned Tommy and briefly explained the situation. Of course I didn't need any extra words. He immediately told me to come over that evening. Charles was still at home so I asked him if he could see to Annie's needs that evening. I received a slightly querying look but an, 'Of course,' followed. Bob was in charge of Robert so that was all arranged. All I had to do was collect Annie after her rehearsal. Charles had already told her about her Grandmother's death. I would have liked to know about her reaction to the news but thought it better not to ask. She didn't seem to be anything but her usual self as we went to school. She chatted away about 'Joseph' and I was grateful for the distraction. Charles had already told me that Annie wouldn't be going to the funeral, which was after the final performance of 'Joseph'. My reaction to this news was ambivalent. Would it not be better for her to learn what actually happens at a funeral, even if there had not been any emotional attachment? It wasn't my decision, so I tried to stop thinking about it. Almost simultaneously, I knew that the reason for our trip to the stables was of a therapeutic nature. Cristabel had an almost uncontrollable need to be with Pablo. If I am totally honest, I am indifferent, emotionally, to the death of this grandmother. The only pain I experience is the connection it brings to the death of Lily and I was just managing to come to terms with it. 'Coming to terms with it' – in itself a phrase impossible to define. Does it mean to accept something rationally, coldly and unemotionally? No, I must think about Cristabel and be grateful that she trusted me enough to admit to her bout of binge drinking. In a perverse way it was a good thing as she has obviously cut down dramatically otherwise why would she feel so ashamed of herself at the lapse.

Now I must get everything ready for our stable outing tonight without Charles suspecting anything untoward is happening. He does know there are subtle changes evolving around his wife. It is just such bloody bad timing that his mother popped her clogs at this time. If that sounds disrespectful, then so be it. I don't know what respect is anyway, only that it has to be earned and Grandmother certainly didn't earn any from this quarter. I will keep quiet and the cork must be tightly wedged into this bottle of opinions.

The C.B's have a couple of weeks to get the funeral arrangements confirmed. One good thing is that Annie might meet her cousins and their parents at some time. She won't be writing in her diary tonight so I will continue this when we get back. I know, for some reason, that it is imperative to write everything down that is going to happen. It's almost like being in a dream, surrounded by imaginary people. The knowledge that everything is going to evolve in a disconnected and surreal atmosphere, has given me unexpected thoughts that appear like darts attacking my head. How unusual it is not to have any power over one's feelings. A certain detachment is rather pleasant to have imposed on me.

Well, we are going to the stables tonight. Charles is in charge for the evening, a fact that Annie will love. I hope she doesn't spill the beans over where we are going in such a rush. It really is of no importance anyway. I will wait until Annie has written her thoughts down before I record my own after the extra trip to the stables. I think it is probably a good thing that I accompany Cristabel tonight or it might cause suspicion as I'm sure Cristabel has never gone out by herself in the evening. I wonder what she'll tell Charles.

Last night was great fun because Daddy was in charge. He laughed when he told me that he felt important and that I'd better be on my best behaviour. I asked him if he felt sad that his mother had died and he went very quiet and stared at me. I don't think he was being jolly to stop me getting upset but then we had a really good talk. He told me about how he was very unhappy when he was a little boy and that his mother, my Grandmother, didn't see him very often. I asked Daddy why that was and he said that he didn't think Grandmother liked children very much. I said that I agreed with him but that she can't have been a very happy person as most mothers like their children, even when they are naughty. That's what Charlie says anyway. Daddy said that my Grandmother's own mother had somebody else looking after her children as soon as they were born. She was my great grandmother and sounds horrible. As Daddy was telling me about her, I imagined her as an old witch with a black cloak and tight, black lace-up shoes. She was wearing a pointy black witch's hat and she had a pointed nose. She was like the bad owner of the Gingerbread House and I expect she would have cooked Daddy if she hadn't given him to somebody else to look after. I'm glad my Daddy likes me and isn't going to send me away. Daddy said that he regrets that he never sees any of his uncles, aunts or cousins. He told me that I might meet some of my cousins that I haven't met before and that it might seem strange. Daddy doesn't even know how many there are but all the families are being invited to the funeral anyway so we will find out then. Daddy has got special invitations and they have black edges. He has told me about the service and that we will be having a reception in our house afterwards. Some men are coming to talk about something, oh yes, the order of service. Daddy said something in a quiet, mumbly voice but I think it was, 'They'll want to see what's in it for them afterwards, I expect.' It was to do with The Will. What's a 'Will' Charlie? I hope there won't be loads of relations and their children or it will be too confusing. I can't think about it too much because I need to concentrate on the school show. I need to practise some of the songs, especially the duet that Jessica and me are doing. I dream that I'm singing it when I'm asleep and the tune is still going round and round in my head when I wake up. Daddy said that he thought Mummy and you were going to the shops to see about suitable clothes to

318

wear for the funeral. I nearly laughed but I managed to keep the secret. I know that you have been to the stables. It gives me an important feeling that I have been given a secret that I mustn't tell anyone. I think Daddy suspects that Mummy is doing something because he asked me if I'd noticed anything about her. I was very good and just said, 'She is happier at the moment but I'm not sure why.' Then Daddy gave me a very long stare but didn't say anything else, thank goodness. I hope he doesn't smell a rat. I like that expression. We had it in school today. We had to think of all the strange things people say, like 'chin up', and 'best foot forward' and one that I like best which is, ' don't cross your bridges until you come to them'. We had to talk about what they all meant. 'More haste, less speed', was another one that Miss said all the class need to think about. I can't remember any of the others but I wrote them down in my book. It took ages but Miss said that my writing was getting much better. You should see Jessica's writing, Charlie. She does all sorts of curly things on the end of some letters and Miss said it was looking like Chinese. My hands don't tremble quite so much now but I still feel as if everyone is better than me. Well, I know they are all better than me, but it doesn't matter so much now as I can sing better than everyone apart from Jessica. I think Jessica will be surprised when she sees what I can do on Poppy. Perhaps she will be brilliant at that as well. There must be something that she isn't good at. When Mummy came home from the stables she had taken off her riding things so Daddy wouldn't suspect anything. I was very pleased to see her because she looked so happy and her face had a sort of glow on it.

Well, that would describe it perfectly. When we arrived at the stables, Tommy was waiting and told me to go to the farmhouse where his wife would make me a cup of tea. I asked him if I could watch for a bit if I kept out of the way and he agreed. He also whispered, 'She's lucky to have you.' At least I think that is what he said. I went to stand behind a tree after I had given Alana a stroke and a bit of apple. Pablo was standing at the top of the field. He was totally motionless, possibly asleep. I heard Tommy talking to Cristabel and she told me on the way home that she had confessed to drinking a whole bottle of wine after seeing her mother-in-law dead. She also told him about not having any attention as a child and that made her feel cold towards other people. She dried up then but I was amazed that she had managed to use those words to him. Apparently, Tommy told her that she wasn't particularly unusual and that he knew there were things in her life that were too painful to talk about but horses have an uncanny instinct to empathise with humans and can alter their whole outlook and emotional well-being just by being in close proximity with them. Well, Cristabel listened to what Tommy said and then, slowly, walked up to Pablo. She said something to him but I couldn't hear what it was. He lifted his head and looked at her. He didn't move for a minute and neither did Cristabel. Then he slowly walked nearer to her, near enough for her to touch him gently on his neck. Then he appeared to be looking at her intently and she started talking to him. Again, it was obviously very private and Pablo was the consummate listener, hardly moving a muscle. Then, in their private world, he moved closer and again stood very still. Cristabel was wiping her eyes and, even at a distance, I could see she was almost emotionally overcome. I was unable to move, my gaze fixed on what was happening at the top of the field. The two of them stood in a combined and personal space, and some sort of healing was happening. I don't know what else to call it. All I know is that something unique was passing between them and I was a privileged observer.

It's only two more practices before the performance of 'Joseph'. Mummy and Daddy are coming and so is Charlie. Bob is looking after Robert. I know Mummy will look very smart and another word like glammy, oh yes, that's it, glamorous. Daddy always looks very proud of her when she's in her best clothes. Sometimes I think she is happier in other stuff. I think she looks most happy in her jodhpurs. I want to keep all my thoughts in my head about all the things that are happening and then write them all down at the same time. When Grandmother's funeral is over I will feel as if I have been let go. I have to try on my frock for Joseph now. Jessica and me are both wearing the same as Miss says if we look too glamorous people will look at our frocks and not listen properly to our singing. I think I must be growing because the sleeves feel tight and more of my legs show. I can't have grown that much in just a month, can I? Can you loosen it a bit for me, Charlie? Miss said today that my writing with a pen was getting very much better and Jessica better watch out or I would get better than her. Jessica gave me a sort of frown, so I think Miss said the wrong thing. I know that I will never get any good at writing with a pen but I'm getting much faster on the computer. I just wish I could see when I spell a word wrong. Sometimes Miss puts a word spelt wrong next to the same word spelt right and asks me which one is the right one and I stare hard at them both but still can't tell. They seem to have all the same letters and I know they must be different but the more I stare at them, the more muddled they look. I wonder if there is anyone else in the world that has this strange way of seeing things.

Daddy told me that he can't spell and when he was at boarding school one of the masters hit him with a cane because he got all his spellings wrong. I didn't know that teachers were allowed to hit children. I know they never do it at my school. Daddy told me that the teacher that hit him had to leave. He said he was an old fogey anyway and couldn't have taught a fish to swim. I knew what he meant and I felt pleased. Why would anyone want to hit somebody just to get them to do something they find difficult? It would make me so frightened that I would never learn to do anything. I wonder if Mummy had nasty teachers like Daddy had? I don't think I'll ask her. She is smiling more and I don't want that to stop. If I start asking questions it might open up a can of worms. That's what Miss said today when I asked her if she would tell me about her schooldays when she was little. I'm not sure but I think it means you might hear something that you're not supposed to. Now I must sing.

Yes, she must! So much to do and so little time to actually feel as if we have done everything expected. We can only do our best, and I know Annie instinctively understands that is what matters. She looks so charming in her plain little frock, with hairband of flowers; very appropriate for the historical context. Her hair is long and brushed simply. She must remember to take her watch off. Jessica has ear

322

studs which will have to be removed. I don't think they had pierced ears in biblical times, but perhaps they did. Perhaps a little row of pottery beads would be seen as authentic; best to keep it as simple as possible. The note that came home from school just stated the barest minimum; a simple frock down to the ankles, plain with no frills or flounces and a hairband of small flowers, no jewellery or special footwear. Miss was making some special flipflops for footwear out of braid and cardboard. Let's hope some of the more boisterous boys don't wreck them. When I peeped in to one of the rehearsals, I was impressed by the total concentration that the cast were giving to the performance. I know there are at least six boys that could spoil the whole thing with no effort at all but there they were, eyes looking at the conductor, singing their hearts out. So much for my opinion that boys won't or can't sing; an inspirational teacher is all that is apparently needed. I believe that all the children in the school are in the show, even if only as a part of the scenery. It has been made very clear to them all that each and every one of them is important. I am not surprised that Annie wanted Liam to be included. The children all appear to feel needed. I wonder if, for some of them, this event is the only one during which they feel really wanted. Watching some of the children coming out of school, it is noticeable that they have dull expressions on their faces. There is a mini-bus waiting for a group of them and they troop on in a melancholy way, to go to after school care, I suppose. They are probably the same children that come to school early to have breakfast. Will these grow up into the disaffected youth of tomorrow? It makes me admire the work that the school attempts to do with the most deprived group, of which a fair number are from well- heeled middle class families. Emotional deprivation isn't confined to the poorest. I will always take Robert to school and collect him. In years to come if it means Bob and I have to pull our belts in a bit and my hours have to be cut with the C.B.'s then so be it. Nobody else is going to enjoy my child's development, or company and if it means we have to share fish fingers then it won't be the first time. By taking and collecting Annie from school, I have learnt so much by watching children coming out. There are a lot of grandparents picking them up but it is the minibus children that are the most noticeable. I bet, if they were asked, they would all say they would like their mum or dad to pick them up.

There is only a short time left until Annie starts her secondary education. I am dreading it and know that there will be many questions to consider before a final decision is made as to the most suitable placement for her. Now there are other things on which to concentrate and one of them is finding time to have a private conversation with Cristabel which, hopefully, would be a continuation of the one we had before we went to the stables. This morning she seemed to be back to her more cheerful persona, but it could have been an act. Nothing will be written here until after the performance of Joseph. I shall keep everything crossed that Annie will sing like a nightingale and, of course, everyone else will be perfect, but especially Annie. It is so important, at this precise time, for Cristabel and Charles to see the potential of their lovely daughter.

I was so amazed at the performance of Joseph. The audience clapped and clapped for ages. There was a man from the newspaper that took lots of photographs and he wanted one of me and Jessica on our own. I don't know why but I saw him talking to Mummy and Daddy afterwards but they wouldn't tell me what he said. All they said was that the photographer was very impressed with the singing. It was very quiet on the way home and Mummy blew her nose as lot. I hope she wasn't getting a cold. She was smiling so she can't have been crying. Charlie said we were all wonderful and I must be very proud of myself. I think all the school were proud but I just wish that Liam could have been there to see us but really I wish he could have been part of it. I do wonder where he is and what he thinks about. Does he think about his friends at my school or has he made new ones? I hope they are kind to him. I am very tired tonight so I can't write any more. The funeral is in two day's time but I'm not going.

No, she definitely isn't going. Annie's euphoria over the last few weeks mustn't be spoilt. I have come to the conclusion that foisting a funeral service with all the hypocrisy involved would be wrong. I will be in the background, observing and completing my normal routine. The reception back at the C.B.'s will be more than enough to cope with. There is a team of caterers already standing to attention. What a load of nonsense. There is no affection between these people and never has been, but they are going to act out their roles as characters from a closely united unit. They are more like caricatures. It makes me so angry, knowing the damage they have done to each other, generation after generation. I expect they will all be appropriately kitted out in designer black ensembles. Let's hope the veils are thick. I sound so bitter but it is only my resentment over the ridiculousness of it all and the double standards. I think Charles has more than an inkling about the way I feel. I will, however, be interested in the various never seen remnants of this family. Perhaps I'll be pleasantly surprised and there will be a few children at least that appear to be able to behave in a responsive way.

Chapter Thirteen

I'm writing this after Grandmother's funeral. We had lots of stuff to eat afterward and I met some very strange people. I had some cousins that I had never met but they were all looking at their mobile 'phones all the time and two of them had bigger things called tablets. I thought they were things that you took if you were ill. I thought they were very rude and I think Charlie did too. Mummy and Daddy seemed so different from all the other people because they tried to talk to them but nobody seemed to answer properly. Mummy came to talk to me a lot and said she was sorry that my cousins were so rude. That surprised me because Mummy has never really wanted to talk either. We ate lots of food and I watched the adults, in their strange black clothes and hats, stare at all the things in our house. They went from room to room looking at everything. I ran up to my bedroom and locked my door from the outside and hid the key. Not one of my cousins bothered to talk to me. There was a girl, about my age, that stared at me. I went over to her to see if she wanted to come up to my bedroom and play but she turned away from me when I got near to her. Why would she do that, Charlie? I don't understand things at all. Daddy said he would talk to me after they had all gone. I saw him speaking to one of the grownups. They were both very serious and glum. Daddy kept trying to move away but the other man kept following him. Gramps was lovely and rescued Daddy from him. Everything seemed to go on forever and all I wanted to do was play the piano or go for a swim. After ages and ages, they all went away. Mummy laughed when I told her I'd locked the door. We sat on my bed and Mummy tried to be very nice to me. I think she was ashamed of her relatives, actually they are mine as well but they don't seem like it. She read lots of books with me and when I asked her why my cousins spent the whole time on their mobile 'phones or the other things she said it was because they didn't know any better and I wasn't going to have one until at least the time when I went to senior school. I don't want one anyway. All my best friends don't bother with things like that. We prefer to talk to ponies and people, don't we Charlie?

Annie is developing some seriously interesting opinions about people which I find fascinating. She has been affected by the way her relatives ignored her and, luckily, is condemning in her attitude towards them. She hasn't, as yet, realised that it might be connected to her awkward way of moving around. To them it is not acceptable to be seen as anything but perfect. What they don't realise is that this little girl has more potential in her little finger than all of them put together and it won't be too long before she will show the world. That is my wish for the future. I know in my bones that something special will happen. I just wish I could have a very small clue as to what it is going to be. My overriding impression of the ghastly people at the reception was of immobile people, dressed in black, standing around staring at all the opulence. Not one of them had the ability to speak. Or so it seemed. The occasional squeezed mouth squirted a phrase out but it was as if they were puppets, nailed to the floor and could only move if someone pulled their strings. I studied all their mouths. With no exception they were small, tight lines rigid with boredom. The only time they moved was to place minute pieces of canapés into the tiny, waiting gap. What was so ridiculous was how they all resembled each other to such an extent that they were almost carbon copies. Even the children were miniature of the adults, self absorbed and disconnected from the present. Why the hell were they all there? Obviously they were expecting something out of the Will. I did so hope that Gramps had been brave enough to guarantee these parasites received nothing. I wonder if there had been time for him to update his Will? I did notice him talking to Charles one evening and the next day disappearing with him up to London for the day. The thought of Annie's absent family reaping any benefit from Grandmother's death was repulsive. I am fully aware that it is nothing whatever to do with me but I've been a member of this family for so long that I feel protective, probably overly so. Since the death of Lily, I suppose I've been anticipating another approaching trauma. Being so busy is a bonus as there is precious little time for brooding.

Cristabel and I need to visit the horses again very soon. I find I am developing an increasing need but can't think of a logical reason for it. Tommy possesses a specific ability, a gift really, that enables him to understand with few words what a person's problem might be. I almost envy his wife. Surely, when Daisy was born and he was told of her disabilities, he must have felt intense pain. It seems incredible to me when I see him with his wife, that they are so accepting and don't seem to pay any extra attention to her. Perhaps that is the secret of life; acceptance and lots of love towards whatever it throws at you. It would be interesting to hear what his own thoughts are in respect of little Daisy, who, in my opinion, is at a far greater disadvantage than Annie due to her greater physical difficulties. I have a sudden thought attacking me that I'm totally wrong in every respect. Now it's time to hide my part of this history away.

It's Saturday tomorrow and Daisy and me are going riding in the morning and then she is coming to my house to swim and then she is staying for a sleepover. Daddy says that he never had anything like that when he was a child and he suspects that we won't get to sleep until after midnight. We are going to be allowed to take food up to our bedroom and Mummy said it is called a midnight feast, so we had better eat it before then. I'm pleased that Daisy is allowed to come as it means we can get on with our story. We are up to page seven now and Chapter Three. Charlie knows it is a secret and isn't allowed to see it until it's finished, are you? I know the spelling is rubbish but we keep looking words up but it gets very boring and stops me thinking of things to write. It seems a bit like putting the brakes on when I'm free-wheeling downhill. I am better on a pony. I wonder what it's like to gallop? I have a picture in my head of Daisy and me on a sandy beach galloping side by side along the edge of the water and everyone is watching us. In my picture, our hair is stretching out behind us, actually much longer than it really is. We are riding horses not ponies. How old do you have to be before you can ride a horse, not a pony? I expect Tommy will let us when we are bigger and better riders but Daisy is much better than me anyway and she still is on a pony. I want to talk to Mummy about her riding lessons soon. I sense that she will talk to me when she's ready. I know she trusts Tommy to teach her to remember all the things she learnt when she was small. I wish I knew all about the things Mummy did when she was little but I don't think she wants to tell me until I'm older. There are so many things that she is going to tell me then. I expect it will take days and days.

It is rather good having Gramps staying with us and I suspect it will turn into a permanent arrangement. He has perked up no end since the funeral and Charles has been taking him into work with him some days. Cristabel seems to get on with him also and I've seen her watching Charles and him chatting together. I'd love to know what was going on in her head. Well, tonight is our riding evening and time is dragging deliberately slowly. We are both like schoolchildren off on a special school trip. Cristabel is getting home early from work again. I have never been as well organised as on our riding lesson days. Necessity, I suppose or perhaps desperation to make the time go quickly and push away any thoughts of obstacles. I know Cristabel's needs are greater than mine but I feel mine are increasing rapidly.

At school today Miss asked us to talk about the best thing in our week. I told everyone about my riding lessons and I noticed that Miss gave a couple of nods to my helper. I wonder why she did that? I told the children about all the different smells and all the jobs I had to do around the stables. Jessica put her hand up and told everyone about the galloping she has been doing. When she was talking I had a nasty feeling about her because I think she was showing off. I don't think I want to ride with her. She will make me feel I am a bad rider. Tommy says that the best riders always take their time to get to know the pony and they never, ever, use a whip. I know that Jessica had a whip for a Christmas present. I'm trying to remember the name that Tommy looks after his horses and Charlie has just told me but she says she doesn't really understand it properly. It's called keeping horses 'At Liberty'. I really love those words. I think it must be why all his horses and ponies are so happy and quiet. Mummy says that they can understand people and their feelings but it has to be at the actual time they are together, not later. I know Poppy remembers me as soon as I go near her because she whinnies.

The only way I can describe this evening is magical. In the last few days my emotions feel as if they have been shredded, and then repaired. I think I'm getting as much from our contact with horses as Cristabel and Annie; something I never imagined I would ever think. Of course Tommy is the catalyst. Tonight he made Cristabel stand in the far corner of the field. I heard him tell her to think about her worst fears. I saw her face cloud over and she stood very still for at least a minute, then she slowly walked up to the top of the field and stood, immobile, in the corner, facing away from everything. I began to have the tiniest sliver of understanding of what Tommy was doing. I stood, transfixed as Tommy led Pablo through the gate. He ignored Cristabel completely which was unexpected. Then, she turned and started to walk slowly towards him. He lifted his head and moved smoothly towards her, stopping when he was within touching distance. There they both stood, in their own bubble, neither moving now but with such an obvious contact that nobody would dare to interrupt. Cristabel put her hand out eventually and touched Pablo's head. He seemed to sway slightly from side to side as she caressed him. Tommy, during all this time, was observing silently.

Eventually, it was my turn. Tommy had put some poles out in the bottom field and I had to first groom Alana and then tack her up and lead her to the field. I had to step over the poles thinking of Lily. Tommy had told me that I didn't have to do it until I was ready, but I knew the time was right. As I stepped over the parallel poles I remembered the intense pain I had felt when my little baby had died of meningitis. It was almost unbearable to bring back all the unhappiness but I knew I must try to come to terms with my grief in a more complete way. In the back of my mind was the memory of Cristabel's little baby, who she couldn't even be bothered to name. The baby, whom I have helped to nurture for the last nine years; the baby that had been damaged by the mother's selfishness and my baby that I had lost through no fault of my own. As I stepped over the poles slowly, one by one, I knew my head was full of vicious resentment. It became almost unbearable and I was on the point of returning to the gate when there was some presence next to me and Alana was there nudging against me. She had stepped over the poles and followed me without my noticing her. I stroked her neck and it was as if something fluid was being poured into me, down my shoulders and filling my whole body with a calmness that I haven't ever felt since Lily died. I was unable to move for a few minutes. Actually, I didn't want to move ever again, but eventually I noticed that Cristabel was at the bottom of the field watching, seated on Pablo. She called out to me to get ready to go for a ride. I didn't know how long we had been in the field but I did as instructed and led Alana back to the stable to get ready. I was clumsy and uncoordinated I know and probably looked like a sack of potatoes on Alana but I knew it didn't matter one jot. We walked the horses round the field together. I noticed Tommy watching from a safe distance with a massive grim on his face. When we had finished our little outing, he came across to us and said, 'Well done, you two,' in a teasing sort of voice which made us all laugh. I know I have never felt so happy and relieved at that point in my life and would never be able to explain why. Tommy was talking to Cristabel before we left and I was wondering what he was saying to her that was so obviously private when she turned to me and said, 'Tommy wants to train Annie and Daisy for the Paralympics.' It wouldn't be for another eight years at least and it would all depend on the whole family's commitment. She said she had never thought about anything like that for her daughter but then, with the biggest smile I have ever seen said,' Whatever you think best for her will be wonderful, I'm sure.' Now, that was really amazing as Cristabel's experience of giving compliments is not very well developed. We drove home in virtual silence, but of the type that is completely comfortable. I think we probably both had silly smiles on our faces. When she dropped me at my house, she touched me on the arm and gave me a fragment of a squeeze. She didn't have to say anything at all and neither did I. Bob kept giving me funny looks all evening so I told him about the experience we'd had at the stables and the incredible effect Tommy had on us both. He is such a good listener and seemed genuinely interested. He'd bought a 'Horse and Pony' magazine when he realised that I was serious about going riding with Cristabel and there had been an article in there about the healing effects of being in contact with horses. It seemed to be a ridiculous coincidence but there had been a programme on the television about naughty children that had been expelled from school. One of the boys had been taken to some stables and his reaction when in contact with horses had as great an impact as Cristabel's and my own. He had been diagnosed with ADHD but where did this hyperactivity disappear to when he was with a horse? The boy was calm and controlled. He had a permanent smile on his face. Perhaps all 'naughty' children should be re-diagnosed and their doses of Ritalin abandoned, substituted by riding lessons. It would save the National Health a packet and possibly make the experts reconsider their diagnosis. I laughed as I had these thoughts but, when I told Bob, he agreed. He said that he has always thought that being in contact with animals and out in the open air was very therapeutic for almost anything. I asked him what he thought about Tommy and training his daughter and Annie for the Paralympics in the distant future. He thought it was a brilliant idea but was slightly worried that it might mean I would become even more involved and that it would mean less time I could spend with him and Robert. I assured him that I would be especially careful not to overdo the 'horse' time. I knew Robert would want to come to all that was going on anyway and I determined to gently persuade Bob to increase his interest also. All the grandparents too, I thought as my imagination was getting carried away with the euphoria I felt. For the first time for as long as I can remember, I felt a total happiness, as if the memory of Lily was shut away in a corner in a tiny protected carapace, one that would always be there but with a soft barrier of perpetual love not needing my continuous thought. This was also the first time that I had managed to use words to my husband, Bob, without accompanying them with floods of tears. Gratitude is a weird emotion and I knew it was owed to Tommy and Bob but the words I needed to express it were still underdeveloped. Saying, 'thank you,' was transitory and inadequate. I went over to where Bob was sitting and put my arms around him. He held me tight and we stayed there for several minutes before he said, 'Well, if going to the stables results in this show of affection, you can go and move in.' He roared with laughter and I loved him so much at that point that it almost hurt.

Being so happy is something that will worry me as there must be a down side and it will be the blackest slope. We are going to my parents this Sunday which will be good as Robert is making such rapid progress that they will have even more fun with him. Bob's parents are coming in a couple of weeks as it is his mother's birthday and we are going out for a meal in the early evening with Robert. I can't face leaving him with anyone. It is stupid, I know but, after Lily's death, I feel uncomfortable leaving him. It will get better when he is older, I'm sure.

Mummy was very cheerful this morning. I saw her chatting with Gramps and the words were not so stiff. I know that's a strange way of explaining but she actually laughed with him. Charlie says it is better to laugh with someone rather than at them. I definitely know what that means. On Saturday I am going to the stables for the whole morning because Tommy is doing some special balancing work with Daisy and me. He told us that we have to stretch out on the ponies across their backs and then roll under their tummies. I expect he will explain it to us on Saturday. I think it is something to do with the pony trusting us. I know he has been talking to Mummy about something but it is all a long way away. Daisy and me will be teenagers. That is at least four years away. I wonder if I'll be better then. Perhaps I'll be able to write properly and not have to use the special computer all the time. Mummy says that she never writes anything now; everything is done by email or on-line. She said that her writing is really untidy and her spelling even worse on the rare occasions that she has to use a pen. I was very surprised as Mummy seems very perfect sometimes. Perhaps she just said that to make me feel better. Mummy and Daddy were doing lots of whispering last night and

Mummy was giggling. I have never heard that before. I think they might have a secret. Will you try and find out, Charlie? I am writing a letter to Liam to tell him all my news. I am giving it to Charlie as I think she might be able to get it to him somehow. So many things seem confusing at the moment and I have lots of questions that don't have answers. Mrs. Winter, my helper at school, says that life is one big question until you get older and even then lots of questions don't have answers. Mrs. Winter is such a nice lady. When I told her that I was writing to Liam, all she said was, 'Good for you.' Her face was a little bit serious though. In my letter I shall tell Liam that I don't expect an answer.

The onus is on me to try to see if there is any possibility of getting Annie's letter to Liam. I suppose it will depend on what she includes in it. I will make an appointment to see the Social Worker again. Robert is starting at the Nursery attached to the school for two mornings a week from next week so that would be a good opportunity. I will stay with him on the first morning but I know he will love it and two mornings is as much as I want to be apart from him. He always tries to go into school with Annie and we have looked in the nursery many times so I think he'll settle quickly. I know it is important that he meets other children of his age but it is getting the balance right. I will never allow him to be farmed out like some of the children I see. He is the happiest little chap imaginable at present so I intend to keep it like that. If he doesn't settle at Nursery, then I'll take him away and try again when he's three. Annie is really excited about her added time at the stables. I wonder if it will really result in the two little girls reaching the ambitious target of the Paralympics? It's such a mighty task, but one in which Tommy must have confidence to have suggested it in the first place. Annie is such a lucky little girl in many ways.

I know there is something in the wind between Charles and Cristabel too. There seem to be smartly dressed visitors arriving regularly. They appear to be Estate Agents but nothing has been said to me yet. Cristabel gave me a funny look yesterday and just muttered, 'All will be revealed soon.' There was a massive, glossy booklet on the kitchen table which I opened. What was inside were details of what looked like a country estate. I quickly closed it up feeling insecure. What was going on? That Cristabel is up to something is a certainty but I'm sure she will tell me when she's ready. There are subtle changes in her demeanour, which Annie has picked up on but I don't think she's been told anything yet or she would have burst to get it written down in her diary. I would dearly love to know if the family are aiming to move. It couldn't be to anywhere larger or with more facilities so, if my deductions are accurate, and the Estate Agent brochure is anything to go by, a farm is being considered; one with facilities for horses. Oh, my goodness, I hope it won't mean Annie moving school. I must stop imagining the worst scenario. There are a few places with land on the outskirts of this area and I'm almost sure that the C.B.'s wouldn't dispense with my services after all the years I've been with them. What would happen to Bob? He has been Charles' right hand man for just as long and they have developed a deep friendship. Now I must stop writing as my imagination is running away with me.

Mummy has said that she has something to show Charlie and me so we are going to do this diary very quickly tonight. Mummy always works on her tablet as soon as she comes home from work as she says it means that she can get everything organised for the next day and then spend time with me. I like the sound of all of it. Do you know what the surprise is, Charlie? I hope it's something really exciting but not something that will make me feel that things are going to change. Mummy was all sort of twitchy and couldn't keep still. Shall we stop this and go and ask her?

Now we know what the 'Master Plan' is and it could be very exciting. Tommy has a brother who is selling some land that is part of his farm next to where Tommy has his stables. His brother is quite a lot older than him and is finding all the work very difficult. Cristabel says we can go and have a look at it after riding on Saturday. She says that Daisy can come too. Charles is going to have a look if Cristabel thinks it is a good idea and if she thinks it is the right thing to do. I noticed that Cristabel's eyes were all twinkly when she was talking and all her words sounded careful.

I'm not sure what Mummy was trying to tell me. She was talking in a different voice from what she usually uses. I need a word that tells you that she feels a bit slow and confused but not unhappy. Can you tell me one, Charley? Oh, 'thoughtful'. Yes. That will have to do. Sometimes, when she talks her words get a bit jumbled, but it's strange because it only happens in the evening. I expect it is because she's tired after work.

At my riding lesson on Saturday, Tommy told me that horses are very forgiving. It made me almost sad to think of that. He said that they live in the present and whatever is happening at that precise moment is what they react to. I think I understand that too. I would like to talk to Mummy about it but I don't know what is stopping me. Whenever I think I'm going to start talking to her about something serious, my voice doesn't let me. The words are all there but I can't seem to make my mouth say them in the right order. It's as if something had shaken up my thoughts in my head and muddled them all up together. The more I try the worse it seems to make it. At school it is better because I'm given more time to gets things in order. At least that's what Mrs. Winter says. I can talk to Poppy, the pony, properly. I have noticed Tommy watching me and he probably thinks I'm peculiar because I talk to her all the time and she pricks up her ears. She knows lots of my secrets, just like you do, Charlie. Daisy and me are going to be doing lots of balancing work on our ponies and Tommy says that, in the winter, we will be going into the barn to practise. There are some Pony Club events for that long word like parachute and Daisy and me are going to go to one.

Tommy is setting up a scheme for disabled children and young adults. It is something he has wanted to do for a long time and Annie coming along when she did has triggered him into action. Annie doesn't really understand what the outcome of all this training will eventually be for, and it might not happen at all. There are many years to get through and I'm sure hurdles will appear to prevent it happening at all. It is irrelevant anyway as the positive benefits of the connection with the horses for all of the family is increasingly apparent almost on a daily basis. It has a profound effect on my attitude to life also and I find it an essential part of my weekly routine. On returning from the stables, I'm relaxed and Bob has noticed that my 'thoughtful' periods have almost disappeared. Can a horse help a person to become more accepting to grief, I wonder?

Cristabel has told me that the family are going to buy a field next to Tommy's riding school. She has just showed me the plans given to her by the Land Agent. There are five stables and an outdoor riding area which looks as if it is made of bits of rubber. The fields are massive but look in very well-kept condition. There are gates and fences which look a bit rickety but Cristabel says that is easy to remedy. She is very over-excited about all this and I tried to calm her down a bit by saying it is 'early days' for making any big decisions. She answered by telling me that the decision had been made and that the property had been bought. She was so animated that I feared she might burst a blood vessel. What I really feared was that she would need a vat of wine to get her through this obviously traumatic event. How wrong was I? As the days pass, she appears tranquil, happy and sober.

We visit the stables nearly every evening, taking the children to walk around the fields that are in the process of acquiring a new owner. Annie is ecstatic.

She pulls Daisy along with her and together they crash and tumble in the long grass, laughing. This happiness level cannot last and it is cut short suddenly by Daisy falling on a bit of broken glass. I expected a great fuss but she got up, with difficulty, and saw that she was bleeding badly. I carried her to her father so he could look at her foot. She whined a bit but then stopped as if it was too much bother. Tommy looked at the cut and calmly got out an antiseptic wipe and a plaster and that was the end of that. Annie was more concerned about it than Daisy. I remember, as a child, milking a similar situation to the maximum possible. It makes me ask myself if a child with a serious disability makes less fuss than a more 'normal' one, having become used to the need for extra effort to overcome problems.

I know this diary will have to stop for a while. Annie will be starting a new school in under a couple of years. Robert will also be starting Infant School and I wonder if The C.B.'s will really need so many hours from Bob and me. It is as if I have been on a long journey with many twists and turns and as if I'm trying to pull myself up a spiral staircase but the curves of the metal stairs extend as soon as I think I've reached the top. There is always one more corner to navigate, just like real life. The aim of training Daisy and Annie to compete at the Paralympics in the year so far ahead, that it seems irrelevant, is something to which Tommy and the rest of his family will need to devote much time if he is to succeed. He is the sort of character that doesn't take anything on unless he knows it is worthwhile so it will be interesting to see how things develop, especially the physical aspect of Daisy and Annie's ongoing needs. I would love to project myself into the future to see, just for a tiny moment, what Annie and Daisy will look like in eight year's time. I feel as if I'm on the outside of something, looking in as a stranger. I see a scene composed of people I don't recognise. They seem unable to respond to my presence. Then I pull myself together and cut the daydreaming short. It would be interesting to transport myself into the future, but then rapidly return to the present. This would be a total waste of eight years and all the involvement with reacting to the various progressions that will be made. Of that I am certain. I must not forget Robert in all my mental meanderings. In eight years he will be at the end of his Primary School life. Will we still be so closely involved with the C.B's? I would never have imagined, eight years ago, to being this closely involved with them in any circumstances. I disliked Cristabel intensely when Annie was born and had very little understanding of the damage that she had suffered herself by her own bad parenting. Working in the maternity unit came to an abrupt end as my whole life was disrupted in order to support what I thought was a most unpleasant mother. Things have improved out of all recognition and I find that I am increasingly drawn to this family, especially Annie. In all probability I believe that my little family will be closely involved with them for always; a ridiculous idea if it had been suggested to me nine years ago. That's how quickly time passes. Exactly the same amount of time from now and we will be in the future that is full of mystery.

I went to find Mummy tonight when we went to the stables and she was standing in the far corner of the bottom field all on her own. Her head was down and I didn't dare go any closer. She looked so sad that I very nearly called to her. Tommy came and stood next to me and said that everything was going to be all right. We just stood there and waited. It seemed a very long time. Then Pablo, who had been in the other field, right at the far end where he couldn't see Mummy, came slowly through the gate and walked up to her and nudged her with his nose. I saw that Mummy was crying and I didn't know what to do. I knew that I mustn't interrupt so Tommy and me stood like statues. In a few seconds Mummy put her arms round Pablo's neck and stroked him. I felt jealous because she has never stroked me. She has kissed me recently though, but never really, really held me as if it is important to her. Do you see what I mean, Charlie? Anyway, Mummy and Pablo stood there for such a long time that I thought they were never going to move but then Pablo shook his head as if to say, ' That's enough,' and they came walking towards us. Mummy was smiling a lot and she came over to me and hugged me. I was very surprised, but I hugged her back and it didn't feel weird. Do you know, Charlie, that it was the very first time that I knew Mummy really wanted to touch me.

That was almost too emotional for me to write. When Annie was telling it to me and I was typing it, there was an atmosphere of something almost surreal around us. I had to keep very quiet as I knew it was important that this little girl expressed her thoughts with no interruptions from me. Could it be the breakthrough? Could Cristabel feel comfortable with her past and come to some sort of agreement with the demons that persecute her? Was it really possible for a massive four-legged creature to have such a profound effect on a person? It certainly appeared it was indeed the case. Annie, Daisy and Robert went off with Tommy to work with the ponies, and Cristabel and I tacked up and went for a hack around the farm. Robert is now riding a small Shetland pony and it is amazing how quickly he has adjusted to balancing perfectly on top. This particular Shetland pony is old and very placid, as are all the animals at the stables. Robert helped to put the reins and leading rope on the little pony, called, ominously, Scamp. Tommy explained to me that small children have an inbuilt instinct to adjust themselves, the stirrups being accepted without any questioning. See how the horse terminology has started to become part of my language. Cristabel was calm and chatted away as if the last hour has never happened. She was like a butterfly emerging from the chrysalis. The problem with that analogy is that butterflies don't last very long, so I must find another.

We trotted for a bit and Cristabel taught me how to get into a rhythm of lifting my bum up at certain times. I found it really difficult but Alana didn't seem to mind when I bumped down on her a bit hard. Tommy's wife came out of the farmhouse and watched us. We walked over to her and she asked if we would like a cup of tea when we had finished. It passed through my mind that in the winter we wouldn't be able to spend so much time at the stables as it would be dark and I would be needed at home. That fact gave me a sinking feeling which was followed by the knowledge that it really didn't matter at all as we had managed far more difficult situations before. There was a complete confidence in my thoughts that nothing could possibly go wrong. Robert would be given the same amount of love and attention that he had always had and I was being stupidly oversensitive. Look at all the mothers with little children that are farmed out at a very young age and, even after starting school, picked up by an after school care system. Are they harmed? Yes, I think they are, irreparably. Cristabel is an example. If I was ever in any doubt about the importance of good parenting I have the proof at first hand. I'm starting to feel sad about the lot of many children and this gives me strength to make certain that we give Robert all the love that he needs, however inconvenient it might be to our own diaries. I will give up riding in the winter and take it up again in the longer evenings when Robert is in bed. There!

I feel much more relaxed about it now. Guilt is a toxic weapon if it is allowed to fester. As we returned from our short hack we were met by three children on ponies. Robert had Tommy next to him but he was sitting like a king on a throne, nobody holding on to him at all. Tommy silently clapped his hands and pointed to Robert, indicating that he thought the little chap had done really well. I would never have allowed my little boy to do what Tommy had just showed us and it was a lesson in expectations for me, just as his attitude towards his daughter relates to his treatment of her as a perfectly normal child. I wonder if he has just a few worries deep down. He comes across as the calmest and most well-adjusted person imaginable. There must have been times in the past, when Daisy was born, when it was obvious that her physical needs were going to be serious and lasting, that he questioned the situation. His wife must have been concerned about their ability to cope. Daisy has the determination that I've noticed many times with Annie. Perhaps part of it is genetic but part is possibly developed by the parents not erecting barriers and being overprotective. The more I come into contact with Tommy's family, the greater my admiration grows at his ability to take a step back from potential problems and allow a natural course of events to take place. I must ask him if there have ever been times when he or his wife have felt despair. At least that is what I imagine asking him. It would be too impertinent to invade his privacy with a question like that.

We had a relaxed half hour in the farmhouse and I listened with amazement as Cristabel chatted confidently about the land that they had bought from Tommy's brother. I found that I was almost speechless in a most unusual fashion; something that has never happened to me before. I played with the two little children as Daisy and Annie disappeared upstairs. I sat on the floor as I had a sudden need to be inconspicuous, helping the two toddlers build towers with some bricks. I listened to the information that was racing out of everyone's mouths apart from mine. Where had I been during the last few weeks to have missed all the recent activities? I knew, of course, that the land had been bought and that the C.B.'s were planning to build some new shelters on it but I hadn't understood the extent of the plans and how they extended far into the future. It seemed that new ponies were being bought plus a horse for Cristabel. She was cutting down her work hours considerably in order to spend more time with the animals. I glanced at Tommy and saw how energised he was also with all the myriad of plans gushing forth. Tommy's wife suddenly laughed and said, 'Well, that's just about taken care of the next ten years.' I saw her raise her eyebrows as if to say she wouldn't have expected anything else from him. He went over to her and gave her a squeeze, saying,' What would I do without you?' I noticed that Cristabel looked embarrassed. Showing emotion in public was not something she had been brought up to copy, having probably never experienced it. I did notice Cristabel glancing furtively round the room, taking in the sloppy untidiness. This day, I knew she was surprisingly comfortable with the lack of concern about things being in their proper place. Again I warmed to her, knowing this environment was another one that was a rarity in her cocooned life. I knew that I was the privileged one in the present scenario.

Life seems to throw almost accidental hurdles over which a person can jump, avoid or knock down. It seemed appropriate that jumping appeared to be the most popular at the moment. A wave of contentment washed over me and I felt completely relaxed. What is it about Tommy and his wife that seems to filter calmness, as if by osmosis, into all in their presence? It is almost a spiritual feeling, one without a name, but something I intend to investigate further. I returned to the present easily as if I had been floating along on a distant collection of thoughts. Tommy was speaking about the Olympics in eight year's time and I saw him look at Cristabel. She had a silly smile on her face and said, ' Anything that you will think will help Annie is fine with us.' She quickly added, 'and Daisy of course.' That pleased me as she was not usually particularly interested in anyone else. They then started talking about the acquisition of the fields that Tommy's brother had sold to them. I noticed that Annie and Daisy had crept closer to the adults and were listening avidly. The atmosphere in the room was full of expectations, and looking at the little girls' faces was enough to reassure me that there would be no resistance from either of them in this master plan. The little girls, having heard everything that was of interest to them, disappeared. Tommy saw them go and said, quite bluntly, to Cristabel, ' It will be a good opportunity for you to work with Pablo a bit more. I expect you'll want to buy a horse for yourself eventually but, if you take my advice, it would help your confidence if you continued with Pablo a bit longer. It's good to see how you are making such a connection with him. 'Cristabel took a breath and slowly and thoughtfully answered,' You will never know how much the last few months have helped me.' Then she hesitated, looking worried as if she had admitted something of which she should be ashamed. Tommy quickly filled the space with, 'You don't realise what amazing progress you've made. Don't forget, you've not ridden since you were a child.' Tommy didn't mention the help that Pablo had given her with her problems, but Cristabel didn't need any more words. She knew exactly what Tommy was saying to her. All this time Tommy's wife was a spectator but I sensed that she understood what was happening in that room and the importance of it. I noticed that she smiled at Tommy when he made the remark about Cristabel's progress. Unexpectedly she said, 'When Daisy was born and we weren't sure if she would live, we found that the horses sensed our anxiety and quietly comforted us.'

Cristabel almost shouted, 'But it wasn't your fault. It was totally my fault that Annie was born with all her problems. Don't you see?' Tommy's wife leant over to where Cristabel was sitting and touched her so gently on the arm that Cristabel looked down at the place where the hand rested. Tommy's wife quietly said, 'You are making up for the past now, don't you see?' Cristabel looked at the floor and I think I heard her mutter, 'Oh, I do hope so' Then the little girls came back into the room and it was the perfect time for us to leave.

Charlie and me have had a brilliant day. Mummy has smiled a lot as well and it was a proper smile with all of her face. When she reads this diary she will be surprised because it says how much she has melted. Stop laughing at me Charlie. You know what I mean. Daisy and me are going to work really hard with our ponies because Tommy says that we are going to be in the Lympets. I thought they were things in the sea but Tommy has told us all about the competitions that everybody can enter and there are special ones for riders like Daisy and me. Everyone in the world can have a turn but we have to work very hard indeed. There are medals that you can win. There are gold, silver and bronze medals. Daisy and me are going to train for something called a funny word like 'dresshours.'

You are laughing at me again, Charlie. I'm going to ask Tommy all about it. He is going to talk to Mummy about the way he looks after his horses. I know it's called 'At Liberty' and it means that the horses don't have shoes on. Sometimes he doesn't even put a bit in the horse's mouth and I've seen him ride with no saddle. Is that why all his horses are so gentle and kind Charlie? I bet he could be the best rider in the whole world if he wanted to. I watch how Mummy seems to be part of the horse when she is standing next to him and how Pablo seems to know that something is wrong with Mummy. He helps her, doesn't he Charlie?

Oh, indeed he does. The more I see the reactions of the horses at the stables the more I am astounded by their ability to absorb any negative feelings surrounding the humans. They manifest an incredible sensitivity towards us. It can be almost overwhelming. I am almost overcome but stay quietly affected by their influence and instinctive power to empathize. Having witnessed it, I will never underestimate this gift, for that is what it is. The feelings of peace that permeate through all the senses are just beginning to have their effect on me. Cristabel is a few weeks ahead of me in whatever is happening to us. It must appear rather ridiculous to an outsider but I know we both have a feeling of complete trust in our horses, knowing they understand that both Cristabel and I have 'luggage'. What a few months this has been!

Chapter Fourteen

There is something I have to tell Charlie and she might be a bit cross but I hope she'll understand. If I tell her now she can write it and then I can watch her face and stop if she looks angry. She never gets angry so I know it will be fine. Well, when I was playing at Daisy's house last Saturday, we went on her computer and we tried to find out where Liam lived. You remember him, don't you Charlie? Well, it was almost by accident because Daisy said we should try to find out on her Facebook page. I've never done that so it was new to me. It was amazing because his name came up and Daisy asked to be his friend and then she had an answer and now we can send him messages. She is much better than me at typing but I can tell her what to say and Liam can reply. He said that he is only allowed to go on his computer for an hour at a time and his new parents are really kind and he is very happy. His brothers are happy too and their real mummy comes to see them once a month but she can't have them back because she's having another baby.

Annie is right. I have learnt that there isn't much point in getting cross. This bit of news took me by surprise though. In a way I'm pleased that Annie and I can talk about things that might cause friction between us. Liam is such a dear little boy potentially and there may be a chance for him in this obviously nurturing new family. They have my total admiration for taking on three boys. Their experiences in their young lives will not have left them with very good memories. I hope the damage their mother did to them hasn't ruined their chances for later. I have my doubts though. I feel as if there has been a knife sliced through my bond with Annie. I know this sounds dramatic but it is a sign of things to come and I know that there will be many times that Annie will prefer to be with other people in different situations that don't include me. This is a natural progression to her development and I must be pleased. I must not interfere and be too inquisitive as to what this Facebook thing involves. I don't want to be part of it as it might take up too much of my time. I have read that it can become obsessive. So, I'll be a good listener instead and hope that the girls will tell me anything that they think I should know.

It's amazing because Liam has a brand new computer and he can do all sorts of things on it. His new Daddy takes him and his brothers out into the countryside cycling and they go swimming too and lots of other things. Liam is very good at writing his news and he can spell now. He wrote that he thinks of the music we did at my school and he misses it so his new Mummy is going to get him guitar lessons. Me and Daisy write to him and tell him all about what we are doing. Daisy's Daddy has set up her Facebook page for her but I don't think you'll do it for me will you, Charlie? I know Daisy's Mummy is always interrupting her when she is on Facebook because she says there are some 'funny people about' and she needs to keep an eye on it. I think I know what she means. Mrs. Winter has talked to the class about it. She had an unhappy face on when she was telling us.

Facebook is another nail in the coffin. I will try to set it up for Annie but not yet. There are too many other things to do, as Annie has said. It is only a matter of time. Annie is getting much more efficient at typing but her spelling is still pretty awful. She really doesn't see when a word is spelt inaccurately. The letters are in quite bizarre orders and she can't 'spellcheck' every word or she would stop trying altogether. Her reading, however, is coming along very well indeed. If she sees a word thousands of times and can read it with little difficulty, surely it will eventually be installed into her memory accurately. Well, our next riding 'lesson' is in a couple of days and the long road for Daisy and Annie is stretching ahead. Today, Herta telephoned to ask to come to see us all. We haven't seen much of her recently as she has been studying for her finals. She will make a wonderful doctor. Her husband is a kind gentle man, just what she deserves.

Herta came to see us tonight after I'd got home from school. She is going to be a doctor. Mummy had a long talk with her and I knew it was about their plans for me training for the Lympets. It is a longer word than that and it sounds like parachute. We are going swimming in a minute and then doing some exercises. Robert joins in too but he is very funny as he keeps falling off the balancing beam and Herta kept catching him. He was doing it on purpose. Mummy was laughing, properly, again. I have a piano lesson tomorrow so I am going to practice after our exercises. Herta told me that she is nearly a doctor.

She has to work for another year and then she will be a proper doctor. She helps me a lot when she comes here but I know she can't see me very often because of her training. She says Daisy and me have to send her a ticket for the Lympets. I really don't understand about it but it is a long way away. Mummy was whispering to Herta about something but I couldn't hear but Herta's face was shining and alive.

So it goes on. The patterns of everyday wend their way inevitably forwards a few steps at a time. I know there will be times when life seems impossible but the balm will be in an accessible field.

Chapter Fifteen

Eight Years Have Passed

Two identically dressed young ladies were waiting on shining horses outside the competitors ring. A voice is heard from the loudspeakers.

'Annie Courtney- Browne on Sunrise'.

In they come with precision and confidence. They stand, as one, waiting for the signal to start. There is a hush then a very thin buzz as people are saying things to each other. There is nudging and pointing. What can be the matter?

The horse has no bit and is unshod. Has there been a mistake?

Then the sign comes for Annie to start. She proceeds round the ring, in perfect control without seeming to do anything. Horse and rider work in perfect unison, moving and completing the required elements harmoniously in magical time with the music, one of the young lady's favourites, the slow movement from Mozart's clarinet concerto. Her face is set with an ecstatic smile and the routine is completed with hardly a mistake. When she finishes and stands motionless in front of the judges to tip her head, there is a silence, complete and frozen. It seems to last forever. Then, as if the watching spectators sense that something extraordinary is happening, a roar of applause crashes into the void. As we look at the people watching we can see familiar faces, all with tears streaming down, clapping as if their lives depend on the amount of noise they can make. Liam is one of the most enthusiastic. He is shouting, 'I knew you could do it'. There are other people, Gramps, Herta with a baby and a toddler, Cristabel with Charles standing next to Tommy and his wife and little boy. There seem to be some people missing from this scene. But no, there they are, hugging each other. Charlie, Bob and Robert.

If it hadn't been for them, this unique scene wouldn't have happened.

Then another young lady enters the ring. It is Daisy on Midnight and she has the same calmness about her; her horse smoothly standing waiting for the signal for her to start her sequence of movements. The crowd again know they are experiencing something special. Midnight is bitless and unshod. Daisy is announced and walks Midnight serenely towards her first required task. She has also chosen a beautiful piece of music from Beethoven's 7th symphony. The onlookers wonder at the ability of the horse to have perfect timing. Again, there is silence at the end of the routine and the crowd's admiration is tangible. There is the sudden explosion of applause and cheering again. Daisy smiles and looks up and searches for her father who waves at her frantically. How brave he is- the only familiar person not weeping. He knew that his horses wouldn't let them down. His pride and total confidence was there to see, head held high.

There were three small eighteen year olds that won medals. The bronze medal winner was a young boy, the silver medal winner was a young lady called Annie and the gold medal winner was a young lady by the name of Daisy. The two young ladies were hugging each other, leaning over from their horses and very nearly falling off.

The horses, standing very still and close together, seemed to be smiling.

I think they had the last word.

About the author

Having worked for Oxford University Press for many years on educational material, I now need to explore a more imaginative genre.

I have worked with children that have experienced different degrees of difficulty- emotional and developmental. The positive changes that can occur if the child is given appropriate help is heart-warming. My interest now is to write about how a child's early experiences can have a profound and lasting effect on his or her future.